OTTAWA TITANS

ROUGHING

SARAH HEGGER

DEDICATION

*There's only one person I owe this book
to, and that's my dear friend Tara Cromer, the best hand holder,
commiserator, and ass kicker I could ask for.*

*Once again, I owe a debt of gratitude to the proof reading dream team of
Anna Sharpe and Debbie Fuller. You ladies are the absolute bestest
EVAH!*

COPYRIGHT

❀ Created with Vellum

CHAPTER
ONE

A PRIMAL SCREAM shattered the peace in the kitchen. Followed by a bellow of unbridled rage. Standard background noise for *Hockey Night in Canada*.

Elizabeth took her roast out of the oven for basting while Jane snapchatted her newest manicure to her adoring public. At least her sister's habitual teen scowl was downgraded to indifferent scorn.

"Kill him! Smash his face until he cries like a little girl. Fight him, you pussy." Hockey was sacred in the Rogers household and, Dad believed, dependent on his active participation from his favorite lounger. "I'm gonna need another beer in here."

"Janey?" Elizabeth looked up from the beef roast. "Do you think you could take him one?"

Perched on a stool at the kitchen island, Jane cocked her hand for a better angle and sent another snap. Jane had pretty much been on a hormonal rampage since she'd turned twelve.

"Jane?" Elizabeth balanced the roasting pan and spooned juice over the joint. One wrongly worded request and Jane would open a can of vitriol that would ruin Saturday night dinner.

Family dinner, always subject to *Hockey Night in Canada*, and Mom had found a way to merge the two.

Keeping her tone pleasant, she tried again. "Jane?"

"What?" Jane stared at her screen and smirked.

"Dad would like another beer."

With an impatient huff, Jane looked up. "He's not crippled. If he needs another beer, he can get it himself."

Jane was right, Elizabeth knew she was right, but Dad came from a generation of men who barbequed burgers and took credit for the entire meal. She grabbed a Molson from the fridge and took it to her father in the living room. It was only a beer. No big deal.

Yeah, right. She was such a pushover.

Dad took the beer without taking his eyes off the screen. "What the hell!" He half rose in his seat. "Where's the defense? Get them out of the paint."

"Dinner in twenty minutes, Dad." Elizabeth scooped scattered chips off the table and back into the bowl.

"When the game's done." Dad growled at the screen.

The hockey went to an ad break and Dad scowled at the bowl in her hands. "I'm eating those."

"Dinner is nearly ready." Elizabeth nailed a smile on her face and kept on beaming at him. Mom had put up with thirty years of scowls and indifference before finally walking out three months ago. Someone needed to hold the remnants of their family together. Even if the remnants were not cooperating.

Dad gaped at her. "After the game." He jabbed his Molson at the bowl. "Get me some more chips, won't you?"

"Who's playing?" She liked hockey. Kind of. She used to like it more.

The ad break ended, and Dad went back to the television.

Elizabeth watched the game for a second. There you had it. She should have known which game had Dad glued to the television.

"Oh, look." Jane lounged against the doorjamb and glanced

at the television before going back to her phone. "It's the son he'd like to have."

Number ten for the Ottawa Titans hit the ice, and Dad straightened in his chair. "Come on, Sam, son. Show them how it's done." He chuckled and rubbed his hands together. "Sam will get the job done."

It was bigger than Elizabeth, positively Pavlovian. The sight of that number with Stone printed above it and she wanted to swear. Also the reason she used to like hockey more. "Dick," she whispered.

"Elizabeth." Jane gave her a theatrical gape. "Aitch-ee-double hockey sticks, did you use the dee word?"

Elizabeth blushed. Somebody had to set the example for Jane on swearing, but Sam was totally a dick.

"Do you mind?" Dad glanced over his shoulder. "I'm watching the game here."

"Sorry." Smile stuck in place, Elizabeth headed back into the kitchen. She wanted them all to sit down, chat over dinner, behave like a family, and not three people regretting they shared DNA.

"Go, Sam!" Dad yelled, leaning so forward in his lounger, the footrest snapped back down. "Yes, Sam, yes!"

Apparently women from here to California screamed much the same on a regular basis. Elizabeth snickered into the carrots. Not that she kept track, but last she'd heard Sam was dating some former Disney, now turned screen vamp, movie star.

Elizabeth watched the game through the doorway. If Sam was playing, then that meant Craig Dawson was also on the ice. Dark brown hair, gorgeous hazel eyes, chiseled jaw and sensual mouth, the six three of power packed muscle and sinew that made up Craig Dawson made up for having to watch Sam.

The camera zoomed in on Sam in a faceoff. Intense blue eyes blazed over his faceguard at his opponent. The puck dropped. Sam won the faceoff and snapped the puck to Dawson.

Opposing defense converged on him. Dawson took a rattling slam into the boards.

Dad groaned.

But Dawson kept the puck and passed to Sam. Sam took it up the ice and even Elizabeth had to admit Sam Stone on ice was a beautiful thing to behold. The quickest forward in the league, with a magical pair of hands that could find the back of the net through the eye of a needle.

In this garden, Sam had worked on that shot. Her dad still hadn't recovered from the glory of her Sparkly Fairy Play Palace dying under the relentless assault of puck after puck fired at it from Sam as a boy.

On screen, Sam powered a shot from the hashmarks and lit the lamp.

"Yes!" Dad leaped out of his lounger. "Goal." He turned to her with a grin. "What did I tell you?"

"That you wanted another beer?"

"Eh?" Dad looked momentarily confused. "No, that Sam would sort them all out."

"Oh, right." At least her play palace hadn't collapsed in vain.

At the time Dad had stared at her aghast as she sobbed over the demise of her play palace and asked where else she thought Sam could practice.

Whelp! There you had it. A career in the hockey league demanded sacrifice. Her play palace had died at the altar of Sam's hockey career, along with her Celebration Two Thousand Barbie (head used in lieu of a puck), Chester the stuffed raccoon (another puck substitute) and her favorite Kim Possible T-shirt (ripped to shreds to tape a stick handle).

After all, a boy with Sam's talent couldn't be expected to adhere to the same rules of behavior as any other child. To be fair, his mother had done her best. But as a single mother, Danica had often been working.

Dad had been more than happy to step into the breach once Sam's mad hockey skills had made an appearance. The same good old Dad who flapped his hand at the coffee table. "Where are my chips?"

No way she was filling the chip bowl. Not when she'd spent all this time getting dinner ready. Of course, her surge into assertiveness would be more effective if she wasn't playing proxy little woman in the kitchen.

"Chips!" Dad hollered. "Also gimme some dip with them."

No. Only two letters that when strung together made a helluva impact. "Right away."

Dammit. The same two letters that hardly ever found their way out of her mouth.

"Beth." Winsome expression on her face, Jane sidled into the kitchen. No had been the first word Jane spoke and she was still proficient at it.

Jane's expression warned Elizabeth it was time to practice her new word.

"Beth." Jane wrinkled her nose in a way that took Elizabeth right back to what a gorgeous baby she'd been. Ten years Elizabeth's junior and so pretty and sweet and cute. Other girls had made do with doll pretend babies, she'd had Jane. "While you're here, can you iron my new shirt for me?"

Elizabeth gave it her all. "No."

"What?" Jane blinked at her.

She wavered under the crestfallen beam of Jane's huge green eyes. "I don't have time. I need to finish dinner and get back to my apartment. I have things to do."

Jane's gaze grew wounded. "What things?"

"The retirement center." Elizabeth faltered. "They need a new bus and I'm helping them fundraise. Plus I have a women's auxiliary meeting this week and the Humane Society is relying on me—"

"But those things are for strangers and you know I can't iron." Jane's mouth turned upside down. "Mom always used to do the ironing for me." Tears welled in Jane's eyes. "I miss her so much."

No backbone. She had no backbone because Elizabeth's mouth opened and what came out? The same thing that always came out. "Sure, Janey. Put it in the laundry and I'll do it before I go."

"Thanks." The sun shone behind Jane's momentary rainstorm. She snatched her coat off the peg by the back door and shrugged into it. "See you later."

"But dinner is almost ready." Elizabeth stared at her beautiful roast, currently nestled between crispy skinned, golden roasted potatoes. She had green beans and carrots to go with it. Maybe Dad would open a bottle of red, and it would feel like home again.

Jane wrinkled her nose. "Yeah, I'm not staying. I'm a vegetarian anyway."

"Since when?"

"Jesus, Elizabeth." Jane snorted. "Since forever." Eyes glued to her phone, she sauntered out of the kitchen. "And dad wants another beer."

The door slammed behind her.

"No!" Dad's agonized shriek sent Elizabeth running.

Standing, he was pale with sweat beaded on his forehead.

"Dad?" Elizabeth crept closer. "Are you all right? Tightness of chest? Nausea? Difficulty breathing?"

"S-Sam." Dad wagged his hand at the television.

Elizabeth turned and caught the replay.

Sam shot across the ice and connected with an opposing player. The same player who had taken Dawson to the boards.

Sam's shoulder slammed into the player's jaw. Mouthguard, spit and a spray of bright red blood arced through the air. Oh boy, that wasn't good.

Don Cherry appeared on the screen, dressed in his signature eighties living-room-curtains suit, this one shocking pink with palm trees on it. By contrast the immaculately dressed man next to him looked straight off the pages of *GQ*.

"In my book, that's a dirty check," Don said, stabbing his blunt forefinger into the shiny desk surface.

"This is not the hockey of today," said *GQ* man. "We're looking at a major for that, at least. I'm even thinking the league is going to have something to say."

"Shut up, Gracie," Dad howled at the screen. "That was a legitimate hit. A legal hit."

"No doubt about it." His name, Marc Gracie, popped up beneath him. "Stone has gone too far this time. And this from a player who makes too far part of his game plan."

"You know nothing." Dad slashed the air with his hand. "Nothing."

The screen went back to another replay of the hit.

"See there," Marc Gracie spoke over the footage. "Stop it there."

The picture froze on the moment Sam made contact. Sam's shoulder slammed into the other player's jaw.

"And that, my friends, is an illegal hit." Gracie sounded delighted about it. "Stone has wriggled out of this hit too many times now."

"Shoulder first." Dad shook with anger. "It was a shoulder check. Stupid shit dipped his head and got it on the jaw. Sam did nothing. Nothing."

The slo-mo footage rolled across the screen another time.

Nope, Elizabeth was going to have to disagree with the parental unit on this one. Sam had cleaned that player's clock for him.

Bam! Elizabeth flinched. That had to hurt. The footage rolled forward to the player hitting the ice like a felled tree. The referee blew the penalty and chaos broke out on the ice.

Two of the downed player's teammates surged for Sam.

Helmets dropped, gloves hit the ice, and fists went flying.

Gracie appeared back on the screen and smirked. "Sam Stone has done it this time. Can anybody say league suspension?"

Don Cherry nodded his agreement. "You put a hockey stick in the hands of a thug, he's still just a thug."

"N-o-o." Dad folded into his lounger and dropped his head in his hands. His shoulders shook. "You can't do this to me."

"Pretty sure that line belongs to that poor guy being helped off the ice." Elizabeth read his name off the back of his jersey. "Karlov."

Dad turned on her, eyes gleaming wrathfully. "Karlov's a girl. Nothing but a girl."

"Isn't he lucky." Feminism came to die at her father's feet. "Dinner will be ready in fifteen."

Springing to his feet, Dad glowered at her. "What are you talking about? How the hell do you expect me to eat now?"

CHAPTER
TWO

ELIZABETH'S CELL WOKE HER, and she fumbled for it and hit Answer.

Mom's voice dragged her out of sleep lethargy. "Elizabeth, are you awake?"

She was now. Coffee sounded like a great thing to do and she stumbled out of bed. "Hey, Mom. How's Paris?"

"We're in Amsterdam now and it's lovely. I wish you were here to see it, Elizabeth. They have all these cute houses packed together and everybody rides bicycles, and oh, Danica and I are off to see the tulips tomorrow."

"That's awesome." Mom sounded happy, a lightness to her voice that hadn't been there in a long time.

"But now we might not get there." Mom's voice hitched. "Elizabeth, love, I hate to ask this of you. You already do so much for other people. Only..."

Mom really wouldn't ask if she had an alternative. "What?"

"It's Danica. She's getting desperate. Desperate enough to come home early."

Her mother and her bestie, Danica, had been planning this trip for years. "How early?"

"Like right away." Mom lowered her voice as if someone was in the other room. "She's worried about Sam."

"Sam?"

"Sam."

Elizabeth braced her hands on the kitchen counter. No good ever came of Sam being anywhere in her vicinity. "What's he done now?"

The possibilities were endless.

"She can't get hold of him since he had his accident on the ice."

Elizabeth could barely hold her scoff in, but Mom liked Sam. "You mean when he laid a dirty hit on another player?"

"It looked like a fair hit from here." Mom grew snippy. "Danica and I have watched it on the iPad."

Sometimes it felt as if she was the only person who really saw Sam for what he was. "That was over two weeks ago. Why can't she get hold of him?"

"He's not answering any of her calls. Last we knew he was having a horrid time and he asked Danica if he could stay at her house for a bit." Mom lowered her voice to a hoarse whisper. "He's been staying there since the league suspended him."

"And?" Oh God, please let her be wrong about this. Just this once.

"Somebody needs to go around there and check on him." Mom waded in with the body check. "Once Danica knows he's okay, she can relax. And we can go and see the tulips."

No! Say no! You need to stop letting people drag you into stuff. But it was Mom and Danica and they both deserved this trip. This was bucket list stuff they were doing. "Okay, Mom." *Sucker!* "I'll pop around on my way to the women's auxiliary and see if he's all right."

Mom breathed a teary sigh of relief. "Darling, I would be so grateful if you would, and so would Danica."

"But I'm sure he's fine. Probably sacrificing virgins or something." Elizabeth stomped into her bedroom to get showered and dressed.

Mom giggled. "Stop it, Elizabeth. Sam is a lovely boy."

"Sam is a—" She breathed deep. "I'll call you later. Better yet, I'll take a picture of him and text it to you."

Thirty minutes later Elizabeth parked outside Danica's house.

She had about twenty minutes to snap her shot of Sam before she was due at her women's auxiliary meeting. Being the first Sunday in the month, they were expecting her. Mostly, they wanted the muffins she always brought, but sometimes they let her have an opinion.

Cold sharp air hijacked her breath as she climbed from her car. Instead of being out in below freezing, she had planned to be tucked in the cozy meeting room behind the public library and weighing in on whether they should do a bake sale or a knitted goods stall at the upcoming high school fundraising fair.

Nobody had shoveled the walkway since Danica had left a month ago, and she carefully placed her feet in the snow holes made by someone before her. Snow clung to her leggings and the wool tops of her boots.

Reaching the porch, she stamped snow off her boots. Using the key and barging straight in would be rude. Also, she could never be quite sure what he might be doing in there.

Icky, sordid Sam-type things, which did not bear thinking about.

She shuddered and pressed the bell.

"Go away," Sam yelled from the other side.

At least she could now reassure his mother he was alive. "It's Elizabeth. Open up."

"Get outta here."

Same old charming Sam.

Elizabeth rang the doorbell again. Unfortunately she needed more than proof of life.

"He's not answering." A woman emerged from the large rhododendron guarding the right side of the door.

For the life of her Elizabeth didn't know how Danica got her rhodos through an Ottawa winter. She focused on the woman. "I'm sorry?"

The woman heaved a huge sigh, which pushed her breasts perilously close to spilling over the gold corset top peeking out from beneath her red shaggy jacket. Elizabeth experienced a pang of ta-ta envy. Those things defied gravity and they looked real.

"I can feel his pain," she of the terrific ta-tas said. Actually she had pretty banging legs as well, lovingly covered in black stockings and showcased by her bright red and black micromini skirt. "I've been here since"—she leaned forward, ratcheting up the chance of wardrobe failure, and dropped her voice—"*it* happened."

"It what?" Elizabeth's imagination rapidly cycled through cataclysmic hurricanes, genocide, pandemic plague, and finally hit on the answer. "Oh, you mean since Sam got tossed off the ice?"

"Shhh!" Ta-tas—and Elizabeth suspected she was developing a mammary obsession at this point—pressed long, bright red fingernails to her equally red mouth and flinched. "It's agonizing for him."

Agonizing her ass. Elizabeth snorted and ground her finger down on the bell again. "Well, he should have thought of that before he checked that guy's lights out, shouldn't he?"

"Who are you?" Ta-tas looked hostile and squinty eyed. "It's clear you're not a fan."

"Nope." Not even a little bit, and proud of it. Elizabeth rapped on the door. "Sam! Open the damn door or I'm coming in there after you."

The response came through the shut door loud and strong. "Fuck off."

"Charming." Elizabeth glared at the door then gave it a

healthy pound. "As much as I'd love to comply, your mother is worried about you, which means my mother is worried about your mother, and wants to come home." She took a deep breath. Losing your temper when dealing with Sam didn't work.

Ta-tas watched her with huge, thickly lashed eyes and blinked.

"And my mother is not coming home." Elizabeth punctuated each word with a pound on the door. "My. Mother. Is. Going. To see. The tulips."

Thirty years of living with a man who treated you as nothing more than a convenience deserved a walk in the tulips, and a whole lot more.

"You know his mother?" Ta-tas dialed down on the hostile. "She should come home. He needs her."

"Like hell she's coming home." Elizabeth tried not to glare at Ta-tas. She really couldn't keep calling her that. "What's your name anyway?"

"Maddison. Maddy." She eyed Elizabeth's hand as if it might bite and then slid hers into it. "I'm a fan of Sam's."

"I got that much." Elizabeth dived under the rhododendron. The oval rock was right where it should be. She lifted it and dug out the front door key. "I, however, am not a fan of Sam's." She brandished the key at Maddy. "But I am going in there. You coming?"

Maddy lit up. She really was an extraordinarily pretty girl. "I'd love to." She indicated her outfit. "I'm wearing the team colors." Her smiled died. "Do you think that might upset him? Should I change?"

"Sam'll be fine." Because in order for things to be upsetting you had to have at least the sensitivity of a cockroach, which Sam didn't, ergo Sam would be just peachy.

She turned the key in the lock and opened the door.

It jammed on the security chain and held.

"Dammit!" The security chain gave her a three-inch peep into the house. Pressing her face against the opening she tried to catch sight of him. "Sam! Open the door."

"Not happening," Sam slurred. "I w-want to be alone."

Great, he was drunk, which would increase his obnoxious quotient to around four billion.

"I told you." Maddy looked crushed. "We've been waiting outside his house for two weeks now."

"We?" Elizabeth stared at the chain. There had to be a way into the house. Then the rest of Maddy's statement penetrated. "You've been waiting outside this house for two weeks?"

"Not me personally." Maddy blushed. "There are a group of us. We're here for Sam and we want him to know it." She looked coyly from beneath her lashes. "We call ourselves the Stone Cold Foxes."

"Wow." Elizabeth didn't have much else. She stepped off the porch and circled the house. "What is a Stone Cold Fox, exactly?"

Deeper snow crept over her shins and tried to work its way into her boots. "Great!"

"We're Sam's superfans. Mostly we shorten it to the Foxes." Maddy followed, doing a noteworthy job of walking through snow in five-inch heels, but she had to be feeling it through those sheer black stockings. "What are we doing?"

"Right now we're looking for an open window." The curtains were shut on the lounge and dining room windows, so she couldn't even see inside. She rounded the corner to the back of the house. "And what does a Fox do?"

"We run a Facebook page, an Instagram account and a Twitter feed that's all about Sam. Post pictures of him. Sightings of him out and about." She smirked. "We even get to party with the team sometimes, because Sam knows us, and we don't bug him."

Elizabeth bet Sam knew Maddy, and the others if they looked anything like Maddy. Then she felt like a bitch because Maddy was rather sweet.

"Should we be doing this?" Maddy stopped and stared at the closed house. "Part of being a Fox is respecting Sam's privacy."

Elizabeth gave a casual wave. "It's totally fine. I'm a very old family friend."

Friend was pushing it. She'd known Sam far longer than she cared to remember, nearly in vitro if their mothers were to be believed. She and Sam had pretty much disliked each other from that point as well. Sam's very first fight on the ice had been with her. He had pushed her, and she had whacked him with her hockey stick.

Good times!

"I think he wants to be left alone." Maddy stood on tiptoe beside her as they peered over the windowsill into the open plan family room and kitchen.

At least Sam had shelled out for a great house for his mother. A great house he was now squatting in, refusing to answer the phone, not letting anyone in and generally causing his mother to freak out.

"His mother is worried about him." Elizabeth looked mournful. She wasn't proud of herself but if Maddy's deplorable taste in professional hockey players would help her get into that house, she would use it. "She's going to fly back from Europe, ruin the trip of a lifetime, if we don't reassure her that Sam is all right."

"But Sam's not all right." Maddy sighed.

"Think of her pain, " Elizabeth said. Danica would be in true pain if she could see the way her son had treated her house. Pizza boxes, beer bottles, glasses, takeout containers and plates hid the square walnut coffee table in front of the oversized TV. Of course, he'd bought that for his mother. So she could better view the awesome that was Sam.

Maddy chewed her lip. "You should tell her to come home."

"No." Elizabeth needed a quick recovery. "She doesn't need to. Because you and I are going to make sure that not only is Sam all right, we're going to cheer him up."

"We are?" Maddy blinked at her.

Elizabeth infused her voice with can-do and delivered the deal clincher, suppressing the desire to dry heave around the words that next came out of her mouth. "We're going to save Sam."

Fervor gleamed in Maddy's big brown eyes. "Yes, we are."

"And to do that." Elizabeth pressed her advantage home. "I need to get into the house."

Maddy took a deep breath, and Elizabeth sympathized with straight men everywhere. It was hard to know where to look. "Let's save Sam," Maddy said.

"I'm guessing he's in there somewhere." Elizabeth kept looking.

"Why's there a deck chair in the kitchen?" Maddy pointed to a deck chair with its back to them positioned in the sunlight streaming through the floor to ceiling glass doors leading to the pool.

The deckchair sprouted an arm with a Baileys bottle dangling between long fingers.

"Got him." Elizabeth stared at the tangled top of Sam's head.

Things must be bad if he'd resorted to Danica's stash of Baileys, kept for secret, giggly tipples over the bridge table.

But one only, because ladies didn't drink and get trashed, and Danica Stone was an old-fashioned lady of the sort who never left the house without her lipstick intact and her pantyhose waistband pulled up to her bra.

Elizabeth would never be able to climb in through the window and it was locked tight. That wall around the pool, however, presented definite possibilities. Especially if you knew that the latch on the French doors leading from the pool to the kitchen was faulty and that Danica had been meaning to have it fixed for months.

The same broken latch which you'd had fixed for her, and now kept the keys in your purse for when Danica got back from Europe.

With Maddy trailing her she walked the length of the wall guarding the pool to where a lilac tree abutted it.

She grinned at Maddy. "I'm going in."

———

Sam winced around a sugary mouthful of Baileys and swallowed. He raised the bottle and toasted himself. Sam Stone, right winger on the first line for the Ottawa Titans, picked fourth in the oh-eight draft, the not-so-much phenom of the ice, and now a drunken suspended has-been soaking up the wintry sun in his mother's house because he was too chicken shit to face the world.

What a guy!

The bare branches of the lilac tree on the other side of the pool enclosure shook like a bear was climbing them.

Weird.

If he could sober up for long enough, he could make a run for some decent grog, and lose the Baileys. Sobering up, however, meant dealing, and he wasn't ready for that yet.

There actually was something in the tree. He didn't think it was a bear. It looked definitely human. Maybe Maddy and the rest of the Foxes had decided to take a more aggressive approach.

A warm female body might do what the Baileys was failing to and offer a moment or two of oblivion. Except he'd have to brush his teeth for that, and the bathroom was all the way at the end of the hall, and he wasn't sure he could make it there in one piece.

Besides, it wasn't the Foxes' style to shove themselves forward like common puck bunnies.

But he knew who would consider climbing a tree if he locked her out.

A booted foot appeared on the top of the wall, followed by its twin. The feet edged forward, tottered, and then Lizzie crouched into view.

She clung to the top of the wall for a moment and examined the drop on the pool side.

Yup, it was a bit higher than on the other side.

Lizzie swung her legs over the wall. She was dressed in those yoga leggings that made smart men do stupid things. Lizzie had great legs, long and shapely, which was a pity because of the toxic brain that drove them.

She inched over until she was lying on her stomach and dangled. Her jacket snagged on the wall and revealed her ass sticking straight up in the air.

Along with those nice gams, Lizzie had a killer ass on her, round and full and juicy.

Of course, to get your hands on that ass you would have to run the gauntlet of her personality and that was a hard no.

Her entire body stretched down the wall.

Although for those legs and that ass it might be worth it. Except she'd probably mate with you and eat your head afterwards like those praying mantis things.

Dropping the final foot to the ground, she nailed her landing.

Sam toasted her with Baileys and regretted the action as soon as the sweet blasted his taste buds.

Lizzie wriggled her coat down and smoothed her hair. Not even her climb over the wall had managed to disrupt her neatly contained brown hair or dirty her coat.

She turned and their eyes locked over the length of the pool.

Puck drop!

CHAPTER
THREE

ELIZABETH ALMOST TOOK a victory lap around the pool. Sam thought he could lock her out, did he?

She met his eyes over the pool and smirked. "Got ya."

The French doors were open, so she didn't need Maddy to toss her the key.

"Nice ass." His gaze raked her from top to toe. "Glad to see you haven't lost the best part of you."

"Funny guy." Elizabeth tossed her head. She refused to let Sam's opinion of her get to her. She held up a finger. "Wait! Let me see if I give a crap what you think." She grimaced. "Nope. Not a crap."

He swigged and maintained eye contact. "Aren't you worried your twenty nice cats will starve while you're not there?"

"Again." She shrugged. "Not a crap."

Sam watched her as she walked toward the open door. She put a little swing in her step. His opinion meant nothing to her.

As she got closer, he glanced at the doors.

"Don't bother," she called. "I have the key."

He looked like crap, lounging in the green and white striped deck chair in a pair of track pants and what looked like Danica's pale blue satin bathrobe. Elizabeth refused to look at the strip of bare skin peeking out between the robe's edges. He probably used spray tan to highlight those abs anyway. Except his tanned skin didn't carry the telltale orange of spray tan.

"My eyes are up here." Sam smirked.

He was so vain, but those abs were enough to make any girl lose her way. Except for her and she forced herself to meet his mocking gaze. "I like the new look, Sam."

Around two weeks of beard accounted for the mess on his face, and his hair hadn't seen a comb in as long.

"Ah, Lizzie." He ran a hand over his chest and down over those abs and tucked it into the waistband of his sweats. "You say the sweetest things."

She would not look. She would not look. She would not—

Dammit!

Raising his eyebrow, Sam pulled a cellphone from his robe pocket and dialed.

Elizabeth dragged her brain into the game. She knew that look. It was the same one he'd worn when he had pushed her in the pool at her sweet sixteen. He still owed her for a dress.

"OPP can I help you?" a woman said over the speaker on Sam's cell.

"Don't you dare." Elizabeth ran the remaining distance.

Sam smirked. "Yes, hello this is Sam Stone. Fourteen Montgomery road. I need to report a prowler."

"Hey, Sam. Are you all right?"

Elizabeth recognized Chris's voice and grinned. "He's fine, Chris. I'm his prowler."

"She climbed the wall and broke into my house." Sam looked petulant. "It's your job to get over here and arrest her."

"Yeah, yeah." Chris sighed. "And if I do that, next week she'll be calling me to tell me you're stalking her."

Sam snorted. "She should be so lucky."

"You'd arrest him for me, wouldn't you? Bestie?" Elizabeth let her smug shine through.

"Stop wasting police time and sort it out, children," Chris said, and hung up.

"What are you going to do next?" Elizabeth propped her shoulder against the doorjamb.

Sam sipped his Baileys and grimaced. "I can still throw you in the pool."

"Right." Elizabeth drew the word out. "I'd be surprised if you could throw yourself out of that deck chair."

Sam looked down at himself and then the deck chair. "You're right." He sighed and looked up at her, all cockiness gone. "What do you want, Lizzie?"

"I want my mother to stop calling me." She stepped into the kitchen and recoiled. "Damn, it stinks in here, Sam."

"Window's open."

"And it's freezing."

He took another swig. "You should feel right at home."

"And my mother is not going to stop calling me until your mother stops trying to get on a plane and rush home to you." She shut the door and picked up a beer bottle at her feet and then another, and another. The itch to tidy roared through her, too strong to be denied and she grabbed another bottle and dropped it in the recycling bin beneath the sink.

What the hell. She took the bin out and picked up an empty Jack Daniels bottle.

"What are you doing?' Sam scowled at her.

"And your mother will only stop threatening to come home when she knows you're all right."

Sam clutched his Baileys to his chest. "So tell her I'm all right and go away."

"Wow! When you sulk, you go all out, don't you?"

"I'm not sulking." Sam sniffed. "What the hell do you know about it anyway?"

"As much as I need to." Elizabeth scooped empty cans off the table into her bin. "Which is a lot more than I want to know."

She took the box to the main recycling outside the kitchen door and emptied it with a clatter.

Maddy popped her head around the corner of the house and looked at her hopefully.

"In a minute." Elizabeth motioned her to go around front. "Let me have a chat to him first." And get him to pick his dropped lip up off the floor.

Sam glowered at the pool, and still managed to look ridiculously sexy. Supporting her long-held theory he was one of hell's minions.

"Unfortunately, your mother is not going to settle for me telling her you're okay." She trashed the Styrofoam takeout boxes. Really! Styrofoam! Hadn't they heard of recycling? "Because she knows as well as we do that I really don't care. No, it's going to take some proof."

"What are you babbling about?" Sam sneered at her. "You're the last thing I need right now."

"Right back at ya, big boy." Elizabeth loaded up pizza boxes. "And I'm not here for you. I'm here because of my mom. She needs this holiday, which means she needs your mom not to come rushing home to her precious little boy."

"Screw you."

"Not if you were the last man on earth." It must be the alcohol because as Sam insults went, it was like he wasn't even trying. "So, I tell you what." She stood over him and stared down. "We get you cleaned up. Starting with those teeth. Snap a shot of you looking fine and dandy and you and I go back to pretending the other doesn't exist."

He rolled to his feet and towered over her a good ten inches. She also got more of a sense of how wide and muscled he was when he stood. Her stomach clenched, but she couldn't step back. He'd read that as giving ground, and he'd be right.

"What's wrong with your mom?"

He smelled…awful. "Sam! That breath could kill a cow."

Swaying slightly on his feet, he gave her a flat stare. "I like your mom. I might do it for her."

The implication being not for Elizabeth, but she could work with that. "She divorced my dad."

"Eh?" Sam blinked at her. "I thought she'd done that years ago."

"She should have." Elizabeth didn't like talking about this, so she tidied. It's not like the place didn't need it. "But she finally got around to it earlier this year."

Sam whistled and staggered over to the coffee pot. He swayed over it looking mystified. "There isn't any coffee."

"I'd be happy to make some for you." She held up a hand. "If, and only if, coffee is a precursor to you getting prettied up and letting me take the picture that will put your mom's mind at rest."

He blinked at her. "My mom is really threatening to come home?"

"Go figure." She shrugged. "I'd let you rot, but then I'm not your mother."

"Thank God for small mercies."

"That's the ticket." She punched his shoulder. "Now you're starting to sound more like yourself."

"And you'll go away if I do this?"

Elizabeth nodded. "With pleasure."

He stood there and thought about it. "Make the coffee."

"You'll do it?"

"For your mother." He jabbed a forefinger at her face. "Not for you."

"Got it!" She saluted him and fetched the coffee grounds.

Before he lumbered out of the kitchen, she stopped him. "Sam! Can I get a picture of you like this, for the old scrapbook?"

He gave her the one-finger salute over his shoulder. Definitely not on his A-game, but coffee would help.

Maddy was waiting on the front porch and Elizabeth let her in. "It's worse than we thought."

With a look of horror, Maddy surveyed the kitchen. "How much worse?"

"Sam looked worse than the kitchen."

Maddy's big browns filled with tears. "Poor Sam. This is awful for him."

"He'll rally." Probably. But as long as he did so for long enough for her to get her photo, what did she care? Actually, she sort of cared. A tiny bit. It would take all the fun out of bitching at him if he became a broken-down old wreck. "But first, we need to make sure his mother thinks he's fine."

"What do we do?" Maddy perked up.

"I'm going to send a picture to my mom." The next part was the clincher. "And you said you run social media groups for Sam?"

Maddy nodded.

"The best thing to do would be to make sure a picture of Sam got on one of those. That way his mother won't suspect I'm faking it and she might believe it."

Frowning, Maddy tapped her chin. "Why would his mother not believe it if you were involved."

"Sam and I...have history." Elizabeth loaded glasses and plates into the dishwasher.

Maddy gaped at her. "Romantic history?"

Elizabeth gaped right back. "Dear God, no."

———

Sobering up hurt, and Sam's hands shook so badly, he cut himself three times while shaving. Popping Tylenol with the coffee Liz had made him, he downed six glasses of water before he started to feel partly human.

Missing his track pants already, he pulled on jeans and a sweater.

The man staring back at him from the mirror still looked like shit, but at least he now looked like respectable shit.

Elizabeth moved about the kitchen, speaking to someone. He stopped and listened.

Maddy. His favorite Fox—he suppressed a shudder that Lizzie had heard that name—Maddy never hung on him, and in the five years she'd followed him around, had never once hit on him.

He could deal with Maddy.

The other viper in his mother's kitchen might take more strength than he had right now.

The smell of bacon got him moving and he hit the kitchen salivating.

Elizabeth and Maddy had worked a miracle in the kitchen and were making another one happen in the family room.

"Sam." Maddy teared up. "We've been so worried about you."

If they'd been alone, he might have wallowed in the comfort offered by one of the nicest women he'd ever met.

As it was, he put on a big boy face and accepted Maddy's hug. "I'm good, Maddy. Just spending this time reflecting."

"Really?" Maddy stared into his face, trying to read his thoughts. "Because we want you to know that you're not alone going through this."

Elizabeth snorted and made a clatter shaking the garbage bag and tying off the end.

"Something got you in a tizzy, Lizzie?" He might still feel like four-day-old roadkill in the noonday sun, but his game was heading back to him.

Liz gave him the look of death, sweeping up from his toes to his hairline and back again. "Absolutely nothing."

He didn't bite, and mainly because Lizzie was the source of the bacon smell. Bacon, which she was now plating and putting on the island. He nearly cried when she put a set of cutlery beside it and motioned him to the island. "Eat."

Sam grabbed a stool. You didn't have to put food in front of him twice. At least not the same food.

Maddy sat beside him and watched him eat.

Elizabeth poured him a glass of juice and another cup of coffee. She also watched him eat, but not with the wide-eyed adoration beaming from Maddy. Nope, good ole Liz was giving him the stink eye with both barrels.

"So." He shoveled up bacon and eggs. "What's the plan?"

"Why don't we begin with basic table manners?" Liz curled her lip as she watched him eat.

As he was two-fisting toast and bacon, his mother would have smacked the back of his head. But this was Lizzie, and he grinned and chewed.

She rolled her eyes and turned her back.

"Well." Maddy eyed the two of them and then the door. "I can take a picture of you and post it, and then Elizabeth can tell her mother, who can show your mother."

Sam held his arms out. "Take your picture."

"Not in here." Elizabeth peered down her nose at him. "It needs to be outside. You doing something that will reassure her you're not sitting in her bathrobe drinking yourself into an early grave."

"Ooh, Lizzie." He mimed getting shot. "You wound me."

"Really?" She brightened up. "Say it's true. Don't toy with me like that."

"Ummm." Maddy held her hand up like it was school. "Maybe we could get a shot of Sam playing hockey. That would tell everyone he wasn't sulk—that he was alright."

"I'm not playing hockey." His okay mood crashed back into fucked off again.

Lizzie cocked her head. "That gives me an idea."

"No." Sam stood up so fast he knocked the stool over. It clattered to the ground behind him. "I am not playing hockey."

Maddy squeaked and dashed for the far side of the kitchen.

Not so Lizzie. She squared her shoulders, rounded the island and stared him down. "What's wrong, Sam? Too good to play hockey when someone isn't paying you millions of dollars to do it."

"Back off, Liz." Damn woman didn't know when to stop pushing a man.

Maddy cleared her throat. "Maybe we should—"

"Or what, Sam?"

Damn it to hell but she went toe to toe with him. He could and did say what he wanted about Lizzie, but the girl had guts.

"You going to stamp back into your mommy's room and put her robe on again?" She made a surprised face. "Or maybe you'll punch someone." Her eyes went squinty as she moved in for the kill. "Tell me, Sam? How did that work out for you last time?"

"Sam was provoked." Maddy rounded the island and hovered in their peripheral vision. "Karlov hooked him."

"So Sam broke his jaw. Seems a little disproportionate don't you think?"

No, Sam didn't think that at all. Karlov had a glass jaw and you had no business being on the ice if you couldn't take care of yourself.

"Well." Maddy's voice wobbled. "Maybe it was a little...but Sam has a temper. Everybody knows not to mess with him."

Liz widened her eyes. "I'm shaking in my shoes."

"You should be." Sam gave her his best look. The one that made six four, two-eighty-pound defensemen pale.

Liz was tougher than Philly's goon-squad defense, because she almost had her nose pressed to his as she whispered, "Chicken."

"Say that again."

"Pak!" Liz flapped her elbows. "Pak paaak. Pak, pak, pak. Paaak."

And damned if he didn't want to laugh. Liz did the worst chicken ever. "You still can't do that properly."

"I know." She wrinkled her nose. "Come on, Sam. Don't be a big baby. We take you to the pond, take a photo of you chatting to all the little wannabe Sams and then I get out of your hair, and leave you to Maddy's tender mercies."

"At least Maddy has tender mercies." He sneered. "Not that freezing no-man's land you got going on."

"Whatever." She waved him off. "But you'll do it, right?"

God, he hated giving in to her, but he really did like her mom, and his mom had been talking about this trip to Europe for years. Many, many years. "I'll do it."

CHAPTER
FOUR

VICIOUS MORNING SUNLIGHT bounced off last week's snow and jabbed Sam in the eyes as he sat folded into the front seat of Elizabeth's compact car. A little green pine tree dangled from the rearview mirror, making the car smell like a formaldehyde rainforest. If he didn't think she'd lose her shit, he'd open the window and toss it out.

As if reading his thoughts, she cut her pea-green's his way and said, "Don't."

Even he wasn't that balls to the wall. Things he'd learned about Lizzie's crazy side. One, nobody messed with her car. That lesson he had learned due to a teen dating miscalculation on his part involving beer, curry, and Lizzie being the only person he had been able to think of to call for a ride home. Second, and in no way of less importance, Lizzie took her commitment to the environment seriously. Only a man with a death wish used a straw around Busy Lizzie. Littering would earn you an all season pass to Hurtville.

Pretty face alight with the joy of living, Maddy sat in the back and leaned forward through the front seats. She kept her voice low enough not to hurt his fragile ears. God, the drinking thing had a savage payback. Not being much of a drinker, he had forgotten what a hangover felt like. Which almost took him back to the aforementioned Curry-pocalypse of '07.

When you'd been in training since you were twelve, alcohol hit your system like a Canadian National freight train.

Lizzie drove like she did everything else, on the cautious side and strictly by the rules. She must be the only person he knew who actually went forty kilometers in a school zone. Every single school zone, and he'd never noticed before how many schools there were in this place.

Canadians were a law-abiding group, as a rule, but even then, most people hovered somewhere between forty and fifty.

Not Lizzy. She tapped the breaks and kept the needle at forty like the thing was Superglued there.

It reminded him of an old joke.

"Hey, Maddy?"

She craned forward. "Yes, Sam?"

"How do you get a hundred Canadians out of a swimming pool?"

Maddy twinkled at him, and damn was she pretty with her eyes sparkling like that. "I don't know, Sam. How do you get a hundred Canadians out of a swimming pool?"

"You ask them." Lizzy dropped the punchline.

Big surprise. She always did like to rain on his parade. He never got why everyone else thought she was so sweet and generous and kind, like the Tooth Fairy and Pollyanna, all rolled into one sexy package.

Sue him, Prissy Lizzie was sexy, in an if-you-touch-me-I'll-deball-you kind of way.

Maddy giggled, because she didn't save her sweet for everyone else but him.

The bright winter sun turned Lizzie's skin marble white and it was as smooth and beautiful as he remembered. Thinking of Lizzie as beautiful would only get his nuts mangled, so he went for the distraction. "Have you ever gotten a speeding ticket?"

"No." She side-eyed him.

"Parking ticket?"

"No." She frowned. "Are you bugging me about my driving?"

"Of course he isn't." Maddy patted Liz's shoulder. "You're a wonderful driver. I feel perfectly safe."

Lizzie wasn't a bad person; she was just a bit uptight. He didn't blame her growing up the way she did, but he did resent that she couldn't be nicer to him. Then again, Paul had pretty much ignored his daughters and paid more attention to him. "How's your dad taking the divorce?"

Lizzie flinched a tiny bit and Sam wanted to kick himself. Her dad was always a touchy subject between them. And that was saying something. He and Liz could argue about the color of the sky. "He seems okay."

Sam was willing to bet Paul Rogers was fine. The guy had been good to him once his hockey talent had showed up, but that didn't make Sam blind to his faults. Paul Rogers was the most self-absorbed man on the planet, and this coming from Sam Stone.

The way he treated his wife and daughters had made an impact on Sam even as a kid. The I'll never treat any woman of mine like that kind of impact. He'd eat his skates if Paul had even noticed his wife was gone.

Lizzie turned into the parking lot for Brock Park and found a space. She eased her compact straight in and equidistant from the cars on either side.

"We're going to the pond?" He had been quite clear on the no playing hockey thing in the kitchen.

Lizzie threw him a bright smile. "Yup. I thought it would make a great photo. You outside, little Sams playing hockey, big Sam smiling and being encouraging."

That he could do. Actually, it was an awesome idea. The internet ate this shit up. Sam opened the car door. "Let's do this."

"Perfect." Maddy hopped out beside him. She took a deep

breath of the fresh air and smiled. "It's so pretty here."

"Yeah. I used to play pond hockey here as a kid." It was working a winter wonderland theme this morning, all sparkly clean white snow and powder draped trees.

Lizzie came around from the back of the car with a large tote bag. As long as he'd known her, Lizzie had toted shit around. He'd given up asking what was in her wide array of bags.

He took this one from her and followed them on the path toward the pond.

"Every winter they turn the duckpond into an outdoor rink." In that way women had, Lizzie and Maddy seemed to have hit it off.

Maddy glanced behind at him. "And you played here?"

"Yup." Lizzie's must be carting bricks in this bag.

"Sam started playing hockey here," Lizzie said. "You'd never guess it to look at him now, but he was quite a sickly baby."

"Really?" Maddy ran her big brown eyes over him. "Not anymore."

"Nope, not anymore." Sam wasn't a big fan of discussing this, but Lizzie was on a roll and stopping her now would make an even bigger deal.

"His mom and mine have been best friends since they were at school." Apparently, Lizzie was going to do the entire family history for Maddy. Yay!

Lizzie giggled. "You won't believe this, but my mom was pregnant with me when Sam was about eight months old. They actually had this plan that Sam and I might grow up and get married."

They broke into cackles, laughing so hard they had to lean against each other.

Hardy har har. "They didn't think that for long."

Not when, as the story went, their first play date had involved a set of plastic kid's skittles. He'd wanted the blue one Lizzie had, and when she wouldn't give it had whacked her with the red one. Typical Lizzie, she'd schooled him right back with the blue one.

The path wound through a stand of towering spruces. Shouts and laughter from the pond drifted over with the scratch of blades on ice.

"The doctors recommended to Danica that she get Sam into sport." Lizzie shrugged. "She put skates on him, and the rest is history."

Not quite the entire story, but he appreciated Lizzie not going into it. Mom had stood pond side and flinched every time he fell off his skates or got bumped by another player. On one ego-shriveling occasion, she had even run across the ice and berated another boy for checking him.

Jesus, that day had sucked. It had also been the birth of years of teasing. Some of those pond hockey kids had followed him into the peewee leagues and so had his reputation for being a momma's boy.

Well, he'd shut them up. Amazing what a couple of good hits will do to close a set of flapping lips.

They broke free of the trees into a natural depression in the undulating terrain of the park.

The pond hadn't changed at all. A squat brick building with glass windows housed the skate rentals, bathrooms, and a small restaurant. Rubber matting led from the hut, as they called it, to the ice.

A teen girl crab walked her way down the matting toward the ice. She clung to the young guy with her, giggling and giving him big eyes.

Sam knew that play. The let's go skating, I'll hold on to you, so you don't fall play. He'd gotten his first kiss behind the hut from a grateful skating companion.

Little kids stayed to a small side section of the pond that housed the fountains in summer, clinging to their skating frames. Moms and dads hovered around them. Young studs weaved through the slower traffic. To the center a few couples held hands and did the whole let it snow romance thing. Cue Harry Connick Junior.

Beside the pond, and their destination, was the outdoor rink. On the main pond it was free skating, all comers welcome. But the rink was hockey only. If you graduated to the rink beside the pond you carried a hockey stick and needed to use it.

A kid's game was in progress as they approached.

Sam had played some of the best games of his life on this rink. The bigger kids always looked out for the little ones. They had played until the sun went down and the evening cold drove them all home. Then arriving home, exhausted and chilled to the bone with only enough energy to shower and shovel food down your face before hitting the sack.

A kid in a blue coat cranked a snapshot into the back of the net. Cheers and groans filled the air.

Not bad. Neither was the kid's drop to one knee slide with a fist pump celly. Sam had been hours perfecting that move in preparation for when he scored his first league goal.

"Hey!" A boy yelled and pointed. "It's Sam."

"The whole town knows him," Lizzie said to Maddy.

Maddy beamed like a proud parent. "Of course they do. They must be very proud of you."

"Did you see my snapshot?" The kid in the blue coat turned an eager face up at him.

Sam couldn't help but smile. The love of hockey transcended age. "I saw it. You keep that up for a few years and I might have to watch my back."

"Are you here to play?" A bunch of other eager faces joined the kid in the blue coat.

"Nah." Sam shoved his hands in his pockets. "You guys are too good for me."

"No." Lots of heads shook at once. "Come and play with us."

"I would guys, but I'm with my friends here and I didn't bring my skates." He hooked Lizzie around the nape and hauled her into him.

She surprised the hell out of him when she slipped an arm around his waist, her curves pressed against him slowing his brain down for a few fatal seconds. "Funny you should say that, Sam."

A nasty feeling wormed up through his gut and he tightened his grip on her.

Lizzie gave him her sunshine and unicorn rainbow-farts smile. "Your skates are in the bag."

CHAPTER
FIVE

THE RINGING PHONE woke Sam the next morning. He scrabbled for it and answered. "What?"

"Sam?" His mother's concern crept down the line. "Did I wake you?"

"Uh...no." He checked the bedside clock. Half past eleven and time he was up and about. "I was reading."

"Oh." She took a breath. "I've been trying to get hold of you for two weeks."

"I answered." He chugged the glass of water by his bedside.

Mom got soft and wounded. "You texted me."

Guilt body checked him.

"Yeah, sorry about that." He scrubbed his face and tried to wake his ass up. "I needed time."

"From you mother?" *Bam!* Into the boards again.

"From everyone, Mom." From himself mostly. After Maddy had left last night, he'd climbed into a leftover quart of Jack Daniels that Way-too-Busy Lizzie hadn't discovered. She'd even tossed his Baileys out. "It's been a bad couple of weeks. I needed to get my head together."

"Oh, Sam." Mom sighed, and her voice wavered. "I've been

so worried about you since I watched the game. Then I couldn't get hold of you."

He worked saliva back into his desiccated mouth. "Sorry about that, Mom. Sometimes a guy has to do what he has to do." What a dick thing to say. He could imagine what Liz would have to say if she'd heard him.

Mom was a lot kinder than Liz, and probably a lot kinder than he deserved. "I was so relieved when I saw that photo of you in the park last night."

He didn't know what she was on about. Then it hit him. The park, yesterday, Liz and Maddy and damn Liz pushing all his buttons.

"I've been trying to get out there. You know, spend time with people." Was that ass burning sensation his pants on fire?

"Really?" Mom didn't sound convinced. Then again, she had known him since his ass was cracked. "Because Mrs. Koenig says she hasn't seen you outside the house in two weeks."

And Mrs. Koenig would know. Nosy old biddy probably had her binoculars trained on their house all day and night.

"You know Mrs. K." He kept it light. "She probably went for a nap and missed seeing me."

"Hmm. She doesn't miss much." Mom took a breath. "Anyway, seeing you with those children did my heart good."

As much as he really, really didn't want to, he had to give that one to Lizzie. Taking him to the park and making him talk to the kids playing pond hockey had been inspired. Even if the sneaky bitch had suddenly produced his skates, and he had spent the next two hours playing pond hockey with the under-eight contingent. Side note and not worth mentioning to Lizzie, he'd had a blast.

He missed hockey. Its absence in his life ached like a sore tooth. Yesterday had brought everything he had to lose rushing back.

"I'm fine, Mom." He managed to sound convincing. "I'm

suspended for twenty games, but after that, I'll be back on the ice."

"Oh, that's good, Sam. I don't know what you'd do without hockey," Mom said.

Neither did he. He also didn't mention that his twenty-game suspension was only the penalty imposed on him by the league. His coach had sent him away with a clear message. Straighten up and fly right, or he was grounded. Forever. His agent had gone one further. Once the Titans were done with him, there was nobody else who would touch him.

For the first time since his mother had laced him into skates at three-years-old, he was staring straight into a future that didn't include hockey. It seemed everyone was tired of Sam Stone's crap. Even Sam Stone. Especially Sam Stone.

After chatting with his mom a bit longer, and even managing some enthusiasm for her visit to the tulips, he lay in bed and stared at the ceiling of the spare room.

He'd bought mom this house when he'd first been drafted by the 'Cudas. As nice as it was, and as much as Mom loved it, this house wasn't home to him. Neither was his apartment in the ByWard market.

He missed his bedroom in their old house. The one with the huge posters of Gretzky, Roy, and Lemieux. The room that had always stank of hockey gear. Back then he had lived and breathed hockey with a passion bordering on obsession. When Mom got him his first brand new Bauer stick, he'd slept with the thing.

Too restless to sleep, he climbed out of bed and wandered through to the kitchen naked. If Quizzy Lizzie climbed the wall this morning, she'd get a real eyeful. He'd changed since they used to bath together as tots. So had she, and in ways he wouldn't mind catching an eyeful of.

Another side note never to be mentioned to Lizzie.

She and Maddy had done a good job of the cleanup yesterday. He put some coffee on and gave the countertops a careless swipe. He'd have to get a cleaner in here before Mom came back.

His cell rang and he checked caller display.

Coach.

Heart pounding, he took the call. "Hey, Coach."

"Stoney, how you doing, big guy?"

Stoney? Big guy? A jovial coach made him twitchy. "Fine, and you?"

"Can't complain." Coach chuckled. "Well, I could but what fucking good would it do me? Am I right? Tell me I'm right."

Oh-kay. Last time he and Coach had been together, they hadn't parted buddies. "Team's doing well?"

"Yeah, not bad. Playoffs are looking doubtful though." Coach had his management shit-eating voice on. "We're missing our big guy."

Fucking time out here! "What's going on, Coach?"

"What, I can't call one of my favorite players and see how they're doing?"

Sam rolled his eyes. He hated this side of pro sports. Even a gruff old war horse like Coach had to pull the schmooze wagon. "Considering you called me a shit for brains, fuck headed goon the last time we saw each other, I'm a little dubious."

And then coach had said the thing that made him itch for the bottle again. "Stone, you're a two-hundred-and-seventy-degree player. It's all there but the ninety degrees that would make you a hall of famer."

Coach did his warthog grunt. The one he used when he'd been caught out or embarrassed. "Had a chat to the league this morning. They asked after you."

"Yeah?" He needed to sit down.

"They're reviewing the duration of your suspension."

He grabbed a kitchen stool and dropped on it. "And?"

"For the first time they might be thinking a shorter term."

"Yeah?" He couldn't get any more words past the constriction in his chest. "What did they say?"

"Look, Stoney, they're not promising anything but they like the direction they see you going in, and they would certainly be amenable if they were to see more of the same."

The only direction he had been going in was right to the bottom of the Jack Daniels bottle. Pushing on through to the end of *Orange is the New Black*. Except for yesterday.

"What did they like? Specifically?" He needed to play this cool or he'd blow it.

A second call bleeped. His agent. Another stalwart soul conspicuous by her absence for two weeks.

Coach cleared his throat. "The whole thing. You playing with the kids. Out there being an ambassador for the sport even when you're suspended. The cute girl who doesn't look anything like a hooker."

Holy Fuckballs! The only woman he hung out with who didn't look like a hooker was Lizzie. He almost snorted. They wouldn't say that if they'd clocked her ass coming over his wall yesterday.

"Whoever she is, she's good for your image," Coach said. "Gives the right impression of who you really are. Off the ice."

"Right." Liz would bust a gut laughing if she could hear this conversation. "She's just a friend."

"Ke-rist, Stoney! I don't give a crap who you're fucking. Keep that shit to yourself."

Only Coach had brought it up, but what the hell. "So, what you're saying is that the league likes the way I'm handling my suspension."

"Yep." Coach sniffed. "Seagulls like it too. Made sure to send the message down the line. They like to see you looking like a team player."

Part of that missing ninety degrees Coach went on about. Apparently Sam was not a team player. Also the reason often cited for why he had been traded as many times as he had.

Management was looking kindlier on him, and if Coach was making this call—which he was—he was doing the same.

"Well." Sam gave it all the sincerity he had in him. "I wasn't happy about the suspension, but I've been using this time to think. Get back to the basics. Touch base with my love of the game."

"Right." Coach cleared his throat. "Whatever the fuck that means. Do more of it."

After Coach hung up, Sam padded through to the laundry and found a pair of boxers. Only then did he dial his agent.

"Sam!" Tammi had a voice made for phone sex and the toughest head in sport. "I'm gonna send you a fruit basket, you clever, clever boy."

"What bit of genius are you referring to this time?"

"The pictures." She sounded surprised. "The ones that hit the old inter webs yesterday evening and have been zinging all over the twitter-facebook-insta-snapchat-verse ever since."

Maddy had taken pictures that he hadn't bothered to look at.

"Tell me, for realz, did you set them up?" Tammi giggled, bringing to mind a smirking boa constrictor. "Don't tell me. I don't wanna know."

"I…um…it happened."

"Well, it happened in the right way at the right time," Tammi said. "Even Marc Gracie had nothing shitty to say about them."

"Huh!" Marc—fuck nuts—Gracie. The bane of Sam's life, and the most respected sport's journalist in hockey. Gracie had been making byline after byline on Sam's suspension. A big advocate for cleaning up the on-ice fireworks, Gracie had made Sam his poster boy for everything wrong with hockey.

"A couple of the other guys had some stuff to say." Tammi read him a few snippets.

Sam let her roll. Getting a word in with Tammi took skill his pre-coffee brain didn't have.

Somehow Lizzie had hit on the magic key to unlocking his chains. His suspension had come on the back of several questionable hits last playoff season. To be fair, only some of those hits were his, but when you were big, fast and not afraid to drop gloves, you earned yourself a reputation.

The league had come under heavy fire for not doing anything. Mothers against violence in sports—MAVIS—had been knocking on influential doors and turning their focused maternal eye his way. When MAVIS yelled, people paid attention.

"Anywho, baby blue, what you need to know is that your star is on the rise again. Up, up, up and away." Tammi laughed like grating steel. "And I'm calling to impress upon you, in the strongest terms, to keep on keeping on. Following that yellow brick road. Rolling down that river."

The coffee had dripped enough for Sam to get a mug under it and take a slug. "You got something for me?"

"Nothing definite but the sharks are circling."

"The Sharks?"

"Not the actual sharks." Tammi tsked. "But there are teams looking to drop their hooks in the water."

She went on in that vein for a bit longer while Sam finished his coffee and went for another. Once he'd hung up, he hit Twitter.

Maddy had excelled herself and the Foxes had taken the threads and run with them. One picture had gotten the most traction. The sky was blue behind them, the snow Tide detergent white. In the foreground rosy cheeked kids played pond hockey. And right slap dab in the middle was him, with his arm around Liz's neck as he whispered in her ear.

Liz's big green eyes sparkled. Her wide mouth was split in a laugh. She looked hot. Not that he would, but still hot.

They looked like a couple sharing a private moment. If say, the reality the picture did not reflect was that one member of that loving duo had the other in a headlock and was whispering, "You're going to pay for this, Dizzy Lizzie."

CHAPTER
SIX

ELIZABETH LEFT work about five minutes to seven the following evening. Thus far today had been the Mondayest Monday ever.

Dad had been balled out by a client for a shoddy job done of cleaning their offices, which had somehow become all Elizabeth's fault.

The Humane Society had called in a panic asking her to help them sift through applications. She'd used her lunch break to drive out there and pick them up. If it were up to her, she'd take all the dogs, all the time. This way she could still help the puppies out.

Now the women's auxiliary was deadlocked over baked versus knitted goods at their stall for the high school fundraiser. Libby Singer had threatened to resign her presidency, for the eighth time this year and it was only March, and current treasurer Elene Clemmens had her foot in Libby's back, shoving her out of the president's chair. Auxiliary members hovered between those two camps, many changing sides. Elizabeth had managed to get the rock and the hard place talking to each other, and tensions had eased somewhat.

To top off a fantastic day, Jane had stomped into the kitchen as Elizabeth was sliding dinner into the oven for them.

"You need to cover for me." In a poured-on dress that left nothing to the imagination and glaring at her from between road markings of black liner, Jane had stormed into the kitchen and struck a defiant pose. "My friends and I are going downtown for a pub crawl."

If Mom were here, she'd handle her gently but firmly. "Janey, you're not old enough to drink and none of your friends have their full license yet. If they're caught drinking, you know what the repercussions will be."

"I have a fake ID." Jane looked at her as if her head might explode. "And we won't get caught. We'll take an Uber."

Even as she said the words, Elizabeth braced for the hideous fallout. "I'm sorry, Janey, but I'm not going to cover for you. I'd be worried sick about you, and if anything happened to you, I would never forgive myself."

Jane's eyes narrowed like a striking viper's. "Are you fucking kidding me?" She pulled her lips back in a snarl. "I wasn't asking for your permission. You're not fucking Mom."

"No, I'm not Mom." She refused to rise to the bait being doublehanded about. "But just because Mom's not here, doesn't mean we can do what we want."

"I'm eighteen. Nobody can tell me what to do," Jane bellowed.

"And the drinking age is nineteen." Elizabeth put the salad in the fridge. "I'm not telling Dad you're with me."

"Jesus, Elizabeth. Were you always so fucking lame?"

She probably was. She set the timer for the oven to turn itself off, because nobody would bother if she didn't. "And don't you have school tomorrow anyway?"

"I'm going!" Jane stormed out of the house, slamming the door hard enough to make the windowpanes rattle.

Elizabeth finished making dinner for her father and left it on the counter. She also left a note telling him Jane was out with her friends. She tried to introduce her concerns around Jane's plans without being alarmist. Dad wouldn't listen anyway, but she had to try.

That done, she had a date with Haagen Dazs Belgian Chocolate and the adoption applications for the Humane Society.

Jane worried her. Even before Mom had left, Jane had been doing pretty much as she wanted. Dad left it to Elizabeth to try to check the runaway train of teen willfulness that was Jane Margaret Rogers.

In her car, she put in a call to Mountain Vista.

"Elizabeth," Carol sounded tinny over the Bluetooth connection. "How are you? Busy as ever?"

She went with her standard response. "It keeps me out of trouble."

"And us grateful," Carol said. As director of the retirement center, Carol was always scrambling for volunteers. "Are we seeing you tomorrow?"

Every Thursday evening for drama night. "Yup."

"Elizabeth." Carol sighed. "Don't get me wrong, we couldn't do drama night without you, but isn't there some stud whose libido you should be torturing?"

If only. Not since Peter anyway. Peter had been a nice guy but there had been no libido torturing for either of them. "You know me, a sucker for a show tune."

"Ha!" Carol snorted. "You're a pushover and we all take shameless advantage of you."

Carol said much the same most times they talked. "Anyway, I called for an update on the new bus."

"About that." Carol sighed. "So far, we've raised seventy-eight dollars and twenty-five cents."

Elizabeth waved to the Jessop family in the car next to her. Three of the four boys were on Chris's hockey team. She rolled down her window and mouthed, "Hockey forms," to Debbie Jessop.

Debbie nodded, waved, and they both drove on.

She turned her attention back to Carol. "Somebody donated a quarter?"

"They told me every drop counts," Carol said. "And they're not wrong."

At this rate the retirement village would have its new bus by the time she took up residence there. "All right then." Elizabeth turned into her street. "I'll put my thinking cap on."

The residents really needed this new bus to get to their shopping days, and for excursions out of the center. The old one was on its last legs and had never had enough space to meet the senior's needs.

"I'd appreciate that," Carol said. "I don't know what the residents would do without you."

Walking everywhere seemed a certainty. "You won't have to find out," she said.

She hadn't meant to get dragged into fundraising for the new bus, like she hadn't meant for Thursday night drama club to become a regular thing.

Drama club had started as Christmas caroling two years ago. Somehow their caroling group had been persuaded to come back for New Year, and then Perry Staven's birthday the following Thursday. At which stage most of the other carolers had seen the pattern and dropped out, leaving her and Leonard Smytkowski. As a child, he'd been in the New York Ballet's *Nutcracker Suite* for three years running and liked nothing more than to "immerse himself in the glory of the theatre."

Which reminded her she needed to have the script for *South Pacific* copied, because Leonard's idea of glorious immersion didn't include the grunt work.

Chris never got why Elizabeth enjoyed working at Mountain Vista, but both Elizabeth's sets of grandparents had died before she'd gotten to know them. She loved hearing the resident's stories, and spending time with them. They were a charming mixture of wisdom, fragility, and past giving a crap. Some residents, mostly those in pain, could run the gamut from crotchety to mean, but they didn't bother her. Most had earned the right to a little bad temper.

Elizabeth turned into her condo parking lot and stopped. "Damn it!"

A red minivan in Elizabeth's spot meant Bonnie from 4B had her boyfriend over for the night.

"Once." Elizabeth glared at the minivan. "I said you could park there once."

She idled behind Bonnie's minivan, trying to work up the righteous indignation to get Bonnie to move her car.

Nope. She didn't have it in her. A request to move the car would result in a debate, possibly tears on Bonnie's part and belligerence from Randy.

Elizabeth parked in a visitor's space and grabbed the box of sign-up sheets to Chris's team from her backseat. Once she was done with the adoption applications, she could start getting the team paperwork together. It didn't matter how many times you told parents they needed to sign the waiver, there was still the chase to get it done. As a cop, Chris didn't have the time.

Also, and more to the point, Chris lacked the patience with the parents, but she was great with the kids, and Chris's kids needed the team.

Rounding the corner from visitor's parking, she saw Sam sitting on the stairs leading to her condo. She stopped and her blood pressure shot up.

"No." She shook her head because her hands were too full for appropriate hand gestures. "Whatever you're doing here, and whatever it is you want, the answer is no."

"Lizzie." Sam stood and spread his arms wide. Dressed in jeans and a Nike sweatshirt beneath his open coat, he looked well. Delicious. Better than he had the last time she'd seen him. "You haven't even heard what I have to say."

"I don't need to." She climbed the few steps separating them and sidled past him. "My mother hasn't called, which means your mother is fine. We're done."

"Where's your car?" He took the box of signups from her.

After a brief tussle, Elizabeth let him have it. "Parked around the side."

"But isn't that your spot?" Sam jerked his thumb at Bonnie's minivan.

She wasn't getting into it with him. She wasn't getting into anything with him. "Yup."

"Why are they parked in your spot?"

Elizabeth dug her key from her purse. "Go away, Sam."

"I will, if you tell me why someone else is parked in your spot."

"Why do you care?" Elizabeth turned the key. It jammed in the lock and stuck. "Damn it!"

"I don't care." Sam shouldered her out of the way, tucked the box beneath his arm and took the key. "But if it was me parked in your spot, you'd have keyed my door by now."

Damn lock slid back as if it hadn't spent the last three months jamming for her. "Bonnie's a single mother, and Randy is the best boyfriend she's had in a while. He's good to her."

Smirking, Sam opened her door and motioned her to precede him. "Of course."

"You're not coming in." Elizabeth barred his path. "And what does of course mean anyway?"

"Busy Lizzie's bleeding heart to the rescue." Sam sidestepped her. "This won't take long."

She didn't have a bleeding heart, but life had been really shitty for Bonnie with her ex, and Randy—parking stealing aside —took care of Bonnie and her four-year-old twins. Bonnie certainly didn't need an uptight, picky neighbor getting in her face. It took a couple of minutes extra—tops—to walk from visitor's parking to her door.

Of more immediate concern was Sam's intrusion in her space. He took up too much real estate and her condo felt too small to contain him. As much as she wanted him gone, that set to his jaw said he wouldn't be going before he said his piece, and she certainly couldn't pick up all six three, two hundred and ten pounds of him and toss him out.

So what if she had his stats memorized, most of greater Ottawa did and he didn't need to know that.

Slipping out of his coat, he looked around him. "This is nice."

Elizabeth snatched his coat off the back of her couch where he'd tossed it and hung it by the door. Her condo was nice. It was her space, handpicked by her to make her feel as if she was in her own private oasis. Neutral walls, and hardwood floors gave the condo an elegant feel. Elizabeth had scattered brightly patterned green accents throughout, with a bit of over the top here and there.

"I actually came by to thank you for yesterday." Sam put the box of forms on the kitchen counter.

Now she knew he wanted something, and it was a big enough favor he was prepared to kiss ass, her ass at that, to get it. She folded her arms and stared at him. "Uh-huh?"

"Mom called me this morning and she's staying in Europe." He held out his hand. "We did good work there."

Elizabeth eyed his outstretched hand. If she took that, he'd take a mile. No way. "How long have we known each other, Sam?"

"Since we were babies." His expression grew guarded.

A pain in her ass, but never stupid, he knew when to get wary. "In all that time have we ever worked well together?"

"Well, th—"

"Sam!"

"Okay, we suck at teamwork." He realized his mistake and tried to backtrack. "Or we did until yesterday."

"Nope." She shook her head. "Try again."

He met her stare, challenge glittering in his blue eyes. "I'm here to express my gratitude?"

Like hell. She snorted.

"Bury the hatchet?"

"In my back?"

"Talk about old times?"

"I don't want blood on my walls."

"Kindle an old flame?"

She mimed dry heaving.

"Okay." Sam held up his hands. "I'm here to ask you for a favor."

"Ah hah!" Now that had the ring of truth to it and Elizabeth walked into the kitchen. She grabbed her ice cream and a spoon and sat down by her island, facing him. "What do you want?"

"Is that Haagen Dasz?" Sam zeroed in on her ice cream.

Elizabeth dug her spoon in and popped it in her mouth. All that rich chocolatey bitter and sweet creaminess exploded on her tongue. "Is there any other type of ice cream?"

Sam studied her mouth, then rounded the island, grabbed himself a spoon from the drawer and sat beside her. He wagged his fingers for the carton.

Elizabeth glared, and then handed it over.

He slid a full spoon into his mouth, closed his eyes and groaned. "That is the bomb, right there."

"Yup." Elizabeth reclaimed her ice cream. Sam's mouth was hard like the rest of his face, but when he smiled it spread wide and surprised you with its warmth. "Get to it, Stone. I'm tired, I've had a shitty day, and I've got a life to live."

"Your shitty day have anything to do with whoever stole your parking space?" He jerked his head in that direction.

His sable hair caught the light and looked soft and silky. It was so unfair how men got the hair and the eyelashes. Especially unfair when that man was Sam. She should have shaved his head when they were kids.

Oh, that's right, she had.

She smirked and pushed him the ice cream. "Nah, that's just the cherry on top."

He looked at her. Sam did a great look. It silently demanded you tell him stuff.

Elizabeth resisted for thirty seconds, and then caved. "Car belongs to Bonnie, my downstairs neighbor. When her boyfriend comes around, he uses her spot and she takes mine."

"And you let her?" Sam gaped.

"I let her once." Okay and then there had been the time Randy broke his finger. "Okay twice she asked, and I said yes. Now she doesn't ask anymore."

Sam shook his head. "So tell her to move her car."

"She's a single mother."

"And?"

Damn he could gnaw a thing to death. "It's not easy to raise two little boys without support."

"I get that Lizster, got all the love in the world for a single mother, but what does that have to do with her taking your parking?"

They could go back and forth all night with this. "Because I'm tired, all right. I haven't had the best day and all I want to do is eat my ice cream in peace, put on some TV and relax."

"No date?" His eyes gleamed. "No Lizzie getting busy?"

"Ugh." She snatched her ice cream back. "You're so annoying." Which raised another point. "And didn't you hear the part about me wanting to eat my ice cream and relax. Alone."

"I heard you." He grinned, his annoying smug, too charming grin. "But I'm ignoring that. Back to the neighbor."

"No, I don't want to talk about that." She shoved her mouth full of ice cream.

Sam snagged her carton. "Then I'll talk." He winked. "I'll even get to the point."

She rolled her eyes because words were wasted on him.

"You know I got suspended?"

"Yup."

"Well, there's a chance I can get that suspension lifted. If I toe the line and play nice." Sam shifted his gaze to the side. His tell for when he wasn't giving her the entire truth.

She poked his shoulder with her spoon. "You're not telling me something."

"I'm telling you everything." He ostentatiously brushed the spot where her spoon had left a small mark on his shirt.

"Nope." Elizabeth dug out more ice cream and ate it. Keeping her gaze on his, she shook her head slowly.

Sam scowled, as he made up his mind whether to come clean with her or not. If he did or not would tell her how important this favor was to him.

He opened his mouth and shut it again. Then took a deep breath. "Okay I'll tell you, but this is not public knowledge and I don't want it getting that way."

She crossed her heart with her spoon. They may hate each other but she wouldn't blab his secrets. She liked his mother. And her mother loved his mother and the whole thing would get nasty.

"My team is pissed at me." He clenched his jaw. "They are talking about not renewing my contract."

That did surprise her. Since the day he'd stepped on the ice, teams had been chasing Sam. Girls too. Except for her. "Are they threatening to trade you?"

Sam cleared his throat and grabbed the ice cream. "My agent says interest is low."

Elizabeth let that sink in. Sam lived and breathed hockey, and he was incredible at it. She couldn't believe somebody wouldn't want him. "What does that have to do with me?"

"The pictures you took yesterday." He lost all cockiness and met her gaze. "Everybody liked them. They want to see more of them and if they do, it would go a long way to reassuring everyone I've learned my lesson."

"Have you?" She really doubted that.

Sam smirked. "You know me better than that."

"So you want me to take more pictures with you?"

"Partly." He side-eyed again. "Maybe also you could let me hang out with you. Doing the things you do. Being all fucking saintly and everything."

The insult was too old to hurt. "So, you want us to pretend to hang out and be friends?"

"And." He took a breath. "They might have assumed we were more than friends."

It was her turn to gape. "Why would they assume that, Sam?"

She'd kill him if he had said something.

Sam took out his phone and thumbed it open. He showed her a picture of the two of them.

Elizabeth looked at it and looked at it again. It did, sort of, look like they were more than they were. Maybe even a bit couply. *Somebody pass the eye bleach.*

"I'm not pretending to be your girlfriend." She handed his phone back to him. "One, because I'm not that good of an actor, and two because I already have someone in my life."

"Who?" He frowned. "And why isn't he here now then?"

"He's busy." She made a cutting motion with her hand. "I'm not talking about Peter to you." Mainly because she and Peter had ended a couple of months ago, to what she suspected, was mutual relief. "Besides which, I watch chick flicks. I know how these things end, and even the chance we might get together…" She shuddered.

He glared at her. "Lots of women. Lots. Would love the opportunity to be my girlfriend."

"Then find one of them." Gotcha, and she smirked.

Sam backed down. "I can't. Because they've already seen you and they like your image and what you say about me."

She wanted to hear this. "What do I say about you?"

"That I'm boring as fuck."

"Out!" She stood and pointed at the door. He'd crossed the line.

"I'm sorry." He leaped up and grabbed her pointing finger,

his grip warm and calloused. "Force of habit. You made me look like I'm a nice guy who cares about people and my community."

She snorted. "Nobody can do that."

"Look, Elizabeth." Using her name the way she liked it used said he was desperate. "I need this, and I'm prepared to make it worth your while. Tell me what you want in exchange."

He'd dropped a cherry in her lap, and she needed a moment to capitalize.

"And you don't have to pretend to be my girlfriend," he said. "All you have to do is hang out with me, pretend you're having a good time, and if anyone asks, we'll say we're just friends."

"Which they'll assume to mean something more," she said.

"We say nothing." He pulled a face.

She played for time. "What do I tell Peter?" No way she was letting Sam know there wasn't anyone in her life. She couldn't risk him thinking she was hanging around waiting for him to wander into her life.

"The truth." He shrugged. "We go way back and we're hanging out together."

"I need to think about it."

"I'll introduce you to Dawson." His face got cunning.

Damn, that was hitting below the belt. There wasn't much a girl wouldn't do to meet Craig Dawson. "I can't promise any more than to think about it."

Sam's face cleared into a smile. "Great! We can discuss terms tomorrow night. Over dinner." He strode for the door. "And wear something sexy." He grimaced at her sensible navy pencil skirt and white shirt. "I have my reputation to protect."

Asshole! Elizabeth chased after him to tell him she'd changed her mind, but he already had the door open and was trotting down the stairs. "I'll pick you up at eight."

"No, I—"

"Eight, Lizzie." He stopped outside Bonnie's door and banged on it.

The door opened and Randy stood there. "What?" His mouth dropped open and he stared. "Are you—"

"You're parked in my friend's spot." He pointed to the mini-van. "Don't be a dick, man. Move your car."

"S-sure, Sam Stone. Sure." Randy yelled for Bonnie and the keys.

Sam looked up at her and smirked. He drew a one through the air. His round.

CHAPTER
SEVEN

NEITHER ELIZABETH, nor any of her friends, knew how to dress for a date with a professional hockey player. If it was a normal meeting with Sam, say one of the forced get-togethers their mothers had pioneered over the years, no problem. Diarrhea day track pants and that sweater you kept in your pajama drawer would do.

But they'd made a deal and Elizabeth had worked out her price. She needed to show Sam what he was getting, in the "just friends" department. Also, what girl didn't want to have her Cinderella moment? If only shove it down Sam's throat.

She needed to call in the big guns, and before she could overthink it, she dialed Maddy.

"Hi, Maddy, I don't know if you remem—"

"Lizzie!" Maddy squealed.

Elizabeth winced. "Only Sam calls me Lizzie, and he does it because I hate it."

"Oh." Maddy's voice got small. "I didn't know."

"That's okay." Being a gigantic bitch was always a killer way to start a request for help. "I don't really mind, but Sam thinks I do."

"I like Elizabeth better," Maddy said. "It's sort of queenly, like you."

Elizabeth looked down at her tatty sweatpants and T-shirt and grinned. "So, I was calling for help with—"

"Yes," Maddy said.

"I'm going to dinner with Sam tonight, and—"

"Eek, that's so romantic."

"And I'm not sure what to wear. I don't really have that sort of wardrobe." Elizabeth got the words in fast.

Maddy sucked in a breath and then gave a breathy giggle. "Oh, Elizabeth. I'll be right over."

Her phone rang, and she spent five minutes updating Ashley, who ran the Humane Society, on the new potential adoptees. Leonard also needed about seven minutes of soothing over some shoddy painting of palm trees on the sets for *South Pacific*.

Jane texted to harangue Elizabeth for not ironing her shirt the other day, because a day without getting the shaft from her family wouldn't be a normal day. She sent Jane a YouTube video on ironing and got a *WTF* in exchange. Pretty much a normal day in the Rogers clan.

Maddy must have dropped everything because she appeared at Elizabeth's apartment in fifteen minutes. Even more impressive was the generous armload of clothes and shoes she'd brought with her.

Elizabeth eyed the bounty with reservations. "Are those yours?"

"Yes." Maddy beamed and bumped the door closed with her hip. "I'm sure we're the same size."

Elizabeth restrained the urge to snort laugh.

"I brought my makeup kit as well." Maddy brandished a family sized valise. Looking uncertain, Maddy slid the valise behind Elizabeth's couch. "I mean, I don't want to overstep or anything. I assumed—"

"You're wonderful." Elizabeth gave in to the urge and hugged her. Maddy had the sweetest, loveliest heart, and was turning out to be the best part of busting in on Sam. "Where do we start?"

A knock at the door had Elizabeth praying it wasn't someone else wanting her to do them a favor. She hadn't gotten around to working on her no yet.

Looking sheepish, Randy stood on her doorstep. "Hey, Elizabeth." He jabbed his thumb over his shoulder. "I parked in the visitor's today."

"Thanks, Randy." In the eight months he'd been dating Bonnie, he'd never spoken to her. She was surprised he even knew her name.

"You're welcome." He beamed. "So, the thing is, and I don't know if you know this, but I'm a big hockey fan. Huge."

She wasn't even having dinner with him yet and Sam had shoved himself into her life. "Yes?"

"Hi." Maddy nudged her away from the door and held out her hand to Randy. "I'm Maddy."

Randy did an admirable job of keeping his gaze above Maddy's chin, but ultimately it was a doomed effort and his eyeline drifted south. "Hi."

"Sam's fans are super important to him," Maddy said. The quiet authority took Elizabeth by surprise. "Now, we can't offer you tickets to a game, unfortunately." Maddy batted those lashes, probably starting a typhoon on the other side of the planet. "And gosh wouldn't that be the bomb dot com if we could?"

"Er...yeah." Sweat slid down Randy's temple as he kept his eyes locked somewhere in the region of Maddy's right ear.

"But I can certainly hook you up with a signed jersey." Maddy made the pronouncement as if she was offering Randy the Holy Grail.

By the look of awe on Randy's face, he thought so too. "Seriously?"

"I'll make sure you get it as soon as I can." Maddy winked at him. "Sam is so appreciative of his hometown support." She leaned in and whispered, "You local fans are super special to him."

Now her willing slave, Randy stared at Maddy with stars in his eyes. "Is there any chance Sam will be back here?"

"Now, Randy." Maddy pressed her hand to her cleavage. "I can see that you're a sensible fan. Not one of those crazies who doesn't think Sam has any right to his own time."

"Er...gurgh." Randy's gaze got stuck.

"And we wouldn't want Sam thinking he couldn't pop around and spend time with Elizabeth whenever he felt like it."

"Nuhaghyon." Randy blinked rapidly.

"I knew I wasn't wrong about you, Randy." Maddy pressed her hand to his chest and encouraged him out the doorway. "I'll make sure you get that signed jersey."

She shut the door.

Elizabeth had a whole new level of respect. "You're an evil genius."

Maddy grinned. "Wait until you see what I can do with you."

Three hours later, primped, powdered, plucked and pouffed, Elizabeth walked down the stairs from her apartment to Sam's car.

Maddy had insisted she not wait for Sam to come to the door. Chivalry took second place to strategy with Maddy. "Give him time to get a good look at all you got going on."

Poured into a little black dress, her eyes smoky and her lips full and red, Elizabeth clung to the balustrade and hoped like hell the heels and stairs equation didn't bite her in the ass.

"Work it!" Maddy hissed from the crack in her apartment door. "You own the sexy. Be the sexy."

It did Elizabeth's confidence no small amount of good that she and Maddy were the same size. So, she lifted her chin and owned the heck out of her sexy...ish.

In a suit and open-necked shirt, Sam strolled around the hood of his car toward her.

Her confidence took a hit. She might not be a Sam fan, but

the annoying boy had grown into a fine-looking man. Tall, broad shouldered, and as fit and muscular as only a professional athlete could be, he provided a treat for the eyes.

The right eyes. Eyes that gave a crap that was.

It helped to picture him as a towheaded eight-year-old blowing spit bubbles and telling fart jokes. It gave her the confidence to put an extra swing to her hips. "Sam."

"Lizzie." His deep blue gaze did a slow meander from her shoes to her hair. "You look ho—lovely this evening."

She almost bought it too. He might have succeeded if she hadn't caught the flash of his eyes to the side.

"You can't lie to me, Sam. You were about to say something else." She brushed close to him where he held the door open. For good measure she allowed the dress to slide an extra inch up her thighs as she sat. Whatever Sam had to say, she would not let it dent her confidence.

From outside her apartment, Maddy bopped up and down behind Sam giving her the thumbs up. She sucked in a bit of courage from Maddy.

Sam climbed behind the wheel and glanced over at her. "I'm being serious, Lizzie. You look very nice."

"Uh-huh." He really did think her stupid. "You going to spit it out."

"There's my Quizzy Lizzy." He eased the car onto the road. "All this because I said you looked lovely. Which you do. You've always been a great looking girl, Liz."

"I know you were about to say something insulting." Despite lying through his teeth, Sam smelled good and Elizabeth took a discreet sniff of his fresh, sharp aftershave. The last time she'd seen Sam in a suit had been their prom. They'd both had different dates, but their mothers had insisted on a joint photo opp. He filled out his suit a lot better now.

Sam gave her the side eye and took a breath. "You're right." He cleared his throat. "I was about to say you look hot."

"What?"

"Hot."

"Who me?"

"Yes, you." He glared at her. "You look hot for fuck's sake."

The bizarreness of the situation got the better of Elizabeth. Sam and her all dressed up and going out to dinner, like they were on a real date.

Elizabeth couldn't stop the laughter that bubbled up inside her. "This is weird."

"Yeah." Sam flashed her a wry grin. "I promise not to pull your hair tonight."

"Wow." She widened her eyes at him. "You are on best behavior."

Sam did his eye slide. "I know how to behave."

"But do you?" She grinned to let him know she was teasing.

Sam laughed and the atmosphere in the car eased into something more familiar. It lacked the usual antagonism though, and that still left her feeling slightly off balance.

Sam drove the forty minutes into Ottawa and took her to an upscale restaurant in the ByWard market. A perfect place to see and be seen, which was the point of tonight anyway.

His hand spread over the small of her back as they followed the maitre d' to their table. Her dress seemed an insubstantial barrier against the warmth of his touch and she shivered.

Heads swung and gazes locked on them as they took their seats.

"Ignore it," Sam whispered as he slid her chair in for her. "They'll have a good look, maybe take a picture or two, and then forget all about us."

"On with the show." Elizabeth smiled at Sam, the sort of smile she imagined a girl who wanted to be out with Sam would give him.

"Dude!" A young guy sidled up to their table. "You're the fucking bomb."

Sam gave him a fist bump. "Thanks, but the bomb is now sitting next to the ice."

"Don't stress it, Stoney." The guy grinned. "They'll be begging you to come back."

"I appreciate the support." Sam motioned her and leaned into the guy. "Not to be rude, but I'm here with my girl."

Elizabeth choked the 'my girl' down with a hefty sip of water.

"Oh, sure." The fan looked at her. "Got it."

He drifted away.

"What did I say about pretending to be your girlfriend?" She didn't put much heat into it, because the notion was so ludicrous there was no need to get bitter and twisted about it.

Sam lifted one dark eyebrow at her. "I didn't specify in what way you were my girl."

"In no way." Elizabeth picked up the menu. "And for that, I'm going to order the most expensive thing on this menu." She peeked over the top at him. "And getting through dinner with you will require wine. Lots and lots of wine."

Sam shook his head, but he was smiling as he picked up his menu.

"Sam!" Elizabeth couldn't believe what she was reading. "Have you seen the prices?"

He stared at her, mystified. "Yeah. And?"

"And?" Outrage welled in her. "And it's daylight robbery is what. Do you know how many shelter dogs I could feed with the price of the steak?"

Looking amused, Sam put his menu down. "Comfort yourself in the knowledge that it's my money you're spending."

"It helps." She couldn't let him know not even that swayed her. "But still…"

"Tell you what." Sam went back to his menu. "I'll donate the same amount I pay for this meal to the dog shelter."

"In that case." Elizabeth didn't feel nearly as bad anymore. The man made a ridiculous amount of money. "I'm starting with the lobster and moving on to the chateaubriand."

"There you go." Sam winked at her. "Make sure to order French wine while you're at it."

"Good idea." She sat back and looked about her. A couple of gazes slid their way and away again. It was the sort of restaurant people went to in order to impress. It didn't feel like Sam. Make no mistake, he had his faults and she had a detailed list of every one of them, but Sam wasn't pretentious. "Why this place?"

"It fits." Sam put his menu down. "We want to be seen together. This is that sort of place."

That made sense. "Speaking of which." She sat forward. "We haven't come to terms yet. Tonight is starting to look alarmingly like a free pass."

"Dear God. Not that." He rolled his eyes. "Lay it on me twisty Lizzie. What do you want?"

"I hate those rhyming things you do."

"I know."

Again, a fight they'd been having for too long for her to get bent out of shape about it.

"Good evening, Mr. Stone." The waiter appeared at their table. He oozed bonhomie at Sam. "Might I say how delighted we are to have you with us tonight."

Sam gave the man a polite smile.

"If there is anything I can do to make your evening more enjoyable"—the waiter laid his hand over his heart—"you need only to ask."

"Tell you what, Tyrone." Sam handed his menu to Tyrone. "Why don't we order?"

Tyrone brightened as if Sam had made his life worth living. "Perfect."

They ordered dinner, and Elizabeth went with the salmon and a soup to start.

"Lovely." Tyrone gathered their menus. "I will be right back with your drinks."

"Thanks, Tyrone." Sam motioned him closer. "And there is

one favor I would like to ask. My...friend and I would like to have a quiet evening. I know you take my meaning."

"Of course." Tyrone drew himself up and went pink. "You will not be disturbed. You may rely on this."

Sam winked. "I knew that."

Elizabeth shook her head at Sam's antics. It was good to be king. She waited for Tyrone to leave before pinning Sam with a hard look. "I'll agree to be your photo friend, but in exchange the retirement village is going to need a new bus."

Sam gaped at her. "A new bus?"

"Not a big bus." She didn't want him thinking she was going to be unreasonable. "About a fifteen-seater. To get the residents to and from events and stuff."

"Not a Lear jet?" He raised a brow at her.

"Oh, could you?" Elizabeth simpered and batted her lashes at him. "That would be super."

Sam grunted. "How much is the bus going to set me back?"

"We only need a second-hand one," Elizabeth said.

"Done." Sam grinned like a shark. "Selfie time."

He came around the table and draped an arm over her shoulder. Pressing his cheek to hers he grinned at his phone. "Sell it, Lizzie. Make them believe you want to be here."

Elizabeth pressed closer. Sam's mouth was so close she could shift her head to the left and touch it with hers.

And why the hell would she want to do that?

She twinkled at the camera and Sam took the shot. Clearing his throat, he swallowed and eased away from her. He kept his gaze on his phone, but he looked a bit flushed. "What are we thinking for hashtags?"

"BFF? Besties? Oldfriendsarethebestfriends?" If she had been his girlfriend, she would have taken that left shift and kissed him.

"You're good at this." Sam's fingers flew over his phone.

Tyrone slid her wine in front of her, and placed Sam's beer in front of him. He gave her a conspiratorial look and mouthed. "Lovely couple."

If only he knew. Elizabeth resisted the urge to laugh.

Sam took a slug of beer. "Give me your next shot."

"Oh, boy, Sam. You're in trouble now." Elizabeth couldn't stop her evil chuckle. The Humane Society always needed money. "I would like an item of your clothing to auction off for the Humane Society."

He grimaced. "Does it need to be sweaty?"

"Sweaty would be lovely." Elizabeth smiled at his look of distaste. "I know." She shrugged, the only sane woman in this crazy world. "There is actually someone out there who would be prepared to pay money for Sam Stone's sweat."

"Ah please." Sam sat back and folded his arms. "My jock strap is worth the national debt of a small nation."

Sometimes he set himself up so beautifully. "That's probably because it's a small jock strap."

"Damn!" He winced and grabbed his chest. "Shots fired!" Leaning his elbows on the table he stared at her. "How many of these conditions are there?"

"A few more." She avoided eye contact. The trick to Sam was not to show weakness. Or let him play with your toys. The image that popped into her mind was warning enough to keep her from thinking Sam and toys in the same mind drift. "Item three is about Chris's hockey team." She took a sip of her wine. It was really very good, and she hummed her appreciation.

Sam's gaze flicked to her mouth and away again. "I didn't know Chris had a hockey team."

"It's a kid's team she inherited about two years ago." Elizabeth let Sam take a sip of his beer before she hit him with the full demand. She'd been on the receiving end of him spitting his drink before and she didn't want to undo all Maddy's hard work. "They're really bad." Chris would admit as much herself. "But they could really do with a few tips from you."

Rubbing his chin, Sam groaned. "Are you really going to

make me coach kid's hockey?"

"Yup." She gave him a bright smile. "And for that I might even let you get a bit handsy with me. For the cameras."

"How handsy?" Sam's gaze sharpened and he leaned forward.

Heat climbed into Elizabeth's cheeks. "Not like that. I meant maybe an arm around my shoulders. Or maybe even I'd put my arm through yours. You know, a bit more like a couple."

"For coaching kids I'm going to need hand holding and kissing," Sam said.

"Kissing?" Was he insane? "I'm not kissing you. You know what happened—"

"We don't go there." Sam jabbed his forefinger at her. "Ever!"

He was right. They had a deal. They'd even pinky-sworn on it. "Sorry." She backed right down. "I can offer you a cheek peck."

"I'll take it, and also one mouth at a time of my choosing."

That seemed harmless enough, and really Chris's team could do with all the help they could get. "Done."

Tyrone sailed over and put their starters on the table. At a discreet signal from Sam, he refilled her wineglass. Sam asked for water.

"Item four is tiny." Elizabeth tasted her soup and moaned. "This is delicious."

Sam waggled his fingers for a taste, and she held her spoon out for him. He sucked her spoon into his mouth, tasted and nodded. "It is good."

His mouth was the only softish feature in the carved lines of his face. It saved him from looking too severe. She'd heard sensible women eulogize over Sam's mouth. Maybe because they hadn't heard all the crap his lovely lips could spew.

"Tell me about item four?" He ate his carpaccio quickly and neatly. "And by the way, these had better be some smoking pictures you're committing to. I might have to rethink the pretend boyfriend thing."

"Not a chance." She raised an eyebrow and dared him to argue. "Item four, high school dunk tank."

Sam gaped. "It's winter."

"They do it inside and they heat the water."

For several breaths he looked like he might balk and then he nodded. He sat back in his chair.

Tyrone slid in and removed their empty plates.

"You know, Quizzy Lizzie, if you wanted to see my body, you didn't have to invent a wet T-shirt scenario."

"Really, Sam." She let her voice go all breathy. "You've made me the happiest girl alive. Especially if that body of yours looks better than it used to." She faked a wince. "I mean, it couldn't get worse."

Sam threw back his head and laughed. Ego not even slightly dented. Then again, he did have that killer bod to prop it up. Or so she'd been told. Okay, she may have googled. Also might have snuck a look at the pictures from a vacay he'd taken Danica on to Turks and Caicos.

"Dunk tank it is." He threw an arm over the back of his chair. "Final demand. You better make it a good one, Lizzy."

So far, he'd been more than reasonable. "This one really is easy," she said. She was having a good time too. "There's a charity walk for the children's hospital. It's a sponsorship thing and I thought you could walk it with me."

With a slight frown, Sam sat forward and pulled her list toward him. He read it in silence. "These demands are all for other people."

"No, they're not." She pointed out the items. "Chris is my best friend. If you don't buy the bus, I'll be fundraising for the rest of my life. I belong to the women's auxiliary and they run the high school fun day, and I visit a couple of the children in the hospital." She sat back with a smirk. "And the clothing auction is an opportunity to make you squirm."

Sam grinned at her. "Gosh, Lizzy, who knew you were such a self-centered, selfish bitch."

CHAPTER
EIGHT

"YOU'RE SO VAIN" being played at ear drum bursting volume wrenched Sam awake. He shot up in bed and searched for the source.

"Oh, hi." Liz leaned against his doorjamb with her cell phone in her hand. "Glad you're awake."

"What the fuck?" Not even on his best day was he a morning person, which of course, Liz knew. He dropped back to the pillows.

Dressed in jeans and a sweater that loved the curve of her breasts, Liz sauntered closer and put a coffee mug on his bedside table alongside the Beats Pill she must have put there earlier. "I thought we might go shopping."

"Eh?" Sam reached for the coffee like a dying man. "Even for you, Liz, this is a new low."

"Thank you." She beamed at him. "It took a bit of planning on my part. Lucky for me you didn't put the security chain on this morning."

"So say stalkers everywhere." Sam sipped his coffee. She really did make great coffee. "Did Mrs. K see you?"

"I waved to her on the way in." Liz perched on the edge of

his bed. "Right now, she's telling your mom, who is telling my mom."

He'd slept soundly last night for the first time since his suspension. "Is that wise?"

"It's strategic."

He couldn't wait to hear this. "Oh, yeah?"

"With both our moms daydreaming about the heady prospect of little Sam and Elizabeth babies"—they both shuddered—"the moms will spend less time obsessing about your mental anguish." Leaning closer she nabbed his mug and took a sip.

Taking a man's coffee first thing in the morning was not right. He reclaimed his mug. "It beats me why everyone thinks you're so sweet."

"I am sweet." She looked affronted. "With you it's self-defense."

"Uh-huh." And if he believed that she had a piece of swamp to sell him. "More like you hide your Mister Evil behind your Mary Poppins." Last night came back to him. "Are you really going to make me coach kid's hockey."

"Yup." She gave him a bright smile.

He might have given in too quickly last night. "I'm thinking in exchange for kid coaching, we should up our couples' game."

"Eh?" She looked horrified at the idea.

He almost laughed, but the opportunity to give her shit got the better of him. "I mean, if being photographed with you has brought me such a positive response, what about some canoodling shots."

"No." Lizzie shot to her feet. "I'm not intensifying our couples' game because we're not a couple. I'm helping you because my mom asked me to, and also because of the charity auction, and Chris's hockey team, and the bus. Nothing more."

"Come on, Lizzie." Wearing only his boxers, he climbed out of bed and took a long, slow stretch. "Are you sure you don't want to get a bit handsy with me?"

He meant to tease her, but she was really looking at him. And not looking like a friend looking either. Even weirder, he really liked her looking at him like that. The low hum of libido crept through him.

She snatched up a T-shirt lying at her feet and slapped his gut with it. "Quite sure. Now get dressed and buy me a bus."

"Last chance," he called as she stalked out of the room.

She slammed something in the kitchen, loud enough for him to count the win.

By the time he'd showered and dressed, Lizzie had cooked him eggs and was plating them with toast. At least she followed dragging a guy out of bed—where he had been having a most enjoyable dream that may or may not have involved some double-jointed cheerleaders—with breakfast and more coffee.

Taking his reproductive health and possibly his life into his hands, he sidled up beside her and nuzzled her neck. "You can wake me up any morning you like, Lizzie."

"Ugh." She slid away from him and brandished the egg pan his way. "Stop it."

"Stop what?" He spread his arms wide, ruining the innocent act with the grin he couldn't stop.

"Eww." She shuddered and looked ill. "Do not give me your sex face."

He couldn't remember hearing anything about it before. "I don't have a sex face."

"Yes, you do." The pan hovered too close to his jaw. "You've got it on now. It's the face you make when you're going to ooze over to some poor girl and hit on her."

Sam checked his reflection in the microwave door. "I don't—what the hell? I do! I have a sex face."

"Damn right you do." Lizzie slammed his plate on the counter and poured another cup of coffee. This one she kept for herself. Shuddering, she wrapped her hands around the mug. "Don't ever give me that face again or I don't care how many buses you buy me, the deal's off."

"According to last night's negotiations, I might have to give it to you in public." Sam sat down to his breakfast. The eggs made him moan. She got the perfect balance between silky and properly cooked.

Elizabeth held up her forefinger. "Nope. I can't guarantee my reaction if you give me the sex face."

"As in you might rip off my clothes and have your way with me?" Sam bit into his still warm toast.

Liz curled her lip. "As in, I might vomit."

Oh, he couldn't let her get away with that one. "And yet you looked at my naked body this morning as if you wanted to lick me up and down like an ice cream cone."

"You're delusional."

"You're smitten by my boyish good looks."

"I'm bored of this conversation." Liz sipped her coffee.

Fair enough, but he knew what he'd seen, and she knew better than to think he would forget. Feeling reconciled to being woken at the ass crack of dawn, Sam finished his breakfast. He rinsed his plate and put it in the dishwasher.

Liz was drinking her coffee and reading her phone.

"You said something about bus shopping." He helped himself to another cup.

She looked up and then ducked her head again. "Um…yes. You said you were okay with buying the bus for the retirement village."

"That's what I said." He tried to get a bead on the sudden reticence. "And that is why you broke into my home this morning."

"I know." She bit the inside of her cheek and held up her phone. "But I've been pricing them online, and now I'm changing my mind."

"Why?"

Rolling her eyes and trying to pass it off like it was no biggie, she said, "It's a lot of money, Sam. Too much money."

"Hmm." He pretended to give it some thought. "You may

have a point." He counted items off on his fingers. "There was that exorbitantly expensive dinner last night. My usual monthly expenses; the hookers, the blow, the maintenance payments to all twenty of my illegitimate children. I'm tapped out, babe. Would you accept a hover board as a replacement?"

She threw a cloth at him. "Don't be a dick. I'm serious here."

"So am I." A deal was a deal. He stood right in front of her and for the hell of it put his hands on the counter, bracketing her hips. "As you have pointed out on numerous occasions, I make a stupid amount of money for chasing a piece of vulcanized rubber around the ice. I can afford to buy your wrinklies a bus."

"But Sam." It must be bad for her not to rise to the term wrinklies. "What if you get...fired?"

The last thing he ever wanted to think about. "Then it's not your fault. Come on, Lizzie, don't get yourself in a tizzy. You're the first one to point out this is my fault."

"I never said that." She frowned.

That's right, she hadn't said that. He didn't want to think about that, or he might start liking her. Too late, he did already sort of like her, or he certainly liked getting under her skin. "Let's go and spend some of my ill-gotten gains."

"For the wrinklies." She clapped a hand over her mouth and looked horrified.

Sam laughed so hard he thought he might bust a gut.

Elizabeth had woken Sam first thing this morning because she knew he hated mornings. He'd taken it remarkably well, and she'd gotten an eyeful that kept parading through her mind.

It would have helped if Sam could have been his normal asshole self, but bus shopping with Sam had turned into fun. He had the salesman talk him through all the aspects of each bus. He checked the mileage, the warranty, the safety check, the ramps...everything.

By lunchtime, she knew more about buses than she had ever hoped to. Normally she would blame it on him trying to annoy her, but that didn't seem to be the case. In fact, it looked like he had forgotten she was even there.

"Babe." He beckoned her over.

Elizabeth slapped a smile on her face and trotted on over. Later, when they were alone, they were going to have the boundary chat.

"Babe." He flung his arm over her shoulders and tugged her closer. "Brian has been telling me about the bus you like."

"Really." She managed a smile for Brian, who was so star struck it had taken him ten minutes to produce an articulate sentence.

Sam pulled a face. "And I'm afraid it's not going to do it for me."

"No?" She had no idea where he was going with this, but the prickling of her Sam-sense put her on full alert.

He cupped her nape, the callouses on his hands not an unpleasant abrasion against her neck. "It doesn't have a ramp, or any of those tie-down areas."

Now he was going to try and get under her skin by pretending he knew about buses for the disabled. "Yes." She gritted her teeth into a smile and gave him hell through the eyes. "But this bus has enough room for most people, and we can make a plan."

"Babe." Sam loaded the reproach into his tone. "What do I always say?"

Oh, the dizzying, endless possibilities and his grin dared her to go there. "What do you always say...Muffin?"

"If a thing is worth doing, then it's worth doing properly." He leaned forward and winked at Brian. "I know you feel me on this, Brian."

His palm landed on her butt in a resounding smack.

Elizabeth breathed deep. And then deeper. But she still wanted to kill him.

Brian must have read the murder in her eyes because he paled. "Umm...I believe Mr. Sto—"

"Brian!" Sam spread his arms like he was working the shopping network.

"I mean...er...Sam." Brian went scarlet. "I believe Sam thought we might buy a new bus."

Elizabeth shook her head to clear her thinking. It didn't help. "Eh?"

"Yes, babe!" Sam gripped her waist and tugged her in. "A new bus would have a lift ramp, the tie down area for wheelchairs, and seating for twenty."

"But, Muffin." She got her arm around him and squeezed right back. "A new bus is not in our budget."

"Sugar Lips." He kissed her temple. "Don't worry your pretty little head about budget. Big Daddy Sam the Man is here, and he's going to make the whole thing go away."

Brian's eyes started out of his head. He trotted for his office, yelling over his shoulder. "I'll get some brochures."

"You're insane." Elizabeth disentangled herself.

Sam tugged her right back and grinned. "Upping our couples' game."

"Sam." Elizabeth took a deep breath and kept them on topic. "A new bus is far too expensive. I never asked you for that."

"Elizabeth." Sam shoved his hands in his pockets. "I can't have people saying I'm cheap when they see the ratchet-assed bus you had picked out."

Sure, it wasn't the most beautiful bus. "The bus I selected is perfectly adequate for our needs."

"But I'll look cheap." Sam grimaced. "Can't have people saying I'm cheap as well as a thug. It defeats the purpose of what we're doing here."

Elizabeth's bullshit meter twitched. Sam didn't give a shit who thought what about him. If he was buying a new bus for Mountain Vista it was because he wanted to. "Sam." She dropped the attitude and appealed to him honestly. "That's a lot of money, and so much more than I asked for."

"Are you feeling guilty for twisting my arm?" Sam bent his knees so he could meet her gaze.

She totally was. "Never."

"Remind yourself about how useless my job is and how much they pay me to do it anyway," Sam said.

She did that and it still didn't help. "Yes, but Sam, a new bus—"

"Look, Sugar Lips." He took hold of her shoulders. "Think of it this way. Now I can have them paint a decal of me in all my glory all the way down the side." His eyes lit up. "A bigger bus means more decals. I can plaster the damn thing with them."

"Sam." He needn't think he could fool her. She'd known him too well for too long. "This is so kind of you."

And then because the man was going to spend a small fortune, she hugged him. A small fortune that meant Carson and his buddies could get to their Friday night darts game at their local pub, and that Gloria and her girls could go shopping on Wednesdays.

Her breasts mashed up against his hard chest. Like granite, his thighs met hers as she reached up, and up some more, to wrap her arms around his neck.

And, oh my, did he smell good.

"Thank you, Sam." Her voice got a bit breathy and she cleared her throat. "I didn't expect this."

She stepped back, but Sam caught her hips and held her close. "You are most welcome, Sug—"

"You fucking suck, Sam Stone. I hope the Titans never take you back!" A man ran past.

He tensed and Elizabeth tightened her hold. "You don't suck all the time, Sam. Sometimes, and don't quote me on this because I'll deny it, you're a lovely man."

CHAPTER
NINE

FRIDAY NIGHT, and Elizabeth was home alone. Peter had texted to ask her out and she had turned him down. They hung out as friends from time to time but even that was waning and she just didn't feel like spending time with Peter tonight.

Someone pounded on her door. "Ottawa Police! Open up!"

Yes! And Elizabeth flung the door open to her best friend.

"Chris!" She avoided the bags in Chris's hands and gave her a hug. "You've saved me from a sad singly Friday night."

Raising a brow. "We are sad singlies." Chris navigated past her and put her bags down on the kitchen counter. "And speaking of who is single and who isn't, I feel it's fair to warn you I came to interrogate you."

Elizabeth had expected as much. What with the pictures on the internet, the hanging out with Sam, and the best friend who knew more about her than she knew about herself thing. She dived into the bags Chris had bought. "That all depends on what you brought."

"Wine." Chris produced a bottle and put it on the counter. She unpacked the bags. "Cheese, baguette, crab dip, chips, crackers and hummus. The hummus cancels out the chips, so we're golden on the calorie front."

Elizabeth leaned closer. "That'll do it. What are we watching tonight?"

Tapping a finger on her chin, Chris thought it over. It was really hard to be friends with someone with Chris's flawless skin. Doubly hard when that rich creamy skin covered delicate, finely chiseled features that had yet to see the touch of makeup. "I'm feeling *Bridezillas*."

"You're on." Elizabeth got wineglasses and plates and put them on the counter.

Chris perched on a barstool and gave her the steely gray stare. "But first." She raised her finger. "I need to know what gives with Sam."

"Not much." Elizabeth shrugged. She liked to make Chris work for the information.

"Liar." Chris jabbed a forefinger at her. "I know for a fact you're not his girlfriend. Yet..." She produced a picture of Sam and Elizabeth at the dealership. "The evidence against you is mounting."

Sam had his arms around her. Hers were draped around his neck and they were laughing. The picture didn't capture how good Sam had smelled and felt, but her imagination happily filled in the blanks.

"Not bad." Elizabeth studied the image. "We almost look like we can tolerate each other."

Chris snatched her phone back. "You look like you're boning each other. What gives?"

"Boning?" Elizabeth played dumb. "Isn't that a tad strong?"

She got the look of death in response and laughed.

"Okay." She cut the baguette into rounds. "Sam and I are pretending we're a sort of thing."

"Oh, no." Chris shook her head as she poured the wine. "We've watched the chick flicks. We know where this is going."

"Ordinarily, I would agree with you." Elizabeth carried their snacks over to the coffee table in front of her television. "But this is Sam we're talking about. No danger of the chick flick factor coming into play."

Dressed in her usual off-duty uniform of track pants and a T-shirt, Chris settled on the couch and crossed her legs. She helped herself to a wedge of cheese. "But Sam is hot."

"Yeah. If you like that whole rippling muscle, athletic thing he has going." Even Elizabeth couldn't say that with a straight face. "Except, when I look at him, I see that, but I don't."

"Uh-huh." Chris rolled her eyes. "You're suddenly blind?"

"No." Elizabeth climbed onto the coach next to Chris. "You were there almost from the beginning. You know it isn't pretty when Sam and I get together. Plus, there's no mystique. I've known him forever and I still see him as that kid."

Chris pinned her with a stare and then grabbed her phone and brought up the picture again. "This is you seeing him as a big, goofy kid?"

"I'm acting." Mostly. "And anyway, you should be thanking me."

"For?" Chris cocked an eyebrow.

"As part of my deal with Sam, he's going to work with your team."

Gaping, Chris dropped a chip. "Say what now?"

"I'm going to have to tell you everything. Sam did his Mike Tyson impersonation, and then went dark. Danica panicked when she couldn't get hold of him and threatened to come home. Danica coming home meant Mom coming home."

Chris grimaced. She got it.

"To keep them both in Europe, I promised to help Sam clean up his image." Elizabeth kept her shrug light.

They locked gazes and then Chris said, "You know what I'm going to say."

"I know." Elizabeth sipped her wine. "And I don't let people take advantage of me. I do these things because I want to. Anyway this is completely different."

Chris raised an eyebrow.

Honesty demanded Elizabeth amend that last statement. "Mostly. I do these things because I mostly want to. And anyway, now you can get some help with your team."

"Babe." Chris looked perturbed. "That really is the sweetest thing."

"But?"

"But my kids are bad, babe. Really bad." Chris winced. "And I hate even saying that about them because they love to play so much." She fiddled with the crackers. "And Sam was not suspended for being the nicest man in the league."

Elizabeth saw where she was heading. "You think he'll be bad for them?"

"I'm worried he won't understand how fragile they are."

Now Elizabeth felt like the worst kind of friend. "I didn't think of that. All I thought is how much they would love to be coached by a real league player."

"I know that." Chris squeezed her hands. "And I love you for that."

With a nod, Elizabeth made a decision. "I'll get a different favor out of him."

For a moment Chris looked thoughtful and then shook her head. "You're right, they will love it. These kids are the ones nobody would take on their team and having someone like Sam spend time with them, will do more for their confidence than anything I can do."

"I'll talk to him first." The doorbell rang and she and Chris stared at it. Elizabeth got up to answer, part of her wondering if Sam had dropped by.

She opened the door to Maddy.

"Hi." Maddy looked uncertain, also stunning in a pair of poured on jeans and a tight cropped sweater. No muffin top, not even the shadow of the thought of one. "I dropped in to see how your date with Sam went."

"Nondate." Elizabeth needed to get that straight before Maddy had them as BAEs and started shipping them. "More of a business meeting."

"But you looked hot." A hint of mischief lit Maddy's brown eyes. "And so much better in that dress than I ever have."

Honestly, she tried, but the snort got away from Elizabeth. Not a hint of insincerity came from Maddy. Something this gorgeous couldn't be sweet as well. "Would you like to come in?"

"Um...no." Maddy fiddled with her purse strap. "I don't want to interrupt your evening."

"You're not." Elizabeth stepped aside. "And there's got to be more you can do with your time than watch Sam's house all the time."

Stepping into the apartment, Maddy pulled a face. "Can I be honest?"

"Always." Elizabeth led the way into the apartment.

"It is getting a bit boring." Maddy slipped her shoes off. She even had adorable feet with toenails painted pink. "It's not like the days when he used to party all night long."

"Hi." Chris stood up from the couch. Her face flamed red.

Maddy stopped and went pink. "Hi."

Chris stared at Maddy.

Maddy stared right back.

Stepping into the loaded silence, Elizabeth introduced them.

"Hi." Chris sounded gruff.

Maddy went pinker than her toenails and her eyes rounded. "Hi."

"Why don't we all sit down?" Elizabeth steered Maddy closer to the couch and maneuvered her into it. All with Maddy not taking her eyes off Chris, and Chris looking anywhere but at Maddy.

"I'm Maddy," Maddy whispered.

Elizabeth controlled her eye roll. She'd already covered that much.

Flushing, Chris cleared her throat and managed an eyelock. "Chris."

"So." Elizabeth couldn't believe what she was seeing. "Maddy is a super fan of Sam's."

Maddy nodded. "We call ourselves the Stone Cold Foxes."

"Really?" Chris looked blindsided. "I like hockey."

"I like hockey too." Maddy perched like a bird about to take flight on the edge of the couch. "I like to hang out with the some of the players. Just hang out though." She blushed. "Nothing else. Not like a groupie and I run the Ottawa chapter of Sam's fan club."

Sam had fan club chapters? Who knew? They obviously hadn't heard him belch Mississippi, or maybe they had.

"Great." Elizabeth went for another glass. She came back and sat right next to Chris, forcing Chris to shift closer to Maddy.

Chris went magenta. Despite her tough girl exterior, Chris was pure marshmallow. She was also painfully shy.

Shoving wine at Maddy, Elizabeth hoped she was more forthcoming.

"Chris and I were about to watch *Bridezillas*." She got comfortable and flipped through the channels. The show in her living room looked a lot more interesting however. "Would you like to stay?"

"I've never seen it before." Maddy sipped her wine and slid another glance at Chris. Taking a breath, she turned her full body to face Chris. "Will I like it?"

Nearly disappearing into the cushions, Chris nodded. "Uh-uh."

"Then I'll stay." Maddy shifted an inch closer to Chris and spread an arm over the back of the sofa.

"Great." Elizabeth got the show started.

Somewhere between the atrocious behavior on the screen and the second bottle of wine, Chris unwound enough to relax and be more herself. Beneath the shyness, Chris was the best woman Elizabeth knew, funny, clever and with the biggest heart of anyone.

Maddy was smoking hot and so sweet it almost made you want to hate her.

Who knew she'd spend her Friday night playing matchmaker? Judging by the sparks flickering around her living room, both Chris and Maddy were onboard.

The show ended and an uncomfortable silence settled between them.

"So." Elizabeth had another idea and it was a good one. "As you both love hockey so much, and I'm supposed to be Sam's friend why don't you give me a crash course on the team. Other than Craig Dalton, I don't really follow the players anymore."

Maddy blinked at her. "You don't watch hockey."

"Not if she can avoid it," Chris said. "Something to do with the way she and Sam have been rubbing each other the wrong way since they were kids."

"Why is that?" Maddy stared at her.

"Our mothers were always together, so we were always together." Elizabeth couldn't really point to a time when it had all begun. The tension between her and Sam had always been there. "He was a brat and I was perfect." Chris's look made her laugh. "Okay, I might have been a bit bossy."

"You'd make a cute couple." Maddy wrinkled her nose.

Chris groaned. "Spend more time in their company and you won't say that anymore."

"Anyway." Elizabeth found the hockey channel and turned up the volume. "Let me know what I need to know to fake it."

Marc Gracie appeared on the screen. Chiseled features, close cropped hair and a pair of shoulders filling out his beautifully tailored suit. He had a deep, rich voice with a touch of gravel around the edges. "The Titans are surprising themselves with what they can do without Stone in the lineup."

"Ugh, Marc Gracie." Maddy made a face.

"Really, they don't need him," Marc Gracie said. "Players like Sam Stone are a throwback to the bad old days of hockey before we wore helmets, and frankly, the game doesn't need to go back to that."

"Wow." Elizabeth paid closer attention. She really hoped Sam wasn't watching this.

"Don't get me wrong." Marc Gracie flashed a megawatt smile. "I like the game fast and hard." That sounded dirty to Elizabeth. "But hits that threaten the career of a young player, hits like Sam Stone enjoys handing out, don't belong in hockey."

No wonder Sam had been hiding in his mom's house. Gracie was mean.

"He hates Sam," Maddy said. "After Sam's suspension, he's been worse than ever."

"To be fair." Chris shrugged. "Sam does give him plenty of material."

"Sam's a tough player, but that doesn't mean he earns everything Gracie says about him." Ire lit Maddy's dark eyes. "It's like Gracie stays up all night and waits for Sam to screw up."

The flirty atmosphere was disintegrating. Elizabeth tried to recover it. "Maybe we shouldn't watch the hockey.

Chris stiffened. "That last hit of Sam's was dirty as they come."

"Please!" Maddy threw her hands up. "It was bullshit. Sam connected with his shoulder not his head."

Gaping at her, Chris shook her head. "Not from the replay I saw."

"I have ice cream." Elizabeth waded into the growing tension. Shit! No, she didn't. Sam had eaten most of it when he'd come over. "Why don't we go out for ice cream?"

"Karlov deserved an Oscar for his performance." Maddy crossed her arms and set her jaw in a harsh line.

"Really?" Chris scoffed. "He must be the most amazing actor ever to be able to produce blood on demand like that."

Maddy stood. "You don't get Sam at all."

"I've known Sam since I was five." Chris stood as well. "I would say I know him a helluva lot better than you."

"You may have known him as a boy, but you don't know the man, and you sure as hell don't know the hockey player," Maddy's voice rose. Apparently even the sweetest girl got her lioness out in defense of someone she valued.

"I've watched every game Sam's played." Chris stuck her jaw out at an angle Elizabeth knew meant war to follow. "This whole damn town has lived and breathed Sam Stone since he first showed promise." She jabbed a finger Maddy. "And I can tell you, he's never lived up to that potential."

Eyes wide, Maddy opened her mouth and shut it again. Hot color rode her cheeks and her eyes flashed her anger. "That is so unfair." Her voice rose. "So unfair! How is he supposed to play his best hockey when everyone keeps treating him like an enforcer and ignoring what a powerful forward he is."

"Because he can't keep his gloves on long enough to finish a game." Chris sneered. "If he doesn't want to be treated like a goon, then he should stop using any excuse to hand out a bit of pain."

Even when he wasn't in the room, Sam could create a battleground. Elizabeth had to give salvaging the night a try. "Look, we can all agree to disagree."

"Thanks for a lovely evening." Maddy's face tightened into a grim smile. "But I really should get going."

Chris clenched her jaw. "Great to meet you. See you around."

"Right." Maddy sneered.

Grabbing her shoes, Maddy slid them on and picked up her purse. The door shut behind her with a careful click that held all the intention of a slam.

She loved Chris to death, but sometimes Elizabeth wanted to shake her. Turning, she glared at her best friend. "Really?" Her voice rose. "Really? The hottest woman you've met in ages. Ages, Chris. And you choose to get into an argument with her about Sam."

"Someone like that wouldn't look at me twice." Chris hunched into the coach. "Nobody that perfect can be real."

"She is real." Elizabeth poked Chris's folded arms. "And she was sitting right here, all but eye humping you."

Chris went red enough to spontaneously combust. "You imagined it."

"No, I didn't." Elizabeth wanted to shake Chris, and then she wanted to hunt down Chris's ex for the number Alena had done on Chris. "She liked you. I mean really liked you."

Shrinking further into herself, Chris dropped her chin to her chest. "You think?"

"I saw it." Elizabeth's anger dissolved into sadness. Since Alena had left and taken Chris's sense of self with her, Chris had been hiding from relationships. Terrified to put herself out there in case it ended like the last time. Well Maddy had been as thunderstruck as Chris and neither of them better imagine for a minute this couldn't be fixed. She curled up next to Chris and gave her a hug. "Now stop being a sulky bitch and teach me to be the perfect Ottawa Titan's girlfriend."

"I thought you weren't pretending to be his girlfriend."

Elizabeth let her feelings be known in her glare. "Stop being a smart ass and make me hockey smart."

CHAPTER
TEN

THREE DAYS after his dinner with Elizabeth, Sam had reached the end of the available seasons of *Orange is the New Black* and was tired of staring at his phone waiting for Elizabeth to call. She had promised to help him, extorted favors out of him for her help and now she didn't call. Sitting around waiting for Elizabeth left him with too much time to think.

He lay on the kitchen floor and tossed a tennis ball into the air, the aim being to get it as close to the ceiling without connecting and making a mark. This sort of thing was great for hand-eye coordination. It also stopped the bullet train in his head that kept heading for a reality in which he never got to play hockey again.

In desperation, he had even dispensed with the idea of getting in a cleaner and gone with cleaning up after himself. Cleaning, however, left him too much headspace to turn over the all too real possibility that after the league lifted his suspension the Titans wouldn't want him back.

Elizabeth had said she wanted to get stuff done and now she didn't call. All those people who relied on Elizabeth to do things for them should know that she didn't call.

He tossed the ball up. It got to within three inches of the

ceiling and came back at him. Mom would have his nuts if he got ball marks on her ceiling.

Ball marks! He snickered and whipped the ball up.

Dear God, he was annoying the crap out of himself.

The ball came down faster this time and dinged him in the forehead. Even the tennis ball thought he was a dip shit.

Rolling to his belly, he studied the grout between the tiles. It never stayed clean, the grout, and Mom was a clean freak. Someone should develop a stain free grout. He'd get right on that if his hockey career went down the shitter.

While he was down there, he did ten pushups, and then ten more. And another ten because he couldn't think of a reason not to and it felt good to work his muscles.

He should go for a run. That would fix his antsiness.

After changing, he let himself out into the early morning.

Mrs. K peered through her kitchen window and he waved. She ducked out of sight.

He headed for Lizzie's place.

The weather had stayed reasonably mild for March. Ottawa mild that was, which meant it wasn't turning your nose hairs to icicles on contact this morning. He was wearing long thermal running pants with running shorts over the top. Nobody wanted that porno crotch shot of a man in spandex tights. A long-sleeve thermal workout shirt meant he could sweat and not freeze and because they hadn't kicked him out of the team yet, he had covered that with a Titans T-shirt.

Being out of the house improved his mood already. Sun sparkled off the white snow and a few cloud wisps drifted across a wall-to-wall sky.

The chilly air hit his lungs with claws attached and he breathed deep. The sidewalk had been cleared of ice and he didn't need to watch his feet.

Two kids arguing in their yard stopped as he approached and gave him the big eyes.

"Hey, guys." He nodded.

The smaller of the two went pink and squeaked a reply. The other stuck out his chest and deepened his voice, "Hey, Sam."

Two blocks over and his body chattered to him about every minute spent binge watching the girls in Lichfield, every beer and every sip of Jack Daniels. Another four blocks and he swore he could still taste the Baileys.

Fuck a duck, he wouldn't last two minutes on the ice. He'd keel over before the penalty kill was finished.

A pickup came down the road and slowed. A bearded face hung out the window. "You suck, Stone!"

Gotta love a fan. Sam showed his appreciation with the one-finger wave, which reminded him of Elizabeth. Mainly because flipping the bird was an instinctive twitch whenever she was around.

It wasn't right that he was out here pounding the pavement, and quite possibly, freezing his balls off, and Elizabeth was probably all tucked up in a Snuggie watching *Little House on the Prairie* reruns.

He took a left at the next corner and headed for Elizabeth's condo.

Love Actually was more her style, but he bet she had the pink mermaid Snuggie. He may have spent more time internet shopping recently than he cared to admit.

He took the stairs to her condo two at a time.

Randy had gotten the message and the red minivan was still parked in visitor's parking. As if Sam's thoughts had summoned him, Randy poked his head out his door. "Morning, Sam." He sipped from a large white mug. "Good to see you keeping up your condition."

"Thanks, Randy." He loved being referred to as if he was a fucking racehorse. Irritation put an extra zest to his pound on her front door. "Let's get busy, Lizzie."

It was Saturday morning. No way she was out. Unless she'd had a hot date with Peter the night before and was sleeping it off. Dear God, what if Peter was there and he would have to face the man who had been getting his leg over Lizzie all night long?

Asshole had no business crawling into Lizzie's bed when she was Sam's fake friend.

Randy ventured further out and peered up. "Did you watch the game last night?"

"Yup." He'd watched the Titans obliterate the Clash and heard Marc Gracie talk all about how his team didn't need him. "Great result."

He hammered at Liz's door again then looked at Randy. "She in?"

"Oh, yeah." Randy crossed his arms over his chest and shifted from one bare foot to the other. He'd get frost bite if he didn't go in soon. "She had some friends over last night. One of them was the chairman of your fan club or something." Randy rubbed one foot on the top of the other. "She left first."

Maddy must have been over.

"So." Randy cradled his coffee mug as if he could draw the warmth down. "What do you reckon to the playoffs? Gotta chance?"

"Sure." Sam could see the hockey talk fervor building in Randy. He didn't want to talk about how his team might make the playoffs without him. Might even win the cup while he warmed the bench. It still felt like an exposed nerve ending. "Lizzie Baby!" He put some power to his door pounding. "Get your sweet ass out here."

"What?" Liz wrenched open the door and glared at him.

"Babe." He winked at Randy. "Look at you all warm and sexy. Want me to come in there?"

Randy cackled and gave him the thumbs up. "Go get her, Sam. You're the man."

Liz crossed her arms over her rack, which objectively speaking, were some fine-looking lady bumps. Even braless they sat up nice and pretty, with her nipples almost poking through her pajama top.

She narrowed her eyes and hissed the words at him. "Stop staring at my boobs."

"What?" He gave her a casual shrug. "They're right there looking back at me."

Liz grabbed the door and swung it. "You're a pig!"

"So true." He grabbed the door before it could shut in his face and stepped inside her apartment.

Randy was still watching and getting every detail down.

"What the hell are you doing?" Liz glared at him from beneath a serious case of bedhead.

Sam shut the door and leaned on it. He played it cool. "Our deal?" A raised eyebrow added the right touch of condescension. "We made a deal. I even shelled out for dinner. Then I bought a bus." He managed to add a little wounded to his expression. "Now, it's been three days and nothing from you."

"It's eight am on a Saturday." Liz scowled at him. "Get out of my apartment."

"Opportunity waits for no one." He managed to keep a straight face. "We could be out there, right now, showing the world my new face." He spread his hands in front of him. "We made a deal, Liz. Two deals in fact."

She glared at him, and then caved on a guttural, inarticulate yell and stomped into the kitchen. The thing with Liz was that she always played fair. It gave her a distinct disadvantage when dealing with a dick like him. He almost felt guilty taking advantage of her.

Liz downed a glass of water. He really liked those cute plaid pj bottoms she had on. Especially the way the waistband dipped to below the jut of her hipbones.

"Okay." She put the glass on the counter. "What's the plan?" Her focus sharpened on him. "And why are you dressed like that?"

"Because this is the plan." He widened his arms and let her get the full extent of super-athlete Sam. "We're going running together."

Her mouth dropped open.

"We will be one of those cute couples who exercise together." His enthusiasm for his idea grew as he spoke. "You in those yoga pants that hug your ass, and me looking all manly and sweaty."

Liz laughed. "You're joking, right?"

"No." He loved this idea more and more. "This will be perfect selfie material. I'm a pro athlete so obviously, exercising is my thing and there you are, my "just friend" exercising right alongside me. Supporting me."

"I don't run, Sam." Liz sneered. "Unless something is chasing me."

"But you do have those hot yoga pants, right?"

She eyed him suspiciously. "Yes."

"And trainers." He pointed at his feet.

"Maybe."

He gave her arm an encouraging squeeze. Liz had a killer ass and chasing that for a mile or two sounded better and better. He bet she worked out all the time. "It'll be great." He yanked open the blind over her kitchen sink. "It's a beautiful day out there and I'll go slow." Then he delivered the knockout. "Come on, Lizzie. I bought you a new bus. I went above and beyond."

She huffed, crossed her arms, uncrossed them and then glowered. "Fine! But I hate exercising and I hate you more."

He could afford to be magnanimous in victory. "That's my girl."

"I'm not your girl." She stomped off to her bedroom.

"You know that, and I know that, but the rest of the world thinks we're adorable. I'm thinking this might have YouTube potential."

———

Elizabeth kept the exercising in her life to a minimum. Because she hated it. Sweating was for sauna's and running was for motors. This trailing after Sam, lungs burning and everything else bouncing and quivering, made her want to break something. Preferably the man-machine gliding along the road in front of her.

He wasn't even sweating, and she could see her life flashing before her eyes.

Turning and running backward, he frowned at her. "You don't do much running, do you?"

She heaved up a reply that came out more grunt than word. There was a reason why she enjoyed yoga and not this crap.

"With your body, you look like you work at it," he said and spun again and kept them running down the sandy path that circled the pond in Brock park.

Not even that veiled compliment would get him off the hook for this. She should have asked for an entire fleet of buses. Then one of them could come and pick her up and end this torment.

Sam ran up to a bench beside the park and did pushups against it. "Come on, Lizzie." Biceps bulged as he pumped his perfectly straight body up and down. He turned and started doing triceps dips.

The only reason she knew those things were called triceps dips is because she liked to watch beautiful men workout videos on Instagram.

Liz took the opportunity to rest. Hands on her knees she hung her head and prayed for God to take her now. They'd been at this for—she checked her phone. "Ten minutes!"

The phone must be faulty. Sam had been torturing her for at least three hours.

"Let's do this!" Sam gave a spry little leap that made her want to kick him and set off again. He increased his pace to a sprint, then stopped, dropped to his front and did a pushup. Rolled over, another pushup and stood. He sprinted back to her and did the whole stupid thing again.

That tore it. Elizabeth stopped running. Every muscle she owned sent her a profound pulse of thanks. Her lungs heaved to get enough air in them, and her face felt like it might combust.

"What are you doing?" Sam stopped and put his hands on his hips. Narrow man hips that he got from doing all this silly crap.

Elizabeth sat on his bench and sucked back water.

"We've still got another hour to go." Sam ran on the spot. "We can't stop now."

"Yes, we can." She wasn't moving from this spot without a latte and doughnut.

Sam leaped onto her bench and down again, shaking the entire thing as he did step-ups.

If she could catch her breath, she'd yell at him. She settled for baring her teeth instead. The entire morning was an exercise in humiliation and physical pain. She should sue him for unnecessary duress.

She shoved him off the bench.

"Hey." Quick as a cat, Sam caught his balance and started that pig stupid roll over, push up, sprinty thing again. Whatever those were called, she hated those too. "You'll never get your heart rate up like that."

"Go away, Sam." Watching him be all super athletey only made her madder.

Sam did walking lunges around the bench. "We're cute workout couple." He poked her shoulder. "Come on."

Not if her life depended on it. "Leave me alone."

"You're mad." He stared at her and then laughed. "You're really mad." He lunged past and gave her thigh a poke. "You can't be mad at me."

Poke.

"Is this because you can't keep up with me?"

Poke.

"I've never seen someone so red in the face." He chuckled.

Elizabeth tried to kick him, but he danced out of the way. If she could stand, she would, but then she'd never catch him anyway.

He danced outside of her reach looking smug and grinning at her.

Elizabeth whipped off her shoe and threw it at him.

His eyes widened as he ducked out of the way, so she threw the other one at him. "What are you doing?"

"If I could catch you, I'd smack you."

Shaking his head, he laughed harder and picked up her shoes. "You know you're having a grownup tantrum, right?"

"Yup." She lobbed her water bottle at him. "But I'm tired and I'm sweaty and I hate this and I don't care."

"Liz." He brought her shoes to her and sat beside her. "You get that I do this for a living, right?"

She made some sort of noise and turned her head away.

Hand beneath her chin, Sam turned her head back. "You could have said if you were tired."

"Would you?" She crossed her arms. "If you were me, and I was you. Would you?"

"Probably not." He lifted her foot to his lap and put her shoe back on. Then the other one. "Shall I buy you breakfast to make up for it?"

"Maybe." She could eat.

He nudged her shoulder. "With bacon and pancakes."

"I want maple syrup."

Standing, he held his hand out to her. "Then you shall have maple syrup."

A man ran past them, stopped and jogged back. He glowered at Sam. "You're Sam Stone."

"Yup." Sam stood and put himself between her and the man.

"Yeah, well, you're a dickhead." Aggression poured off the man. He stepped right into Sam and shoved him. "You're not that tough, Sam Stone. I could take you."

"What are you doing?" Elizabeth leaped to her feet. She couldn't believe what she was seeing. "Sam doesn't want to fight you."

"Step away," Sam said, his voice quiet. "I'm not going to get into this with you."

"Because you're a big fucking pussy." The guy shoved Sam again.

Sam rocked back but held his ground. His jaw was clenched, and his eyes went icy blue.

"Stop it." Elizabeth got in front of Sam.

He tried to get around her. "Liz."

"No, Sam." She moved back between them and glared up at the man. He was much bigger than her, and part of her brain was screaming that this was one of her worst ideas, but Elizabeth hated a bully. "Get away from Sam."

"You let a girl do your fighting for you, Stone?" The guy shoved past her shoulder at Sam.

His watch strap caught in Elizabeth's hair and yanked. "Ow!"

He tried to pull away and ripped out a hank of her hair.

Sam growled and lunged for the guy. He was lighting fast, and Elizabeth almost didn't catch the back of his shirt in time. He could not be seen fighting in a public park, not with his suspension and all.

Elizabeth got tugged forward a few steps before Sam stopped.

Glaring over his shoulder at her, he said, "Let me go."

"No." She tightened her grip. "You can't fight him. It will only make things worse for you."

"Pussy!" The idiot danced back into Sam's reach.

Sam cocked his fist and Elizabeth dived for the guy. Her shoulder connected his stomach and drove him back. They both went over in a tangle of arms and legs.

"Get off me, you crazy bitch." The guy shoved at her.

Going on pure instinct, Elizabeth opened her mouth and screamed.

"Jesus!" He shook his head and scrambled away from her. "What the fuck is wrong with you? Shut up."

Eyes locked on him, Elizabeth screamed louder.

The guy bolted.

She stopped screaming and drank from Sam's water bottle.

"He was right about one thing." Sam held out his hand and helped her up. "You are one crazy bitch."

Then he laughed, a gut deep belly laugh that rolled over her.

Her own laughter burst out of her. She couldn't believe she'd done that.

They laughed so hard they could barely stand and stood there howling with laughter and clinging to each other.

Eventually Sam straightened and wiped his eyes. "Did you rescue me?"

"Maybe." In hindsight it was silly. Sam could have taken care of himself, but she hadn't thought it through. "All I could think was that if you got into a fight it would make things even worse for you."

"Ah, Busy Lizzie." Chuckling, Sam cupped her nape and rested his forehead against hers. "That will definitely get you maple syrup for breakfast."

CHAPTER
ELEVEN

AS AGREED, the next Saturday Elizabeth went to pick up Sam for Chris's team practice.

"Morning." Sam hopped into the car bringing the fresh smell of a winter morning with him. He pointed to the coffee she had stopped to get along the way. "Is that for me?"

"Yeah." She handed him the bagel. "I brought you breakfast as well."

"I love you." Sam bit into the bagel and groaned. "I'm starving."

"You owe me."

He chuckled and ate the bagel. "I'm good for it."

She and Sam arrived at the rink to the delight of all of Chris's players.

Sam smiled, joked and signed stuff.

Then the kids hit the ice.

Ten minutes later Elizabeth wasn't smiling. Not at all. In fact, she was reminded of all the reasons she didn't like Sam, beginning with his arrogance, his selfishness, and his insensitivity.

They stood on the ice and watched Chris's team play.

"Jesus." He muttered and crossed his arms.

To their left, Tyra skated in circles and sang her own song.

She came because her parents said it would be good for her, but she hated hockey and Chris let her do her own thing.

Granted, it wasn't what Sam was used to. Not even in the same universe, but still.

It made her want to cry how quickly everything had gone bad.

Truthfully, she hadn't been to a practice in a while, and she'd forgotten how bad they were. Still, they were kids and most of them only cared that they got to play on a team. That had to count for something, right? Except for Mr. Big Shot Hockey God who stood there sneering at everyone.

Like he'd never made a mistake. Everyone in this rink knew that wasn't true. The reason he was standing here now was because of a mistake he'd made. If she was a shitty human being, she'd point exactly that out to him.

Anton, all of ten, and more comfortable in front of his Xbox than on the ice took a swipe at the puck, missed and landed on his butt.

"You've got to be kidding me." Sam looked disgusted. "Can't that kid stay on his skates?"

Flushing, Anton stumbled back to his feet, but his skates went out from under him and he landed on his knees.

Sam shook his head. "Apparently not."

"Whoa there, Tiger." Chris skated up to Anton and helped him to his feet.

Anton sent an agonized glance at Sam and hung his head. His skinny shoulders hitched.

"Hey, there." Chris skated him a little bit away from the others. "We all fall. It's okay. You'll get the hang of it."

"No, he won't." Sam snorted. "Someone should take his skates away from him."

"Hey!" Elizabeth rounded on him. She couldn't believe what she was hearing. Except, maybe she could because Sam had never had any time for anyone who didn't excel at sports. She lowered her voice so Anton wouldn't hear her. "Not everyone is going to make the hockey league, but that doesn't mean they're not entitled to play the game."

"Trust me, I can see that." He threw Anton a disgusted look. "And Chris is not helping him by encouraging him. She should tell him to give it up." He grunted. "At the very least tell him not to cry on the fucking ice."

"You're mean." Chloe said. Eight and the best skater they had on the team, the only reason she stayed was because her twin brother wasn't good enough to play on any other team with her.

Sam stared down at her aghast. "The truth isn't mean. It's the truth. My coaches don't tell me I'm doing a good job when I'm not. They tell me the truth."

"No." Chris's eyes went almost black with anger. "They tell you to get the hell off the ice. And now I'm telling you the same."

"What?" Sam gaped at her. "I came here to help."

"Well you're not helping." Chris folded her arms and faced off against him. "You're upsetting my team and I want you off the ice."

"What do you expect me to do with them?" Sam motioned the kids, who stood about gaping at him. "I'm a professional. I can't work with this."

"That's it." Elizabeth had brought him, and she would take him away. Chris had been afraid of this happening, but she hadn't listened. This was on her. "You're leaving."

She shoved his chest.

Sam rocked back but didn't move. "What are you doing?"

"So help me, Sam." Elizabeth got toe to toe with him. "If you don't get the hell away from these children, I'm going to release every one of your naked baby pictures to the media."

The team whispered and snickered.

Elizabeth raised her voice. "And you were not a pretty baby."

"Liz—"

"You had no hair." Elizabeth raised her voice. She had to give these children some recovery from this disaster. "And your ears stuck out."

Giggles erupted behind her.

Sam frowned and looked confused. He dropped his voice for her ears only. "You're seriously kicking me out?"

"I'm seriously kicking you out."

He glared at her and then glanced at the children.

The team gave him the stink eye.

"Fine." Sam threw up his hands and skated off. "Your loss."

Chris and her team broke into cheers.

————

Sam was done with being fired. It sucked, and today had been the last straw. He was a professional hockey player, for fuck's sake. What did Lizzie expect him to do with that bunch of lame ducks?

She had no right to fire him, and he drove to her condo to tell her so.

Randy stopped him before he'd even climbed the steps. "She's not there." He held up his beer. "Wanna come in for a brew?"

"Another time." It made him mad that she wasn't there as well. "Do you know where she is?"

"It's Saturday." Randy sniffed. "She'll be over at her old man's cooking for him and that bitchy sister of hers."

Sam got back in his car and headed to the Rogers house. It looked the same, with its neat white wooden siding and bright green trim.

Giving his car door a good slam, he trudged through the snow to the door. Paul hadn't shoveled the walk yet. Actually, if memory served, Sue had always shoveled the walk, which meant Lizzie hadn't gotten 'round to it yet.

Stamping snow off his boots, he hammered on the front door.

A young woman opened it wearing sprayed on jeans and a

tight sweater. Her brown hair was pulled into a messy knot on top of her head and heavy, black makeup ringed her eyes.

She pushed her hands into her back pockets and thrust her breasts at him. "Well, look who arrived on my doorstep."

"Jane?" He peered at her to be certain. Last time he had seen Jane she'd certainly not been wearing makeup or had any of the other parts tenting her sweater.

"Of course it's Jane." She dropped the Jessica Rabbit routine. "What do you want?"

"Liz in?"

"E-liz-a-beth is in the kitchen." Jane went back to draping herself across the doorjamb. "But you'd much rather see me."

"No." He slipped past her into the house and took his coat off. He'd spent large portions of his childhood in this house. Whenever his mother had to work, holidays so they didn't have to spend them alone, birthdays and times when his mom needed her friend.

Sue Rogers was like a second mom to him.

When he got to the kitchen, Liz had that shapely ass facing his way. She straightened, closed the oven door and caught sight of him.

Her face went cold. "What are you doing here?"

"We need to talk about what happened." He yanked out a stool and sat. Funny, he'd gone straight to the stool he had always sat on as a kid. "You should have warned me those kids can't play hockey."

"They can play hockey." Liz slammed a bowl on the table. "They don't play it well, which is why Chris took on the team in the first place."

"Eh?" That didn't make much sense. "Why would they want to play if they're no good at it?"

Liz glared at him and hauled salad fixings out of the fridge. "Why do you have to be good to play?"

"Because it's more fun that way."

She tore lettuce and flung it in the bowl. "You're such a dick, Sam."

"No, I'm not." He dropped a stray lettuce leaf into her bowl. "Despite my mother, I've always been good at sports, and I've always enjoyed playing them. So were you."

Liz attacked the tomatoes with the knife in a way that made him sit back. "Well, kids like Chris weren't."

"Yeah, I know that." He chuckled. Two left feet and zero hand eye coordination. "Do you remember that time she beaned you in the head when—"

"I remember." The knife flashed in Liz's hands and the cucumber went the way of the tomato. "And I also remember Chris always feeling like a loser because she wasn't any good. Nobody wanted her on their team, no matter how much she wanted to play."

"Huh." He could see by her face that she meant it. "So, she coaches a team for kids like her? I didn't know that."

"Well, now you know." She scooped the cut veggies into the bowl. "And they did not need some dick like you making them feel useless." She slammed the knife on the cutting board. "They have little enough confidence and it's all Chris can do to get them motivated and enjoying the game." Hands on hips, she got up in his face. "I remember a kid who used to get laughed at for being a mommy's boy. What if one of his idols had stood in front of him and laughed at him about it?"

Sam winced. Lizzie did not pull her punches, but she'd also made her point. He replayed the day in his mind, this time with her spin on it. There was only one thing to be said. "I was a dick today."

"Yes, you were."

"I want make it up to you." His behavior today made him cringe. "Ask me for another of your favors."

She looked at him with the coldest eyes ever. "I don't want anything else from you."

"Come on, Lizzie. There has to be something."

"It's those kids you owe, not me." She finished the salad and made the dressing before looking at him again. "Do you have any other reason for being here?"

"Do you cook dinner for him every Saturday?" He wanted her to stop fussing with food and have a conversation with him. Mostly, he wanted her to tell him how he could make it right with Chris's team.

"Mom always used to do Saturday dinner before we went our separate ways." She came up with her face flushed from the heat. "He doesn't know how to cook."

"He could learn." Paul might even find he enjoyed cooking. Sam did.

Lizzie put the knife down with a careful attention to detail that made him nervous. "Did you come here to piss me off? Because if you did, you're exceeding expectations."

"No." Sam kept his eye on the knife. "I came here because I was mad about you firing me today. Now I realize I deserved getting kicked off the ice." She moved away from the knife and he breathed easier. "Can I stay for dinner?"

"Why?"

"So I can pester you into forgiving me."

She rolled her eyes and did something on the stovetop that involved banging lids and stirring.

Sam took the opportunity to know more about the grown-up Lizzie. "Do you still work for your dad?"

"Yup."

Her sweater had ridden up in the back. Girls with asses like Lizzie's should never cover them up. If he told her that, he was pretty sure that knife would come into play. "You used to hate that job."

"I still do." She whipped around, her face flushing. "I mean, I don't hate it. Actually it can be very rewarding."

Sam didn't bother to keep the skepticism off his face. Lizzie was smart, way smarter than anyone else they'd gone to school with. "Being your father's secretary is rewarding?"

"Office manager." She spun away from him and disappeared into the fridge. Beer in hand, she came back up and handed it to him. "I like organizing things."

"Lizzie?" He really didn't have to say it because she knew.

Slamming her hands on her hips, she glared at him. "How come this is about me and what's wrong with me now?

"Come on, Liz. For as long as I've known you, you've worked for your dad and hated it." He took a carrot out the salad. He was taking the beer as a sign she'd let him stay for dinner. There were worse things than sitting down to Lizzie's cooking. "And now you're here taking care of him like your mom would. She walked out of this. We both know she'd hate to see you taking her place here."

"You know what I hate?" Her eyes narrowed in a way he knew meant he really didn't want to know what she hated. He kept quiet and still. Dinner was looking iffy. "I hate the way my life goes to crap any time you're near me."

Damn but that hurt. He, for sure, wouldn't let her know, but that found a chink in his armor and scored. Pushing his beer toward her, he stood. "Thanks for the beer, but I'm good. You live your life any way you want to, but even I think you're worth more than a man who treats you like crap."

CHAPTER
TWELVE

"GRIND HIM INTO THE BOARDS," Dad yelled from the other room. "Break the little shit."

Just like every Saturday of her life. Until Sam had appeared in this kitchen an hour ago with his judgy eyes staring at her, she'd been fine.

Okay, not totally fine. She had been experiencing a few pangs of dissatisfaction, but she refused to feel guilty about upsetting Sam. He had been awful with Chris's team.

And he'd apologized.

But still, he'd followed that apology by picking on her.

"I told you I'm a vegetarian." Jane's diatribe was getting old. "I'm not going to eat whatever disgusting dead thing you're sacrificing."

"Really?" Even for Jane that was over the top.

Jane had the decency to look embarrassed. "I don't want to stay. It's Saturday night. The last thing I want to do is spend it here. Lame."

Elizabeth was well aware of that. It was lame, and it was lame for both of them.

"Is that beer coming?" Dad yelled.

"We need to stick together." Elizabeth kept it calm and

reasonable. Yelling at Jane never got anywhere. Although, maybe a bit more—as in any—yelling when Jane had been little might have helped curb her now.

"Why?" Jane folded her arms and stuck her hip out. "It's not like he cares if either of us are here."

Elizabeth didn't want to believe that. Now Sam was getting in her head too. "Of course he notices," she said, but even to her it lacked conviction. "He misses Mom, but he's too proud to show it."

"No, he doesn't." Jane gaped at her. "And the only person who thinks that is you."

"They were married for thirty years, of course he misses her." He had to, because Elizabeth hated to think of her mother trapped in a marriage to someone who didn't even love her. Dad's lack of respect had been obvious, but she'd always chosen to put it down to his personality. Dad was cold and liked things his own way. He also didn't mind trampling other people's feelings to get things his own way.

"I really don't give a crap." Jane scooped up her phone. "I'm going out anyway. The atmosphere in this shithole is totally toxic."

"Which is exactly why you need to stay." Even knowing she was going to lose this skirmish, Elizabeth followed Jane into the hallway.

Dad peered over the top of his lounger pointedly. "Beer."

"In the kitchen," Elizabeth said.

Dad stared at her. Even Jane stopped walking and gaped.

The doorbell saved her, and Elizabeth went to answer it.

Wine bottle in one hand and flowers in the other, Sam stood on their doorstep. "Hi."

She had enough on her hands without him there. "What do you want?"

"I came back."

"Why?"

Jane gaped at her.

With a nod, Sam said, "I behaved like a shit."

"Which time?"

Sam pushed the flowers into her hands. "Both. All of them."

Before she could respond, Dad broke the land speed record reaching the front door. "Is that Sam?"

"Paul." Sam gave him a tight smile. "Looking good."

"What are you talking about?" Dad flushed and shifted his feet. "I'm getting old and it shows."

"Nah." Sam's response sounded forced. "I bet you could give all of us some stiff competition."

Elizabeth wanted to puke on them.

Dad turned and glared at her. "Don't block the doorway. Let Sam in."

Sam stepped into the house and stared at her. "Give me five minutes."

"You can have more than that." Dad waved a dismissive hand. "You're welcome here anytime." He handed the wine to Elizabeth. "I'm watching the game. Beer?"

Sam shifted. "Actually, I need to talk—"

Tossing his hand over Sam's shoulders, Dad marched him into the lounge and called over his shoulder, "Beer, Elizabeth."

"Sam knows where it is." She'd be damned before she ran around after Sam.

Jane loitered in the hallway. "What time are we eating?"

"I thought you were going out."

Sam came back to the hallway and gave the kitchen door a significant look. "I'm getting that beer."

"Good." She had nothing left to say to him.

"Five minutes. Please." Sam strode into the kitchen.

Eyes glued on Sam's ass, Jane smirked. "I've suddenly developed a taste for roast chicken."

Elizabeth wanted to smack her. "Won't your friends be waiting for you?"

"So?" Jane shrugged and stared after Sam.

That! That right there was how everything went to shit when Sam was around.

"Sam," Dad yelled. "You're missing the game."

"Coming, Paul." Sam reappeared and took the wine bottle from her.

Still clutching the flowers, Elizabeth followed him. She should throw the stupid flowers away. Sam needn't think he could barge his way in, and all would be forgiven because he brought flowers.

They were pretty, though. Irises, her favorite. It wasn't their fault Sam had brought them. Elizabeth hunted for a vase under the sink.

A cork popped and Sam poured a glass of wine. He put it on the table. "For you."

"Thank you." Damn it, but between the flowers and the wine, she didn't want to kill him quite so much anymore.

He took an appreciative sniff. "What are we having?"

"Chicken." She concentrated on putting the flowers in a vase.

Sidling close enough that she could smell his fresh, crisp aftershave he whispered, "With those roast potatoes you make?"

"Stop it." Elizabeth clung to the disappearing tendrils of her anger. "Don't come in here and be all charming. I'm mad at you."

"I know." He grimaced. "And I'm trying to make you unmad." He shrugged, innocent and harmless, and aw-shucks-don't-hate-me. "I seem to make you mad a lot."

"You were mean to those children." She sidestepped him and grabbed her glass of wine. "This is not about me. It's about them."

"I'll make it up to them." He followed her.

When he wasn't around, she always forgot how tall he was, and how broad. "How?"

"I'm not sure yet." He shrugged. "But I'll think of something."

"Sam," Dad yelled. "What are you doing in there?"

"Talking to Lizzie."

"Why?"

Sam swore and dropped his head. Then he called back, "I like talking to Elizabeth."

"No, you don't," she said, but she did appreciate him standing up for her.

"Actually I do." Sam clinked his beer bottle against her wine. "When we're not bickering."

Elizabeth couldn't hold back a snort. "And when would that be?"

"Granted, not often." He grinned.

She found herself grinning back, but she didn't care, and she sipped her wine. It hit her palate in a burst of blackberry richness. "This is good."

"Tim at the LCBO said it was your favorite."

It was hard to stay mad when he did things like that. But she managed a theatrical groan. "Now everyone will be talking about you buying me wine."

"Pretty sure that horse has bolted." He sipped his beer. Sam's mouth was almost girly in the uncompromising harshness of his other features. "What with the internet pictures and all."

"Why did you come back, Sam?" Liz dug a bag of frozen peas out of the freezer.

Sam pulled a face. "I was a dick." He held up a hand before she could respond. "First with the kids and then with you. I'm sorry."

"Sam." Dad sounded agonized. "You're missing the whole game."

"You better go." Elizabeth motioned the lounge. "We can talk about this later."

"Let's talk about it now instead." Sam grabbed her hand. "Tell me what I gotta do to make this right?"

She really wanted to stay mad, but he was sincere, and she knew him well enough to know that. "I'll let you know."

"You do that." Sam refilled her wineglass and nodded at the

peas. "Are you going to do that cream and butter thing you do with those?"

———

With Sam at the table, Elizabeth had no trouble getting Dad and Jane there.

Jane wedged herself in the seat next to Sam and made eyes at him from beneath layers of black eyeliner.

Looking mildly uncomfortable, Sam kept his distance from her.

Dad sat at the table head and beamed at Sam. "How's the suspension treating you?"

Elizabeth caught the slight tensing in Sam at the mention of his suspension.

"As good as can be expected," Sam said and helped himself to peas.

Yes, she had done the thing with the cream and butter for him, but only because she liked it too.

Jane picked at a roast potato.

Cooking for Sam was never a hardship, because he always ate what she put in front of him and enjoyed it.

"Where's the carrots?" Dad glared at the table.

Taking a deep breath, Elizabeth said, "I didn't make them today. I made the peas instead."

Dad looked thunderous.

"That Sam likes," she added before Dad said anything more.

Across the table Sam raised an eyebrow.

She pulled a face at him.

Drenching his chicken in gravy, Dad shook his head. "Completely bullshit call on that hit, by the way. I watched the entire thing and it was crap."

"Thanks for the support, Paul." Shoulders tense, Sam kept his eyes on his plate. "But I've got the reputation I earned and that makes calls like that inevitable."

Elizabeth took pity on him and changed the subject. "Any word on the bus?"

"Tomorrow." Sam's smile lost its restraint. "I forgot to tell you in all the earlier excitement, but they're delivering it tomorrow."

"What bus?" Dad's gaze snapped between them. He hated being left out of any conversation with Sam.

"Sam bought a new bus for Mountain Vista," she said. "The old one gave up the ghost a few months ago and now the residents can't get to their classes or their weekly grocery shop."

"Jesus!" Jane rolled her eyes. "Only you would care about a bunch of old people. Where could they possibly want to go anyway?"

"They're old, not dead," Elizabeth said. Even for Jane that was crossing the line. "They've worked hard all their lives, and now they deserve a bit of consideration."

"Whatever." Jane pulled her phone out.

Elizabeth had to try. "Not at the table, Jane."

"Says who?" Jane snorted.

"Dad?" Appealing to her dad was likely to be a waste, but she'd cooked their meal and it was supposed to bring all of them together.

"Eh?" Dad frowned at her.

Elizabeth motioned Jane. "I think we should put our phones down at the table."

He looked at her as if she'd lost her mind. "Who cares?"

Mom had cared. Elizabeth clenched her jaw before she blurted it out. Mom had cared and she cared.

Across the table, Sam's expression softened as if he might say something.

"Bet the team is champing to have you back." Like a scud missile, Dad went right back to his target. None of Sam's discomfort registered with him. "Of course they do. Not the same without you."

Nodding politely to Dad, Sam turned back to her. His eyes twinkled at her across the table and Elizabeth braced.

"I had them paint a decal of me down the sides," he said. "A montage of me in action."

"Hell yeah!" Dad thumped the table. "That's the ticket, right there. This town doesn't do enough to recognize our greatest resident."

Sam gave a tiny wince.

"Maybe we should have a statue of Sam erected in Brock Park." Elizabeth couldn't resist. "Something that captures the spirit of Sam Stone the hockey player."

Sam Stone the hockey player raised an eyebrow at her and dared her to go there.

With pleasure, and Elizabeth beamed at him. "You know, with his gloves off, punching the crap out of someone."

"Elizabeth!" Dad jabbed his forefinger at her. "You don't understand hockey, and your ignorance doesn't give you a free pass to make asinine, insulting statements."

Even when they were kids, Dad had rushed to defend Sam.

"Seriously, Paul, it's okay." Sam's voice held an edge of irritation. "Liz rags on me all the time and I rag on her. It's what we do."

Dad forced a chuckle, but his gaze still shot daggers her way. "So long as the ragging doesn't turn bitchy. I've told both my girls. I won't tolerate a bitch in this house."

"Wow!" Jane rolled her eyes at her phone. "Toxic masculinity at work."

"Watch your mouth, missy." Dad turned on Jane.

Probably only because he was trying to impress Sam with his paternal prowess.

Jane didn't give a crap and the look she gave Dad screamed that. "Or what? You gonna keep making me feel like shit until I walk out that door? Like you did to Mom?"

"So." Sam raised his voice. "What do you think of the Pumas this season, Paul? Their D could do with some work."

Since Mom had left, Elizabeth had been making Saturday dinners, trying to keep her shattered family together. Why exactly she'd decided to take that on, she couldn't fathom.

Dinner dragged on with Dad holding forth on every team in the league, Jane doing her best to either piss him off or get Sam's attention, and Sam looking like he wished he'd made a different decision on coming over.

When it was over, Jane bolted for the door, and Dad went to watch hockey.

Elizabeth cleared the dishes and loaded the dishwasher.

"Here." Sam handed her glass of wine. "You need this."

After that dinner, she certainly did. "Leave the bottle."

Chuckling, he cleared more dishes from the table and brought them to her. "Man." Shaking his head, he propped his hips next to the dishwasher as she loaded. "When your mom was here, she kept the worst of it under control."

"Yeah, she did." A wave of longing smacked into her. Without Mom, it had degenerated into a house full of people who didn't like each other. "She was the glue that held us all together."

CHAPTER
THIRTEEN

ELIZABETH LOST it when she saw her bus. Technically the bus for Mountain Vista, but she had an emotional investment in it.

It was big, black and sparkly new. It even had that new car smell. And no decals of Sam down the side. She almost didn't want to touch it in case it disappeared. "It's perfect."

"See." Sam wasn't having the same hesitation as he showed it to Carol in the parking lot of Mountain Vista. "It's got a hydraulic lift here, and a tie down area that can take three wheelchairs."

Carol beamed at him. "It's perfect, Sam. More than perfect."

Elizabeth would see a lot better if her eyes stopped their damn leaking.

"And it's got seating for at least fifteen people." Sam jumped into the bus. He reached out and helped Carol into the bus.

Elizabeth kept on nodding as he went through the features of the bus. It was so much more than she'd asked for, and it would make such a difference to so many lives.

"So?" Sam popped up in front of her. "You like?"

More nodding because she couldn't get words past the lump in her throat.

"Lizzie?" Sam bent his knees and looked into her eyes. "These are happy tears?"

She sniffed and nodded.

"Good." Sam pulled her into a spice-scented hug, his body hard and strong against hers, and Elizabeth got a bit lightheaded.

Her arms tightened around his slim waist and she pushed her face into his neck. Because of the bus. The bus and nothing else.

Behind Sam, Carol raised her brow. Yeah, she didn't believe it either.

———

Sam hadn't reached out to any of his teammates since he'd left Ottawa that crappy night. He did now and Luke Riggs, a senior defenceman on the team, along with veteran goalie Guy Pelletier surprised him by offering to come down and see him.

They made plans to work out in the gym Sam had installed in Mom's basement. He suspected he might be the only person who ever used it.

He opened the door to Riggs sporting a black eye and Guy looking tired.

"Stoner." Riggs pulled him into a man-hug. "You look better than you deserve to."

"And you look like shit." Along with that black eye Riggs had a split lip and another bruise along his jaw. He also favored his left leg.

Riggs pulled a face and pushed a hand through his shoulder-length blond hair. "Yeah, well you left me to keep those young dicks in line. And we got our asses handed to us last night by the Raps."

"That's on me." Guy followed Riggs in and shook Sam's hand. "Yeah, last night I let five in."

"Not your fault, Trapper." Riggs clapped Guy on the back. "If the offence doesn't generate goals and our D gets sloppy, that isn't on you."

The Raptors were old rivals and the games always got chippy.

Sam handed them a water and they hit the gym. "Hamstring bothering you?"

"Yeah. Took a bad hit last night." Riggs had a recurring injury that flared up from time to time.

Hell, they all had recurring injuries that flared up from time to time. The longer you stayed in the game, the more of those you racked up.

"Couple of the boys say hello." Guy rattled off the names of a few teammates. Mostly older players like them, men who'd been in the league long enough to have the cocky ground out of them.

As they worked out, they caught him up on all the gossip. The rookie goalie was looking good, nipping at Guy's heels to take his place, but Guy had been playing this game for too many years to let that faze him. Management had their eye on a prospect out of Finland, a center with a wicked shot and a sixth sense for the puck.

"What about you?" Riggs took a swig of water. "Rumor had it you got yourself settled with a nice girl down here."

"Elizabeth?" He played it cool. "Yeah, she's just a friend."

Riggs didn't look convinced and Sam hid a grin at how Lizzie would have reacted to their interchange.

"I've been doing some stuff around the community," he said. "Need to clean up my image and I like it. The people around here have always supported me. I owe them a bit of my time and effort."

His phone rang and he checked caller ID and then picked up. "Hey, Lizzie. We were just talking about you."

Riggs went back to working out.

Guy made no pretense of not watching him and listening to the call.

Down the line, Elizabeth sniffled. "Sam." She caressed his

name in a way that felt like a velvet glove up his spine. "The Mountain Vista residents took the bus for a movie outing. They loved it so much." She gave a little sob. "I sent you some pictures."

"Damn." He couldn't stop his big grin. He'd made her so happy she was getting all weepy. Lizzie did that when she got emotional. "Imagine how happy they would have been if I could've gotten some decals on it."

"Oh, Sam." She giggled. He liked that better than her weepy. "They keep going for drives around the block. Every time a new person sees it, they all load back up again and take it for another spin. Cameron won't let anyone else drive it."

He could picture the scene and it made him grin wider.

Riggs had joined Guy and they shared a look and then went back to gaping at him.

"Tell the old fart not to crash it," he said to Elizabeth.

"I will." She gave a breathy little laugh. "And thank you, Sam. It's perfect."

As soon as he put the phone down, Riggs pounced. "And this is the girl who is just your friend?"

Guy shook his head. "Man, if I met a girl who put a stupid grin on my face like you're wearing, I'd either run from her or marry her."

CHAPTER
FOURTEEN

SAM DIDN'T EXACTLY HIDE behind Liz as they made their way to the ice the next Saturday, but he did let her take the lead.

Picking where she put her feet, Maddy followed them, iPhone at the ready to capture the moment.

He hadn't seen Lizzie for the remainder of the week, although she did blow up his phone with pictures of the bus. On one she even drew stick figures that were meant to be the decals of him playing hockey down the side of the bus.

Damn she made him laugh. Not a lot of people saw the quirky in Lizzie, or that flash fire temper that showed up around him.

"Did you tell Chris I was coming?" Ahead of them, the kids clustered on the ice around Chris.

Maddy gripped his shoulder to keep her balance. "I'm sure they'll be very happy to see you."

Even Maddy didn't sound all that certain and he grabbed Liz's elbow. "Chris does know?"

She glanced over her shoulder at him. "I may have mentioned it. And do you mind? Personal space bubble."

Lizzie smelled good too. Not of perfume like Maddy, but the light scent of something flowery and soapy.

He carried her bag and his, in which he concealed part of his recovery strategy. "Did Chris say it was okay?"

"Not exactly," Lizzie said. "Wait here."

Sam stood there, stupefied, as she trotted through the stands to the ice. Not exactly was not at all the answer he'd been looking for.

She got there and spoke to Chris.

Chris whirled, pinned him with a look and scowled. "No."

"Chris will come around." Maddy made it sound like a dearly held wish.

Dragging his attention away from Chris and Liz, he stared at Maddy.

Maddy's chocolatey gaze stuck on Chris, the longing on her face unmistakable.

It took him a moment and then he got it.

Chris and Maddy. He liked it.

Liz gestured emphatically as she whispered something else to Chris.

"I don't care." Chris raised her hands to her sides.

Leaning in, Lizzie spoke again.

Chris opened her mouth, huffed and then frowned. She glanced at the kids. Finally, she looked at him. "All new sticks, all new pads, and all new skates."

"Done!" Relief surged through him and he jumped down the remaining stairs to the ice.

Maddy gasped. "That's a lot. You should ask one of your sponsors."

He could do that, but it felt wrong. "I'm good for it."

All gazes hostile, the team turned and glared at him. He went for the standard approach. "Hi."

More evil eyeing.

"What do you want, Sam?" Chris folded her arms. She caught site of Maddy and blushed. "Er...hi."

"Hi." Maddy breathed. She held up her phone. "I won't be any trouble. I'm here to take pictures. Of Sam. Sam and Elizabeth, and maybe the children. If you don't mind."

"No." Chris almost yelled the word. "No bother. It's fine."

Three of the kids gave him the once-over and found him lacking.

Behind Chris's back, Lizzie gave him a look that encouraged him to get on with it, which comprised an eye roll and a rude hand gesture.

"First off, I came to apologize," he said. "I behaved badly and there's no excuse for the way I treated you."

"That was lovely, Sam." Maddy beamed at him like a proud parent.

Chris snorted. "Not that lovely."

"Are we going to play hockey today?" Chloe nudged her brother and they both scowled at Sam.

Sam gave her his most dazzling smile. "I would really like it if you would let me play with you."

"You said we suck." Chloe was tougher than a lot of her gender when it came to Sam's smile. "Why should we play with you?"

"Because I'm really good." Sam shrugged. "And maybe I could show you a thing or two. Mostly because I'm really sorry and I'm asking you to forgive me."

Chloe thought that over.

The rest of the team looked at him.

Damn, tough crowd.

"I was wrong to say what I said." He glanced at Lizzie and she gave him a nod of encouragement. At least he chose to think it was encouragement. She might be leading him to his doom. "Look, I shouldn't have said what I said, but your skating...it could be better."

Even Maddy looked disappointed in him.

"Sam." Chris's held a distinct warning. An I've-been-trained-to-make-convicted-felons-cry edge.

He put a couple of feet between him and Chris. "I want to help you skate better. It all starts with skating."

"Why should we trust you?" This from Anton, the kid he'd belittled.

"Because I owe you this," he said. "I can't promise you'll ever be great, but I can promise to get you on your feet for long enough to put up some competition."

Lizzie stepped forward. "And because he promised me he wanted to help," she said. "And I've known Sam since we were your age. He's not always nice, but he doesn't lie."

"If I was a liar, I would have said you skate well and play hockey better," he said.

Chris closed the distance between them and turned her back on the kids. She pitched her voice for his ears only. "I'm gonna let you do this, but not for you." She jerked her head. "You'll do this for them, because they deserve this from you, and because it will make them all feel ten feet high to have the coolest assistant coach there is."

"Assistant?" He met her hard gaze. "Coach."

"Assistant," Chris said emphatically. "Or you can take your pretty, pampered ass out of my practice."

"Assistant." He nodded because he could work his way up from there. He had major bribery in mind, but he would have these kids eating out of his palm. "And at least it's a pretty ass."

"Does nothing for me." Chris snorted and clapped her hands. "Listen up," she said to her team. "I don't agree with the way he treated you, and I for sure won't let him do anything like that again. But he is Sam Stone and he does play for the Ottawa Titans, and think how jealous the other teams are going to be."

That did the magic and some of the frost melted off young faces.

He took a seat and laced into his skates.

On the ice, he held out his hand for the whistle. With a glare, Chris handed it over.

"Right." He blew the whistle. Sure they were all paying attention already but a whistle...the power was heady.

"This is what we're going to do. If by the end of practice today, you can all skate forward and turn left and right, I'm taking you all out for pizza." He dug in his bag and hauled out a T-shirt. "And you get to wear these."

Chloe tilted her head and read the words on the T-shirt. "Sam Stone knows nothing." She smirked. "We really get to wear that?"

"If you earn it," he said. "Show me I'm wrong and show me you deserve to be on the ice."

A couple of the kids looked ready, a couple nervous, but most looked uncertain.

"Are we skating drills?" Anton glanced at Chloe and chewed on his lip.

"Drills." He snorted and rolled his eyes. "Those are so boring. We're going to play tag instead."

An excited murmur rose from the kids.

"I like sharks and minnows." Anton was holding tough.

"We're playing tag," he said. "And I'm catching."

"No way." A heavyset boy with flushed cheeks put his hand up. "You'll catch us too fast."

"Maybe." He gave a casual shrug. "But there are a lot more of you than me. And you get to count to ten and come back on the ice." He pointed to Chris and Lizzie. "And they're on your team and allowed to run interference and call a foul against me."

The kids all stared at him.

"One." He raised the whistle to his mouth. "When I get to ten, I'm coming after you."

Lizzie gave him a smug smile. "I didn't bring my skates."

"Funny thing that." He enjoyed this more than he should. "Your skates are in the bag."

To give Lizzie her due, she took it well and put her skates on.

Kids scattered in all directions as Sam counted.

"Ten." He turned and looked about him. He chose Chloe. She looked like she could skate.

She shot off across the ice, and Sam chased. The kid had good legs and changed direction on a whisper.

Lizzie shot across his path and forced him to slow down. She glanced over her shoulder and smirked at him.

Oh, it was on. He grinned back.

Sam put on the speed and headed for Chloe. He ducked past Chris when she tried to distract him.

Chloe glanced over her shoulder and shrieked.

Bending, Sam scooped her off her feet and carried her to the side. She giggled in his arms and he put her down on the side of the rink.

And so he went, taking out the stronger skaters first, so he could give the weaker ones as much practice as possible.

It didn't take long for the kids to get into the swing of it. Their shouting rang out over the ice.

"You can't catch me."

"Here, Sam!"

"Come and get me."

He surprised the hell out of himself by having a good time. It had been so long since he'd skated for the hell of it. The looks on the kids' faces reminded him of why he had wanted to skate for a living.

Wind whipped past his face as he skated. He drove the kids to turn left and right, scooping them up and putting them on the side. Little stinkers started to cheat and the minute his back was turned they were back on the ice.

Even Chris laughed along with them after a while.

It took him back to a time when he and Liz had skated together as kids. He'd forgotten what a good skater she was.

Fast and agile, she helped the kids who fell and shielded the cheaters.

She looked damn pretty with her cheeks flushed and her big green eyes sparkling.

Eventually the kids tired and the ice cleared.

Only him and Lizzie left. She skated toward the bench.

"Not so fast." Sam moved to intercept her.

Eying him suspiciously, Lizzie slowed. "What are you doing, Sam?"

"You have to get past me." He waggled his fingers at her. "Let's see what you got."

She scoffed at him. "No way. I'm not playing that with you."

"Really?" He cut her off when she tried to go left and clucked like a chicken.

Laughter came from the kids and then Chloe yelled, "Show him, Elizabeth."

"Yeah, show me, Elizabeth." He gave her his cockiest grin. "Bet you can't get past me."

She rolled her eyes. "Really, Sam, I have nothing to prove."

"Do it!" Anton called. "Then you get a T-shirt too."

"Is that true, Sam?" Her eyes sparkled at him. "Do I get a T-shirt?"

The idea of Lizzie's round parts in a tiny T-shirt filled his mind.

She shot past him and very nearly succeeded.

Damn she was fast, but not fast enough, and Sam grabbed her from behind and lifted her off her feet.

Lizzie shrieked and laughed.

Her hair smelled like flowers. Her ass fit neatly against him. Lust rolled through him and he tightened his hold. Fuck! This was Lizzie in his arms.

Lizzie!

And he wanted to press her closer and run his hands over the soft parts rubbing against him.

"Sam?" She went still against him. "What are you doing?"

An excellent question and Sam forced his arms away from her. His voice came out in a croak. "Got ya!"

CHAPTER
FIFTEEN

ELIZABETH CALLED AHEAD to Dino's to warn them about the crowd on its way. According to Sam, everyone qualified for pizza after practice. As parents trickled in to pick up kids, the party swelled.

People forgot prior engagements and commitments in favor of pizza with Sam Stone. Dino's was close to her house, so she dropped her car off at home and walked back.

A cold, crisp night surrounded them as she, Sam and Maddy walked back to Dino's.

"That went well," Maddy said to Sam. "And I got some great photos." She held her phone up to Sam. "The ones with the kids in them are getting a lot of hits, but this one is doing the best."

Sam peered at Maddy's phone and laughed. He turned to her with a twinkle that had her bracing for trouble and handed her the phone. "What do you think, Lizzie?"

In the photo Sam had both arms around her, his body cradling hers, and his head was tucked in besides hers. It looked intimate, sexy, like a couple. Heat spread over her cheeks and she gave the phone back to Maddy. "That looks like more than just friends."

"Yeah." Maddy giggled. "But the fans are eating it up." She

frowned at her phone. "Most of them are anyway. Some of the female fans are feeling a bit jealous."

Elizabeth needed to know what they were saying, and she reached for Maddy's phone. "Let me see that."

"Nah." Sam intercepted her hand and twined his fingers with hers. "Some of that crap is toxic and there's no point in reading it. It will only upset you."

"Sam's right." Maddy put her phone away.

When they arrived at Dino's, the place was packed. Some of the faces she didn't know. It seemed as if word had gotten around that Sam was coming for pizza. Looking frazzled but delighted, Renee, the owner bustled up to them. "I'm glad you called ahead," she said to Liz. "I managed to get a couple more staff in."

Chris surveyed the crowd with a look of dismay. "This was supposed to be pizza as a reward for the team."

"Yeah." Sam's expression darkened. "Would it help if I said I was sorry about this too?"

"No." Chris shook her head. "Because this isn't your fault. It's the downside to what you do."

Maddy gave Chris a sweet smile, and Chris blushed but smiled back.

At least that was moving in the right direction.

Elizabeth followed Sam into the restaurant. Not that she had much choice with him still holding her hand. Maddy's picture bothered her. The way she and Sam looked so wrapped up in each other floored her. Even more worrying—as clearly revealed by that picture—was that she had reacted to Sam's embrace.

Even thinking about it now brought more heat flushing through her body.

Sam was big and strong and hard, and all that plastered against her had made her girl parts sit up and pay attention.

To Sam!

Dear God, this couldn't be happening. She couldn't be attracted to Sam. Except, there had been that time years ago when they had crashed into a lip lock. She'd always dismissed it as teen hormones, and easy proximity. Since neither of them had shown any enthusiasm for a repeat, her theory had never been challenged.

Sam tugged her into a booth.

Maddy piled in behind her and then came Chris. A couple of the kids joined them and pressed her thigh to thigh, shoulder to shoulder with Sam.

"Lizzie," Sam whispered in her ear, his breath warm on her neck. "Are you climbing on my lap?"

Her face combusted. "No!" It burst out of her so loud several gazes snapped in their direction. She lowered her voice. "It's crowded in here and people are pushing me against you."

"Did I say that I minded?" His laughing blue eyes met hers and stuck. In any other man she would say he was flirting with her, testing the waters to see if she would bite, but this was Sam.

She swallowed to ease her dry throat. "Okay."

For the duration of pizza, she kept her attention on Maddy and Chris. They sat close together, heads bent toward each other and spoke quietly.

Sam nudged her. "How about that?"

"I know." She hoped this worked out for Chris. She'd been lonely for too long, and Maddy looked as if she wanted to be the one to end that loneliness. "You didn't know Maddy was gay?"

"Nope." Sam handed her a piece of pizza and grabbed one for himself. "It's not the sort of thing that ever came up." He bit into his slice. "I assumed, because she liked to party with the team, she liked men."

"Huh." Elizabeth had made much the same assumption.

"Sam!" Anton demanded his attention from across the table. "Who is the best hockey player ever?"

"That's easy." Chloe thumped his arm. "Gretzky."

"Sure. He was okay." Sam leaned forward. "But what about Sam Stone?"

The kids all laughed.

"He sucks!" someone said, and they all cheered.

Sam laughed along with them.

For the rest of the evening he chatted with the kids, sometimes their parents, but mostly the kids. Sam was good with people. He put them at their ease and did a lot more listening than speaking.

Elizabeth didn't have the heart to tell Maddy to take pictures, not when Maddy and Chris were almost nose-to-nose.

When Renee brought the bill at the end of the evening, Elizabeth intercepted it. Sam had promised the team pizza, not the entire town. Only when she was satisfied, did she hand it to Sam.

He chuckled at her and gave Renee his card. "It's just pizza, and we got a discount."

"It doesn't matter." Fair was fair in her book. "You didn't offer to take them, and they all came along anyway."

"So fierce." But his smile softened his words.

That smile wriggled under her guard and she stood to hide her reaction. Sam would die laughing if he caught a hint of what was going on in her head. It must be a full moon.

She looked at Maddy. "I'll drive you back to the hotel if you're ready."

"Um…that's okay." Maddy glanced at Chris.

Chris looked everywhere but at Elizabeth. "I can drive her. I mean, I've got to go home anyway and it's not out of my way."

With her no-nonsense exterior, most people had no idea how painfully shy Chris was. Elizabeth chose not to mention that Chris lived in the opposite direction. "That's great."

Sam dropped into place beside her as she left the restaurant.

A family called goodbye to Sam and he waved.

The night had turned colder, and Elizabeth shoved her hands into her coat pockets. Spring might be around the corner, but for now, the Ottawa winter still reigned supreme.

Their boots crunched on the salted ice as they trudged down the road to her condo.

Sam cleared his throat. "That went well, I thought."

"Yes." Elizabeth didn't get this sudden awkwardness between them. Even when they insulted and attacked each other they were comfortable together. Now she was super aware of where her body parts were in relation to his. Like if she moved an inch to the right, her shoulder would brush his. Or if she took her left hand out of her pocket, it would be close enough to his right hand to hold.

"That little blond girl, Chloe," Sam said. "She reminded me of you when we were kids."

She couldn't think why. "In what way?"

"You were fierce like that on the ice." He chuckled. "None of us wanted to get in your way or play defense against you."

"This from you?" She scoffed. "You never met a board you didn't want to slam someone into."

"Ha." He nudged her shoulder with his. "I was not the one who cracked someone over the head with their stick."

"True." She had to wear that one. "It bugged me that I couldn't catch you on skates. Boy, was my dad pissed about that."

Lights blinked on in the houses as they walked. The calm still of a cold winter's night surrounded them, broken only by the sound of their footsteps.

Sam looked at her. "Is that why you hate me?"

"What?" Elizabeth nearly missed her footing.

He caught her elbow and righted her. "Is it because your dad is the way he is with me that you hate me?"

"You mean how he likes you better?" His face made her laugh. "Or how he wishes you were his son?"

"Never mind." He hunched his shoulders and jammed his hands in his pockets. "I always wondered why you hated me so much."

"You hated me as much." Elizabeth wasn't sure she had an answer for him. "You were always trying to make me angry or breaking my stuff."

"That's because you ignored me," he said. "I would try to get your attention, but you would stick your nose in the air and go and do something else."

"I did not."

"Did too." He grinned. "I wanted you to pay attention to me."

"I think Dad did enough of that for our entire family." The burn did still linger. "And maybe I was jealous of that. I always had to try so hard to get him to notice me, and you only had to walk in the room."

"I didn't ask for it." His breath misted in the air. Faint ambient light outlined his stark profile. "I don't think I encouraged it either."

"No, you didn't." To be fair, it had always made Sam a bit uncomfortable. "And I didn't hate you. I don't hate you now either."

He scoffed. "Really?"

"Okay, maybe I hate you now a little bit." She bumped his shoulder, harder than he'd bumped hers. "It pisses me off that you got rich and famous. It pisses me off even more that I don't have a gift like you do."

"It's a curse." He managed to say it without cracking up and then ruined it with a chuckle. "I'm one of a lucky few who gets to make money doing what they love to do."

"Yeah." She'd never found that thing she wanted to do.

"What about you?" He glanced at her. "Didn't you want to be a veterinarian?"

"When I was eight." She laughed. "And only until I realized how much math and science I would have to do to be one. Not to mention my aversion to blood." The silence between them was more comfortable now. "No, but I would like to work for a charity. I like feeling like I'm making a difference, and organizing is my superpower."

"More like nagging." Sam sniffed. "Why don't you do that

then? Instead of working for your dad, because I know that you—"

"Don't start that again." She couldn't have that conversation with him because she didn't have the answers. "I'm only starting to hate you a bit less."

"Good to know." They reached her complex.

She motioned her car in its spot. "Randy hasn't parked in my place since you spoke to him."

"Good."

Elizabeth knew she should go in. It was cold anyway. "I should go." She jerked her thumb at her door. "You did good tonight, Sam. You turned it around."

"I think it was the T-shirts." He shoved his hands into his pockets.

Their breath ghosted between them. "The T-shirts and the pizza helped," she said. "But mainly it was you. And I don't want this to go to your head, but you might even have improved their skating."

He shook his head and laughed. "It's cold tonight."

"It is."

Dropping his head back, he stared at the moon. "You know, during the season I'm often too busy to do things like this. Just take a walk on a beautiful night with a…friend."

"Don't get ahead of yourself, Sam." She poked him. "And you'll be back to being busy and famous soon."

"I sure hope you're right." He caught her finger and held it. "For the record, I never hated you."

"Bull." She regained her finger before she decided to leave it in his grasp for the rest of the night.

"It's true." He spread his arms and shrugged. "You can ask my mother if you don't believe me. I used to bug you because I had a crush on you and wanted you to notice me."

"No, you didn't." He had to be teasing her with his crap. "You're just saying that."

"Ask my mom." He raised his brow. "Anyway, what's next on our agenda?"

It gave her a particularly evil pleasure to say, "The high school dunk tank."

Sam grimaced. "Oh, joy!"

CHAPTER
SIXTEEN

ELIZABETH PARKED outside Danica's house and braced to go in there and haul Sam out of bed.

Tapping on her window jerked her memory away from the last time she'd hauled Sam out of bed. Clutching two travel mugs and a kit bag, Sam peered in through the window.

Elizabeth unlocked the doors and he slid in. "Hey."

"Hi." Her voice came out not sounding like hers at all.

Sam gave her a what-the-hell look, handed her one of the mugs and tossed the kit bag into the back seat. "Caramel creamer, no sugar."

"Yes. Thank you." The sweet way he remembered stuff about her really wasn't helping. Nor the way he always quietly carried bags and other stuff for her, opened doors, hovered about her on icy ground. These were the things nice guys did. The sort of nice guy she'd like to date.

"It's a cold one today." Sam rubbed his hands in front of the heater vent.

And did he have to smell so freaking good? "Ready to get naked?"

"Don't I get dinner first?" Up went one of his eyebrows.

Her face burned all kinds of hot, and she pulled away from

the curb rather than face him. Sam and naked were not paired concepts that should exist in her mind. Ever!

She hated him for every mud pie she'd made and he'd thrown at her. For every time he'd teased her when she was a painfully shy teen. For the way he insisted on calling her anything but Elizabeth.

"Lizzie?" He cocked his head and studied her.

There, see! She hated being called Lizzie. "What?"

"Your face looks weird."

He may be hot, but Sam came with his own libido extinguisher. "You say the sweetest things."

"What did I do now?" He crossed his arms and stared at her as she drove. "You've got that look you get when you're about to rip me a new one."

"I don't."

"Do too."

He could keep this up for hours. "Anyway, the dunk tank. It's to raise money for a local feeding scheme the high school supports."

"Cool." He sipped his coffee. "But I'd still like to know what I did wrong. You hate creamer now or something?"

She was being a brat, and she had to laugh at that. "No, I still love creamer. My jeans, not so much, but my taste buds adore it."

"Lizzie." He leaned back and studied her from top to toe. "Your jeans look fine from where I'm sitting."

Elizabeth didn't dare take her eyes off the road. She didn't need to see that look to feel the way it slid down her body. Dear God, she couldn't do this. "Are you flirting with me, Sam?"

"Why yes, lovely Lizzie." He chuckled. "I am most definitely flirting with you."

She braked too hard for the stop sign, and both of them jerked forward. "You see." She faced him. "That's what's wrong. The flirting." She ran out of words and fluttered her hand between them. "This new us. I don't get it. It's like the rules have changed, and I'm over here trying to play the old game."

The car behind her honked and she got underway again.

"You want us to fight all the time again?" Sam kept watching her. "Because I'm not sure I can do that. I like the way things are now."

She also liked the way things were now and didn't know if she wanted to go back to the bickering and bitching either.

"I like the way you laugh at my jokes," Sam said and sipped his coffee. "I like how despite the way we fight that you get me. And I get you. We don't have to explain ourselves to each other." He chuckled. "And I like how you know the worst of me, and I don't have to pretend to be someone else around you."

Put like that it made so much sense and was even more confusing at the same time. "Me too," she said. "I do like all of those things, but it still confuses me."

"You're confused?" Sam shook his head. "Lizzie, you're going to hate this, but I have to tell you that I most definitely am flirting with you. If you had any idea of the thoughts I've been having, you would toss me out of your car right now."

Shock kept her eyes glued to the road. Sam was having thoughts about her, and she was having thoughts about Sam. Thoughts that could lead to dark, wet, delicious places together. "Me too," she whispered.

"Say what?" Sam leaned closer to her. His attention entirely focused on her. "Say that again."

Elizabeth thanked God she had the road providing a legitimate excuse for why she couldn't look at him. "I've also been having...thoughts."

Sam groaned and leaned back in his seat. "Damn, Elizabeth, you can't say stuff like that to me."

"I just did." She felt so much better now the air was cleared. Still confused, and uncertain of how to go forward but also clear she wasn't the only fool.

They drove in silence for a while, both of them locked in their own thoughts. Not those kinds of thoughts. Okay, not only those kinds of thoughts.

The high school appeared in front of them.

Sam cupped her nape and startled her. His long fingers speared her hair and the warmth of his palm made her want to purr. Sam's touch had never done this to her before. Then again, she'd spent years making sure he never got near enough to touch.

Had her subconscious always known more than she did?

"I have an idea for how we play this," Sam said. "We're both stumbling around in the dark here, but there's no reason to rush into anything." He stroked her neck to beneath her earlobe. "Thoughts are not actions. Why don't we both chill and see where, and if, whatever this is goes anywhere?"

"Gah." Elizabeth cleared her throat. The neck stroking made her want to arch like a cat. "Good idea."

"You think?"

She nodded. "I definitely think."

They parked and headed inside to find the dunk tank. Chris was meeting them there.

"Hey, Sam!" A middle-aged man called. "You did pro hockey a favor by taking out that wuss."

Sam waved and kept on walking.

A woman sidestepped them and sent Sam a vicious glare, clearly a Karlov fan or someone who only listened to Marc Gracie.

"How do you get used to it?" Elizabeth gestured the watching gazes following them. "The fame and the having everyone up and in your business."

He shrugged. "There are good and bad points to it. Luckily I play hockey, and for the most part, we stay grounded. There isn't a lot of time for the kind of crap young kids get into when someone suddenly throws a lot of money at them."

"And the criticism doesn't get to you?" Elizabeth really looked at how many people saw Sam and recognized him.

"Sure it gets to me." Sam put his hand in the small of her back and guided her past a knot of staring teen boys. He gave them a nod. "As much as you develop a thick skin, there are still those things that sting. Most of those come out of Marc Gracie's mouth."

"He really doesn't like you." Elizabeth appreciated the hand he left in the small of her back.

"It's worse because he's right." Sam pulled a face. "I screwed up badly. He's not saying anything I don't already know."

"So, if you know all this, why did you continue to make all those hard hits?"

Sam winked at her. "Now that is the question of the hour. And we'll have to figure it out before I get back on the ice."

The we sounded really good to her, and she couldn't even summon any concern about that.

Chris waved to them from her position beside the dunk tank. On her other side, Maddy looked stunning in her shaggy bomber jacket and jeans.

A hand painted sign read, "Take your shot at sinking Sam Stone. $1 a ball."

"I like to think I'm worth more than a dollar a ball." Sam grimaced.

"You're here." Chris grinned at Sam. "I thought, for sure, you'd renege on us."

"Balls to the wall." Sam draped his arm around Chris. "That's me."

"It would be a lot easier to like you if you didn't talk about your balls," Chris said.

"Hey, Sam." Maddy went up on her toes and kissed his cheek. "This is great that you're doing this." She waved her phone. "And I'm ready to capture the moment."

A kid wearing a Boston sweatshirt and a snarl slouched over. He gave Sam a scowl of teen derision. "Is this thing, like, starting soon?"

"Right now." Sam smiled back. "Think you can dunk me?"

The kid scoffed. "Sure I can."

"Hope your aim is better than Tremblay's." He named the Boston center. "Because he can't hit the side of a barn."

"Oh, dude!" The kid gave Sam an evil smile. "It's on now."

"Wish me luck, Busy Lizzie." Sam tapped his cheek.

Lizzie's face heated, but she rose on her toes and kissed Sam's smooth-shaven cheek. He didn't use aftershave and smelled of soap, toothpaste and musky man scent. "Don't freeze."

He turned to Maddy and tapped the other side. "And you, Maddy."

Chris crossed her arms and glared at him. "Don't even think about it."

With a laugh, Sam stripped his sweater and his jeans. He stood there in a swimsuit and a white T-shirt, pumping his arms to warm himself.

"Right." He climbed the ladder to the dunk seat. "Hey, Boston!"

The kid looked up.

"Let's see what you got."

"Oh dear." Maddy bit her lip. "He's going to trash talk the room."

"And you know this how?" Chris tried to sound stern but the calf-love beaming from her eyes deflated the effort.

Maddy twinkled back. "I've watched more hours of that man play than I care to admit." She snuggled closer to Chris. "And he's good at pissing other players off."

Boston kid bought his first three balls and fired them at Sam.

The first two missed, which only seemed to embolden Sam to keep taunting the boy. "I'm over here, Boston."

The third ball sailed past his head and hit the backboard.

"Great shot." Sam faked a yawn. "Almost as scary as Tremblay's slap shot."

A crowd gathered around the dunk tank and the line for taking a shot at Sam grew longer and longer.

Another contender stepped up to dunk Sam.

"What's your favorite team?" Sam called.

The man told him, and Sam got his trash talk on.

Four shooters and Sam still sat high and dry and cracking jokes.

Mostly people laughed. All of the original four bought more balls and joined the back of the line. Some shouted a question to Sam, which he answered with a lightning quick comeback.

Maddy sidled closer to Elizabeth. "He's making a lot of money."

Glancing at the growing crowd, Elizabeth had to agree.

The crowd egged on the shooters, yelling encouragement and groaning as ball after ball missed.

Sam kept the trash talk flowing, and he kept it clean.

Eight shooters, and Sam still hadn't taken a bath.

A tall, well-built man stepped up to the plate.

"Uh-oh." Maddy laughed. "Sam is going down."

"You!" Sam pointed at the new shooter. "You're disqualified. Lizzie!" He glanced her way. "Make him pay double."

"Who is he?" Elizabeth whispered to Maddy.

Chris turned and gaped at her. "That's Guy Pelletier."

"Goalie for the Titans," Maddy whispered.

Guy had all three balls in one hand. He tossed one from one hand to the other and grinned at Sam. "Hey, Stoner!"

"Don't do it." Sam tried to sound serious, but he was laughing. He raised his voice. "Who thinks professional athletes should pay a hundred dollars a ball?"

An affirmative chorus swelled around them.

Guy smiled and it made his grave, almost stern, face surprisingly handsome. "Make it two hundred a ball. It's worth it."

The crowd cheered, and Sam laughed.

Sam wiggled his fingers. "Come on then, Trapper! Let's see if you can fire as well as you block."

Bouncing one ball on his huge palm, Guy focused on Sam. He aimed, drew back and fired the ball.

The target pinged and bobbed. The trap opened and Sam hit the water with a huge splash.

The crowd roared its approval.

Sam swam to the surface of the tank and hauled himself out. His T-shirt clung to every line of his torso. Every. Single. One.

Elizabeth's mouth went sandpaper dry. Holy crap that was a thing of beauty.

"Shut your mouth. You're drooling," Chris hissed in her ear.

She refused to apologize. That body deserved to be ogled. "Damn!"

"She's a goner." Chris nudged Maddy.

Maddy gave Sam a look and a lascivious grin spread over her pretty face. "Come on, Chris. You'd have to be dead from the knees up not to get a charge out of that." Putting two fingers in her mouth, Maddy wolf whistled.

The crowd laughed and several people joined in.

Climbing back onto his seat, Sam blushed and laughed.

Guy held up his hand with the remaining balls in it. "I still have two shots."

The hall erupted in cheering and Sam went swimming twice more.

CHAPTER
SEVENTEEN

SAM STAYED in the dunk tank until his fingers had pruned and it would take a bottle of scotch to warm him up again. He ducked into the nearest bathroom to get changed.

Someone from the school had called Lizzie away. She would warm him up fast enough. The look in her eye when he'd been dunked and gotten wet had been worth the entire thing. It had almost gotten embarrassing as well. Only the presence of a crap ton of gawkers had kept his reaction under control.

"Stoner!" Guy strolled into the bathroom, handed him a towel and a punch to the shoulder. "This is a nice thing you're doing here."

Sam scrubbed his cold skin with the towel. "You think?"

"Yeah, I think." Guy was one of the largest reasons for the Titans success. Large in both stature and ability, calm and easy going, he provided the chill energy in the dressing room the team often needed. "How you doing, anyway?"

Sam shrugged. They went way back, him and Guy, and there was no bullshitting each other. "This whole suspension and banishment from the team sucks."

"Yeah." Guy nodded. In one word he conveyed the depth of his understanding. When your life had revolved around hockey for so long, it was difficult to think of a time when you wouldn't play. "But you're doing all the right things."

"I hope so." Sam stripped his T-shirt and found a dry one in his bag. He leaned against the sinks and looked at Guy. "I don't know who I am if I don't play hockey."

Guy gave that some serious thought. This is part of why he was so well loved on the team. The man was a thinker and more often found with his head in a book. "Sooner or later that happens to all of us."

"I know." In his thirties, Guy was closer to that point than most. "What will you do?"

"I have this land." Guy smiled. "I want to build my own house on it. Sit on the porch I've built and give that very question some serious thought."

Sam laughed. He could see Guy doing that. "No lady by your side?"

"Hard to find the right one." Guy shrugged.

Sam sensed a whole bunch of stuff that Guy didn't say, but the man was private about his personal life and Sam respected that. "I've been working with these kids. They totally suck at hockey, but they still love it."

"I've seen the pictures on Instagram," Guy said.

"I was a complete prick to them at first." He didn't like thinking about that part. "But once I got over myself, I liked working with them. There's something magical about watching them get it, seeing the way every small victory counts for them."

Guy raised an eyebrow. "Why not work with kids with talent?"

"Because there are enough people to do that." Sam shimmied out of his wet swimsuit and found a pair of boxers in his bag. He pulled them on and felt better for having gotten rid of the wet suit. "Nobody gives a shit about these kids. This is Canada." He shrugged. "Hockey is like a religion and if you're good at it, there are hundreds of people ready and willing to show you the way. But these kids, nobody gives a crap, which is sad because they fucking love the game."

Chuckling, Guy shook his head. "This is a side of you that I'd almost given up on."

"Probably because it didn't exist before." Sam dried his legs and hauled on his jeans.

Guy grunted. "Nah, Stoner. This side of you always existed. When you were a kid you were always the one helping out the weaker players."

The praise made him uncomfortable and he buried his head in a towel. "What are you doing here anyway?"

"Stoner." Guy's bass rumble filled the room. "Why the hell would I miss the chance to dunk your arrogant ass?"

"You playing Montreal tonight?"

"You know it." Guy cracked his knuckles. "I got a yen for a shutout."

Sam laughed. "Do it."

"I gotta get moving." Guy checked his watch. "I wanted to come down here and see you. Let you know you're not forgotten."

That meant more to Sam than he could say. He held out his hand. "Appreciate it."

Guy grabbed him and hauled him into a rough hug. "Look forward to welcoming you back, Stoner."

———

After his shift ended in the dunk tank, Elizabeth lost sight of Sam.

The big Titans goalie approached her with a warm smile. "Lizzie?"

"Elizabeth." The correction came automatically.

Guy chuckled. "Well, Sam told me your name so he can eat the complaint."

"He's always called me that." Elizabeth responded to his

smile. Guy had the sort of smile that teased you to come along and join in the joke.

"Well, he calls me Trapper." Guy shrugged. "At some point I gave up on getting him to call me anything different."

"Same." Beside Elizabeth, Chris squirmed and whimpered.

Chris gazed at Guy with the sort of unmitigated fervor reserved for tweens and boy bands.

"Um...Guy." She motioned Chris. "This is my best friend, Chris. She's a huge hockey fan."

"Chris." Guy held out a huge paw. "You coach the kids' team Sam got involved with?"

"Ergh!" Chris flushed cerise.

"She...er...has coached them for a couple of years now." If Chris didn't get it together, she was going to miss the chance to meet her hero. "They're the kids who were turned away from any other team."

Guy gave Chris that knee trembling smile, and Elizabeth felt the warm weight of it from beside Chris.

Chris squeaked out an affirmative noise.

"Guy!" Maddy tripped over on her high-heeled boots with her arms held wide.

Guy swept her into a hug and lifted her right off the ground. "Maddy, baby! Looking fine as always."

"Big flirt." Maddy kissed his cheek. "I see you met my girl, Chris."

Chris gaped at her. "Your girl?"

"Aren't you?" Maddy cocked her head, a small smile on her face.

Openly grinning, Chris laughed. "Well, sure I am."

"Tell me more about your team," Guy said. "I like what I'm hearing."

Elizabeth kept an eye out for Sam. He must have gone to get dry. A flash of black drew her eye as Jane slipped into the men's bathroom.

"Guy?" *Please let me be wrong about this.* "Sorry to interrupt, but is Sam in the men's?"

"Yeah." Guy pointed at the door Jane had disappeared through.

"Excuse me." Elizabeth flew into action. As she swung the door open, Elizabeth heard Sam say, "Jane, you need to step back, sweetie."

Jane had Sam backed into the counter, her arms on either side of his hips. "Come on, Sam. I know all about you players."

A man pushed through the doors, looked at Sam and Jane, then at Elizabeth and backed out again.

"Elizabeth." Sam paled and slid away from Jane. "I didn't—"

"I know that." There were times when she wanted to strangle Jane. An attitude readjustment was way past due. She glared at her sister. "You are coming with me."

"Jesus, Elizabeth." Jane rolled her eyes. "You don't own him."

Elizabeth slid past annoyed into pissed off. "Get in the car. Now."

"Or what?" Jane stuck her hip out, but doubt flickered in her eyes.

"Now!" Elizabeth stalked her. "Or I am going to make you so sorry you didn't."

Jane looked sulky, but she moved for the exit. "You can't do anything to me."

"Try me." Elizabeth herded her into the hall.

Surrounded by people, Jane made a bid for freedom. "You're not Mom. You can't do anything to me."

"I can take away your allowance." Elizabeth stepped into her space. "I can get you grounded for the foreseeable future." She played her ace in the hole. "And I can tell Mom how out of control you are."

Going pale, Jane got moving again.

Elizabeth prepared to follow.

"Lizzie?" Sam grabbed her arm. "Okay?"

"Yeah." At least it would be once someone shortened Jane's leash. "I'll call you later."

"Thanks, Lizzie." His face softened. "I appreciate you not jumping to the wrong conclusion."

Given their past, she totally got that. She managed a small smile for him. "You're welcome. Can you ask Chris for a ride home?"

"Sure." Then he called after her, "Go easy on her, Slugger."

Elizabeth gave him a wave over her shoulder.

Still sulking, Jane waited by her car.

They drove home in a tense silence, which lasted until they reached Dad's kitchen.

Safe in her own space, Jane made her stand. "You can't tell me what to do, you know."

"Someone has to." The problem with Jane was that too many times their parents backed down. "What happened with Sam is totally unacceptable."

"He wanted it." Jane crossed her arms.

This much Elizabeth knew without doubt. "No, he didn't, and it's lucky for you Sam is who he is, or you might have bought a whole lot more trouble than you're prepared for."

"Oh, that's right." Jane sneered. "Go ahead and blame the victim."

Elizabeth couldn't believe what she was hearing. "How are you the victim in this?"

"You blamed me for what happened. Like I'd lured Sam." Jane entrenched herself deeper into her faulty logic.

Elizabeth wanted to slap that belligerent look off Jane's face. She used words instead. "You followed the man into the men's room. I'm guessing you waited for him to be alone in there before you did. You pinned him to the countertop, and now you're claiming to be the victim. Explain."

"Sam wants me." Jane tossed her head. "A woman always knows."

"A woman might." Elizabeth enunciated clearly, to make

sure her sister got the next bit. "But a spoiled little girl who thinks the world revolves around her wouldn't know any difference between what she wants and what the rest of the world wants."

"You're such a bitch," Jane yelled. "You want everything for yourself. All the time."

Dear God, that was a good one. "How do you work that one out?"

"What the hell is all the screeching about?" Dad stomped into the kitchen.

"Yes, Elizabeth," Jane sneered her name. "What are you screeching about?"

"Jane tried her charms out on Sam." Elizabeth was through protecting Jane from the consequences of her own behavior.

Dad looked confused. "What are you talking about?"

Taking a deep breath, Elizabeth caught Dad up. "Sam did a stint in the dunk tank at the high school fundraiser."

"Why?" Dad glared.

Not about to tell him about their deal, Elizabeth said, "I asked him to do it for charity, and he was happy to."

"Have you lost your tiny brain?" Dad's eyes bulged. "You asked Sam to get dunked in your ridiculous high school fundraiser?"

Jane smirked at her from behind Dad's shoulder.

"Yes, I did." Elizabeth held her ground and her father's hard stare. "And he did it without flinching. Then, Jane followed him into the bathroom as he was changing and went all teen temptress on him."

Dad swung his incredulous look at Jane. "You went into the men's room."

Jane didn't look nearly so smug now. "Only Sam was in there."

"Only Sam?" Dad sputtered. "Only Sam! The greatest hockey player of my time?"

That might be overstating it, but Elizabeth knew better than to try to stop the avalanche of Dad's hero worship. "When I got there, he was doing his best to get away from her."

"You're both idiots." Dad threw his hands up. "What the hell were you doing bothering Sam? Because you knew him as children doesn't give you a right to hang all over him and get on his last nerve."

If she hadn't heard it so many times already, it might have smarted a bit more.

Having it directed her way for the first time, Jane's eyes filled with tears. "Daddy," she whispered. "Sam is special to me too."

Dad sighed. "Janey."

And Elizabeth wanted to puke. She let herself out the back door.

"Elizabeth!" Dad yelled out the back door. "What's for dinner?"

She didn't even bother to turn around. "Whatever darling Janey or you can make."

Slamming her car door made her feel marginally better. She really needed a new shtick. This people pleasing good girl gig was clearly not working out for her.

As she parked, in her spot, thanks to Sam, her phone buzzed with a message from Peter.

She hadn't texted him since the Friday Chris and Maddy had met, and she read his text.

Hey there! Long time no speak. Smiley face emoji. *Fancy dinner sometime next week?*

She had turned him down last time.

After a few moments of the three dots, Peter's next text arrived. *I miss my friend.* Sad face emoji.

On the cusp of texting back a no, she let her people pleaser butt into the conversation. She and Peter had been together for over a year, and they had sworn to stay friends.

Sure. When? she replied.

They made a date to meet and Elizabeth got out of her car.

Randy popped his head around Bonnie's door, saw her, and his face dropped. "Sam not with you?"

"Not today." Elizabeth managed a tight smile. And Sam wasn't with her in that sense. Which brought up their conversation driving to the high school. Her heart beat faster. Sam had more than hinted at something else between them.

And that thought left her with equal parts terror and excitement.

CHAPTER
EIGHTEEN

ELIZABETH PUT Chris's sudden desire to go shopping down to the new woman in her life. As she could count on one hand the number of times Chris had allowed her to update her wardrobe, Elizabeth had no trouble picking Chris up after work and taking her to the mall.

Dad had been particularly toxic at work all day, and she was glad to get the hell out of the office. His mood could be because she'd had trouble concentrating all day. Sam had taken to texting her funny messages and jokes.

Instead of being adult about it, she'd spent the day checking each notification on her phone.

Chris was waiting on the porch when she pulled up.

"Hey." Chris slid into the passenger side. "How was work?"

"Crap!"

With a sigh Chris shook her head. "Your day was shit because you hate your job and your dad is a prick."

She opened her mouth to defend both statements, and then snapped it shut. She did hate her job, and her father had definite prickish tendencies. Imagine what he'd say if she slept with Sam.

Heat prickled beneath her skin.

"Hello?" Christ stared at her. "What's with you?"

Her cheeks heated. "Nothing."

"I call bullshit." Chris folded her arms. "And I think I know what has you looking all hot and bothered."

"Really?" She gave Chris a skeptical look. At her job, Chris was a veritable super sleuth, but personal stuff…not so much.

"Uh huh." Chris looked smug. "Maddy thinks you and Sam have got a thing for each other."

Elizabeth snorted to cover her embarrassment and then tried to flip the conversation. "Is that what Maddy said? Why don't you tell me what else Maddy said?" She snapped her fingers. "Or why don't you tell me what's going on with Maddy?"

"Maddy likes me." Chris smirked at her. "Like Sam likes you. Sam and Elizabeth sitting in a tree—"

"Stop." Elizabeth had to yell over her and ended up laughing. "Shut up about Sam or I'll let you buy a pair of jeans that make your ass look fat."

At the mall, she parked near a department store entrance. A spring freeze had locked the air outside into a bitchy cold that only got worse when the wind blew. She and Chris rushed across the parking lot. Inside, a blast of hot air hit them and they both sighed with relief.

"Oh, Canada!" Chris stomped snow and ice off her boots. "Where nobody comes for the weather."

Elizabeth pulled her tuque off. "And if they do, they don't stay long."

They walked through the men's section as they headed for the women's.

"Hey." Chris stopped so suddenly Elizabeth collided with the back of her. "Ow!"

"You suddenly stopped."

"Look there." Chris pointed to a poster of a half-naked man.

The man in the underwear ad looked vaguely familiar. "Nice, but out of my league, don't you think?"

Chris rolled her eyes. "Definitely out of your league as he's a professional football player."

"Really?" Elizabeth peered closer at the man with dark hair and an amazing set of abs. Those sexy lines disappeared into bright pink boxer shorts. "Those are very pink."

"Get your eyes further north." Chris shook her head. "He's not selling underpants. It's a charity thing. Basically they're getting famous athletes and movie stars to wear these bright pink undies for breast cancer awareness." She pointed to the stacks of pink undies for sale. "For every pair sold, they send seventy percent of the purchase price to breast cancer awareness." Chris grinned at her expectantly. "Normal men participate too if they want. They buy these and then take a selfie and post it using the hashtag."

"That's a good idea." Elizabeth took a closer look at hot stuff on the poster.

"And?" Chris gave her an expectant stare.

"Oh." Those abs had slowed her brain down. "You think I should ask Sam to wear these pink undies?"

Chris nodded. "I totally think you should."

The idea of Sam in those made her go hot and cold and then really, really hot. She'd seen enough of Sam's body to know he would rock them. Women everywhere would be going hot, cold and then boiling. "I'm not sure." She might look like a total perv asking him to do it. "Isn't this a bit like objectifying men?"

"It's for charity." Chris got a stubborn look on her face. "And you also promised to help Sam clean up his image. A high-profile effort like this will do as much as coaching thirty kids' hockey teams."

"I'm not sure what size he is." Shopping for Sam's boxers might be crossing an intimacy line.

Chris rolled her eyes. "Well, don't ask me. The last penis I caught sight of was on Game of Thrones and that was enough to stop me from watching it."

Her phone pinged with a message from Sam, *Want to come by later?* He added a sad emoji face. *I'm bored and lonely.*

So you thought of me? Elizabeth couldn't stop the smile as she sent her reply. *How flattering.*

Come over and I'll make it up to you.

It was fate. Sam had texted as she was weighing up buying the pink boxers.

Chris snorted loud enough to drag her attention away from the phone. "Tell me again how there's nothing going on between you and Sam."

Elizabeth's face flamed hotter. "Shuddup."

———

Sam opened the door to Elizabeth looking cold and flushed and fucking adorable. He'd been delighted when she had agreed to come by and had rushed around making dinner for her.

With his schedule during the season, it made more sense to learn to cook for himself.

She brushed past him and shrugged out of her coat. "Damn. It's cold out there."

As he hung her coat up, he whistled the opening bars to "Baby, It's Cold Outside."

"Oh, Sam." Eyes twinkling, she shook her head at him. "That is so unPC."

"Sue me." Damn she looked pretty with her face turned up to him and laughing. He wanted to grab her and kiss her. Drink deep of all the sweet and tart delights of Elizabeth. "You chicks need to get back in the kitchen where you belong."

"Or the bedroom," she said, and then she looked shocked and blushed. Ducking her head, she bustled past him. "Something smells good."

"My version of a beef and ale stew." He followed her into the kitchen, tempted to tease the reason for that reaction out of her. The idea of Elizabeth in his bedroom made him heat up as well.

Same with Elizabeth on the sofa. Over the sofa. Elizabeth on the counter.

He ducked behind the island to hide the evidence of his reaction. This growing thing with Elizabeth felt new and fragile, and he didn't want to screw it up by lunging at her. "Dinner won't be long."

"And in the meanwhile..." Blushing again, she held up a department store shopping bag. "I brought something for you."

He took it from her, glad that she'd thought of him. "You bought me a present?"

"No." She bit her lip. "I'm sorry I didn't mean to make you... it's more of a me thing."

Sam pulled out a pair of tight boxers. His erection returned. If she wanted to up the rate of progress, he was down for that. "You want to see me in these?"

"Yes! No!" She went even redder and threw her hands up. "What I mean is Chris and I want to see you in those."

Now he was confused. He held them up. "They're really pink."

"They're for breast cancer awareness," she said, rushing to get the words out. "You put them on and take a selfie. It gets loaded on a website with other pictures and helps to sell those." She pointed at the underpants. "You could do that instead of auctioning a piece of clothing."

Disappointment tasted like ashes in his mouth. That's what he got for getting ahead of himself. "I vaguely remember something about this. They sent an invitation to the team to get involved. But it was around about my suspension." He took a closer look at the undies to hide his reaction. At least his other problem was now taken care of. Then he checked the label and took another vicious check to the ego. "These are medium."

"Yes." Elizabeth blinked at him. "You're super fit. I would have bought you small but you're also tall."

"You nearly bought me small underpants?" Why didn't she

rip off his nuts and put them in a jar while she was at it? "I do not wear small or medium underwear."

She blinked at him. Comprehension dawned and she laughed. "Oh, come on, Sam. The size of the underpants refers to the width of your hips, not the size of your..." She waggled her fingers in the general direction of his crotch.

"Not entirely." He gave the medium underpants a look of disgust.

Elizabeth yukked it up. Even threw her head back and guffawed. She took one look at his disgusted face and tried to get control of her laughter. "Sam!" She rolled her eyes and chuckled a bit more. "Even if that were true, there's no link between the size of a flaccid penis and an erect one. You could have the biggest penis out there and it could still be tiny when it was relaxed."

Hearing her talk cocks made his flaccid penis want to take a new dynamic shape. "That's bullshit."

"It really isn't." Tilting her head, she put her hands on her hips. "The average flaccid penis is only a touch longer than three inches."

"Nope." If she thought that, he had a piece of land he wanted to sell her. Or a flaccid penis to show her. Too late. He no longer had a fully relaxed cock to show her.

There really was only way to win this stupid argument. Sam unbuckled his jeans and dropped them.

Elizabeth squeaked and turned her back. "What are you doing?"

Sam went commando when he could, and he wriggled into the pink pants of torture. To make sure she got a good eyeful, he tugged his sweatshirt off. He shuddered when he looked at himself. Nobody needed to see that. He looked like he was smuggling a koala in his pink pants. A koala with its head caught in a vice.

He stepped around the island and tapped her on the shoulder.

Elizabeth turned around. Her gaze dropped.

To be helpful, Sam spread his arms.

She clapped her arms over her mouth, went pyrotechnic red and turned away. "Oh my God. I can't believe you did that."

"You weren't listening." He went back behind the island and ripped off the pink constriction undies and pulled his jeans back on. "You can turn around."

Her blush had given way to more laugher and she had to cling to the island as her amusement swelled. "You're such an idiot," she gasped between laughter. "And would it kill you to manscape?"

"Stoney?" Guy called from the front door. He trotted down the hall and into the kitchen. Cocking his head, he raised an eyebrow at Sam's shirtless state. "Am I interrupting something?"

Elizabeth's receding blush flooded back.

"Naughty Lizzie wanted me to wear these." He dangled the pink pants from a forefinger.

Guy chuckled and looked at Lizzie. He tutted and shook his finger at her. "I really didn't have you pinned as a girl with a kink."

"I'm not." Elizabeth sputtered before she got the next words out. "I don't have a kink."

"It's fine." Guy grinned and spread his hands wide. "Nobody here is going to judge you."

"Hey." Sam made his smile as saccharine as he could manage. "I like a bit of kink."

"Oh, for God's sake." Lizzie snatched the boxers away from him and tried to stuff them back in the bag.

Guy snagged them. "What are these for anyway? That cancer awareness thing?"

"Yes." Lizzie beamed at Guy in a way that made Sam want to body slam him. "I thought Sam could take part."

"I'm happy to take part." Sam wanted her attention all on him. "Let me buy the boxers next time. A pair that fit."

"They don't fit," Elizabeth took them from Guy and stretched them. "They're too big."

"I like you, Elizabeth." Guy hooked an arm about her shoulders and dragged her against him. "Count me in for another photo, but I'll also buy my own boxers. Not all of us are...underachievers."

CHAPTER
NINETEEN

ELIZABETH CROUCHED behind her computer and tried to make herself small. Her dad was on a tear for the third time this week. They'd lost another cleaning account because they didn't have enough people.

As it was her job to hire the cleaning staff, his wrath headed straight her way. Pointing out that she couldn't hire good people when she could only offer them slave wages pushed him over the edge.

A couple of gazes slid her away, loaded with sympathy and the profound relief that they were not in the crosshairs.

A murmur of excitement arose from reception and Elizabeth looked up.

Sam sauntered into their office, unzipping his coat.

Vicky took his coat and hung it in the closet behind her reception desk. Eyes sparkling and cheeks flushed she chattered away to him.

Elizabeth sat up straighter. She had no idea what he was doing here, but so far, he was the best part of her day. Of course, he could have come to see Dad, but that didn't mean a girl couldn't hope.

Across the open plan office, Sam's searching gaze found her and he smiled.

As he sauntered toward her, Elizabeth preened a little. It was that high school fantasy about the hottest guy in the world asking you to prom in front of everyone who'd ever been bitchy to you.

Heads snapped around to follow his progress all the way to her desk. She played it nonchalant and pretended the thumping sound wasn't her heart.

"Hey." He leaned down and kissed her cheek.

Elizabeth took a surreptitious breath of him and her eyes nearly rolled back in her head. He smelled of soap and a light aftershave, and best of all the spicy musk that was all healthy male. She managed to choke out a mangled, "Hello."

"I hope you don't mind." Sam straightened and perched an ass cheek on her desk. "I was kind of hoping you hadn't had lunch yet."

"No." She managed nothing more than a breathy whisper. The next part might cost her a limb, but she didn't see any choice. "I don't think I have time today. My dad needs me to—"

"Sam, my boy." Dad boomed across the office.

Sam gave her a flat stare. "Does he have like a radar or something for whenever I'm around?"

"Wouldn't surprise me." And she was smiling. Even after being ripped into in front of the whole office all morning.

Standing, Sam put a smile of his face and extended his hand. "Hey, Paul."

The smile he gave her dad was the one he kept for fans and reporters. It wasn't anything like the warm smile he saved for her, the one that promised he knew a secret and wanted nothing more than to share it with her.

"Everybody!" Dad preened like a barnyard rooster. "I'm sure you all recognize Sam Stone. A close personal friend of the family."

A woman whispered from somewhere near the copier. "Doesn't he play football or something?"

"No." Another woman scoffed. "He's that Olympic swimmer."

"Does Canada have swimmers?"

"Of course they do. He's standing right there."

"Sam plays for the Ottawa Titans." Dad looked like he might explode. "A professional hockey team." He aimed a glare in the direction of the copier. "He's our very own town superstar."

"Don't watch hockey." The second copier commentator sniffed.

Several heads whipped in her direction.

"Of course you watch hockey." Dad's voice quivered with outrage. "You're Canadian."

Elizabeth dared not so much as a glance in Sam's direction. If she did, she would lose it.

"I just popped in, Paul." Sam's voice shook with something perilously close to laugher. "I hoped to take Elizabeth to lunch."

"Elizabeth?" Dad gaped at her. "Why would you do that?"

Sam's expression hardened and his voice grew clipped and firm. "Because I'd like to have lunch with her."

"Oh, of course." Dad stared at her and frowned, as if he really didn't get it at all. He breathed and his frown deepened. "This is about one of those stupid causes of yours, isn't it? You're taking advantage of his friendship to make him do all sorts of ridiculous things." He stepped closer to her. "I won't have it, Elizabeth. If Sam is too nice to tell you no, then I'll do it for him."

"Actually, Paul." Sam slid his shoulder in front of hers and put himself between her and her father. "Elizabeth didn't ask me to do any of it. I volunteered."

Dad scowled at her and huffed. "Well! What are you waiting for? Didn't you hear Sam?"

God give her patience. "I heard him, but you asked me to sort out our staffing crisis, and I don't think I have time for lunch."

"Sure you do." Sam grabbed hold of her chair and rolled it and her away from her desk. "Isn't that right, Paul?"

Dad looked slightly mollified and still not happy. "Yes."

"Come on then." Sam bundled her toward the door. "Let's get you fed. You know you're always better after a good feed. "

"You're very pushy," she whispered to him as, hand in the small of her back, he frog-marched her across the office.

He ducked his head and whispered back, his breath warm against her neck, "You really want to stay here?"

He had a point, so she grabbed her purse and coat from the closet.

As the office door shut and Elizabeth stepped into a crisp, sunny day, a weight lifted off her shoulders. "Did you need a show date for lunch?"

"Nope." Sam draped his arm over her shoulders. "I wanted to see you."

"Oh." That made her all sorts of flustered and she snapped her mouth shut.

He took her to an Italian restaurant near the office. Inside the dim interior, it smelled of bread, garlic and rich tomato sauce.

Elizabeth breathed deep. "I love Italian."

"I remembered." He looked smug. Then he broke it with a grin. "I'm not very good at this sort of thing, so it really was a miracle I did remember."

"Hmm." She slipped into a booth near the back of the restaurant. She wasn't so sure he wasn't good at the remembering and the small meaningful gestures. She suspected his tough guy might only be skin deep.

A pair of teen boys having lunch with an older woman who could be their mother, stared at Sam and whispered to each other.

Sam slid his arms over the back of the booth and nodded to the boys.

They gaped at him and then each other, looking like he'd handed them a free pass to heaven.

"So." Sam watched her with those incredibly blue eyes. "How's your day going?"

Elizabeth didn't want to talk about that, so she waved her hand. "Not great, but I'm sure yours is much more exciting. What have you been up to this morning?"

"Well, now. Let me see." He pretended to think about it. "I woke up. Had breakfast. Worked out and reminded myself how out of condition I am, and then came to see you."

"Sounds fascinating." She helped herself to the breadbasket the waiter had left.

Sam leaned forward and crossed his hands on the table. "Oh, it was. Want to hear about the eggs I made, or would that drive you over the edge?"

"I'm not sure I can stand the excitement." She clamped the niggle of disappointment. "You're bored. That's why you came to find me for lunch."

"I'm bored all right." Sam's eyes darkened into an unreadable expression that made her flushed and breathless. "But that's not why I'm taking you to lunch."

Elizabeth flushed and ducked her head. She didn't know how to handle this Sam. The one who she fought with all the time was so familiar and comfortable.

"You're not going to ask me, are you?" Sam chuckled and picked up his menu. He clucked softly under his breath before putting the menu aside. "Tell me about your crappy morning."

"How did you know I had a crappy morning?" She hadn't said a word.

"You do this thing." Sam imitated her hand motion. "Like your batting away nasty shit and then you turn the conversation to something else."

Did she do that? She didn't think so. "I don't."

"Yeah, you do." He leaned forward and tapped her menu. "Do you know what you want?"

"Yes." She always had the same thing here. "I'd like the carbonara."

"Then I'll have the same." He motioned the waiter over. "Wine?"

"No, thanks." A glass of wine would be great right now. "I have to get back to the office."

"Or, you could play hooky with me." Sam looked hopeful.

Before she could answer, the waiter arrived at their table. Sam gave their order and the waiter trotted off. Probably to tell all the others what Sam would be eating. At the very least to impress on the kitchen how important their next plate of carbonara was.

Not too long ago, that sort of thing had made her want to kick Sam, but it wasn't him. She knew that now. He wouldn't care what the restaurant put in front of him, as long as there was enough of it.

"Tell me what your dad did?" Sam lounged back, the long taut lines of his body making best friends with the fabric of his long-sleeve T-shirt.

She picked up another piece of bread. More to keep her hands busy than anything else. "He's angry about a lost contract." She told him about her run in with her dad.

Sam didn't bother with the obvious response. It wasn't fair and they both knew it, but that was her Dad and they both knew that too. "Why do you work for him? You don't even like the job."

"You know why." She hadn't even admitted this to Chris. "I'm that pathetic little girl who needs her daddy's affirmation. I want him to be proud of me."

"Yeah." Sam took her hands across the table. "And I'm the pathetic little boy who wants to escape his mommy's almost suffocating overprotectiveness, but instead of manning up and talking to her, he beats the crap out of everyone around him."

The waiter interrupted them with their food.

Elizabeth picked up her fork. "We're a sad pair."

"Yup." Sam dug into his meal like he would never have another one. "We should rebel."

"What did you have in mind?" That twinkle in his eye beat chocolate. Chocolate!

"We should run away to Vegas and have sex for a week."

Her fork dropped against her bowl with a clatter.

Sam winked at her and her face grew hotter and hotter. Although nothing close to the heat that seared her nerve endings and lit a fire in her core. Every female part of her yelled, *Yes, please! That! Let's do that!*

———

Lunch ended far too soon for Sam. He wanted to keep her with him for the remainder of the afternoon. Partly because her company pushed back the dull edge of panic around his career. Also, because he hated taking her back to Paul's shitty office.

Sam had only ever met his own dad once, a meeting Mom still knew nothing about, but even he could see that Paul was a shitty dad to his girls. He more or less ignored Jane and let her get away with whatever she wanted. Elizabeth, he treated like an unwelcome slave.

As they hit the street outside the restaurant, he caught Elizabeth's hand in his and twined their fingers together.

She glanced at their hands and then him, a delicate flush staining her cheekbones and making him wonder what she looked like when she was turned on. He'd like to see that. He'd really like to see that, but only if he was the man doing the turning on. He reminded her of their agreement, although that had nothing to do with why he wanted to hold her hand. "Handsy."

Weirdest thing, but he'd never understood why men walked around with their other half gripped by the hand like this. He got it now, that small connection that kept them apart from the rest of the world.

"Hey, Sam!" The kids from the other table tumbled out after them and chased them down the street.

Liz tensed and he squeezed her hand. "What's up, guys?"

"We wanted to...um...say thank you." The taller of the two spoke, pushing a floppy hank of hair out of his face. "For the dunk tank. The other day."

By the time he'd finished, the poor kid was brick red to his ears.

His buddy muscled forward. "I dunked you."

"Did you now?" Sam gave him a stern stare. "You know I'm gonna have to pay you back for that?"

"Sure, Sam." The kid side-eyed his buddy, not sure if Sam was kidding or not. "Of course you do. You're Sam Stone and you always deliver payback."

"You know it." Sam gave him a light punch on the shoulder. "Consider yourself paid back. How much did it cost you to dunk me?"

The kid snorted a laugh. "It took me three goes."

"Then we're even." Sam grinned at both of them.

The mom bustled up behind them. "Sa...Mr. Stone, I hope these boys of mine aren't bothering you?"

"Nope." Honestly, the kids never bothered him. Their love of hockey was pure, and their hero worship not based on what they could get out of him. "Always glad to chat. Although now I've got to get Elizabeth back to work."

"Elizabeth." The mom nodded at her.

The taller boy swallowed and cleared his throat. "We seen you on Instagram."

"Yeah." The smaller stared at her as if suddenly struck. "Are you Sam's girlfriend?"

"Alex." The mom gave him a reproachful look.

Elizabeth looked up at Sam and gave him her big, beautiful smile. "No, we're just friends."

"Right." The mom grinned. She ended on a wink. "Just friends, we get it."

The taller boy gave Elizabeth a slight leer. "Nice, Sam," he said as his face exploded into a fiery adolescent blush.

Sam gave him a stare. "You eyeing my girl?"

"Nah, Sam." Both boys giggled. "We wouldn't dare."

"Right." He gave the mom a conspiratorial smile. "Let's keep it that way."

"Come along, boys." The mom gave him another grin, like they now had a secret code. "We'll be watching the game tomorrow," she said. "Not the same without you, though."

"I appreciate that." Sam shook the woman's hand and then let the boys show him some complicated hand clasp thing before he drew Elizabeth away from them and back to her office.

"Actually." He hadn't lied when he told her he came to take her to lunch to see her, but Guy had suggested something to him yesterday and it occurred to him that it would be that much easier with Elizabeth next to him. "Speaking of the game tomorrow night?"

"Yup." She stared up at him, gauging him.

He intended to make it so she stopped bracing for bad weather around him. Forcing his facial muscles to relax, he said, "Want to watch it?"

"Sure." She looked thrilled that he'd asked. "Actually we should call Chris and see if she wants to join us. Her and Maddy, of course."

"Umm." He tightened his fingers around hers. "I meant go to the actual game."

"Go to the game?" She stopped and blinked at him. "You want to go to the stadium and watch the game live?"

"I'm not sure want comes into it." He dodged the penetrating stare she gave him. "I'm pretty sure being there and not being on the ice is going to suck, but Guy suggested I do it."

Elizabeth frowned. "If he knows how you feel, why would he do that?"

"Because it looks good," he said, and he knew Guy had called this one right. "Instead of me sulking in Mom's bathrobe, I go along to the game and support the team."

She got them moving back toward her office. "I suppose that could be a good idea."

"It'll be a lot easier if you come with me."

Her soft heart came swooping to his rescue and her face softened. "Of course it will. It must be hard for you."

Sam raised her hand to his mouth and kissed it. "It'll be fun, I promise."

"Hmm." She grimaced. "I'm not so sure about that, but I shall do my best to be a proper hockey girlfriend, dutifully by her man's side."

He knew she was being sarcastic, but he really liked the notion. "You'll be a great hockey girlfriend."

CHAPTER
TWENTY

THERE REALLY WAS ONLY one person for Elizabeth to ask about being the perfect hockey girlfriend. Maddy came around and dropped off a selection of teeny T-Shirts.

Sam arrived on time to pick her up. She liked that about him.

He stood on her doorstep in a ball cap and holding up a hockey jersey. "Okay, you can say no, but I thought maybe it would look good if you wore..." He cleared his throat. "I mean, you don't have to, but it would make us look...would you mind wearing my number?" He winced. "Too much?"

"Way ahead of you." Maddy smirked and appeared behind Elizabeth. "Show him."

Elizabeth opened her arms to show him her T-shirt. Figure hugging and the Titan's colors, the T-shirt played peek-a-boo with her belly above her jeans. But the best part. She whirled around to show him the back. "Ta da."

"Um...Lizzie?"

"What?" She peered over her shoulder, nervous about his tone. "Do I have the wrong number? Maddy assured me—"

"No." His tone carried a warm undertone. His eyes hadn't moved off her ass. "The number is perfect, but who the hell would notice that anyway."

Elizabeth couldn't resist preening a bit as she turned back to the front. "You think?"

"Oh, yeah." His gaze strayed to her breasts. "That's a much better shirt than I had in mind."

"Hey, Sam," Randy yelled from right below. He must have been standing there the whole time. "Watching the game tonight?"

"Sure am." Holding out the jersey, Sam said, "You got a home sweater?"

"I do not, Sam." Randy sounded way too eager.

Dropping the jersey over the edge, Sam chuckled. "Now you do."

"Wha—" Randy gasped.

Safely zipped into her coat, Elizabeth locked her apartment. "So where are we sitting? I'm sure the team has a box."

"A few." He grabbed her mittened hand. "But we're sitting with the fans."

"What?" Elizabeth couldn't believe him. "Won't you get mobbed?"

"Nah." He didn't look even a little concerned by the prospect. "Canadian fans are chill, but in case someone wants to be a tough guy, I'm in disguise." He tapped his cap, which shaded most of his face.

"Not much of a disguise." Elizabeth didn't hide her disdain.

Sam gave her a roguish grin that brought a flush to every part of her. Every. One. "Lizzie, nobody is going to be looking at me. Not when you're standing right there."

The strangeness of their situation struck her. This was Sam looking at her with those bedroom eyes and flirting with her. The same Sam she'd been having a vendetta against since they were babies.

Sam jogged down a couple of steps, stopped and looked up at her. "What's wrong?"

"Not wrong exactly." She came down slower. "More weird."

He cocked his head and shoved his hands in his coat pockets. "What's weird?"

"This." She motioned between them. "Whatever it is that we're doing here. Sometimes it strikes me that less than a month ago I was ready to remove your balls with a spoon."

"Damn, Lizzie." He shuddered. "Remind me not to piss you off again."

"Where's the fun in that?" The moment passed, and she stopped on the step above him. He wore a strange expression. "Now you're looking like you find something weird."

"You know I've always had a crush on you, Lizzie," he said.

He looked like he meant it as well, and it was similar to what he'd said to her before. Still, he couldn't have had a crush on her and she'd never noticed. Could she? "I'm not so sure you did."

"Be sure." Grabbing her hand, he walked them to his car. "We can work on that."

The locks beeped and Sam opened the door for her.

Elizabeth slid into the plush interior. "What are my chances of getting you to call me Elizabeth?"

He grinned and shook his head. "Not a one."

———

Elizabeth reckoned she must be one of the only Canadians to have never attended a live game.

Sam had a pass that got them into the player's parking. It made sense as he did still, technically, play for the Titans.

"Sam! Stoner!" The guard grinned at him. "You're late if you're planning on playing."

"Not tonight, Quentin." Sam took his pass back from the guard. "This time I'm bringing the win from the seats."

Quentin fired his forefinger at Sam. "That's our boy. It's good to see you."

"You too." Sam maneuvered through the parking lot.

The subtle lines of tension around his mouth and eyes concerned Elizabeth.

He parked between a Mercedes and a BMW SUV and opened her door.

Their feet clipped across the concrete as he led her to the arena. This time, she took hold of his hand and gave it a squeeze. It would be all right and she would be right beside him to make sure of that.

An elevator took them into the belly of the stadium. People scurried around, most of them too busy to notice another pair of bodies making their way toward the dull roar of the crowd around them.

She lost her way as Sam twisted them around and through a number of corridors and eventually into the lobby.

They startled a security guard by opening the door right behind her.

Looking for people trying to get in, she hadn't expected someone coming from that side of the stadium. "Sam," she whispered. "What are you doing?"

He handed her a couple of tickets. "Looking for my seat."

"You're watching the game?" Hope dawned on her craggy face. Sam nodded, and she broke into a huge smile. "That's awesome. The team has missed you. So have the fans." She reeled off some letters and numbers into her shoulder mic before turning back to them. "I'm getting someone to take you to your seats. I would"—she grimaced at the door—"but someone has to keep a sharp eye out."

"You always do a great job." Sam smiled at her.

She melted into a girly puddle and batted her eyes at him. Her glance strayed to Elizabeth and swept her up and down. Clearly not impressed with a woman accompanying Sam, she watched the busy foyer.

Fans streamed past them in a variety of jerseys, clutching food and plastic cups of beer.

"Wait here." Elizabeth ducked to the nearest concession

stand. The game was due to start and the crowd thinning, so she got to the end of the line quickly and was served almost immediately.

Sam waited by the security guard, hands in his pockets, chin down and his cap hiding his face.

"Here." She shoved a beer and a hot dog at him. "If you're going to be here as a fan, you may as well go large."

The gesture won her a reluctant smile of approval from the guard. She straightened. "There he is."

An older male guard sauntered up to them. "Hey, Lynn."

"What took you so long, Trent?" Lynn gave him a glare that would have scared a braver man. "I called over five minutes ago." She jerked her head at Sam. "VIP needing assistance."

"Eh?" Trent tried to peer beneath Sam's cap. "I didn't hear about any VIPs at tonight's game."

"I'm afraid I didn't let anyone know." Sam looked up.

Trent took a step back, ducked his head and stared at Sam. "Stoney," he whispered. "Jesus, Lynn, it's Stoney."

"I know that." Lynn rolled her eyes. "Now take him to his seat and see that he gets to enjoy the game without this lot bugging him."

"Are you supposed to do this?" Elizabeth whispered as they followed Trent.

He kept his chin tucked in. "I didn't bother to ask."

"Is this what Guy suggested?" People streamed around them, not even looking twice at Sam.

Sam shrugged as they ascended the staircase to their seats. "He didn't go into specifics."

Music pounded through the speakers. Around them, people chattered, laughed and found their seats.

Trent showed them to a pair of seats, tucked against the player's entrance and right behind the glass separating the player's bench.

Leaning in close, Trent lowered his voice. "We'll make sure nobody comes down here who doesn't have a seat."

"Thanks, Trent." Sam held Elizabeth's beer for her while she got settled in. Residual chill from the ice made the stadium cool.

The announcer was reeling off stats as images flashed across the JumboTron.

Some of the crowd responded, others went about their business of getting settled. The excitement surrounded her and stirred inside as Elizabeth looked around her.

"I loved coming to games as a kid." Sam had a whimsical smile on his face as he looked around him. "Of course then I was way up in the nosebleeds."

He'd worked so hard to be on the other side of the glass, given up so many things to make it happen. As a teen, he'd rarely had time for parties or messing around. Always, Sam had to be on the ice somewhere. "You'll be back there soon."

"Thanks." He kissed her knuckles.

She nudged him with her shoulder. "How about we enjoy the game and get back to brooding afterwards?"

The lights dimmed and the announcer's voice filled the space to the rafters. "Ottawa, please welcome your Ottawa Titans."

Along with the crowd, she and Sam cheered and hollered. He put two fingers between his lips and whistled.

The team filtered into the player's box as the opposing team took the ice to a muted response.

"To fun." Sam held up his beer.

Elizabeth tapped her cup against his. "To fun." She peered at the opposing team. "Now, who are we playing?"

"We're playing the Strikers, and we need the two points a win will give us."

Elizabeth stared at the other team in their royal blue and white jerseys. "For the playoffs?"

"Look at you." Sam grinned. "With all the hockey talk."

She laughed and winked at him. "I've been practicing my hockey girlfriend routine."

"Is that what you are now?"

The look in his blue eyes made her breathless. "I am for tonight."

———

The puck dropped, and the crowd surged to its feet with a roar.

Sam went with them, but Elizabeth was ahead of him. Skates scratched across the ice, fans yelled, players thumped into the boards.

At some point in the first period, he stopped noticing that he wasn't sitting beside his teammates where he should be. Sure, he got into the game, but the woman with him made for much more entertaining watching.

"Biscuit in the basket, boys." She sipped her beer and handed it to him so she could clap. "Let's get the biscuit in the basket."

"I'm fairly sure that's what they're trying to do." Sam put her beer cup in the holder and handed her a hot dog.

Around a huge bite, Elizabeth rolled her eyes at him. "Please! Are you watching this D? Why don't they send a written invitation?" The crowd groaned, and she whipped her attention back to the ice.

The Strikers surged on the goal.

Defense crowded the paint and tried to push them out.

The crowd went crazy. Elizabeth going right along with them.

Guy snapped out a glove and saved a helluva shot.

"Yes!" Elizabeth hopped up and down and pointed at Guy. "Yes, Guy. I love you, baby."

If he were on the ice right now, he would have shouted his encouragement to Guy, but it was hard to concentrate on much but the strip of taut, ivory flesh between Elizabeth's jeans and that tiny shirt.

The man behind them had his gaze stuck on her ass.

Sam looked back until the guy gave him a what-you-gonna-do-boy shrug and went back to the game.

Des Jardins, the new power forward they'd taken on this season, snatched the puck on the rebound and took it up the ice.

Lizzie was back on her feet yelling and screaming.

Des Jardins passed it wide to the winger. Cabbot snapped it into the net to bring the Titans up one goal.

That brought Sam to his feet and earned him a happy grin and a hip bump from Lizzie.

The ref restarted the game, and Sam paid a little more attention. The Strikers would surge hard to close that goal gap. The Titans would surge even harder to make it a two-goal lead.

The action on the ice heated.

Sam saw it coming. "Left, left, left!" he yelled, but Des Jardins couldn't hear him.

Crowe, the big Striker's d-man powered into Des Jardins, pounding him against the boards right in front of them.

A minute or so of pushing and shoving, and Des Jardins shoved himself free.

Yeah, if Sam was on the ice, Crowe wouldn't have pulled that shit, because he'd have known that Stone would pound his ass twice as hard.

As if he'd heard him, Mark Crowe glanced into the fans, caught sight of Sam and did a doubletake.

"You suck," he mouthed.

Elizabeth gasped, and before Sam could respond, she'd rubbed her middle finger over her nose and pointed it right at Crowe.

Crowe gave her a grin and skated back to his bench.

"Did you just flip him off?" Sam had never seen this side of Lizzie, and he was digging it big time.

She went a little pink. "Maybe."

"You totally did."

The horn went for the end of the first period and the crowd stirred. One goal up wasn't enough of a lead, especially against the Strikers, and they would need to widen that.

Elizabeth laughed and pointed. "Look."

Normally he missed this part because he was generally having his ass chewed out by coach.

A couple got caught on the KissCam. The girl giggled and blushed and pointed. The man gave her the kiss the crowd wanted.

The KissCam moved on and found another couple.

A very familiar looking couple.

"It's us." Elizabeth turned and gaped at him.

Sam didn't need a second invitation. He dropped his cap, grabbed Elizabeth's face and went to work.

He took her by surprise, and she stiffened momentarily.

"It's Sam Stone!" A man shouted from a few rows above them. The news spread around the stadium on an excited buzz.

Elizabeth's mouth softened beneath his, and she grabbed the front of his shirt and kissed him back.

All the noise and commotion faded away. The taste of beer lingered as he slid his tongue into her warm mouth.

Her soft moan vibrated through him. Her hips lined up with his and he wanted to grab her ass and tighten the fit between them.

The soft press of her breasts against his chest set a flash burn beneath his skin and sent blood surging to his cock.

"Stoney!" A hard tap on his shoulder pulled him away from heaven.

He turned and wanted to punch the grinning, round-faced fan shoving a pen and a jersey at him. "Can I have your autograph?"

"Oh." Elizabeth blinked at him, sleepy and sexy and as affected by the kiss as he.

He snatched the jersey and pen out of the fan's hand and gave Lizzie a hard stare. "We'll circle round to this later."

CHAPTER
TWENTY-ONE

ELIZABETH WAITED for Sam as he went to greet his team in the locker room. Propping her shoulder against the wall, she spent the time watching the hustle and bustle all around her.

Reporters streamed in and out of the locker rooms. Equipment managers had already loaded hockey bags on carts and were pushing them down the constricted hallways.

The game had ended with a four-zero win for the Titans.

Sam had asked her to wait while he went to congratulate Guy on his fiftieth shutout of his career.

It didn't take long before Sam was pushing through the throng, bottlenecking the locker room door. He spotted her and threaded his way toward her.

"Sam!" A tall, dark-haired man in a suit stepped in front of him.

Sam tensed. "Gracie."

"Looking good, Sam." Gracie shoved his hands in his pockets. "This break seems to be treating you well. You appear to be making good use of your time."

It didn't sound to Elizabeth like Gracie meant that the way it sounded. In fact, it sounded a lot like criticism.

Elizabeth moved closer to Sam.

"Excuse me!' A young equipment guy shoved past her with his hands full of sticks.

Folding his arms over his chest, Sam faced Gracie. "I'll make better use of my time when I'm back on the ice."

"You sure that's going to happen?" Gracie gave Sam a slight sneer. "Way I hear it, the team is real happy with Des Jardins."

An unholy desire to kick Gracie rippled through Elizabeth.

Sam gave good face, but she knew that shot had taken a piece off him. Gracie had it in for Sam. Well, not on her watch.

"Hey, baby!" Elizabeth channeled her best Maddy as she slid up beside Sam and wrapped her arms around his waist. "You see the team?"

He dragged his attention away from Gracie. "Yup."

"Ready to go?" She snuggled closer. Tension locked Sam's body tight.

Gracie turned his dark eyes on her. Gaze filled with intelligence, he assessed her. "Ah! The perfect new friend puts in an appearance."

"Well, I don't know about perfect." She giggled at Gracie as if she had missed his sarcasm. "But I've been on his side since he first played peewee hockey." She managed a playful glance for Sam. "Actually before that."

"Really?" Gracie shifted and studied her closer. "So you two have known each other for years? And I take it you're behind this new squeaky-clean Sam?"

"I'd love to claim the credit for that." Beaming at Gracie, Elizabeth patted Sam's chest. "But Sam's always been passionate about giving back to his community."

"Right." Gracie's expression said he didn't believe her for a minute. "Good for Sam," he said. "Judging by the kiss earlier, Sam is certainly passionate about certain aspects of his community."

———

Sam drove them home in silence. He hadn't said much since the encounter with Gracie.

She didn't think she'd done the wrong thing. "Should I not have said anything to Gracie?"

"Huh?" He pulled his attention away from the road. "What? No, that was great."

"Oh." She studied his profile as streetlights flashed across him. "Guy was okay? Everything was okay with the team?"

"Yeah." He sighed. "I'm being moody."

"About going to the game?"

He shrugged and dropped one hand to his thigh. "Yeah, I suppose so. I loved the game. I had a great time. It was just…"

"Being in the locker room with the team made the suspension feel more real to you."

"Exactly." He gave her a grateful smile.

They drove into the night, and the atmosphere in the car got darker.

Sam spoke suddenly. "What if I don't get back there?"

And then she got it. It had taken her a little long, and she took his hand. "You'll get back there, Sam. You're too good not to play again."

"But I screwed up, Lizzie. I had everything I'd ever wanted, and I let it go."

This was a side to Sam nobody ever saw, the vulnerability he kept hidden.

"Sam." She squeezed his hand. "You're human, and that means making mistakes. You're not immune to that."

He eased the atmosphere with a grin in her direction. "Yeah, but I'm a phenom. The normal rules don't apply to me."

She didn't press him. "As my pretty princess play palace can attest."

"Your what now?"

"My play palace." Okay it still stung a bit. It had taken ages to get her father to agree to buy it, and she had loved it. There was nothing like dressing up and hiding from the fighting going on in her home. "You shot pucks at it and destroyed it."

Frowning, Sam gave that some thought. "That big pink, sparkly thing that looked like a dog's kennel on crack?"

"It was beautiful!" In a very pink and sparkly way. "And I loved it."

"Hmm." He stared at the road ahead of them. "Technically, Busy Lizzie, you only have yourself to blame for that."

This, she had to hear. She turned in her seat and stared at the side of his head. "How do you make that one out?"

"You wouldn't let me play inside it with you." Sam shrugged. "You were being mean, and sharing is caring, Lizzie."

"Oh!" It was something Sam the little shit from their childhood would have said.

His shoulders shook as he grinned at the road.

"Are you laughing at me?"

He glanced at her, blue eyes brimming with laughter. "Only a little."

"I'm glad my childhood trauma amuses you this much."

"Ah, Lizzie." He picked up her hand and kissed it. "I'm sorry about your pink unicorn dance hall."

"Pretty princess play palace." He needn't think the hand kissing worked. Okay, it worked a little.

Still holding her hand, he lowered it to his thigh. "How about I buy you a new one? We could set it up in your parking spot." He looked at her as if he'd just had a brilliant idea. "We can invite Randy to tea parties."

"Dickhead." But he had her laughing with him already.

They pulled up outside her condo, and the easy atmosphere crept away.

Elizabeth didn't know what to do. The hockey game was over. She should thank him, get out of the car and go upstairs to her condo. Put on her pjs and mentally dissect that kiss for the rest of the weekend.

Even thinking about it made her skin prickle with heat. Damn, Sam could kiss.

One arm braced on the steering wheel, Sam turned to her. "Don't you hate this part?"

"Yep." Because she really did, but that he got that made it a bit easier. "Thanks for tonight. I enjoyed the game." Then she felt like a shit. "Although I know it was difficult to be there for you."

"It could have been harder." He gave a tendril of her hair a small tug. "Thanks for coming with me and holding my hand through it."

"Any time." And shit, she really meant that. "Are you okay?"

He shrugged. "As good as I can be."

"You'll play hockey again, Sam." She stared at him until he looked at her. "And everything in my dad's life will return to normal."

His laugh didn't have his heart in it. "I hope so, Lizzie. I'm not good at anything else."

"Crap!" Not for a second did she believe that. "You can play anything with a ball and stick. Anything. And I know this because it made me want to hit you when we were children."

"You did hit me." His wry smile took some of his worry with it.

"I'm not sorry," she said. "Someone had to keep you in line. And you're great with people."

That earned her a skeptical glance. "Why don't you check that with Karlov?"

"He's a hockey player." She waved a dismissive hand. "And he knows the score when he laces his skates and steps on the ice. I've watched you with normal people while we've been hanging out."

He looked at her.

"You handle all the different ways they come at you."

With a wince, he shook his head. "That comes with the territory."

"Not necessarily." She tapped his shoulder to get his attention. "And once you stopped being an ass to Chris's team, you were great with them."

"I enjoyed that." Sam smiled. "There's something very satisfying about working with kids like that. Kids that everybody else has written off."

"Like they did you?" She held her breath to see how that would go over.

He frowned at her. "Me? Nobody gave up on me. In fact, it was the opposite. From the first time I stepped on the ice, the scouts started circling."

"No, before that," Elizabeth said, and she remembered this well because her mom had worried for young Sam. "When you were so sick, and your mom wanted to wrap you up and keep you safe." She nudged him. "You decided to prove them all wrong."

"Your mom helped with that." His face softened. "She was the only one who could get my mom to back off long enough for me to get some room to breathe."

"She was good like that." Too good to have been married to Elizabeth's dad all those years. "I wish she'd gotten out sooner."

"Why didn't she?"

Elizabeth shrugged. "She wanted to stay until Jane graduated high school."

"Huh."

They sat in silence until Elizabeth couldn't avoid going into her apartment for any longer. Not without making it pathetically obvious she wanted another kiss. Maybe even more.

That thought galvanized her. As hot as the chemistry between her and Sam was proving to be, her head hadn't quite caught up. Her heart lagged miles behind that even.

This thing between her and Sam defied her efforts to classify it. They had years of history between them, and once they stopped bitching at each other, a solid friendship underlying all that. And now they were having trouble keeping their hands off each other.

At least one of them did.

"Well." She opened her car door. "I should be getting in."

Sam's gaze smoldered. "Or you could invite me in?"

"I could." Her libido cheered that idea. "But would that be a good idea?"

"I think that would be an excellent idea." Sam leaned into her.

Elizabeth got the hell out of the car before she jumped him. "Good night, Sam."

"I'll walk you to your door." He climbed from the car.

That wasn't such a hot idea. What with her willpower tripping and fusing. "It's not far."

"I'm a gentleman." He shoved his hands in his pockets and gave her a look loaded with challenge.

Elizabeth led the way. "That remains to be seen."

"Look, ma, no hands." He raised his hands before jamming them back in his pockets. "However much I want to put them all over you, pretty Lizzie."

That took her breath away, and she had to concentrate on not tripping up the stairs.

She got her door open somehow. No easy feat with her hands trembling and her pulse pounding loud enough to wake Randy.

As she turned to say goodnight, Sam's disgruntled expression stopped her. He looked like he had when she'd stolen his treat when they were kids.

"Hey, Sam." She leaned in. Her lips lingered next to his ear. "You kiss at least as well as you play hockey."

She shut the door as he reached for her. Giggling she pressed her back against it as he swore from the other side.

She risked the peephole.

Both arms braced on either side of her door, Sam hung his head and swore. He looked up suddenly, as if sensing her watching him, and winked. "Game on, Lizzie."

CHAPTER
TWENTY-TWO

THURSDAY NIGHT DRAMA night at Mountain Vista rolled around, and Elizabeth barely had time to get there straight after work.

Dad had taken her time with Sam personally and was behaving like a jealous girlfriend. He didn't mention the kiss at the game, but she was sure he'd seen it. Paul Rogers never missed a Titan's game and barely moved from his lounger for the duration.

Chris had called earlier in the day and assured her not only had the kiss been captured on the JumboTron, but also shared across the hockey channel on television. It was now making the rounds of Twitter. Response was ranging from "aww!" to "get a room."

"Elizabeth." Dad flung open his office door as she was photocopying the script for drama night. "Did you set up that appointment with the town council?"

"Yes, it's in your planner."

"What planner?"

She barely restrained her eye roll. He'd been letting his bully brat off the leash all day. "The one on your computer."

"It's not in my diary." He shook the book at her. "You know I like things in my diary." Tossing the diary on her desk, he upended a cup of water.

Elizabeth lunged for it and righted it before the water could creep over her completed scripts. She picked up the diary to get it out of the mess and started wiping the cover. Then she stopped. Dad was being an ass, and he certainly didn't pay her enough to put up with his shit.

"The appointment is in your computer." She thrust the diary at him. "For reasons you approved of, and if you want it written in your diary, then you do it."

She tossed sodden tissues into her wastebasket.

Dad blinked at her. "But...you're my secretary."

"Office administrator." She scooped up her purse and the scripts. "And that's only from nine until five. As it's now six thirty, I am once more your daughter, and I have somewhere to be."

"Where?" He followed her to the elevator. "I hope you're not crawling all over Sam. Embarrassing yourself and the rest of your family."

That should have stung, but it more irked her. "Oh?" She stopped long enough to meet his angry stare. "I know for a fact Sam would love me to crawl all over him and embarrass our family."

The elevator door shut on him still sputtering.

So childish and yet so satisfying. Apparently she was discovering her inner vixen, and that meant no longer letting the men in her life dictate the terms.

Her phone rang, and she thumbed it open.

"Elizabeth, darling." Leonard Smytkowski's fruity tones oozed down the phone. "I am at Mountain Vista already."

Elizabeth let the pregnant pause stretch for a bit. "Right, Leonard. Tonight is a rehearsal night."

"And you are not here." Leonard cleared his throat like a Victorian debutante. "I am here, and you are not."

"That's because I am leaving work now, Leonard." She wrestled the scripts and her large tote into her car. "Because rehearsal doesn't start until seven."

"Yes, Elizabeth." Leonard got his snippy tone on. "But you are the production assistant, and you should be here already. When the director—which is me—arrives at the rehearsal space, he expects to have the space set up and ready to begin."

Elizabeth started her car and put Leonard on Bluetooth.

"Most production assistants make sure their director is also provided with sustenance before he must work his artistic magic, but you have not worked in the professional thee-AY-tah as I have." Leonard heaved a long-suffering sigh. "Those of us who have worked extensively in the professional thee-AY-tah, Broadway to be exact, do not place our high standards on those who have no—"

Her phone beeped an incoming call. "Gonna have to let you go now, Leonard."

"Elizabeth!" Jane demanded. "What's this bullshit about you kissing Sam?"

Like most teens Jane had a glass-fragile ego, and Elizabeth didn't fancy getting into the truth. Not that she had a great handle on the truth herself. "It was the Jum—"

"You're such a fucking hypocrite," Jane shrieked, her voice reverberating around the car. "You tell me to stay the fuck away from him, and then you go and make out with him in public."

Talk about your overreactions. It was like Jane was reacting to her and Sam releasing a sex tape. "It was a kiss, Janey, and done because the KissCam was on us."

"I hate you—"

Blip.

Rescued by her phone again. "We can talk about this later, Jane, but I'm going to have to let you go."

Elizabeth switched to the incoming call. "I know you're impatient, but I'm coming. Right now."

"Sugar lips." Sam's smooth baritone filled the car like honey.

"You have no idea how impatient I am, and shouldn't that be, I'm coming, Sam. Yes, Sam, yes. I'm com—"

"Ugh! You're a pig." Elizabeth choked back a laugh. "And there are children in the car next to me."

"Then this is sex ed, and it's free." Sam chuckled. "Where are you?"

"Pulling into the parking lot of Mountain Vista."

Sam's tone sharpened. "Something wrong with the bus?"

"Nope." She gathered up her bag, the scripts, and the bottle of juice she'd taken from the office fridge for Leonard. "It's Thursday night."

"Ye-e-s?"

"And it's drama night." She got out of the car and shut the door with her butt. "And we're doing *South Pacific*."

"Does this mean I'll get to see you in a bikini top and grass skirt?"

"That is so politically incorrect." She trotted across the parking lot, nodding to a group of older men arguing over a backgammon board.

"You're right," Sam said. "Skip the grass skirt and stay with the bikini."

"Not me but Gladys O'Leary, and she is making a strong case for her wearing one."

"Wasn't Gladys ninety when she ran the school library?"

"Ageist as well." She tutted. "She was in her seventies. But she makes a remarkably good Liat."

Sam chuckled. "How long will you be?"

"I'll be here until nine."

"Have you had dinner?"

Elizabeth pushed into the lobby and mouthed a hello to Carol standing beside the reception desk. "No time. I came straight from the office."

"Good, then you can come by here and I'll feed you," Sam said. "Besides I have something to show you."

"What?" She hip-bumped open the door to the dining room, now rehearsal space.

Leonard rose and held out his arms. "Elizabeth. My angel!" He took the juice with a misty-eyed smile. "My savior."

"Mixing food with business gives me indigestion," Sam said. "I'll see you later."

"But…"

He'd already hung up and Leonard was clapping his hands. "Elizabeth! We simply must prepare the creative space for the artistes."

———

Elizabeth must have dropped through a hole in the space-time continuum because Sam opened the front door wearing Danica's blue satin bathrobe.

One arm raised, he jerked his chin at her. "How you doin'?"

"I thought we'd retired the robe." She brushed past him into the house. Rehearsal had almost finished the job her father started at work. She was tired, grumpy and hungry. And a drink wouldn't hurt. "Do you have a glass of wine or something?"

"I have a glass of wine." Sam strolled into the kitchen, still managing to look masculine in pale blue satin with ecru lace edging. "How was *South Pacific*?"

"Trying." Elizabeth kept her eye on the prize being poured into one of Danica's "best" wineglasses, the deep-ruby prize Sam handed to her. She took a big sip and sighed. "Leonard is concerned about compromising his artistic vision."

"How terrible." Sam got himself a beer and popped the cap. "No grass skirts then?"

"You and the grass skirts." Elizabeth took another sip of wine. Say what you would about Sam, he had great taste in wine, even if he only stuck to the occasional beer for himself. And Baileys, she smirked to herself, lest she forget the Baileys.

He cocked his head. "What's so funny?"

"Baileys." It drew the first small laugh out of her since... she'd last spoken to Sam. He made her laugh, a lot.

"It was my gateway drug." He gave a theatrical grimace. "I'm moving on to Cointreau."

"Easy there, tiger." The wine helped bring her down but being with Sam helped more. "What's this thing I need to see?"

"We'll get to that." Sam leaned his hips against the counter. The robe opened over his bare thighs.

God, those thighs made her want to dig her nails into them. She'd bet it would be like clawing rock.

"Lizzie." Sam's voice grew smoky. "My face is up here."

She didn't even bother to be embarrassed. She'd been leering and gotten caught and she didn't care. Sam's thighs deserved all the ogling she could manage. "What's with the robe anyway?"

"We'll get to that." He gestured with his beer bottle. "I need to hear Leonard's artistic vision."

"Right." Elizabeth would much rather stare at his thighs and the rigid definition skating had made of his calf muscles. "Leonard feels we are missing the opportunity to highlight the Marxist leanings of *South Pacific*."

Sam nodded and gave that his thinking face. "Right. Right."

"And therefore, he wants to do the whole production on a stripped stage, no props and no set and have the entire cast wear black leggings and T-shirts."

"The man is a visionary." Sam grinned around his beer.

Elizabeth allowed herself the laughter she'd held in throughout rehearsal. "Unfortunately the entire cast went into revolt at the notion."

"How Marxist of them."

"Ha ha." She made a face at him. "The only reason most of them are doing the production in the first place is to wear pretty costumes with flowers in their hair. A direct quote from Gladys."

Sam winked at her. "I said the same thing when I joined the Titans. Nice jerseys, but where are the flowers for our hair?"

"Shuddup." The wine, the laughter, the wink and a whole lot

of Sam made her insides warm and happy. "Now show me the thing and then feed me because I'm starving."

"All right then, but only because you're really scary right now." Sam went for the robe ties. "You got it."

"Whoa! Our moms used to make us bathe together." Elizabeth went hot and then cold and then really hot. "I've seen that already."

Shaking his head, Sam tutted. "You have such a dirty mind." He dropped the robe. "I went shopping."

Elizabeth nearly dropped the wineglass. On a scale of holy shitballs to squirrel, mark her off the charts distracted.

Clad only in the pink undies for the breast cancer campaign, Sam took her breath away. His body was beautiful, a finely crafted machine. Not overly buff but packed with corded sinew and strongly defined muscle. As for the part covered in hot pink spandex…

The words got away from her. "Holy crap."

Fortunately Sam was too busy looking at his purchase. "I got the right ones, didn't I, Lizzie?"

"Uh-huh." That's all she had. She took a slug of wine to save her dry mouth. Right then she'd give up the wine to touch, which, given her day, was saying a whole heckuva lot.

Sam looked up. "Lizzie?"

"Er…" Her speech ability was still missing. "S…sure."

"Lizzie." His expression changed to quizzical, and then grew sensual. "Are you checking me out?"

She went for a head shake, but her heart and her girl parts weren't in it and her gaze roamed all over his beautiful flesh. Her breathing shortened and her pulse double-timed it. A flush spread everywhere. Every. Where.

"I feel so cheap." Sam sauntered toward her, his entire focus locked on her. He placed his hands on either side of her hips. "The way you're looking at me right now, Lizzie. Tell me I'm reading it right."

He was so close that heat radiated off his body and she could smell the musky scent of his skin.

"You're reading it right." She said, "This is getting very complicated."

"No, it's not." He brushed her ear with his lips. "It's about to get a whole lot simpler."

Sensation shot through her core, and she couldn't stop the soft moan. "You would say that."

He skimmed his lips down her throat. "You want me, Elizabeth, and God knows, I want you."

Elizabeth couldn't not touch him, and she put her hands on his broad shoulders. Needing more, she ran them down his defined biceps and over the heavy veining of his forearms. "You know it's not that simple."

"This feels pretty simple to me." Sam pressed his hips into hers.

"Sam." It came out on another breathy moan. His hot mouth on the curve of her shoulder, nudging aside her shirt to find the skin beneath was killing her. Her knees weakened, and she leaned into the counter.

She did want him, bad enough to forget their past, the way their families intertwined. All of it. To say to hell with it and let this man do all the things her body craved.

As if she had no control over them, her hands found the trim line of his waist. "I want to touch you."

"Then touch me." Sam's voice matched all the throbbing desire coursing through Elizabeth, and it almost drove her over the edge. "But Lizzie, don't rub the lamp if you don't want the genie to come out."

It was such a Sam thing to say that it made her want to laugh. It added to her dizzying vortex of lust and apprehension. This was Sam.

Sam!

"Do you?" He toyed with the top button of her shirt. "Do you want the genie to come out?"

"Stoner!" Guy bellowed from the front door. It shut with a bang behind him.

Sam leaped away from her and snatched up the robe. "Fuck!"

Thank God one of them was thinking, because Elizabeth stood there against the counter with disappointment and relief raging an almighty battle inside her.

Guy rounded the corner and grinned when he caught sight of her. "Hey, Elizabeth."

"Hi," she forced out.

Stopping suddenly, Guy looked at her and then at Sam. "Nice robe, Stoner." Shoving his hands in his pockets, he broke into a huge shit-eating grin. "I came to talk to you about that photo thing." He motioned Sam's underpants. "The cock blocking you was a bonus."

Elizabeth's face nearly exploded with heat.

After a scowl, Sam shook his head and laughed. "You're an asshole. Want a beer?"

"Sure." Guy sniffed and grinned. "And dinner. Something in here smells great."

CHAPTER
TWENTY-THREE

ELIZABETH WOKE on Sunday to a crisp, clear day with the temperature hovering around freezing. The weather would help make the annual walkathon for education a success. Of course, the fact that Sam and now Guy would be taking part had definitely raised interest and Chris said the OPP had been called in to manage the flow of people and traffic.

A rumor that CBC would be there had brought an even larger turnout.

Driving to pick up Sam, she had nervous marbles rolling through her gut. She hadn't seen him since *that night*.

If Guy hadn't walked in and then insisted on staying for dinner, things would have progressed between her and Sam. Progressed to a point that made her marbles roll faster and her breath catch.

The reason behind those disturbing symptoms evaded her. Did she want this to happen between her and Sam or didn't she?

Then, what might happen afterward between them got more confusing. It wasn't like they could be intimate and then return to being enemies.

God help them if their mothers ever found out.

She pulled into Danica's driveway.

The door opened, and Sam and Guy tumbled out, shoving and pushing each other like ten-year-olds. It was still a fine sight.

At six-six, Guy was taller and built like a grizzly, but with a classically handsome face and a beautiful smile.

And Sam was Sam. The same sexy, tousled, just-out-of-bed good looks that used to annoy her.

Sam met her gaze through the windshield and his smile broadened. His eyes warmed as if she was the best thing he'd seen that day.

Both men wore hoodies, sweatpants and Titan's toques.

Sam opened the car door and let in a waft of clear, cold air. "Morning, Lizzie."

"Elizabeth." Guy climbed into the back and rocked the entire car with his bulk. "You are looking particularly pretty this morning."

He'd sounded like he meant it, and Elizabeth wanted to giggle like a teen with a crush.

"Hey." Sam leaned over and punched his shoulder. "Stop flirting with my Lizzie."

His Lizzie. The marbles grew into tennis balls and bounced off major organs as they went.

Sam leaned over and kissed her cheek. "He's right though. You do look beautiful this morning."

She snuck in a sniff of his light, citrus soap. The warm imprint of his lips lingered on her cheek as he moved back.

"Aww, look at you two." Guy leaned forward and put his elbows on the back of their seats. "So, what is this thing we're doing today anyway?"

"You didn't tell him?" Elizabeth backed into the road and got them underway.

"Nah." Sam sat at an angle that enabled him to watch her. "I told him the important part. That I'd do it better than him."

"He did tell me that." Guy nodded gravely. "And I couldn't let such a blatant challenge to my masculinity go unanswered."

It would take a lot more than that to challenge Guy's masculinity. Every inch of his huge frame threw out testosterone waves.

Before Sam could start ragging on Guy, she jumped in. "This is a walkathon that takes place every year to raise money for families who are struggling with school expenses."

"That's nice," Guy said, sitting back. "Education is important."

They arrived at the event and sat in the long row of cars waiting for space in the parking lot.

Chris approached them and tapped on her window. "Hey." Her smile included Sam and Guy. "You can go ahead and park in the VIP section."

"Really?" Even feeling a bit guilty about the other people having to wait in line didn't stop her from being glad.

"Yup." Chris nodded and pointed. "Skip the queue and go straight in where that red sign is. Maddy said she would meet you there."

Elizabeth couldn't resist teasing Chris. "Did she now? And when did Maddy tell you this?"

"You're impeding a police officer in her duties." Chris went all kinds of red and strode away.

"I like her," Guy said. "And I like her for Maddy. They make a cute couple."

Elizabeth thought so too, and she smiled at him through the rearview mirror.

"Tell me something?" Sam turned in his seat to speak to Guy. "Did you always know Maddy was gay?"

"D'uh." Guy rolled his eyes. "And also she told me."

"When?"

Guy shrugged. "I don't remember when. At some point, maybe a party or something." He gave Sam a smug grin. "What can I say? Women like me and they tell me stuff."

"Women friend zone you." Sam snorted.

Guy heaved a massive sigh. "Yeah! That too."

Taking the path Chris had indicated, Elizabeth drove them into the VIP parking lot—filled with only them and the mayor's car—and found Maddy waiting.

"Good morning." Maddy looked incredible in yoga pants and a big puffy jacket. Her cheeks were pink from the cold, and her eyes sparkled. She kissed Sam and then Guy before hugging Elizabeth. "Today is going to be so much fun."

Maddy's mood was infectious and buoyed them as they found their way to the group of walkers waiting for the start.

"Up here, Sam!" Dad waved a dapper red flag about. "You and Guy need to start at the front."

Sam took Elizabeth's hand and tugged her with him. "On our way, Paul."

Her father caught sight of her and frowned. "Just the VIPs, Sam, meaning you and Guy."

"But who will kick my butt if I get tired if Lizzie isn't with me?" Sam threw down the charm.

A few chuckles sounded in their wake as they wove through the crowd. Dad looked like he might argue and then shut his mouth.

"So, how's the studying going?" Guy asked Maddy from behind them.

Of course, Maddy had to be smart as well. She couldn't only be a sweetheart in a gorgeous package. "What's she studying?"

Sam shrugged and pulled a face. "You'll have to ask her. Or Guy." He raised a brow at Guy. "He seems to know everything."

"It's because I listen." Guy tapped the side of Sam's head with one hammer-sized finger. "You should try is some time."

"Haven't you heard?" A note of bitterness crept into Sam's voice. "I don't know how to listen."

"I heard that," Guy said and clapped Sam on the shoulder. "But I know you better."

"Hello, Sam." A boy from Chris's team sidled up to them. "I don't know...I mean, I'm sure you don't remember me."

Elizabeth leaned in to remind Sam of the boy's name. Mathew had a hard time at school because he was painfully shy.

"Mathew, right?" Sam got there before she did. "You play defense."

Mathew flushed and his eyes gleamed. He puffed out his chest and looked at the group of boys now gaping at him. "That's right, Sam. Are you going to come and watch our game this Saturday?"

"Yeah." Sam rolled his eyes. "Of course I am. I'm the assistant coach, remember."

"Okay." Mathew let out a huge, quivering sigh of delight. "Then maybe you should come to more practices." He looked horrified at his own daring. "I mean...only if you want and you really are...never mind."

Sam put an arm around his shoulders. "You're absolutely right, Mathew my man. I will be at your next practice, if Coach Chris says I can, and I will be at your game."

"You coach these losers." A larger boy shouldered Mathew aside. "You should come and coach our team. We're top of our—"

"Dude." Sam kept his tone gentle, but he frowned. "I'm already coaching the team I want to coach."

"But—"

Sam raised an eyebrow.

The boy backed off and melted into the crowd.

"Wow." Guy draped an arm around Elizabeth's neck, dragged her closer and whispered, "Whatever you're doing to our boy, keep doing it."

"I'm not doing anything," she said.

Guy gave her a skeptical look, but it was the truth. This was all Sam.

"Seriously?" Sam gave Guy's arm around her a pointed look. "Every time I turn around, you're there."

Sam tugged her away from Guy and tucked her close to his

side. His hard, muscular side. Guy was as muscular, if not more so, but he didn't have the collapsing effect on her knees that Sam did.

"Did I mention you look beautiful today?" Sam whispered in her year.

Elizabeth called his bullshit. "Yup."

"And how good you smell?" He nuzzled her neck. "Or how much your ass in those pants makes me want to touch?"

The knee weakening thing was happening again, and her protest was half-hearted at best. "Sam."

"You're right." He nipped her earlobe. "I'll give myself wood if I keep going this way."

"Sam!" And this time she sounded like she was begging him for more. Which she totally was.

Mathew pressed into Sam's side. "Can I walk with you, Sam?"

"Dude." Sam ruffled his hair. "I'd be gutted if you didn't." He jerked his thumb at Guy. "Because the big guy back there gets tired quickly." Sam winked at Mathew. "He sits in the goal all the time. Doing nothing."

"Don't make me squash you like a bug," Guy said.

Mathew giggled and breathed. "Best day ever."

After a bit of speechifying, with Sam fidgeting worse than Mathew throughout, they set off. The crowd around Guy and Sam ebbed and flowed as people found an excuse to say hi and grab a quick selfie.

Throughout the walk, Sam kept a firm grip on her hand, not letting fans or haters nudge her out of the way.

Mathew grew tired about two kilometers in and Guy hoisted him on his shoulders.

Maddy chatted to Guy the entire time, about her studying—which was going well—about her family—which totally didn't deserve her—and about Chris—who she was head over heels about.

Elizabeth didn't mind the people or how they monopolized

Sam. This was why she'd made him do this. His presence brought more people out to walk, meaning more money raised, and the selfies and videos of him walking were social media gold.

Also, Sam kept a watch on her the entire time and wrapped her in a sense of togetherness.

By the end of the walk, the weather had turned overcast and the temperature dropped. A cold wind coming straight off the Ottawa river discouraged any lingering, and after making sure Mathew was back with his family, she, Sam and Guy piled into her car.

Chris waited for Maddy. Now off duty, she grabbed Maddy and kissed her as if they'd been separated for days.

Sitting in her car and watching them, Elizabeth was so happy for Chris. She would never have pictured her with someone like Maddy, but there they were. Making their way through the parked cars with their hands entwined and their heads close together.

"Damn, Lizzie." Sam shivered. "Turn the car on and let's get some heat in here."

"Wuss," she said, but she could do with the heat as well.

People were still milling about on their way to their cars, and it took a while to weave their way to clear roads again.

Elizabeth glanced at Guy and then Sam. "Thank you for doing that."

"Lizzie." Sam cupped her nape. "We had a deal. All I did was stick to the deal."

Like she believed that was all there was to it. "Sure. But thank you anyway."

"You're welcome, Elizabeth." Guy squeezed her shoulder.

"Hey!" Sam glared at his hand. "What did we say about touching Lizzie?"

"Do it as much as I can?" Guy chuckled.

Sam rubbed his hands and held them over the heater vent. "Why don't you drop Guy off first?"

He must have forgotten the ins and outs of driving around there. "But your mom's place is halfway between here and Guy's hotel."

Sam gave her a hard stare.

Clearly, she was missing something vital here.

In the backseat, Guy cracked up. His loud laughter almost hurt her ears. "What?"

"Sam wants you to drop me off first so he can be alone with you in the car." Guy chuckled.

Now she felt all kinds of stupid. "Oh."

"Yup." Guy stretched his huge arms over the top of the backseat. "Stage one is to get rid of all obstacles." He pointed at himself. "That would be me. Step two is to make his move. Maybe invite you in for hot chocolate or tomato soup and grilled cheese."

Elizabeth's face was ready to explode.

Guy kept on chuckling and Sam turned to scowl at him. "You're such an asshole."

"Me?" Guy widened his eyes, an innocent man condemned for no reason. "I'm helping you along here, Stoner. Making sure Elizabeth gets where you're headed, because your game is pitiful, my friend, pitiful."

"Like you've got game." Sam scoffed at his friend.

Guy sighed. "Sadly, you're right. I have even less game than you."

Elizabeth found that hard to believe, about both of them. They had to be knee deep in puck bunnies and wannabe Mrs. Professional Hockey Players. "You're both bugging me."

She took the road to Guy's hotel anyway. What the hell! It was only ten minutes out of the way, and she preferred this road.

Her conscience smirked at her and raised its eyebrows.

Guy unfolded himself from her car with a kiss on her cheek. "Thanks for everything today, Elizabeth. I hope to see you again, soon." Then he chuckled. "Not as much as Sam hopes to see a lot more of you, but anyway."

The cool air from outside did nothing to cool her cheeks and she sat a moment as Guy sauntered into the hotel lobby and disappeared.

Sam turned in his seat. "Come home with me, Lizzie. And not for hot chocolate or soup."

CHAPTER
TWENTY-FOUR

NOW THAT SHE'D agreed to go home with Sam, the marbles clattered into her tummy. The sexual tension between them was undeniable and the best way to deal with it was to scratch that itch.

Right?

Right! Of course it was. She and Sam would do the nasty and then they'd both know and they could move on with their lives. As friends this time, and drop all the childish animosity.

She parked and got out of the car.

Sam looked at her as if he might say something. Then he turned and walked to the front door.

Standing in Danica's entrance hall, where she'd been so many times before, Elizabeth didn't know whether to leap or wait to be leaped on.

Instead Sam hung his hat and hoodie on the pegs and sauntered into the kitchen. "I know I said no hot chocolate but it's cold as balls out there. Want one?"

"S-sure." It took Elizabeth three tries to get out of her coat. The damn thing kept tangling on her arms and fingers. She hung it on a hook, missed, and bent and picked it up again.

She was losing it. She took a deep breath and then another

and another. This was Sam and nothing would happen that she didn't want to happen.

"I'm going to take a shower." Sam walked down the hallway to the bedrooms. He flipped open a door. "Clean towels and stuff in there."

Okay, this was happening. Sex was happening and she might ruin it all by puking on the floor. First you had a shower, so you were nice and clean and then—

"I'll get you something warm to wear." Sam smirked over his shoulder as if he could read her thoughts.

Leaving her shoes by the door, Elizabeth tiptoed into the bathroom he'd indicated.

Sam appeared in the door with clothes in his hands. He put them on the closed toilet seat. "Here."

Elizabeth went for nonchalant "Yeah! Thanks."

Then she stood there and looked at him.

He grinned. "You need to turn the shower on."

"I know that." Heat flooded her cheeks. "But I'm waiting for you to leave."

Sam grinned. "Right."

The hot water relaxed her a bit and she slipped on the track pants and sweatshirt Sam had left her. Along with a large pair of socks, the clothes looked like they might belong to Danica.

In the kitchen, Sam already had a pot on the stove. Damp hair clung to his head and his long-sleeve Henley found its way to all the fascinating dips and swells of his torso. He also had a pair of track pants on that framed his ass in a way that brought all her nerves rushing back.

She knew what the score was when she'd agreed to come home with him. Not that she was afraid Sam wouldn't respect her wishes, even if she changed her mind.

It wasn't that. The whole idea of Sam wanting to have sex with her stretched incredulity too far. He was gorgeous, famous and a sports star. He could, and frequently did according to the tabloids, have any woman he wanted.

Standing there like a tween wouldn't work either, so she walked closer to Sam.

"I hope you're making your mother's hot chocolate." She peered into the pot.

Sam nodded. "With a few improvements." He flourished a wine bottle. "A touch of red wine and a dash of brandy."

Her laughter sounded forced, because it was.

Still stirring with a wooden spoon, Sam looked at her. "You're nervous."

"Nah." She tried for a dismissive wave and knocked a pot of cooking utensils over. They clattered, clunked and rattled over the granite island and to the floor. She dared to look at Sam. "What gave me away?"

"I'm perceptive." He grinned. His expression grew more serious. "Listen. Let's have our hot cholocate. Watch a little TV and not throw shit around the kitchen."

That sounded like a good idea to her. Elizabeth gathered up fallen utensils. "Isn't there hockey on?"

"Yup." Sam fetched two mugs from the cupboard behind him. The look he gave her was ridiculously hopeful. "We don't have to watch hockey if you don't want to."

"I want to watch hockey." Elizabeth picked the remote up from the couch and flipped on the TV. Surprise, surprise, it was already set to the hockey channel.

Sam put the mugs on the table. "Want me to start a fire?"

"Yes, please." Elizabeth took a seat and tucked her feet under her.

Sam got the fire going and came to sit next to her. He picked up his mug and stretched his legs out in front of him.

On the television, players whirled about on skates, but Elizabeth couldn't tell what was happening in the game. Her awareness was focused on the hockey player next to her who smelled of soap and shampoo.

Sam grunted. "Shit! Where's the defense?"

The humor struck her suddenly. Here she was getting her

panties in a wad about something that showed no signs of happening. And Sam was watching hockey.

Not pretending to watch hockey, mind, but actually focusing one hundred percent on the game.

Not wanting to be that person, she checked out the score on the top left of the screen to see who was playing.

Sam grabbed her feet and put them on his lap. His huge hands almost entirely covered her feet as he held them lightly by the instep.

With the game only being halfway through the second period, and Sam totally focused, it seemed stupid to sit there and stress. Don't get between a Canadian hockey fan and their game. Dad had taught her that much. Elizabeth grabbed her mug and drank her hot chocolate.

Rich chocolate with a slight bitter undertaste cutting the sweet flooded her mouth. "This is so good."

"Told you." Sam glanced at her and went back to the game. "Fuck!" He tossed his hand up. "What the fuck is Hansom thinking? Pass!"

She wriggled her toes in his grip.

His dug his thumbs into her instep, not too hard and not too soft.

Elizabeth hummed her appreciation and got more comfortable on her back with her head propped against the arm of the sofa.

"Want to tell me what's got you jumpy?" Sam kept his attention on the TV.

That and the foot massage made it easier to talk. "A couple of things."

Sam laughed and glanced at her. "Why am I not surprised?" He went back to his game and groaned as someone missed the net. "You don't think you might be overthinking this?"

"It's what I do." She folded her hands on her belly. "It's part of why we fought as kids. I overthink and you don't think enough."

"Hmm." He worked his strong fingers over her feet. "You may have something there. So, a couple of things?"

"First off, I'm not sure what happens after…" Embarrassment won and she couldn't finish that sentence.

Sam gave her a lascivious smile. "You mean after I rock your world and spoil you for other men?"

"Yes." She rolled her eyes and made sure he saw.

Sam stopped massaging and turned to look at her. "I really can't answer that at this point, Lizzie. I can only tell you I'm crazy about you and now that I've admitted that, I'm exercising a fuck ton of self-control to sit over here while you're over there."

"In a purely physical way?"

Sam gave her a hard stare. "You know better than that. If this was some random itch, I'd go and scratch it somewhere else. But this itch is all for you, Lizzie."

"How flattering." She giggled.

Sam shifted to his knees and crawled up the couch until he bracketed her. He lowered his head and kissed her cheek. "Is this okay?"

"Sam." Now he was being silly.

"How about this?" He trailed his lips to her jaw and kissed beneath the hinge. Moving down to her neck, he whispered, "And this?"

Her thoughts scattered and Elizabeth wrapped her arms around his broad, muscular torso.

Shifting his weight until he half covered her, Sam discovered her earlobe and sucked it into his warm mouth.

A soft moan got away from Elizabeth. His mouth, both gentle and firm, heated every place it touched, and the warmth radiated outwards.

Her nipples stiffened and pushed against the sweatshirt.

"That's better." Sam slid his hand under the sweatshirt and covered her ribs with one hand. His mouth lingered over hers. "Shall I kiss you, Lizzie?"

"Yes, please." She speared her fingers through his silky, dark hair and tugged his mouth down to hers. The delicious weight and heat of him made her shift against him, seeking greater contact.

With a groan, Sam sunk into the kiss. His tongue sought entry into her mouth and demanded her response. He kissed her with the same intensity he chased down a puck.

One of his thighs slid between hers, pressing that rock-hard muscle at the junction of her legs. Having danced on the edge of arousal and need for days now, Elizabeth ignited at the touch. She pushed harder against him.

"Damn, Lizzie." Sam broke the kiss. "You're wearing far too many clothes."

He gripped the bottom of her sweatshirt, and doubt crept into Elizabeth's sensual haze.

"Wait." She gripped his hands.

Sam stilled and stared at her. "What? You don't want this?"

"No. I mean, yes I do. But I'm me, Sam."

He raised an eyebrow. "I know exactly who I'm trying to get naked with."

"I mean—" And she took a deep breath. "I'm not any kind of model or actress. I'm a normal girl, and I have lumps and things." Her face was nearly radioactive by the time she'd gotten that out.

Amusement danced in Sam's bright blue eyes. "Lumps and things?"

"Are you laughing at me?" She'd kick his butt if he was.

"Lizzie." He chuckled. The pig. "I'm going out of my mind here because I want to see those lumps and things. And then I want to touch them." He tugged at her sweatshirt. "And after that, I'm going to get my mouth on them. Maybe I'll vary that order, but you get the idea."

"Sam." She gripped his hands tighter. "I'm serious. Under my clothes, I don't look like those girls you normally have sex with." She hated saying it aloud, and her voice dropped to a whisper. "I have a bit of muffin top, and my thighs touch."

Sam stared at her for a long moment, then he sat on his knees beside her and pulled her up to a sitting position.

"First." He raised his forefinger. "Those supermodels and actresses you're talking about. Not as many of them as you seem to think. Secondly." He added another finger to the first. "They also have lumps and things. Nobody's perfect, Lizzie. But thirdly, and most importantly, you're the sexiest woman I know, and I want every bit of you."

"I've seen you." They way he looked when he called her the sexiest woman he'd ever met made her want to wriggle closer to him and make him show her. "You're perfect."

"Really?" Sam hauled his sweatshirt off.

Elizabeth lost the power of speech. Real men weren't supposed to look like that.

Sam pointed low down on his belly. "Here! Appendix scar."

"That's nothing." Elizabeth sneered. Compared to the rest of what he had going on, who even noticed.

"Okay." He half turned and showed her a five-inch scar above his waist. "Clumsy kid got me with his skates."

Elizabeth traced the scar with her fingers. "Did it hurt?"

"Like hell." Sam caught her hand and kissed her fingertips. "I showed you mine."

Enough of her nervousness dissipated for Elizabeth to pull off her sweatshirt. She sucked in her breath then stopped herself and pointed. "Muffin top."

"Damn, Lizzie." Sam's gaze scorched as he studied her breasts and drifted lower to her stomach. He spanned her waist. "You're even better than I imagined." He leaned forward and kissed her shoulder. "And I have a hell of an imagination."

His mouth covered hers in a kiss hotter than the last one.

Slowly he slid his big rough hands up her ribcage and cupped her breasts. "Anything you want to tell me about these?"

Elizabeth's breath came in puffs between kisses. "They're real."

"Thank you, Jesus." He slid her bra cups down and rolled her nipples between his fingers.

Dear God, he did that so well, and Elizabeth moaned. "They're under the influence of gravity."

"Let's see." Sam unhooked her bra with one hand and peeled it from her shoulders. Drawing back, he watched his hands on her breasts. "I'm a massive gravity fan. You're beautiful."

With him looking at her like that, she felt it too. "My thighs are too heavy."

"My shins look like they've been through the plague." Sam ducked his head and sucked a nipple into his mouth.

His hot mouth sent a bolt of lust right to Elizabeth's core and she gripped his head and kept him there. "Sam!" she cried. "That feels so good."

Groaning, he moved to her other breast. He gripped the waistband of her sweatpants and tugged them down.

Elizabeth wriggled to help.

"Your heavy thighs make me crazy." Sam slid his hand between her thighs and cupped her sex through her panties. "Are you wet for me, Lizzie?"

"Yes." She pushed into his hand.

Sam stroked her seam, his thumb circling her clitoris. "Ask me if I'm hard?"

"Are you hard?"

"Find out." He slid his fingers into her panties and touched her. "Touch me."

She needed him naked, and Elizabeth gripped his waistband and tugged. Underneath he was naked and his hard, thick cock sprung free. Elizabeth gripped his hot, velvety flesh.

"Fuck." Sam slid a finger through her wetness and inside of her. "Is this where you want me?"

"God yes." Elizabeth pumped his cock and ground against his finger.

Sam slid another finger inside of her. "This is where I want to be, buried deep inside you."

"Now, Sam." Elizabeth rode his hand.

Sam left her suddenly and lunged for his sweatpants. Out of the pocket, he tugged a condom and ripped open the wrapper.

Elizabeth watched as he slid it over himself. "Sure of yourself, weren't you?"

"Lizzie." Sam dropped on the couch and dragged her closer until she straddled him. "Let's see if we can shut that smart mouth up for a minute or two."

Elizabeth opened her mouth to protest, but his cock was right where she needed it to be.

He flexed his hips and pushed into her.

Not wanting to wait a second more, Elizabeth slid onto him, her body opening and easing his passage until he was buried to the hilt inside her.

Sam flung his head back on the couch. Tendons stood out along his neck. "That feels so good."

"Yes." Elizabeth took a moment to absorb the size of him and how fully he filled her. Then it wasn't enough, and she ground down on him.

"That's it, baby." Sam cupped her breasts and brought them to his mouth. "Take what you need."

She pushed down harder on him, taking him as deep as she could while she rubbed her clit against the hardness of his stomach.

Sam gripped her hips and drove her faster. "Take us both there, Lizzie."

Elizabeth rode him harder. Her orgasm tightened in her belly and exploded through her in waves. She froze and tightened around him.

Flexing his hips, Sam rode it out with her. Then he took control of the pace. "Again."

"I'm not sure I can." She struggled to catch her breath.

Sam drove deep inside her. "I know you can."

His fingers digging into her hips, Sam drove them both forward relentlessly.

Amazingly, Elizabeth felt another orgasm building. This one deeper inside her and sweeping her away with it. It crashed over her in a searing wave.

Beneath her, Sam thrust deep inside of her and came with a shout.

Boneless, Elizabeth collapsed against his sweaty chest.

Sam held her closer and stroked her spine. "Lizzie?"

"Hmm." She didn't have the energy for much more.

"We are definitely doing that again."

CHAPTER
TWENTY-FIVE

ELIZABETH WOKE CUDDLED up next to the furnace called Sam. Turns out a girl could make use of all the stamina that came with a professional athlete.

This morning, she ached in all sorts of delicious places.

Sam lay on his back with his arms tucked behind his head.

For a moment, Elizabeth lay still and waited for the awkwardness to settle in. She waited a few more moments, but it didn't.

This was Sam, not some unknown factor. For the most part she already knew the worst about him, where he came from, what demons rode him, and what each expression he had meant.

The one he was wearing now said he was deep in thought.

"Morning." She snuggled closer to him, tucking her head under his chin.

Sam's arm came around her and tugged her closer. Her libido registered the possibilities of naked Sam and morning sex.

"Morning." He kissed the top of her head. "I have a conundrum."

"You sure do." She cracked herself up. "Your conundrum is nudging my thigh."

"Smart ass." He laughed. "I don't know what to call you now."

"Elizabeth?" She propped her chin on his chest the better to see his sexy, dear face.

"You see when you were being nosy, I'd call you…"

She filled in the pause. "Quizzie Lizzie."

"Right." He tapped her ass. "And when you were getting yourself all riled up—"

"Lizzie in a tizzy. I think I hated that one the most."

"Nah, you only pretended not to like it."

She pinched his side. "I'm one hundred percent sure I didn't like it."

"Tomato, tomahto." He cupped her ass and lingered. "And when you were being crazy or girly, I went with Dizzy Lizzie."

Her irritation was only a vague sense she ought to protest because that's what she did. But with his calloused hand on her butt and his sexy torso beneath hers, it didn't seem worth the effort. "I'm waiting to hear the conundrum."

"Hussy." He flexed his hip. "I've been lying here trying to figure out something suitable to rhyme with Lizzie."

She bit his pec. "Or, and not to keep flogging a dead horse, you could go with Elizabeth."

Sam snorted. "Sexy Lizzie doesn't work, neither does steamy Lizzie. The best I can do is Sizzly Lizzie."

"Dear God, Sam, I will pay you not to use that one." But the idiot could always make her laugh. It was her Achilles heel. That and the incinerating smoke show that was Sam.

Lightning fast he rolled her under him. "You don't like that one?"

"No." She shook her head and laughed at him. "And we both have morning breath."

"Really?" His eyes gleamed with mischief. "Don't you think you should check?"

"No." She tried to wriggle free before he did what she knew he would.

Sam gripped her head. "I think we need to make sure."

The phone rang and stopped him.

Happy with her reprieve, Elizabeth prodded him. "You better get that. It could be your mom."

"Do you want to say hello if it is?" Waggling his eyebrows, Sam reached for his phone. "Tell her her dearest wish has come true."

"I swear to God, Sam—"

His face stopped her.

"What is it?"

"My coach." He looked at her with a face full of longing and dread.

Elizabeth took the phone from him and swiped to answer the call. She held it up for him.

Sam took the phone. "Hey, Coach?"

Elizabeth leaned her ear against the other side of the phone, but she still couldn't make out anything.

Sitting back, she watched Sam's body language for a hint of how the call was going.

Sam stiffened and pushed his hand through his hair.

Ah, shit! But he looked more dumbfounded than pissed or shocked. So, probably not his contract being ended.

He listened to Coach, occasionally nodding and scratching his jaw. There was even some hair tugging tossed into the mix.

"Tonight?" He stared at her as if he needed rescuing. "The thing is, I promised some kids I'd come to their—"

Elizabeth pinched him so hard he jumped and glared at her. "Ask him to give you a second," she whispered.

Her heart pounded so loudly. If she had interpreted right, it was everything he most wanted.

"Sorry, Coach, there's someone at the door. Give me a second." He muted the call and glared at her. "What?"

"Is Coach asking you to meet with him tonight?"

"Umm, no." Sam gave her a boyish grin. "Actually he wants me to come in so they can assess my fitness."

This was better than she'd hoped. "Why?"

"The league has lifted my suspension." His grin broke free. "They want to see how soon they can put me back on the ice."

"Sam!" Elizabeth shrieked and threw her arms around him. This was everything he'd hoped would happen. "You must go."

"But I promised that kid, Mathew—"

"Screw Mathew." And then she felt bad. "Well, not really but I'll explain it to them. Everyone wants to see you back on the ice, and they'll understand." She'd make damn sure they did, and she was fairly certain Chris would be with her on this. "You have to go, Sam."

"Really?"

"Yes." She poked his side. "Now you've left Coach on hold long enough."

Sam unmuted the call. "Sorry about that, Coach, but the guy wouldn't stop talking. So, what time tonight?"

He nodded and ended the call. Then he sat there staring at the wall opposite the bed. "Did that just happen, Lizzie?"

"That happened, Sam." She slid her arms around his waist. "You're getting your second chance, Sam."

He grabbed her and pulled her into a hard hug. "What if I mess this up?"

"You're not going to miss this up." She didn't even have to fake how much she knew this. "Because I've watched you fight for what you want since we were babies, and nobody stops Sam Stone when he wants something."

"I want this, Lizzie." He tightened his hold. "I want this so much. I want to do better."

She wriggled close enough to kiss his jaw. "You will do better, Sam. It might be hard, but remember we've all got your back."

His voice was gruff as he tucked his head into her shoulder. "Thank you, Lizzie."

———

The locker room looked bigger than he remembered it. Sam pulled up his socks and bent to tie his skates. Habit took him through the same order of kitting up.

His name was still written above his stall with all his kit hanging like he wanted it.

"Sam." Kurt, the equipment guy, entered the locker room. "Man, it's good to see you sitting here." He held Sam's favorite stick. "I kept her company for you." He handed the stick to Sam with a roll of tape. "She's been lonely without you."

A couple of his teammates sauntered in, already dressed in practice kit and sweating. Dawson, their captain, nodded to him. "Stoner."

"Tank." Sam nodded back.

Still wearing his skates, Dawson bow-legged it over to him. "You don't look as shit as I thought you would."

"Shit, Tank, don't make me blush." Sam had missed this too. The camaraderie of being part of a group who pit everything they had against an opposing team.

Taking a seat beside him, Dawson studied Sam.

Sam kept taping his stick.

"So, you're back?"

He nodded. "I'm back."

"Gotta ask this, Stoner." Dawson took a heavy breath. "Are we getting the old Sam back?"

"Shit." Nerves attacked Sam. Sitting with Lizzie in his bed this morning, he'd been so sure things would be different. "I fucking hope not."

Dawson barked out a laugh. "We'd like some parts of the old Stoner back."

"Give me a list." Sam lightened the mood with a grin. "And I'll see what I can do."

Dawson chuckled and then looked at Sam's phone. "Someone is blowing up your phone."

What the hell, he had a few minutes anyway and felt sure it would be Lizzie.

It was Lizzie, but not only Lizzie.

Shit! They were going to make him bawl.

Lizzie had sent him photo after photo of Chris's kids. They were on the ice, dressed to play and holding up signs.

Go get them, Sam.

Stone Crush!

And the last one nearly did him in. *We know you can do it, Coach!*

Dawson peered over his shoulder at the photos. He cleared his throat. "That the kids team you coach?"

"Assistant coach," Sam said. "And yeah."

"Are they any good?"

Sam had to laugh. "Nope, they're the crappiest team you've ever seen on the ice. But, Tank, those kids love the game in a way I'm not sure even I did at that age."

Dawson smiled. "Yeah?"

"Every time they touch the puck it's like Christmas. They cheer when they manage not to fall off their skates." Sam thumbed through the photos again. "That's what hockey is about, Tank."

"Yeah." Dawson punched his arm and leaned closer. "Is that your new lady?"

A new photo had come in of Lizzie showing him her tough face. Her sign read *Don't mess up!*

A sappy grin spread over his face. "Yeah, that's my Lizzie."

Dawson studied the photo of Lizzie. "Kind of makes me wish I had one of those."

Sam tucked his phone into his bag. "I need me some ice time."

CHAPTER
TWENTY-SIX

THE NOISE in the Mountain Vista bus was near deafening. Chris's team sat side by side with some of the Mountain Vista residents and they all spoke at the top of their voices, nobody listening to anybody else.

Elizabeth would put up with this and a whole lot more because of where they were going.

"You all right?" Maddy nudged her and gave her a huge smile.

Elizabeth was better than that. Three days of not seeing Sam, only talking to him late at night, and she was more than all right at the prospect of seeing him again. Holding him again. "I'm good."

"Yeah, you are." Chris winked at her before turning to yell at the bus. "Quiet down."

Nobody paid her any mind. They were overexcited. They were going to see the Titans practice, courtesy of Sam, and not a team member would miss it.

She still worried about the number of people, but Sam had laughed at her when she called. "It's a big stadium, Dizzy Lizzie."

Somehow even that name didn't annoy her as much.

The team had a couple of days between games, and apparently the press would also be attending practice.

The bus stopped at the stadium and introspection time ended. Elizabeth helped Chris wrangle Sam's herd in the right direction and into their seats.

The stadium looked kind of naked without all the game hoopla. Dressed in a variety of Titan's jerseys, the team was on the ice, their blades scratching across it.

The coach stood on the ice and yelled, "Close him down! Stay on your man!"

"There he is." Maddy shrieked and pointed. "There's Sam!"

Elizabeth almost gave herself whiplash she turned so fast.

The tribe broke into cheers.

Sam glanced up and raised his stick at them. Then his attention went straight back to what was happening on the ice.

How had Elizabeth never realized how damn sexy Sam was on the ice?

Maddy grinned and nudged her. "You're drooling."

As much as Elizabeth would like to deny it, she couldn't.

A number of other groups of people were scattered around the stadium, including a small press contingent who had their gazes glued to the practice. Marc Gracie sat in their midst, his attention focused on Sam.

She couldn't read anything from his face.

Around her, the children chattered and pointed. They weren't holding any grudges for Sam missing their game.

"Stone!" Coach yelled and they all turned to look. "Close that gap around the net."

Nodding that he'd heard, Sam put on a burst of speed.

"Probably the best skater in the league," Marc Gracie spoke from right beside her.

Elizabeth turned. She hadn't even heard him approach. "Careful, Mr. Gracie, that sounded like a compliment."

"Perish the thought." He gave her the attractive smile that

made him so popular with TV hockey viewers. "He's looking good."

Two compliments in one session. Elizabeth dredged up something to say. "He's been working hard through his suspension."

"It shows." Gracie turned to look at the kids. "Is this the team Sam coaches?"

"Actually Chris is the coach." Elizabeth gestured where Chris and Maddy were wrangling kids. "Sam agreed to help her out."

Gracie watched the practice for a few silent moments. "You know, I think you have the wrong impression of me."

"Oh?"

He flashed his smile, reflected in his deep espresso eyes. "I've never disliked Sam."

As a good Canadian girl, she'd been raised to say nothing if she had nothing nice to say.

"I still don't." His smile widened into something far more genuine. It made her want to like him, or at least give it a shot. "I was playing my last year for the Barracudas when they drafted Sam."

She hadn't realized that. "You played on the same team?"

"For part of a season," Marc shrugged. "Then I got injured and it was my final concussion."

"That's a tough way to have to retire." Sam would hate that. Behind Marc, Chris pulled a face.

"Not really." Marc watched the skaters come close to the glass. "I was getting on and my body was starting to bitch at me about the amount of punishment I put it through." He glanced at her. "And I love what I do now."

They stood in silence for a while. Not wanting to be rude, Elizabeth focused on Sam and tried not to prod Gracie to get to the point.

"Sam was the most talented rookie I'd ever seen," Marc said, his expression softened. "Man, that kid hit the ice and the hair on the nape of my neck stood up. I knew I was watching the sort of player who could shape the way the game is played. He had that Orr magic about him."

None of this jibed with what Marc said about Sam now. "What happened?"

"Sam's head let him down." Gracie tapped his temple. "Great players have the raw skill, for sure, but it's the head that gets them there."

Elizabeth rose to Sam's defense. "Sam has great mental focus."

"It's more than that," Gracie said. "Sam let himself get distracted by the sparkle of being a hockey player. Dating actresses, partying, playing to the crowd."

"Lots of players date actresses and models." She had nothing for the partying and the playing to the crowd. "And I think he's learned his lesson."

Gracie stared at her for a long moment and then shrugged. "We'll see. The reason I ride him so hard is because a waste of that much talent is a goddamned sin." He gestured to the kids around Chris. "How much would any one of these kids give for an ounce of what Sam has?"

Nearly everything. Elizabeth really looked at the young faces absorbing the experience with something akin to worship.

"I've known Sam a long time." She didn't want to give away too much, because although she understood what Marc had said, she still didn't entirely trust him. "He had to fight every day to play hockey. He wanted it bad enough to keep going despite how much his mother desperately wanted him to play some-thing less violent."

Gracie turned to watch Sam with an assessing look on his face. "I didn't know that."

"He's too loyal to his mother to ever say anything, but Sam would get in a car with the devil to get to hockey. He'd beg, borrow and steal to buy his own equipment. My dad was the first adult to help him out."

"And you?" Gracie cocked his head. "Where do you fit in?"

It was a valid question and not one she had an answer for. "I used to provide the Pretty Princess Sparkle Palace that he destroyed with pucks. I was also his first fight on the ice." She smirked. "I won, by the way."

Throwing back his head, Gracie laughed.

"Sam was shorter then," she said.

"Can I quote you on that?' Gracie's eyes still gleamed with mirth.

"Only if you really want to make him squirm."

Still chuckling Gracie nodded. "I'll remember that. So how do you fit in now? Still just friends?"

"Always friends," she said. Gracie was still a journalist.

"You're a great girl, Elizabeth." Gracie shoved his hands in his pockets. "I hope Sam has grown up enough to appreciate what he has. He hasn't always."

Chris closed in on her the moment Gracie turned back to the press cluster. "What did he want?"

Elizabeth summarized her conversation with Gracie.

"Hmm." Chris studied Gracie across the stadium. "You know, he has a point about when Sam first joined the league. There was so much buzz around him."

"There still is."

"Don't snap my head off." Chris rolled her eyes. "I'm not criticizing your precious Sam. I'm saying the buzz around his playing faded and became more about him as a hockey party boy."

She did need to put her hackles down. It wasn't so long ago that she'd have been first in line to take a swipe at Sam. "Sorry."

"Don't get me wrong, he's still one helluva player and every now and again he produces enough magic to keep us all salivating for more."

As she said it, Elizabeth hoped like hell she was right. "I think he's learned his lesson and you'll see a new side to Sam."

When the players left the ice, Elizabeth would have loved to hang around and spend some time with Sam, but she had a busload of little hockey players to get home.

She left a text for Sam and got with herding everyone in the right direction.

They got back home, and she went to the office to finish up some work she'd left hanging while she took the time off to go to Sam's practice. Her dad hadn't objected to her going and seemed a bit better about her spending time with Sam. Still, she didn't want to give her dad anything to bitch at her about.

She got home late and changed into comfy clothes. While she was pouring herself a glass of wine, Sam called.

"Lizzie." He sounded happy. "Thanks for coming today and bringing everyone."

"Are you kidding me?" A warm glow filled her chest and Elizabeth got comfortable on the couch. "I couldn't have stopped them if I tried. And all is forgiven as regards you missing the game."

"I may be missing a lot more of those." He also sounded tired.

Elizabeth wished she could be with him. "Everyone understands. Now tell me how things are going there."

"I'm playing my first game tomorrow."

"Sam!" She almost spilled her wine. "Really?"

"Yup, tomorrow night. Unfortunately it's an away game."

She corralled her disappointment at not being able to attend. "Why unfortunately?"

"I won't get to see you before I go. We're flying out first thing in the morning."

"Ah." She would miss seeing him too. "But I'll see you when you get back, right?"

"Right." He sighed. "Only we go to Pittsburgh tomorrow and then jump a flight to San Antonio after that game. We're only back on Thursday, which is *South Pacific* night."

"Damn." They could always do without her for one night.

"Regardless, I'll only be back in the wee hours of the morning from San Antonio and then we have practice that day. The next night we play here though."

"Friday?"

"It's a home game," he said. "And then you can bet your ass I'm on my way down there to see you."

It seemed like an endless time to wait, but this was Sam's life and giving him crap about it wasn't her way. He didn't make the league schedule up. Besides, this was his chance to make up for lost ground. All that they'd done together had been to get him to this point and now he had to take the opportunity.

Time to show Gracie how wrong he was.

"If you're not too tired, I'll see you Friday," she said. "Or I can come up there and make it easier for you."

He yawned. "I want to see you, Lizzie."

"Me too." She ached to hug him. "I'm so proud of you and I want you to know that."

His voice softened. "Babe."

"You can do this, Sam, I know you can. And I'll be watching all your games. Every. Single. One."

"You will?"

"Damn straight."

He yawned again. "Fuck! I'm tired. I'd almost forgotten how grueling this can be."

"You need to sleep." So maybe it was good he was in his flat in Ottawa, because if he'd been with her, Lizzie doubted she could have let him sleep. "Tomorrow you're going to show everyone who ever criticized you how wrong they were."

"Thanks, Lizzie." He went silent for a moment. "For all of it. Everything you've done for me. I doubt I'd be here without you."

"It was my pleasure." And it really was. She wasn't so sure what that meant for her. Could Sam be done with her? Had he taken what he needed and moved on?

CHAPTER
TWENTY-SEVEN

SAM SAT in front of his stall and got geared up for the Storm game. The Storm was a physical, quick team and wasn't going to give him an easy slide back into the groove.

Neither were the Titans for that matter. Other than Guy and Dawson the team pretty much kept their distance from him. Sure, they were polite and most of them had welcomed him back, but his antics had cost the team.

His suspension had left them with a weakened first line at a critical time in the season. They'd lost ten games in a row and no pro hockey player wanted those sorts of stats. Since that losing streak, they'd made adjustments and clawed their way back into a wild card position. But they wouldn't have struggled so much if he hadn't gotten his ass suspended.

Coach came into the locker room and the chatter died down. "Listen up, boys. Starting offense, Dawson, Larson, Koskinen." Sam cheered along with the rest of the team. "Trapper in the cage."

Sam blew Guy a kiss, which he mimed catching and tucking in his pads.

Coach went on to defense. So, Sam wouldn't be starting. He

should have expected as much, but it still bit. God, he wished like hell he could call Lizzie and bitch. She would know what to say to him.

She'd probably tell him to get over himself. He'd pissed everyone in the Titans corporation off with his antics. He'd have to take his punishment until he could change their minds about him.

Even thinking about Lizzie made him feel better. She would be watching tonight, and he knew what he wanted her to see. Not Sam sulking on the bench because he didn't get to play with the new toys first, but the Sam she believed him to be: focused, motivated and ready to kick ass.

He stood and grabbed his stick. Tonight Pittsburgh was going to see him at his best. If that meant two minutes of ice time or twenty, he would make it count.

"Trapper." He rapped his stick against Guy's pads. "You make sure you give them nothing on your end, and we'll light that lamp up for you."

Guy held his gloves up for a two-handed punch. "Stone Crush!"

———

Sam let himself into his hotel room in San Antonio, a hair after two a.m. His bones ached with the rattling they'd been given tonight.

He stripped of his tie and hung his suit jacket in the wardrobe.

Pittsburgh had been chippy as fuck with him tonight. Not that he blamed them. He'd have pulled exactly the same shit. See how long it took for him to lose his shit.

Ha! The laugh was on them because Sam did not lose his shit. Instead he cost Pittsburgh three penalties. One of which resulted in a power play goal.

His team had been a degree warmer to him postgame. He had sat with Guy during the flight and managed to doze off for a bit. The ability to fall asleep anywhere, anytime was an asset to a hockey player.

It was after three in Ottawa, and Lizzie would be fast asleep. He closed his eyes and pictured her like that. Lizzie slept like a cat, everything neat and tucked away, her hand beneath her cheek.

God he missed her. She would know exactly what to say to make him feel okay with the team's attitude toward him. She could make him laugh about Pittsburgh bearing down on him. And she would say his name in that soft, sweet way that said she had his back.

Unable to resist, he texted her that he'd arrived in San Antonio. She also slept like the dead so nothing—

His phone rang.

Hardly daring to hope, he answered the call.

"Sam." Lizzie's voice reached down the line and touched his bruised body and weary spirit. "I was hoping you'd call."

"It's late for you." He couldn't be more thrilled. Sitting on the bed edge, he toed off his dress shoes and peeled off his socks.

She sighed. "Yeah, but I was thinking about you and I couldn't sleep anyway."

"Leonard is going to be hell to take tomorrow on no sleep."

Her deep Lizzie chuckle stroked velvet fingers down his spine. "Leonard is always hell to take. He's a bit like Dante's Inferno. He has levels of hell."

"Huh." He unbuttoned his shirt and stretched out on the bed. "Is that a pizza place or like one of those smart books that smart girls read?"

"Pizza place on Westminster road. They do a meat lover's to die for."

And like that she had him shrugging off his night and laughing. "Did you watch the game?"

She snorted. "Of course I watched the game. Maddy and Chris came around and we made a party of it."

"Chris and Maddy." He shook his head. Not a pairing that would have occurred to him, but it made sense.

The phone crackled as she moved about. "Yeah, I think they're talking about moving in together."

"That's fast."

"Maybe." Her voice went gentle. "When you know you know. At least that's what I've always believed."

"There's my Dizzy Lizzie, being all sappy and romantic."

"Screw you." She laughed. "The game was incredible, by the way. You were incredible. Even Marc Gracie climbed off your ass."

"Dear God. I think a pig flew past my window."

She chuckled and then said, "You did good, Sam."

"Yeah?" And he grew three feet. "They had it in for me."

"Hey." She got her sassy Lizzie voice on. "You're an annoying guy. Of course they had it in for you."

"Damn, that's harsh and from my girl, as well."

"Your girl?" Her voice got serious.

That shouldn't have slipped out. Sure, Lizzie had been his girl from the moment he stopped wanting to egg her house and wanted to kiss her instead. Still, they'd never had the exclusivity talk or the where-do-we-go-from-here talk. He wanted all those conversations with Lizzie but not at three thirty in the morning. "I mean, if that's okay with you."

"It's weird." She exhaled noisily. "But it's okay with me."

When they were face to face, they could talk about this more but for now, he needed to lighten up. "Does this mean I need to give you a promise ring or you'll wear my jacket?"

"Nah." She went with him on the mood. "But if you have a secret decoder ring, I'd be in for that."

"Hey." He'd forgotten. "Do you remember when they were giving those away in boxes of cereal?"

"Yup. You tried to pour all the cereal out to get them."

Even back then, he'd been a kid with a plan. "I did get them."

"Only the first two." Lizzie sounded really smug. "But I got to the next boxes before you, took out the real ones and put one of the old two back."

"Hey!" Getting the same ring had been horribly disappointing. "Not only did you con me, but you maybe scarred me for life."

"How are you feeling about the game?" She got serious again.

"Honestly." And she was the only place he could be honest. "I would have liked more ice time. Coach is still feeling me out, and the rest of the team is still pissed.

She sighed. "I'm sorry about that, but they'll get over themselves. And you have Guy."

"Yeah, I have Guy. And Dawson is being fairly decent as well."

"Huh." Lizzie paused. "Now I don't feel so bad for thinking he's hot."

"I almost forgot about your little crush." Even knowing his chain was being jerked didn't keep the green-eyed monster in his cage. Dawson wasn't hot. He looked like a lumberjack with that scruff and those barn shoulders. Okay, he might be considered to have something. "How about I rearrange his pretty face for him?"

Lizzie snort laughed. "How did that work for you before?"

"Eh." She had him there, but he didn't have to concede "I play Karlov tomorrow, I mean today."

"Oh." She went quiet again. "I imagine that means you're going to have a target on your back for most of the game."

"I'm going to have a target on my back for the rest of the season, Lizzie." He hated admitting this. "I screwed up and showed my weakness to the whole league. When I lose my temper, I become a liability to my team."

"Sam," she said it soft and sweet like he loved it. "You're not a liability. You screwed up and it was a doozy, but you're also responsible for a fair chunk of your team's points this season."

He wished it was that simple. "My mom called me today."

"How are they?" Lizzie sounded more alert. "I had a text from mine a couple of days ago, but she didn't say much."

"They're in Venice." Sam could picture them there with their sun hats and enormous tote bags, still wrestling with the intricacies of smartphones. "Apparently it's really pretty but smelly."

"Has your mom broken out the Clorox yet?"

That is what made them so special. They knew crap about each other. "Of course she has. Except she has them in wipe form now, so they're lighter and easier to travel with. She even has an on-the-go pack. You know, for those pesky germs that suddenly spring out at you."

"They should have offered her shares in the company by now." A slight pause. "Did she say how my mom was doing? You know with the divorce and all."

"She didn't, babe." And he should have asked. "We don't really talk about stuff like that. Mainly she wants to know if I'm eating right, how many injuries I have, and when I'm going to quit hockey?"

"Still?" An edge of anger laced Lizzie's voice. "I thought she would have reconciled herself by now."

"Nope." His mom wanted to tuck him in cotton padding and keep him safe from the world. "But I did mention we were fucking."

"Sam!"

He had to hold the phone away from his ear.

"You did not do that. Tell me you didn't do that." Lizzie groaned. "Oh God, Sam, please tell me you didn't do that."

As tempting as it was to keep her dangling, he cut line. "Of course I didn't do that but I sure got your attention."

"And now you're about to lose it." She yawned. "Now that I know you're okay, I can get some sleep."

She had been worried about him and that made the center of his chest glow. "I'm good, Lizzie. I'll call you after the game."

"I get back from death by Leonard at around nine."

"I remember." So many things he wanted to say but the moment needed to be right. "Night, Lizzie. Dream of me."

"Night, Sam." She yawned again. "Actually I thought I'd dream about Dawson instead."

CHAPTER
TWENTY-EIGHT

ELIZABETH HADN'T HEARD from Sam since he'd sent her a brief text after the San Antonio game.

Even though Sam had played fine, the rest of the team imploded and went from the four-one lead to lose in overtime four-five.

Dad was in mourning and had been particularly grouchy in the office all of yesterday and today.

For the fifth time that day, he loomed over her desk and glowered. "Where are those quarterly reports I asked you for?"

"On your desk." Lack of sleep several nights in a row stripped her patience. Leonard was channeling Satan and getting steadily worse as the performance date drew nearer. He had been calling her throughout the day. Then she'd waited up until two to hear from Sam and had fallen asleep with the television on.

He'd finally texted her this morning: *Sorry about last night. Caught up here. Will call later.*

It even annoyed her that he texted in curt sentences, like he couldn't take the time to complete one.

A-a-and she needed to sleep. When she sounded like a grumpy old woman in her head, it was time to hit the sack.

Except Dad had other ideas. Five crept closer, and he showed no signs of letting her go for the day.

"Elizabeth," he bellowed from his office. "Where on my desk?"

She damn well refused to get up and point out the reports, which she'd bet a limb were right under his nose. "Right hand side."

The second hand inched closer to the twelve.

"They're not here."

Quitting time. Elizabeth surged to her feet. Maybe she could cast herself on the mercies of Maddy and Chris and spend her Friday night with them. Not obsessing about a man who didn't call. Honestly, did the inability to call come hardwired in the Y chromosome?

"They're right there." She stood in her father's office door and pointed. "Underneath your Starbucks cup."

He looked up at her and scowled. "Where do you think you're going?"

"Home." She wrapped her scarf around her neck and shrugged into her coat. "And then out. It's Friday night."

"But I'm still here." He looked dumbfounded. "And what are Jane and I supposed to eat tonight?"

God, it was so pathetic, she wanted to scream. "I can count on one hand the number of times I've left this office at the end of my working day. This evening I'm tired, and I want to go home, so I am." She buttoned up her coat in short angry snaps of her wrists. "And you and Jane can eat whatever you like. It's about time one of you learned to cook, and if that's too much for you, get takeout."

She strode for the lift with her head held high. The look of amazement on Dad's face had been priceless.

"Your mother taught you better," he yelled after her.

No, her mother had taught her to be a doormat. That with a man like her father it was easier to go with the flow than stand up to him.

It had gotten Mom nothing.

Only after divorcing the miserable old bastard had she managed to go on a trip she'd been talking about for twenty years. Mom was tripping around Venice with Danica, and it was not Elizabeth's job to step into the void she'd left.

Even admitting that buoyed her spirits.

The elevator opened to the parking lot. Her shoes clacked like a triumphant drumbeat on the concrete floor as she went to her car.

She arrived home and parked in her spot. Another boundary conquered, although this one by Sam.

Randy stuck his head out his door. "Yo! Elizabeth! You watching the game tonight?"

"That's the plan, Randy." She let herself into her apartment and was heading for a pair of joggers and Sam's sweatshirt when someone banged on the door.

Chris and Maddy stood on the doorstep, both of them dressed in Titan's gear.

Exactly what she'd been hoping for. Elizabeth yanked open the door.

"Told you so." Chris smirked at Maddy.

"Elizabeth." Maddy's mouth drooped. "You can't go to a hockey game dressed like that."

True that. Her grey A-line skirt and white blouse looked more like a…

Well, like a nun. Wait. "What hockey game?"

"The one we're going to." Chris grinned at her. "The Titans are playing at the Canadian Tire Center so we're going. Tonight he's on home ice for the first time and the entire thing is reaching fever pitch."

God, she wished she could be with Sam right now.

"Go and get dressed." Maddy shooed her. "Wear those jeans and that shirt you wore when they caught you making out with Sam on the JumboTron. That ought to inspire him."

Chris burst out laughing. "If that doesn't do it, nothing will."

Elizabeth headed for her bedroom. She wanted to be with Sam, and if sitting in the stands was the best she could manage, she was still going. "I'll be quick."

"And don't worry about makeup," Maddy called after her. "I can do it in the car."

Elizabeth didn't doubt that for a second. Maddy and her makeup brushes could paint the problems of the world away.

Ten minutes later she sat as still as she could in the backseat of Chris's car while Maddy made her pretty.

"Firstly, we want you to blow Sam away when he looks at you. Close." Maddy did something with her closed eyes.

"Do we want him blown away?" Chris hummed. "I mean, we want to make sure he doesn't lose it in front of the fans. And we can be damn sure the opposition is going to come after him. In none of the games he's played so far, has Sam allowed anyone to crack him. Those Raps dickheads are going to see that as a challenge."

"We have to make sure she looks super hot." Maddy dabbed at her face with something cold. "I've been a Fox for a long time and Sam does his best when he gets to strut his stuff. Seeing Elizabeth looking gorgeous will bring out his swagger."

"Huh." Chris sang along to the radio for a couple of minutes. "How are you doing back there? Team minus five minutes."

"Done!" Maddy clapped her hands. "And some of my finest work."

Elizabeth blinked her eyes open.

The rounded end of the Canadian Tire Centre wove into view, a blaze of lights against the sky.

"Normally I wouldn't do this." Chris edged her car out of the long snake of traffic and into an access lane. "But we'll miss the practice skate if I don't, and that's our best chance of getting Sam to notice her."

"You're so right, babe." Maddy squeezed Chris's shoulder. "Good thinking."

"Let's hope I know the officer on duty." A knot of OPP officers stepped into the road to stop them. Chris slapped the steering wheel. "Score!"

She rolled down her window. "Barker!"

A tall officer stepped forward and his face broke into a grin of recognition as he strolled to the car, hands in his utility belt. "Excuse me, ma'am, but is there a reason for this flagrant disregard of traffic regulations?"

"The best reason in the world." Chris adopted Carol Kane's voice from the Princess Bride. "True love."

Barker peered into the car, did a doubletake on Maddy—because who wouldn't—and glanced at Elizabeth.

Recognition dawned on his face. "Hey! Aren't you—"

"We thought our boy could use a little extra help tonight." Chris winked at Barker.

He broke into a massive smile. "You got it!" He waved them over to an empty parking lot right outside the center. "Take a pew over there and I'll slap an official sticker on your windshield."

"Yes!" Chris pumped her fist. "I owe you, Barker."

He winked at her. "Anything for true love." He nodded to Elizabeth. "Go and give our boy a reason to do good."

Elizabeth couldn't believe Chris. Normally a stickler for the rules, Chris had never have used her position like that.

After parking, Chris leaped out of the car and motioned them to follow. They joined the queue shuffling into the stadium.

The man in front of them turned, spotted her and grinned. "Stoner!" He raised his hands. His friends turned and stared at her. "Tell Stoner the boys from the Bell in Carp say he rocks."

"I'll tell him." Elizabeth's face flushed. This was about as close to famous as she ever wanted to get.

"Move!" Her friend from Carp nudged his friends. "Stone's girl is here."

Chris surged into the gap. "Thanks, guys, we'll get her ringside as fast as possible."

People turned, and Carp guy kept up his shepherding her to the front.

Once through security, they moved with the massive crowd deeper into the center. Chris located their gate and led them through, and then down and down until she stopped right behind the glass.

"Chris." Elizabeth couldn't believe the seats. "These must have cost a fortune."

"Nah." Maddy nudged her from the back. "I called in a couple of favors."

The mind boggled and Elizabeth pinned her with a stare. "What sort of favors?"

"I called Guy." Maddy giggled. "He was more than happy to organize these seats." She winked at Elizabeth. "He likes you. So maybe if this thing with Sam doesn't work out..."

Chris gave Maddy a mock stern stare. "Are you pimping out my friend?"

"Damn straight." Maddy rolled her eyes. "Hockey players make great lays." She nudged past Elizabeth and looped her arms around Chris's neck. "At least that's what all the straight Foxes tell me."

"Nice recovery." Chris hooked her forefingers through Maddy's beltloops and pulled her closer. "So what do they say about cops?"

"The best." Maddy kissed her. "Nothing beats a cop."

Elizabeth took her seat and left them to it. Chris was so happy, and she'd waited so long for someone as special as Maddy to appear in her life.

Seeing the ice made her nervous for Sam. Somewhere down the tunnel to her right Sam was waiting to play.

"Beer." Leonard appeared in front of her. Looking dapper in a sport coat and cravat, he smiled. "You look nervous." He giggled. "Truth to say, we're all a bit nervous, and we thought you could do with some liquid fortification."

"We?"

Leonard pointed.

A group of people stood and cheered. Elizabeth couldn't believe it. She recognized several residents of Mountain Vista, along with a handful of Chris's kids and their parents. There was even a small group of the kids who had dunked Sam at the high school.

She took a hasty sip of her beer. Before she burst into tears. They were all here for Sam.

"Elizabeth." Maddy pinched her arm.

Bodies filled the tunnel and burst onto the ice. The crowd surged to its feet and yelled.

Maddy bounced on her seat. "Do you see him?"

"No. Maybe." Chris scanned the players milling about in the practice skate. "There he is."

Without his helmet, hair flowing, Sam took slow circles around the ice.

"Sam!" Chris banged against the glass. "Sam!"

Elizabeth wanted to crawl under her seat. She really wasn't a limelight sort of girl.

As he crossed the goal, Guy stopped his robotlike jerks and stretches, and yelled at Sam.

Turning so abruptly he made snow, Sam locked eyes on her. He stared and then the biggest, goofiest grin broke over his face.

He beelined straight across the ice for her.

Elizabeth pushed past Maddy and Chris and into the corridor.

The glass in front of her pissed her off and Elizabeth stood as close to it as she could.

"Lizzy." She couldn't hear him well but she lip-read.

Closing his eyes, he pressed his forehead to the glass.

Elizabeth pressed hers to where his pressed and raised a hand.

He took off his glove and put his hand to hers.

"Aww." Someone sniffed from behind her. "It's Sam's girl."

"Nice ass," a man said.

She didn't care.

Sam lifted his head and looked over his shoulder. He mouthed that he had to go.

She nodded and smiled. Then she said loud enough for anyone to hear, "You fucking rock, Sam Stone."

A huge cheer arose behind her.

Laughing, Sam winked at her and skated away.

Halfway through the first period, Elizabeth didn't think her nerves could stand anymore. By the end of the second, she knew they couldn't.

Sam had gotten the ice time he had wished for, but it came at a price. Karlov's teammates were gunning for him. She lost count of how many hard checks he took to the boards.

Once they even tipped him into the opposing bench and he came back up with a split lip.

If it carried on, someone had to die. Elizabeth wondered if Chris had her gun in the car because she couldn't sit there and take any more punishment on Sam.

The only thing that kept her sane was Sam. He showed no signs of losing his temper. He took the checks, managed a few subtle jabs in return, but kept right on playing his game.

The reward for him was one goal about five minutes into the start of the game and another one before the end of the second period.

Someone in the Sam contingent behind her kept her supplied with beer. Trent, who had led them to their seats when she'd come with Sam, kept appearing with another beer.

She was definitely getting buzzed, and her jeans would be way too tight next time she wore them.

Maddy and Chris cheered and hollered and wound themselves around each other.

Elizabeth didn't care. All her attention stayed with Sam. Even when he was off the ice, she watched him on the bench. He didn't look at her, not once, but somehow, she knew that he was aware of her.

As the third period began, the Titans led the Raptors three goals to two.

If she'd thought the first two periods were rough, the third was a revelation in brutality. The Raptors threw everything they had at Sam. High sticks, elbows to the gut, knees to the face, hooking, shoulder checks, tripping.

And Sam took it all. Not that he was an angel. It was hockey after all. But he kept his cool and didn't let them push him into giving away even one penalty.

With five minutes to go, the Raptors scored and brought the game even at three-three.

Then Sam struck. Sam at his most lyrical and dangerous, intercepted a pass and drove it up ice.

The crowd screamed to its feet.

He faked one offenceman and then another. Then he slipped right through the defense, making it one on one with the goalie. Sam put on a burst of speed that set the crowd to raving.

Dawson skated parallel with him on the far side of the goal. Sam lined up his shot, and then passed the puck to Dawson at the last minute. Raptors defense surged at Dawson, who sent a lightning fast puck back to Sam.

Sam tucked it into the top shelf.

The lamp lit. The siren blasted and the Canadian Tire Center went bat shit fucking crazy. Elizabeth along with them.

Hats rained down on the ice.

She hugged stranger after stranger. Tears streamed down her face and made her vision blurry.

Sam had done it and done it in style.

CHAPTER
TWENTY-NINE

CHRIS AND MADDY dropped her off outside Sam's apartment in the ByWard Market. Along with his text asking her to stay in town tonight, he'd texted her the door code, so she let herself in.

A large loft space with exposed ducts and brick walls, the place might have been modern and cool, if it didn't currently have all the appeal of a warehouse.

"Hello," she called, just to hear her voice echo.

One leather sofa squatted more or less in the middle of the cavernous space in front of an enormous television. Even bigger than the one he'd given Danica.

At the far end of the loft, a mattress and base set pressed against a wall. On the floor beside his bed, sat a cell phone charger and a book.

To the right of the door, a huge, modern kitchen occupied the space facing the living area. Top of the range appliances, granite countertops, polished concrete floors, which were warm under her feet so must be heated, made her want to whip up something amazing.

One cup sat on the draining board. An inspection of the cupboards revealed not much more.

In a utility area separated by a wall from the kitchen was Sam's hockey gear. All of it tossed into the room in a malodorous jumble that made her shut the door.

This was not a home.

Sam texted her he would be a while. There was a post-game debrief, and then he had a bit of conditioning work scheduled.

Not knowing what else to do, Elizabeth flicked on the television. Replays of tonight's game, with Marc Gracie holding forth filled the silence.

Next she found clean sheets and made the bed.

Sam's bathroom made her want to girl-squeal. A large claw-foot tub sat in a window box behind one-way glass. You could lie in there and watch the city while you had your bath. A massive shower bristling with stainless steel hardware made her picture Sam in there.

Naked.

And also absent.

Outside the apartment, the city bustled with Friday night partiers. When she found nothing in the fridge, she ventured out.

A nearby shopping center provided her with a big Whole Foods. Elizabeth got enough groceries for a meal and a couple of extras for Sam's fridge. Next she found a liquor commission and stocked up on wine and a six-pack for Sam.

French and English voices rose on all sides of her as Elizabeth hurried through the sinus-numbing cold to Sam's apartment.

She let herself into the apartment and almost tripped over a bag and a coat.

"There you are." Sam strode across the loft toward her. Still in his suit, tie tugged halfway down his chest, he looked grumpy and rumpled. "I thought you weren't here."

"No." Elizabeth indicated her bags. "I went out for a few things."

He took the bags from her and dumped them on the kitchen counter. His mood was a total downer after an incredible night.

Sam turned and grabbed her around the waist. "I'm grumpy because I got home, and you weren't here. I thought you might not have come."

"Sam." She wrapped her arms around his neck. "Where else would I want to be?" Cupping his beautiful face in her palms, she made him look at her. "You were un-fucking-believable tonight."

He flushed and looked a bit coy. "Yeah?"

"You know you were." She called his bullshit. "But your apartment is empty, so I went out for a few things."

"Okay." He grinned.

Their night was back on track. "Okay. Now you owe me a glass of wine."

"Coming right up." He didn't release her but slanted his mouth over hers instead.

His kiss liquefied her bones and she clung tighter to him, wrapping her legs around his waist.

Cupping her ass in his palms, he deepened the kiss and groaned. "I missed you, Lizzie."

"Show me."

Sam whimpered and pressed his forehead to hers. He slid her down his body. "I would love nothing more, babe. But I hurt in every moving part."

She couldn't resist the tease. "Every moving part?"

"Every. Single. One." He let her slide down his body and gave her a lascivious wink. "How about I pop a couple of pain killers while you drink that wine."

"Wow, Sam." She put some sass in her walk as she went into the kitchen. "I thought you were years away from having to pop a couple of pills."

"Ha ha." Sam winced his way out of his jacket and dropped it on the kitchen counter.

He, at least, needed to invest in some stools.

"Here." Elizabeth popped the cap and handed him a beer. "If

you're no good to me as a sex toy, at least tell me about your game."

"Lizzie." He used that tone that made her girl parts wake up. "You keep yukking it up, sweetheart. I'm gonna make you eat those words."

"Sure you are." She rolled her eyes and poured herself a glass of wine. Fortunately, she'd had the foresight to add a couple of glasses to her grocery shop. "Actually start with telling me what's been going on since I last saw you."

Pulling off his tie and tossing it on his jacket, Sam told her about his team practices, the extra hours and effort demanded of him and the games he'd played.

"Were they all like tonight?" Watching Sam take punishment on television made her wince, but seeing it live made her cringe and then want some payback on Sam's behalf.

Sam shook his head. "Tonight was the worst, but there are lots of players with something to prove to me." He hid a yawn behind his beer.

"Why don't we go to bed?" She'd never seen him look so done in.

"I'm sorry, Liz." He yawned again and stood. "I know this is not cool. Me not...you know. But I needed to see you tonight. I needed you."

And what the hell girl could resist that? Not her that's for damn sure. She took her newly acquired toothbrush into the bathroom and got ready for bed. In Sam's dressing room, she dug out a T-shirt and slipped it on.

Sam had dropped to the bed like a felled tree. The clothes he had been wearing lay scattered around the bed like fallen leaves.

Picking up his jacket, Elizabeth read the label. "Sam! This is Armani. You can't drop it on the floor."

Cracking an eye, Sam muttered something that sounded like a sorry and closed his eye again.

Elizabeth tried not to care, she really did, but you didn't leave your clothes on the floor. You especially didn't leave your horribly expensive clothes on the floor. As she finished her wine, she hung up his suit and put his tie away. The shirt she dropped in the laundry.

She shut the door before the urge to make order of his stinky gear overcame her. Nobody needed that kind of punishment. She turned off all the lights and slipped into bed beside Sam.

Beside her, Sam snored softly, dead to the world. City lights painted the loft in multicolored hues while streetlights created intriguing shadows on his back. The sheet draped the perfect globes of his ass.

Yay her! She was in bed with a naked, super-hot jock. And he was fast asleep. There were worse things.

None that her overheated hormones could think of right then.

But they were out there.

———

Early morning light woke Elizabeth.

Sam had kicked off the covers and lay face down and spread-eagle across the bed.

"Shit." In the lightening morning, the full extent of Sam's hard week was revealed. The backs of his legs, where the pads didn't cover were riddled with bruises in varying shades from green to newly gained puce.

She ran her hands lightly over the marks.

Stirring, Sam grumbled and rolled over. He reached for her before he opened his eyes. "Hey."

"You look like you've gone ten rounds with someone," she said, snuggling close to his warm chest.

"Several someones." He kissed her head. "And I feel like it too."

Elizabeth traced the muscles of his chest and then his abdomen. She already knew the hours of work a body like this took, and Sam didn't do it for vanity. Sam's body was a tool.

Speaking of tools, he didn't seem as wiped out this morning.

Elizabeth trailed her hand down to his erection and palmed it.

Sam hissed and pressed his cock into her hand.

Kissing her way down the same path her hand had taken, Elizabeth peered up at him. "All those moving parts still hurt?"

"Not all of them." Sam's eyes were slumberous with desire.

She slid her lips over his cock and took him deep.

Arching his back, Sam groaned. His hands fastened in her hair. "Jesus, Lizzie!"

He grew bigger and harder in her mouth as she worked him over. Hollowing her cheeks and taking as much of him as she could, she used her tongue on the sensitive tip. She learned he liked the flat of her tongue on the underside of his cock, and when she cupped his balls it drove him wilder.

Panting, fingers in her hair, he guided the pace of her mouth.

His balls tightened in her hand.

"Lizzie!" he rasped through clenched teeth. "I'm close."

Close wasn't far enough. Elizabeth wanted all of him, until he came with a shout.

Elizabeth crawled back up him and kissed the underside of his jaw. "Good morning, Sam."

"Christ." He lay lax and sated beside her. "I can't tell you how glad I am you're here."

She laughed, but she was serious when she answered him. "I'm glad I'm here too."

Sam rolled and took her with him. His hard body caged hers as he grinned down at her. "Not as glad as you're going to be." He trailed hot kisses down her neck. "Can't let my girl do all the work and leave my bed not taken care of."

"Am I your girl?" The question popped out of her, and she wanted to kick her ass for sounding so desperate and needy.

Sam raised his head and stared at her. "What kind of question is that?"

"A fair one." Lying against her thigh, evidence that he was

fully recovered got her libido celebrating. "We kind of drifted into this thing, you and I. I'm not even sure what it is."

"There's my Quizzy Lizzie." Sam nibbled her ear and drifted lower. "You like your rules."

Concentrating on rules and boundaries got really hard when Sam put his mouth on her nipple and sucked. Her other breast got his hand.

"You're my girl, Elizabeth Rogers." He grazed her abdomen with his teeth. "My one and only girl for as long as this thing lasts." He pressed her thighs open and settled his shoulders between them. "Meaning I'm the only man who gets to see this pretty pussy of yours." He lowered his head and blew softly. "And the only man who gets to do this."

He lowered his head and showed her. After that, there was slow, sweaty lovemaking filled with laughter and exploration.

Finally, after Sam had shared his huge shower with her, and delayed her coffee even further, they left his apartment hand in hand. And Sam showed whoever saw them that she was his girl.

———

Sam drove her home later that evening. He had Sunday off, and they would spend it at her place. Monday his crazy schedule started again.

"Listen." Sam kissed her hand as he kept his eyes on the road. "The next few weeks are going to be crazy. And if we make the playoffs, they're going to get worse."

"I know." Elizabeth didn't relish the days when she wouldn't see him, but she refused to be that girl. "Make sure you win the playoffs, or my dad will be even worse than ever."

Sam stared at the road, his jaw muscle working.

"What?" She knew that face. Sam had something on his mind.

"I think you should find a new job," he said. "Your dad

doesn't deserve you, and there would be plenty of places that would love to have you."

"Like who?" She had a standard degree in marketing.

"Plenty of companies." Sam intertwined their fingers and rested them on his rock-hard thigh. "Have you ever looked around?"

"Not really." They'd known each other too long for lies. "I drifted into working with my dad, and now I feel like I would betray him if I left." Her laugh had a bitter edge to it. "Not that I think he'd even notice."

"You're worth more, Lizzie." Sam kissed her fingers again. "Promise me you'll look."

"I'll look." That seemed easy enough, despite her churning stomach.

Randy popped his head around the door as Sam parked outside her condo. "Yo! Sam."

"How you doing, Randy?" Sam grabbed his bag from the trunk.

Leaning against his doorjamb, Randy scratched his belly. "Doing good, Sam. You know. Same old shit, different day."

Apparently Randy and Sam were now great buddies.

Sam took her hand. "I hear ya, Randy."

"Great game last night," Randy called as they climbed the stairs to her condo. "Pay no mind to what that shit Gracie is saying tonight."

Despite the light tone, Sam's hand tensed in hers. "He trash talking me again?"

"You know how he is." Randy rolled his eyes and disappeared into his condo.

Elizabeth got the door open.

As she expected, Sam headed straight for the television and flipped to the hockey. Sitting down in front of it, Sam dug his phone out and scrolled.

"Would you like a beer?" Elizabeth stood beside the sofa not really sure whether to join him or not.

Sam kept scrolling. "Sure."

Oh-kay. So much for Gracie not getting to Sam.

Elizabeth took Sam a beer and then surveyed her fridge for something to make for dinner. Calories weren't a problem for Sam, but he did have a quite specific eating plan.

She hauled out some chicken breasts first, then dug through the veggie drawer. The feeding of a professional athlete took a lot of considerate shopping.

"Fuck." Sam had his attention on his phone. The rigid set of his shoulders spoke for him.

Elizabeth got busy on a chicken casserole. She didn't know whether to ask him or leave him alone, and that bothered her. "What is it?"

"Gracie." Sam took a swig of beer. "He's on my fucking case again."

"What about this time?" Elizabeth added carrots, onions and celery to her pot and fried them.

Back to her, Sam stared out her window. Her condo overlooked a small duckpond in the center of the complex and while pretty, was not particularly inspiring. Anger radiated off Sam.

Elizabeth poked at her veggies while her mind raced. His anger didn't bother her as much as her reaction to it. She was dancing around Sam and trying to appease him. When Dad got angry, she did the same. It was something she'd seen her mother do time and time again.

Discomfort with the situation churned in her belly. She was avoiding Sam's displeasure, like she did her father's. She added chicken to the veggies and stirred it around.

Sam's heavy silence hung around her.

"What did Gracie say?"

Shoving his hands in his pockets, he shrugged. "More of the same. How I'm always showboating and how I mistake tricks for talent."

Wow! Gracie hadn't held back. "Sam." She turned her burner

to simmer and approached him. "You have to know that's not true."

He grunted.

Beneath her hand his arm stayed taut and tense. "Why does this get to you so much?"

Spinning, he looked at her as if she'd lost her mind. "I'm human, Elizabeth. Shit gets to me sometimes."

"I know that." She kept her tone gentle, soothing. "But what he said tonight was totally undeserved. You played a fantastic game Friday night, and everyone knows it."

He turned away from her and continued staring out the window. "Apparently not everyone."

"He rides you hard because he thinks you're the most talented player he's ever met," Elizabeth said.

"Right!" Sam's face twisted with skepticism. "Is that what he told you?"

The anger in Sam's face put her on the back foot. She was losing her grip on their conversation, and it made her anxious. The familiar anxiety she'd had growing up around a man she could never please. "Yes."

She carried on preparing dinner. Also familiar, her in the kitchen trying to make sure everyone else was happy.

Sam had never demanded this of her, yet his anger triggered it in her.

"Listen, Lizzie." He strode into the kitchen. "I don't want you to take this the wrong way, but I think I should go back to the city tonight."

"Oh?" Only a bona fide people pleaser could manage to keep the hurt off her face like Elizabeth did.

Sam rubbed at his nape. "Gracie got under my skin tonight, and I'm not even sure why."

"Okay." She wanted to ask him to stay. Invent ways in which she would make it all right for him to stay. And that was precisely the problem.

"Look at me, Lizzie." He got closer to her.

Elizabeth stirred her pot and then did as he asked.

"This is not on you," he said. "But I'm in a stinking fucking mood, and I want to punch something, or pound a treadmill."

She managed a nod. Part of her did get it. "I understand."

And even in that she missed the mark on honesty.

"Cool." Sam kissed her on the mouth. "I'll see you soon."

The door shut behind him, and Elizabeth flipped off the burner. "No point in making a man dinner that he's not going to eat."

Her mother's voice rang in her mind. *Daddy is busy. Daddy's had a hard day. Daddy needs time to relax.* All the excuses made up year after year to deal with a difficult man. Was she signing up for more of the same?

Elizabeth sat on the sofa and picked up Sam's half-empty beer. She pressed her mouth to where he'd had his and took a sip.

Her people pleasing had led her here. She buzzed about making the world better for other people. She did it for her family, for Leonard, for the animal shelter, even for the women's auxiliary. And now she was doing it with Sam.

A knock at the door stopped her nasty mental meanderings toward a distressing conclusion.

Elizabeth opened the door.

"I'm back." Sam stood on the other side looking sheepish.

She held on to the door. "I see that."

"I got halfway home and turned around." Sam dug his hands in his pockets. His breath made vapor clouds in the air. "Then I realized that even though I was upset, the person I most wanted to be upset around was you."

Elizabeth swung the door open. "Good answer."

CHAPTER
THIRTY

SAM SENT a text to Lizzie before putting his phone away. She really liked those GIF things and he liked blowing up her phone with the ones of him.

"Hey, Stoney." Novotny chucked his socks at Sam and said in his heavy Czech accent, "Stop sending dick pics to your girl-friend. They cameras cannot focus that small."

Sam faked confused. "Is that English you're speaking there, Novo?"

"Varg you."

Sam pinched the socks between his forefinger and thumb and tossed them on the rookie next to him. "No thanks, Novo, Lizzie doesn't share."

"Jesus." The rookie went green and pushed the socks away. "Does he ever wash his feet?"

"Nah." Sam loved messing with rookies. They'd believe anything. That kid was a goddamn rocket with a wrister on him that inspired poetry, but still a rookie. "He only wears one pair for the entire season, and never washes them. They bring him good luck."

The rookie rolled his eyes. "Bullshit."

"You kees your ma with that mouth, Rookie?" Novo joined

the action.

"I thought Trapper was kissing the rookie's ma." Dawson chimed in. "They're about the same age, aren't they?"

Guy looked up and grinned at Dawson. "Varg you, kid."

Coach walked in and the laughter died. "Okay, boys. They're fast and their first line has a wicked breakaway. Starting tonight, Dawson, Stone…"

Sam stopped listening. The temptation to text Lizzie almost won out, but Coach would lose his shit and Sam needed to get his head in the game.

He was back in the starting lineup.

———

Elizabeth arrived at work on Tuesday and fought the sinking feeling that had only gotten worse in the last few weeks.

It was as if by acknowledging she didn't want to be there, she'd made it so much worse. She'd promised Sam she would look for something else, but so far, she'd not upheld her promise.

She was scared. Okay, there she'd said it. Not so much scared that she might not find something, but scared that she would. Then she would be out of excuses to hide behind her job.

Her relationship with her dad had also deteriorated. She still went around to the house when she could, but last Saturday night she had spent with Sam.

As she was putting her bag away, Dad walked past her desk.

"Good morning," she called after him and got a grunt in reply. Maybe she would look online for something else today. Looking wasn't committing.

Midmorning, Dad came out and dropped a large envelope on her desk. "I got these from your mother this morning."

The logo on the envelope belonged to Mom's lawyer. This must be the reason for Dad's bad mood. Maybe he'd even had them for a while now and they had contributed toward making him extra difficult. "I'm sorry, Dad."

"About what?" He blinked at her.

Maybe she'd gotten it wrong. She slid the papers out of the envelope. "She sent you divorce papers."

"Yes." He shoved a hand in his pocket. "That's what happens when two people get divorced."

Clearly, she was missing something. "Why are you giving them to me?"

"You're my secretary, aren't you?" He scowled at her.

"Office administrator." Although why she bothered to make the distinction he didn't respect was beyond her. "And I'm also your daughter. The divorce is between you and Mom."

He made a sound of frustration. "Call my lawyers and set up a meeting. Or send them an email or something, but also tell them this is unacceptable. Tell them to let her lawyers know if she wants a fight, she's got it."

All Elizabeth could do was sit there and blink at him. She had nothing. Not one coherent thought, and therefore, no chance of forming a word. "Huh?"

"I've got meetings all morning." Dad threw his hands up in exasperation. "I need you to do your job and call them and tell them what I told you about that woman."

"That woman is my mother."

"I know that." He sneered. "And I'm your father, and more importantly, your boss."

"Holy fuck." It had gotten away from her before she could stop it.

"What did you say?" Dad's face went tight with disapproval. "Show some respect around me."

"Holy. Fuck." This time she'd said it on purpose. "If I didn't know you as well as I do, I would ask if you're serious. But you absolutely are."

"Of course—"

"I'm not calling your lawyers about your divorce from my mother." She flicked the envelope to the floor. "That's my mother, whom I respect and love."

Dad jabbed a finger at her. "Now, you stop right there. You work for—"

"No, no I don't." She grabbed her purse from the drawer. There wasn't much on her desk that she cared about other than the photo of her mother, tucked away in her drawer. She grabbed that and shoved it in her purse. "I'm not working here another minute."

"What is this?" Dad looked so smug she wished she'd chucked the envelope at him. "Is this you showing me how independent you are? You got yourself a big time, big deal boyfriend and somehow you think that makes you worthwhile. But it—"

"I know, I know." Christ, she could script it herself. "It doesn't make me worth crap. Not in your eyes anyway." Hands shaking, she shrugged into her coat. "I don't happen to agree with you. I think I'm worth way, way more. And I know I'm worth more than you have to give."

Anger took her down the elevator and to the street. And then she ran out of steam.

"Excuse me." An irate man in a suit sidestepped her. "You're in the way."

She was in the way. Tears flooded her eyes, and she couldn't get them to stop. After all she'd done for Dad, it still wasn't good enough.

Her entire life she'd tried to make him see her, love her, maybe be proud of her. What a massive fucking waste of time.

That thought shook loose the sobs, and she started to really cry. She kept that up all the way home.

———

"Damn." Chris shook her head for about the twentieth time. "You actually did it."

Elizabeth sipped her wine. "Yup."

She had called Chris from the parking lot.

Now she was having an emergency meeting at a pub around the corner from her condo with Chris and Maddy.

It had taken Elizabeth two glasses of wine before her hands stopped shaking. Whether from anger, fear or a combo, she wasn't sure.

Maddy beamed at her and squeezed her hand. "Well done, you. You cut the toxic thing out of your life."

"Yes, but she still has to eat." Ever the practical one, Chris looked concerned. "And he is her dad, so this could make family dinners really uncomfortable."

"There won't be any family dinners." Elizabeth's wine buzz kept her from panicking. "Because I'm the only one who cooks, and I'm not doing that anymore."

"What made you do it?" Maddy tilted her head. "I mean after all this time?"

Across the bar, a studly suit kept flexing and chin jerking in case Maddy happened to look in his direction.

Elizabeth would have felt more sorry for him if he hadn't been at this for the best part of an hour. At some point, you had to take the hint and give up. "I'm not sure."

Hockey was playing on the screens over the bar, but it wasn't a Titan's game, so it got limited attention.

"Sam has been talking to me about it a lot," she said.

Chris sent Maddy a meaningful look.

"What?" Elizabeth didn't like that look. She also didn't like her best friend sharing secret looks with someone else. This was the downside to Chris being in a relationship. "What was that look?"

"Nothing." Chris sucked at playing innocent, so Elizabeth stared her down.

"It's nothing." Chris shrugged. "A thought I had."

"Well, obviously you've shared that thought with Maddy." Elizabeth tried not to let her hurt show. Chris and Maddy talking about her felt like a betrayal. "So whatever it is, I'd like you to share it with me."

Maddy touched her arm. "We weren't speaking behind your back. Chris loves you, and she shares stuff about you with me. Nothing she wouldn't say to you, or any of your secrets."

"You're concerned about me?" The sting lessened, but still, it smarted a bit. She felt left out. "That I won't get another job?"

"You'll get another job," Chris said. "How many people have tried to steal you away from your father?"

"A few." She didn't want to sound conceited, but she planned to start with those people, first thing in the morning. Burning sense of justice and liberation aside, she did still have to pay the rent. "If it's not that, then what?"

"I've been saying for years that you should resign." Chris fiddled with the stem of her glass.

"And?"

"And now you have."

Elizabeth still didn't see where she was going. "So, you should be glad that I finally took your advice."

"I am glad. I think it's way past time," Chris said. "But it's not my advice you took, is it?"

"What?" Was Chris mad because Sam had said it? "Sam only said what you'd said before."

"Exactly." Chris grimaced. "But you only listened when Sam said it."

She must have been missing something. "I wasn't ready before."

"And now you are?"

Elizabeth shrugged. "Clearly. That's the reason we're having drinks."

"Then let me make it absolutely clear what I mean," Chris said.

Elizabeth nodded, because that would make the evening a lot nicer.

"I'm worried you're swapping one dominant male figure in your life for another," Chris said.

That robbed Elizabeth of thought.

Chris filled the silence. "You've always twisted yourself into knots to please your father. I want you to be sure you're not doing the same thing with Sam. Trying to please him."

"What?" Elizabeth found her voice again. "Sam and my father are nothing alike."

"It's not about that." Expression grave, Chris edged closer to her. "It's about you. It's about how you do for Sam what you do for everyone else, you put their needs in front of your own."

"That's not..." Okay, she might have had a similar thought. But this wasn't the same. "I resigned because I'd finally had enough of my dad's bullying. And yes, maybe being with Sam gave me the impetus to do that. And maybe I do prioritize Sam's needs from time to time. I do the same for you, and I don't notice you complaining."

Chris and Maddy shared a look, and she wanted to smack their heads together.

"Sam is grateful for what I do for him." She struggled to find the right words. "And when he wants something, he goes after it. He's driven and motivated, and maybe some of that has rubbed off on me."

Maddy gave her a soothing smile. "We're not saying you're changing one bad situation for another; we are asking you to think about it."

Now Maddy and Chris were the "we" and she sat on the outside. It hurt and it definitely killed her buzz. She dropped some money on the bar and stood. "I'm going home."

Chris stood with her. "Don't go away mad, Elizabeth."

"Of course I'm mad." She and Chris had been friends for so long. She thought Chris knew her better than that. "You basically told me I'm a doormat."

"I didn't say that." Chris threw her hands up. "I knew you would react like that, which is why I never said anything before."

"Well, excuse me." That came out a bit loud, and heads

whipped their way. "Firstly, I don't like being discussed by you two like I'm the group basket case."

"We didn't—"

"I get that you two are together, but the three of us are friends as well, and from that point of view, it wasn't right. And secondly, I don't appreciate that you've taken what should be a celebration and turned it into some kind of intervention."

Grabbing her coat and purse, she strode for the door. Her mad took her all the way home, and it was only when her condo door shut behind her that she deflated.

Still in her coat, she dropped into a heap on her sofa. She'd lost her job and her friend all in one day.

She dug out her phone. No missed calls and no messages. She'd left a message for Sam earlier asking him to call her because she had big news.

When she dialed him again, it went straight to voicemail. "Er...hi, it's me. I guess I'll tell you my news like this. I quit my job. With my dad. I quit." She went to end the call. "Oh, and I had a big fight with Chris tonight." She stopped herself before she ended the call again. "And I hope you had a good game tonight."

She ended the call and sat on her sofa. Watching TV didn't appeal, and more wine might make her weepy. Mom would only worry, and Jane wouldn't give a crap.

A tsunami of self-pity beckoned. Whenever anybody needed her, she went out of her way to help them. Now when she needed a shoulder, she was huddled up on her sofa and all alone.

And her boyfriend was too busy too.

Okay, enough of that. She got up and took her coat and boots off and put them away. Then she got ready for bed and made herself a cup of tea.

Sam would call as soon as he could. It wasn't his fault he was busy and lots of people wanted a piece of him. It came with the territory of being part of his life.

CHAPTER
THIRTY-ONE

BLEARY EYED, Elizabeth stumbled to answer her front door the next morning.

She opened the door to a frigid blast of morning air.

"Lizzie!" Sam stood on her doorstep, grinning at her. In one hand he had a huge bunch of flowers and in the other a bottle of champagne. "Good morning."

"Morning, Sam," Randy yelled from below. "Great goal last night."

"Thanks, bud." Sam crowded her back into her apartment. "Damn it's cold out there."

"What's all this?" Elizabeth followed him into her kitchen where he put the champagne and flowers on her counter.

"First off, champagne for my kickass girlfriend who told her asshole dad to shove his job." He snatched her off her feet and gave her a smacking kiss. "I wish I'd been there to see it. I want a full action replay later." He kissed her again, slower this time and hummed against her mouth. "I missed you and here you are all warm and half naked."

"I missed you too." Elizabeth wrapped her arms and legs around him and held tight. Things didn't seem so bad with Sam there, and she clung to him.

Holding her as if she weighed nothing, he tightened his hold. "I'm sorry about your fight with Chris, but you guys love each other, and you've been friends for too long not to sort it out."

"Yeah." Elizabeth unwrapped herself and slid to the floor. "What time is it?"

"Early." He grinned. "But I couldn't wait any longer to see you."

Sam's gaze shifted to the side. Ah hell, she knew what that meant.

"What?" She caught his gaze and held it. "What did you do?"

"Umm…" He considered lying—she read it on his face—and then he cleared his throat. "I…er…that's what the flowers are for."

Now he had her undivided attention. "What did you do that would require flowers?"

"Before I answer that, I have a thing tonight." Sam gave her a charming grin as he tried to two-step his way out of her firing line. "It's a dinner thing, at Dawson's house, for the team. I can bring a date. You like Dawson."

Elizabeth crossed her arms. "That will depend on what you've done."

"Well, you know we traveled back late last night?" Sam rubbed his nape. "It happened then."

"What happened?" Elizabeth braced for trouble and folded her arms.

"Okay." Sam blew out a breath. "My mom's been calling, and we've been missing each other. I called her when I got in last night, and it was late."

With Danica in the story, Elizabeth had a strong suspicion coffee might not be enough.

Sam shoved his hands in his pockets. "I was chatting to Mom and I may have…pretty sure I did…let something slip."

"About us?" Elizabeth scattered coffee grounds all over the counter. *Please, let him say no.*

Sam nodded. "I said something about us, and she caught it right away."

"What did you say?" By her calculations, she had three minutes to get coffee down her before her mother called. Mom never called anyone before nine in the morning, but it was creeping close to that.

"I let slip that you'd been at my place, and then she put two and two together." He tried to look innocent. "They'd already seen the KissCam thing."

"Yes, but we convinced them that was a joke." Elizabeth eyed her phone as if it might bite. God, their mothers would be all over it. There would be no end. She could see Mom and Danica right now, picking out baby clothes in France together.

"I came clean." Sam shrugged. "I said you were my girlfriend now."

"Dammit, Sam!" She barely waited for her coffee to finish brewing before she had the cup to her mouth. "Do you know what you've done?"

"I know." He winced. "But on the plus side, we don't have to worry about them finding out anymore."

She got more caffeine down her. "You know they'll be heartbroken when we break up."

"When we break up?" Sam lifted a brow at her. "What makes you think you're getting rid of me?"

It seemed too soon to be having that conversation, so Elizabeth sidestepped instead. The idea of breaking up with Sam made her chest ache. "I can always distract my mom with the news about resigning. Has anybody been particularly mean to you on the ice lately?"

"Hey!" Sam rounded the island. "We have a good thing here, Lizzie." He caged her against the counter. "And I know it's early days, but this feels right to me."

How was she supposed to keep her head when he said shit like that?

"Let's not put an expiration date on this before its time." Sam leaned his forehead against hers. "And now you have no reason not to be my date tonight."

"Maybe I'm mad at you."

"Maybe." Sam took her mug from her and put it on the counter. "In which case, I have all day to get you in a better mood."

———

Dawson lived about forty minutes outside Ottawa in an upmarket suburban neighborhood. It didn't seem the sort of place to find a single hockey player. It was more of a family neighborhood. "Is Craig married?"

"Nah." Sam slowed for some kids walking down the road. "But he has this long-term girlfriend. She threw a shit fit about getting married, and they bought this place last year."

"But they didn't get married?" One huge house after another faced the quiet, tree-lined streets.

Sam shook his head. "They're engaged now, but if you ask me, Dawson is dragging his feet. I think he bought this place to placate her."

Elizabeth didn't know who she felt most sorry for. "How long have they been together?"

"Eight years." Sam found the right house and parked behind a large SUV.

"He should be sure by now." She didn't like the idea of Dawson stringing some poor woman along. "He should marry her."

"He's not sure."

Of course Sam would defend a guy, especially a teammate. "How much more of her life does he want to take before he makes up his mind?"

He blinked at her vehemence. "She doesn't have to stay."

"She loves him."

"You haven't even met her."

Elizabeth took a stand for women everywhere. "No woman stays with a man for eight years and supports his career if she doesn't love him."

"Plenty do." Sam pulled a face. "There are women who like to bag themselves a trophy husband."

"That's insulting."

"It's reality." Sam snorted. "And anyway, I think he stays with her because he wants her to be the one, but she isn't."

"How do you know that?"

Sam took her hand and kissed it. "Because when you meet the right girl, you won't waste eight years and take the chance someone else puts a ring on it."

That shut her up.

"You coming?" Sam stood by her open door.

Elizabeth wriggled out of the car and took the hand Sam offered. It marked their first official outing as a couple with Sam's team.

The door was unlocked, and they entered a vestibule and hung up their coats and toed their boots off. Finding space proved a bit challenging. The party was much bigger than Elizabeth had been expecting.

"Do I look okay?" Maybe she should have opted for something smarter than jeans.

Sam tugged her to him and kissed her. "You look perfect."

The inner vestibule door opened, and Dawson stood there. He was much better looking without helmet hair. "Stoney." He nodded to Sam and gave her a devastating kneetrembler of a smile. "It's nice to meet you, Elizabeth."

She burbled something semi-coherent and got a hard look from Sam.

Not seeming to think anything of it, or maybe he was used to women falling over their tongues when he was around, Craig put his arm around her shoulders and led her into the party.

"Don't worry about these assholes." He bypassed a group of

his team members. "I'll introduce you to the important people first."

Sam followed behind them but got waylaid by the raucous greetings of his teammates. They acted like they hadn't seen each other in months.

Craig led her to three women.

Elizabeth was relieved to see two of them were in jeans and a sweater as well. All three of them were drop-dead gorgeous.

"This is Kathy." Craig put his arm around the waist of a tall, slim brunette who could have been a cosmetics model.

Elizabeth resisted the urge to stare. "Hi."

"You'll take care of Sam's girl, won't you, babe?" Craig kissed her temple.

Kathy gave him a tight smile. "Sure."

She introduced the two blondes with her. The shorter, fairy-like one was Chloe, and the taller one with a Sports Illustrated body was Lisette, and from Quebec judging by her accent.

"So, you're Sam's girl?" Lisette smiled at her, but it didn't quite reach her eyes. "I'm married to Pierre Beliveau. Defense."

Elizabeth assumed she meant Pierre played defense.

"Chloe is married to Greg Fletcher." Kathy pointed to a blond guy talking to Sam. "Wing."

Elizabeth smiled and nodded. "Lovely."

"Okay?" Sam brought her a glass of wine and leaned down and kissed her cheek.

"Fine." She waved him away. "Go and talk hockey. Or whatever else you do when you're not on the ice."

"You know what else I do when I'm not on the ice." Sam leered and drifted away.

The women with her all tittered.

"I remember when that was Greg's favorite thing too." Chloe sipped her drink. Her laugh sounded brittle.

"They really do talk hockey," Kathy said. "We're lucky there isn't another game on, or they'd be watching that."

Elizabeth tried to read the tone. "Well, I suppose if they were doctors, they'd be talking about the bits they cut off people."

"Maybe." Lisette finished her drink and stared across the room at one of the players.

A dark-haired man with a square, stubbled jaw stood and fetched a glass of wine. Pierre, she presumed.

"What do you do?" Elizabeth threw the question to the group.

Kathy spoke first. "I was in advertising, but I had to give that up." She indicated Craig with her glass. "Craig got traded, we moved here. There doesn't seem to be much reason to get another job when it could happen again."

"Craig's getting traded?"

"No." Kathy stared at her, and Elizabeth got the impression she'd missed the point.

"I have four children," Lisette said.

"Wow." That would keep anyone busy. "That's a full-time job right there. Boys? Girls?"

"Four boys." Lisette drained her glass. "And yes, they do all play hockey."

Okay, not what she was going to ask but fine. "Great."

"I don't work." Chloe gave her a neon-bright smile. "I do my best to spend all the money Greg makes."

Elizabeth joined in the laughter, but she wasn't so sure Chloe was joking.

"Do you have a job?" Kathy turned back to her.

"Actually, I was working for my father." Elizabeth wished her wine would magically replenish itself. The conversation felt like work. "But I resigned. This week actually."

Chloe and Lisette nodded.

"I need to start looking for something."

Kathy stared at her. "Why bother?"

"I have to eat." Elizabeth had the feeling she'd missed the point again.

"Your job is hockey now," Chloe said. "And it's full time. All day. Every day. You are now a piece of Sam Stone's hockey equipment."

"I don't think—"

"Chloe's exaggerating." Kathy threw Chloe a look. "But if you and Sam are serious, then it does mean your life will take second place to his. You may as well get used to it now."

Elizabeth wanted to argue with them, but all three of them were veterans. She didn't feel like she had a leg to stand on.

"Guy." She spotted him heading toward her and nearly jumped into his arms.

He arrived with a huge smile and a kiss for everyone. "Come and rescue me," he said to Elizabeth. "All the guys want to do is talk hockey, and Sam told me you resigned your job."

"Sure." Elizabeth jumped at the chance to get away from the happy trio.

"She's my blind." He winked at Kathy. "Don't tell anyone."

Guy led her over to the bar and refilled her wine. "You okay now?"

"Was it that obvious?" God, she hoped she hadn't been standing there looking shell shocked.

"I know those ladies." Guy led her to a sofa and sat beside her. "I've been doing this a long time, and there are two main kinds of hockey wives."

"You make it sound like a club."

"Nah! It's a team." He stretched his long legs out in front of him. "I caught a bit of what they were saying to you, and they're right, to an extent. What we do, Sam, me and the other guys, it's consuming. You can't get to this level without it being that way."

Elizabeth understood that. "I grew up with Sam, remember?"

"So you know what he's sacrificed and how hard he's worked. That's difficult for some of the partners to get," Guy said. "And they can get resentful."

"It can't be easy for them." Chloe, Lisette, and Kathy were speaking freely now that she was gone. None of them looked happy. "Nobody wants to feel like their needs are second place."

"Some women marry the athlete not the man, though." Guy watched the women too. "They marry for the status and resent what that means."

"You're saying they don't love their partners?" Elizabeth was getting outraged for women everywhere.

Guy grinned at her. "Not all the wives are like that, babe. A lot of them are great women who keep their man grounded. Those ones tend to want to stay out of the limelight. Kathy wants to be Mrs. Craig Dawson, and she's bitter as hell that Craig doesn't want the same."

"Sam told me."

"Chloe hates Greg's guts. And he deserves it. He screws around on her."

Elizabeth looked over at Greg. "Does Chloe know?"

"Sure she does." Guy shrugged. "And she really doesn't care." He motioned Lisette. "And Lisette misses her family and hates Ottawa."

"Why are you telling me this?"

"Because you looked like you were about to cut and run, and I wouldn't want you to do that before you'd met the other side of this equation."

Guy introduced her to another couple of wives. Like he said, they were nice women with genuine affection for their spouses.

Shortly after that, Sam claimed her and kept her by his side for the rest of the party.

It was only later, lying next to a sleeping Sam that Elizabeth identified the troubling feeling. She was way, way, way out of her depth.

CHAPTER
THIRTY-TWO

ELIZABETH OPENED her front door to Peter the next day. She hadn't seen him in weeks and weeks. He looked shorter than she remembered. As always, his hair was neatly combed in a side parting as if his mom had dressed him and sent him out to play.

She used to think it was endearing.

"Hi." Peter looked at her sweatpants and frowned. "Are you running late?"

"Late?" It hit her all of a sudden. "Oh shit! Our lunch."

Peter's face tightened in disapproval. "You forgot."

"I'm so sorry." She had forgotten. Totally and completely.

"Well. Never mind." Peter sighed. "I can wait while you change."

Elizabeth wanted to cancel, but she couldn't think of a reason. She didn't even have the work excuse, so she trailed into her bedroom and changed.

She could have invented an appointment or something. Or, and here was a groundbreaking idea, she could have said no. Tugging on jeans, she wanted to slap herself.

Not surprisingly Peter took her to "their" restaurant. It was an upscale steakhouse that had only become theirs because Peter liked it and always brought her there.

He ordered them a bottle of San Pellegrino and sat back. "How are you?"

"Great." She flagged down the waitress and ordered a beer. "You?"

"Great." He gave her a tight smile as if she had erred in some way. "I went past your work. Apparently you resigned?"

"Yup." Peter had been on the receiving end of her work complaints for years. "I finally did it."

"So, what's next for you?" He leaned forward on the table.

"I'm not sure yet." She shrugged. "I have some money saved. I want to look around and do something that excites me. You know?"

His smile told her he did know. Before they'd been tepid lovers, she and Peter had been friends, good friends. They'd wanted to stay friends when the romantic part of their relationship had withered.

As lunch progressed, Elizabeth relaxed. He had some good suggestions for where she should start her job hunt.

Peter sat back and pushed his plate away. "I hear you're seeing Sam?"

"Um...yes." Elizabeth's face heated. "I bet that surprised you."

"It did." Peter fidgeted with his cutlery. "I thought you hated him."

Elizabeth forced a laugh. "So did I."

Peter arranged his napkin. "I take it that means you and I..."

"You and I?" Elizabeth hadn't thought of her and Peter as a couple since they'd broken up, and she had gotten the definite impression neither had Peter. "We're not an us."

"That's what I thought." Peter tittered. "But I wanted to ask anyway. In case you had, you know, changed your mind."

Weird. If Peter was trying to say he had harbored some unrequited feelings for her, she was going to have to call bullshit. She hadn't even thought he cared that much when they were together. "I haven't. I'm with Sam now."

"Okay." Peter dug out his wallet and put a smile on his face. "This was fun. We should do it again."

"Um...sure."

Since it was Thursday, Elizabeth went to *South Pacific* rehearsal that evening. With time running out, Leonard was so stressed he was nearly going into orbit. Elizabeth had weathered a show before with him. Last year in fact, *Sweeny Todd,* and Leonard had almost ended up as a victim.

"How's it going?" Carol popped into the rehearsal room.

Carol had also lived through *Sweeny Todd.* "Not bad." Elizabeth looked up from supervising the costume sewing. "Tonight, we've only had four eruptions and one walk out."

"Progress." Carol looked impressed. "And why is Agnes wearing a muumuu?"

"Because the alternative was a bikini."

"Good call." Carol motioned the hall outside the rehearsal room. "Listen, I actually popped in to chat with you. Got a sec?"

"Sure." Elizabeth made sure the set decorators were still happily adorning everything with garish crepe flowers.

A short woman, and square, Carol looked like she got straight to the point. And she did. "I heard a rumor you'd quit your job."

"I did." Elizabeth should have known word would get around.

Carol crossed her arms. "You in the market?"

"Sure." She'd had a depressing afternoon filling in her CV on an online job site. There wasn't much in her part of the world. She might have to move closer to Toronto.

"Would you consider us?" Carol looked dead serious. "We have an opening here, and I think you'd be great for it. Part fundraising, part administrator and part organizing this sort of thing." She motioned the rehearsal.

Leonard's voice rose from the other side of the door. "I need to *fe-e-el* the sun on your back. I need to *sme-e-ell* the sea breeze."

"Don't we all." Carol rolled her eyes. "The salary's not great." She grimaced. "But we do feed you with the residents, and I think you have what it takes to work here." She grinned. "And there is always the opportunity to nap."

Elizabeth's head reeled a bit. She'd never thought of turning her spare time activity into a job. Despite Leonard, she did like working with the residents. She loved their stories and their life experience. "Can I think about it?"

"Of course." Carol patted her shoulder. "I'll email an official job description with salary and whatnot to you and you can have a look." Her eyes gleamed as she said, "Take your time but not too long. People are beating down our doors to work with Leonard."

Elizabeth got through the rest of rehearsal, but her mind was full of her conversation with Carol. Her volunteer work had always been important to her. Even at school, she'd willingly done her community service activities.

After college, she'd drifted into Dad's company because he seemed to need her and stayed because some part of her thought she could win his approval that way.

But she was free now, and that meant her choices were wide open.

She wanted to talk it over with Sam. He would be off the ice by the time she got home. On her drive home she almost dialed Chris, but they still hadn't spoken since their blow up the other night.

She parked and walked to her condo dialing Sam's number. It rang. Out loud.

Ringing phone in hand, Sam sat on the top step outside her condo.

Elizabeth was so pleased to see him it took her a few minutes to get that Sam looked pissed. Very pissed.

"Hey." She climbed toward him. "You okay?"

Standing, Sam motioned her door. "Inside."

Say what? He must be really pissed. "What's wrong?"

"Inside." He clenched his jaw. "I don't feel like having this conversation with Randy listening."

"Is that Sam's car?" Randy's voice drifted up on cue.

Elizabeth opened her door and let Sam in.

Sam strode into the center of her apartment and jammed his hands in his pockets. "Why did you have lunch with fucking Peter?"

Elizabeth stared at him, not sure whether to laugh or smack him. She didn't think he could be serious.

Except Sam looked serious as a heart attack, those blue eyes snapping fire at her, the muscle in his jaw spasming.

"Um..." Playing for time, she put her stuff on the counter and removed her jacket. "Hi, Sam."

"I'm waiting." He yanked out of his jacket, seriously endangering seams as he went. "I drove straight down after my game."

"First off, that tone? Not a big fan." Amusement still warred with anger inside her. Right then, he reminded her of five-year old Sam when he couldn't get his way. He was totally jealous and that made her feel rather smug and pleased. "And I had lunch with Peter because we're old friends."

"Friends?" Sam snorted and yanked his phone out his pocket. "Does this look like friends to you?"

With his phone shoved in her face, Elizabeth had no option but to look. She and Peter were sitting together at the steakhouse. She was laughing at something Peter had said. She thought it might have been a work story he'd told her.

"Actually, yes, Sam." She really had missed Sam, his strong, handsome face, his gorgeous body, and even his hot temper. But one had to move slowly with crazy. No sudden movements and no loud noises. "It looks exactly like two old friends having lunch."

Sam glowered. "Really?"

"How did you get that picture?" Her money would be on Instagram.

"Somebody called Maddog122 sent it to me."

"Sounds legit."

Sam yanked the image back and stared at it. "You're laughing."

"I am laughing." She spoke slowly and clearly. "Because I do that sometimes. Most of all I do it when I find something funny." It must be a sign of how far gone she was that a good part of her wanted to kiss the hell out of him right then. He was hot as fuck when he was pissed.

Sam glared at her. "Are you humoring me?"

"Do you require humoring?"

"I make you laugh," he said, crossing his arms. His frown deepened. "And if it's all so innocent, why didn't you tell me about it?"

"Because I forgot." Elizabeth opened a beer and handed it to him. "I made the lunch date with him weeks ago, and until he arrived on my doorstep today, I had completely forgotten."

Sam looked marginally mollified by that. He snort-laughed and sipped his beer. "You forgot you had a date with that loser."

The storm front had moved off and Sam's tense shoulders relaxed.

"Is there anything else you would like to know?" Or better yet, anything else he'd rather be doing.

"Do you still like him?" Sam shoved his spare hand in his pockets.

Elizabeth approached him. When he'd calmed down, she and he would have a word about his attitude, but first, the competitive streak three miles wide running through Sam needed to be soothed.

"No, Sam." She stopped in front of him. "Things were over with Peter even before we…" She didn't know what to call them, so she ended on a hand motion. "That day you came here and ate all my ice cream, I lied about him still being my boyfriend."

"You lied." He squinted, hackles on the rise again.

Elizabeth took a sip of his beer. "Yes, Sam, I lied, because there was no way I was admitting to you that I was a loser without a boyfriend."

He took his beer back and stared at her. Uncertainty crossed his expression. "Today was lunch between friends?"

It amazed her that someone that hot could even have a glancing moment of insecurity. Lust and the need to comfort him made uncomfortable neighbors inside her. "In the interest of full disclosure, he did ask how things stood between you and me, and whether that meant he and I were truly over."

Sam's thunderous scowl crept back over his face. "You told him he didn't stand a fucking chance, right?"

"I did." She nodded and stole another sip of beer. "But not only because of you and me, but also because I don't have those sorts of feelings for him anymore. I'm not sure I ever did."

"Hmph!" Sam took his beer back and sipped. He held the bottle up. "It's empty."

"Would you like another?"

"I only had half of that one because you drank most of it."

"Two sips." Now it was her turn to lay down some truths. "Green is a very unattractive color on you, Sam."

"I was not jealous." He glared at her but couldn't hold it for long. "Okay maybe a little."

"How did Maddog send you the photo?"

"Twitter." He shoved his hands into his pockets.

"Let me get this straight." Elizabeth took her time taking the empty back to the kitchen. Let him sweat a bit. "A complete stranger called Maddog122 sends you a picture of me with a man. You don't do what a reasonable person would do, which is to call me and ask about it. No!"

Sam squirmed.

"You tear over to my house and start yelling. You don't even give me the chance to explain before you start hurling F-bombs at me."

Sam muttered something.

Elizabeth cupped her ear. Even after all these years, she still got a charge out of making Sam twist. "I'm not sure I heard that."

"I may have overacted." His dagger gaze dared her to make more of it at her peril.

Foolish man! Like she wasn't going to go there. "May have?" She deepened her voice and made ape arms. "What the fuck are you doing having lunch with fucking Peter?"

"I do not sound like that."

Elizabeth pounded her chest. "Yeah, you do."

"Do not." He kept his gaze on the ceiling and recited in a singsong voice. "I am sorry I charged down here and started yelling."

"What should you have done?"

"Asked you first." His gaze snapped down and a huge grin spread over his face. "I probably should have asked you before I gave the entire President's defense a beatdown tonight."

"Did you give away a penalty?"

"Nope." He looked affronted. "I don't do that anymore."

"Sam?" She sauntered closer to him, putting a swing in her step. "You're really cute when you're jealous."

"Is that so?" Sam raised a brow in challenge, done with her crap and ready to throw down. "You enjoying this, Lizzie?"

She showed him a pinch of air between her forefinger and thumb.

Sam lunged.

She knew his moves, and Lizzie feigned right and went for the gap between Sam and the sofa. She flew past him with a laugh. Oh, too easy.

Sam pivoted and snagged her around the waist.

He took her right off her feet and pulled her tight to his front. "Got ya."

The fight bled right out of her. She couldn't think of anywhere she'd rather be than there.

"I can't stay long," Sam said close to her ear. "I have an early conditioning session."

Being close to him always snagged her breath. "Is everything okay."

"Mmm-hmm." He kissed her neck. "I really am sorry, Lizzie, for behaving like a dick. I saw the photo and lost my shit."

"It's kind of flattering." She hooked her arms around his neck. "In a Neanderthal sort of way."

He took the offering of her upthrust breasts in his palms. "Want to see what else I can do in an entirely Neanderthal way?"

"So much."

CHAPTER
THIRTY-THREE

ELIZABETH WOKE with a grin on her face. Light streamed across her bedroom floor, later in the morning than she generally got up.

Sam had left sometime in the night.

She rolled over and checked the time on her phone. A notification from Sam made her laugh. *Next time you won't get off so easy.*

Damn, but she liked having him in her life. She liked the way he brought so much noise into her existence. Sam had made a stadium game of her life. Lights, music, energy, enthusiasm and emotion played out at fever pitch.

She went in pursuit of coffee.

Her doorbell rang as she was adding creamer.

Jane stood there, scowling at her.

"Jane." Elizabeth hadn't seen much of her since she'd stopped going around to make Saturday dinner. And she could count on one hand the number of times Jane had visited her at her apartment. "Come in."

It was redundant because Jane had already stomped past her.

"Would you like…" She motioned the coffee pot. "Or you could help yourself."

Banging her mug on the counter, Jane yanked open the fridge. She held out the creamer with a look of disgust. "Is this all you have?"

"Yup." Elizabeth cradled her cup of magic elixir and prayed it would give her enough strength to survive the encounter. "The reason that's what I have is because that's what I like."

Jane gaped at her and added the creamer to her coffee. Clearly in the mood to lower her dizzying standards.

She'd love to know what brought Jane there this morning, but she probably wouldn't have to wait that long.

"So what?" Jane snarled. "Are you like fucking Sam now?"

No way she was answering that. "Is that what you came by to find out?"

"I thought you hated him." Jane slouched through to her sitting area. "This place is small."

And getting smaller by the minute.

"You gonna tell me what's happening with Sam?" Jane turned to her and shook her phone. "Or are you going to make me read it on social media like everyone else?"

She had a point, not much of a point, but after last night, Elizabeth was feeling magnanimous. "Sam and I are seeing each other."

"Is it serious?"

"I'm not sure." She very much suspected that for her, she might have crossed into serious a way back. "We're taking it one step at a time."

Jane sneered. "That is so like you."

"Is that all you came by for?" Elizabeth went to the door. She wanted to see if Carol had sent that email about the job.

"Dad said you walked out," Jane said.

"I did." Jane had never shown any interest in her work situation. "I haven't been happy for a long time, and I decided to do something about it."

"Yeah, well, he's been a total bastard ever since you left." Jane scowled at her. "He won't even listen to me."

Welcome to the last twenty-eight years of my life. "I'm sorry about that, but if Dad is angry, it's on him."

"Are you kidding me?" Jane gaped at her. "You walked out on him. Walked out on your own family."

Jane definitely wanted something. She had the familial loyalty of a lizard.

Elizabeth waited.

"You have to fix what you did." Jane hadn't even lasted to a mental ten count. "Because of you, he's been in a pissy mood. He's ruining my life."

Here it came.

"He's trying to lock me in that fucking house until I die." She paced Elizabeth's living room slopping coffee everywhere.

Thank God for hardwoods. "Where do you want to go?"

"It's not only me." Jane looked thunderstruck that Elizabeth should even ask. "There are about five of us who want to go on a road trip." Her expression turned mulish. "We are going on a road trip."

"Where to?"

"Vegas." Jane tossed it out there like she was going around the corner.

Elizabeth went with reason first. "Jane, you don't even have your license. How are you going to go on a road trip?"

"It doesn't matter." Jane sneered. "Bugs and Allie have theirs. They can share the driving, and even though the rest of us don't have our licenses, we can all drive."

"Bugs and Allie have only recently gotten their full licenses." Elizabeth wondered if she was hearing it right. "I'm not even sure they are allowed to carry that many passengers."

"In Canada." Jane rolled her eyes. "But Vegas is in the States. They get their licenses there like at fifteen."

Elizabeth had never thought she would see the day when she and her father agreed, and particularly agreed about parenting Jane.

"I'm sorry, Janey, but I'm not going to talk to dad for you," she said.

Jane stamped her foot. "You have to. You turned him into an asshole, and you have to fix that."

"I didn't do that." Dad had been an asshole long before her resignation, and even before that if memory served. "Also, he doesn't listen to me, so it would do no good if I did speak to him." She held up a hand to stop Jane from speaking. "And, more importantly, even if none of that was true, I think this is a crazy idea. You're talking about five girls, all of them inexperienced drivers, driving thousands of kilometers."

Jane stilled and glowered at her. She stalked for the door, slamming the cup on the counter on the way. "Fuck you, Elizabeth. Fuck both of you."

"Well," she said to the slammed door. "That was heartwarming."

Even knowing it would do no good, she called her father.

The call went to voicemail, and she left a message. "Hi Dad, it's Elizabeth. Jane was here and she wanted me to talk to you about this road trip to Vegas." Elizabeth really hadn't liked that look in Jane's eyes. "I told her I agree with you, but you might want to keep an eye on her. Jane doesn't take well to being told no."

———

As she read the job description Carol had sent her, excitement fluttered in Elizabeth's belly.

She still hadn't spoken to Sam about this new opportunity, but she would. With playoffs looming and the Titans fighting tooth and nail for the wild card spot, their conversations tended to be short and late at night when Sam was tired.

Plus Sam was riding high on the wave of the best hockey he'd played in his entire career. Even Marc Gracie had grudgingly conceded as much. Sam was racking up individual points for every game with goals and assists.

And she couldn't be happier for him.

In life before Sam, she would have called Chris, but the silence between them persisted. Of course, Chris had Maddy now, so she probably barely noticed Elizabeth wasn't there anymore.

The job Carol outlined couldn't have been more perfect for her, and she wanted to bounce it off someone. It wasn't like she doubted whether the fit was good; it was that she wanted that affirmation.

Mom and Danica had moved on to Prague and were extolling the virtues of the city in long Instagram stories. Thus far, Mom had said nothing about Sam. Their silence on the subject shrieked between them.

There was no way Danica wouldn't have shared the news with Mom about Elizabeth and Sam, but Mom might be giving discretion a try.

Well, she was doing this solo. Elizabeth dialed Carol's number.

"Elizabeth." Carol's gritty voice came down the line. "I hope you're calling to let me know you're interested."

"I am." Like a key in a lock she knew it was what she should be doing. "I assumed you'd like me to come in for an interview?"

"Are you kidding me?" Carol laughed. "The job is yours. When can you start?"

That thing flying past Elizabeth's head was the rocket going into the future. "When do you need me?"

"After lunch work for you?"

Elizabeth laughed, although she wasn't entirely sure Carol was kidding. "Monday?"

"See you Monday," Carol said. "And look, I'll do some arm twisting on the board and see if I can get you a bit more money."

Elizabeth hadn't discussed salary. What Carol offered would mean she could keep her lifestyle without too much trouble. More than that though, this job meant another thing in her life that felt right.

CHAPTER
THIRTY-FOUR

ELIZABETH CALLED Sam and left him a voicemail that she had news. Now she had a double reason to celebrate, and she wasn't going to sit there and feel sorry for herself. She ordered pizza from her favorite place and went back to the kitchen.

When the pizza arrived, Elizabeth settled down in front of her favorite chick flick with a glass of wine.

The movie had reached the grand gesture stage when Sam called.

"Hey." Hearing his voice made her feel better.

"Open up for me, I'm downstairs," he said.

He didn't need to ask her twice.

As soon as she opened the door, Sam grabbed her and planted a big kiss on her. "I came as soon as I found out."

"Sam." He made her go all gooey inside. "I'm so happy you're here."

"Me too. I have the best news." He swung her around. "And the only person I wanted to tell was you."

"You have news?" She struggled to catch up with herself. If he had news, then he wasn't here for her news after all. "What is it?"

Sam kissed her again before putting her back on her feet and striding into her condo. "Can I smell pizza?"

"Um...yes. On the table. What news?" Elizabeth trailed him.

Folding a piece of pizza in half, Sam took half of it in one bite and groaned as he chewed and swallowed. "I am so fucking hungry. The Storm made us work for it tonight. After, coach called me into his office, and then I came straight here."

"What news?" Elizabeth fetched him a beer, opened it and handed it to him.

"You're the best." He side hugged her and reached for another slice.

Elizabeth sat on the couch arm, sipped her wine and waited for him to swallow. He was so excited about his news, whatever it was. Did that make her a bitch for feeling disappointed he wasn't there because of her news?

"Lizzie," Sam said, his eyes sparkling. "They are renewing my contract!"

"What!" That was incredible news. "They're renewing you?"

"Yup." Sam grinned. "And my agent says she thinks she can push them a bit on salary."

It was great news and Elizabeth threw her arms around him. After all he'd been through with the suspension and having to fight his way back on the team, his news couldn't be better.

She grabbed his face and made him look at her. "You did it, Sam. You fought your way back to where you want to be."

"I couldn't have done it without you, Lizzie." He slid his arms around her waist and tugged her to him. He kissed her soft, sweet and deep.

When he broke away, Elizabeth's libido had woken up and she pressed herself to him. "How about we relocate this celebration to the bedroom?"

"God, I'd like that." Sam ground his hips against her. Then he grimaced. "But I've got to go. I need to get to the airport because we're flying down to Florida."

"Shouldn't you be there already?"

"I'm good." He kissed her again. "I had enough time to come and tell my girl my news, kiss her and tell her I can't wait to see her again."

"I'll miss you too." Elizabeth unwrapped her arms from him. "Now get out there and earn that ridiculous salary they pay you."

"I'll be back day after tomorrow, and then I have two days off." He leered at her. "And we will be spending those celebrating."

Elizabeth opened her door and waved him through. "Get outta here."

"Bye, Lizzie." He hugged her tight. "I love you, you know."

Then he was gone, trotting down the stairs and climbing into his car while she stood nailed to the spot by three words.

Sam loved her. He'd said so. And that was probably a very good thing, because she loved him right back.

———

Sam called about midmorning the next day.

"Lizzie." He sounded pissed. "What's your big news and why didn't you tell me last night?"

Elizabeth poured hot water over her waiting tea bag. "You didn't have long." Her news had faded into the background. "And your contract being renewed was bigger news."

"Bullshit." From his side of the call came the echoey sounds of skates on ice and men shouting.

"Are you supposed to be practicing?"

"Tell me your news," Sam said. "Dawson likes you, so he also wants to know your news."

A man yelled something.

Sam chuckled. "Guy wants to know as well, and Coach says you better tell us all or nobody will get any ice time this morning."

"I got a new job." She felt shy telling him now. Her new job felt anticlimactic.

Sam whooped and then yelled, "Lizzie got a new job."

Hollers and whistles came over the phone at her. Sam came back on the line. "What new job?"

"At Mountain Vista," she said. "Carol heard that I'd left Dad's company and offered me the job. It's part fundraising and part organizing events and entertainment for the residents."

"You'll be perfect at that." Sam's voice warmed. "You already do it now, and you love it."

"I do." Sam understood her. He got what mattered to her without her having to tell him. "I start Monday."

"That's great, Lizzie, really great news." He cleared his throat. "But next time you have something to tell me and I'm hogging all the attention, tell me to shut the fuck up and listen."

"Sure, Sam." Like she would ever do that.

"Listen, I got to go. Coach is glaring at me." He took a deep breath. "Haven't you got something to say to me?"

"What? Like goodbye?"

"Yes goodbye, smart ass, but also the thing that starts with I and ends with love you too." Sam went balls to the wall on everything.

"Maybe."

"Lizzie!"

She couldn't keep him in suspense and laughed. "I definitely love you too, Sam."

Elizabeth's next call was to Chris. Life was too short for their wounded silence. Elizabeth wanted to share her news with her best friend, and that's exactly what she was going to do.

"Elizabeth." Maddy answered Chris's phone sounding breathless. "I'm so glad you called. Chris is in the shower, but please wait."

Elizabeth had a better idea. "Is she working today?"

"No."

"Do you two have plans?"

Maddy's tone lifted. "None that we can't change for someone if they asked."

"Good." She grabbed her keys and purse. "I'm coming over."

With a squeal, Maddy hung up.

Nerves kicked in for real as she parked outside Chris's small two-bedroom house. Typical of Chris, the snow was all cleared from the drive and the wraparound porch surrounding the square redbrick house.

Maddy answered her knock. "Come in." She took Elizabeth's coat. "She'll kill me for telling you this, but she's nervous."

That made Elizabeth feel better.

Grabbing her own coat, Maddy jerked her head to the inside of the house. "Go on. She's in the kitchen, fussing with cookies on a plate."

"You're not staying?"

"No." Maddy slid her arms into her bright pink Canada Goose coat. "I think it's best if I make myself scarce for a bit."

With a deep breath, Elizabeth stepped into the dining room to the right of the entrance hall and then went through the door to the kitchen.

"Hi." Chris looked up from a plate of cookies. "Maddy said you were coming around."

Now that she was there, she couldn't think of much to say. They'd been best friends since kindergarten, and it made no sense that she couldn't speak. "Hi."

She stood on the far side of the island from Chris.

Chris motioned. "Sit. Please."

"Thanks." The stool scraped over the tiles and Elizabeth jumped. "Sorry."

"No, that's fine." Chris waved a dismissive hand. "I need to replace those felt pads on the bottom of the legs."

Elizabeth perched and sat. She peered at the cookies and her heart melted. "Are those Dares?"

"Yup." Chris pushed the plate toward her. "They're my favorite."

"I know."

"Of course you do." Chris cleared her throat. "I always have them in the house. In case, you know, I want one."

"Yup." Elizabeth nodded, feeling like a dumb puppet. "It's best to keep some here. Because you like them so much."

Dear God, she couldn't keep this up for much longer before one of them started screaming.

"Coffee?" Chris turned and got the coffee going.

"That would be great." One of them had to push through the ice crust. "Chris?"

She turned with an overbright smile. "Yes?"

"I miss you. So much. And I'm so sorry we fought."

"Oh, Elizabeth." Chris dropped her spoon and coffee grounds fell all over the counter and floor. "I miss you too, and I'm so sorry for what I said."

Elizabeth rounded the island, banging her hip in the process. "I'm sorry I got so angry and didn't stay and talk it out."

"Maddy is lovely, and I'm happy with her." Chris pulled her into a tight hug. "But she doesn't replace you in my life. It's different and I need you both."

"I know." Elizabeth returned the hug as hard as she received. "I've wanted to pick up the phone a hundred times and tell you something, and then stopped myself."

"I promise I won't tell Maddy stuff you don't want me to." Chris pushed back from the hug.

Elizabeth needed a tissue, or the snot and tears situation would get out of hand. She dug one out of her purse and handed another to Chris. "It's not that so much. I know Maddy wouldn't betray me or anything. I think I don't like the idea of sharing you with someone. I've had you all to myself for years."

"It's the same for me." Chris blew her nose. "I mean, you've had boyfriends before but nobody like Sam. I know how important he is to you, and I get resentful too."

"Let's not fight again." Elizabeth held out her hand.

Chris took it and shook it. "I'm not sure we can agree not to fight, but I think we should agree not to freeze each other out if we do."

"Done."

The handshake ended in another hug before Elizabeth sat down again. "How about that coffee?"

"Coming up." Chris cleared the coffee grounds away and started again.

Elizabeth helped herself to a Dare Maple Leaf cookie. "How are things with Maddy? She can come back now."

"She's shopping." Chris grimaced and took a cookie. She bit into it and sighed. "I love these things."

"I know."

She laughed. "I got them specially for you. When Maddy said you were coming, I ran out and got them."

"Chris." If this kept up, Elizabeth would start crying again. "All I wanted was to see you."

"Me too." Chris smiled. "As to Maddy. Things are great, better than great actually, but you know how I feel about shopping, so she's more than happy to take this time without me whining at her about going home."

Elizabeth sensed something Chris wasn't saying. "Better than great."

"Yeah." Chris flushed. "I'm thinking of asking her to move in with me."

They knew each other too well for bullshit. "Really? Thinking about asking her, or it's a done deal." She pointed to a wooden tree of brightly colored coffee mugs. "Because that's new."

"Okay." Chris rolled her eyes and blushed deeper. "I asked and she said yes."

"That's great," Elizabeth said and meant it. Chris had been waiting for a Maddy for so long. She deserved all the happiness she could get. "We'll have to have a housewarming party."

Chris put a mug of coffee in front of her. Exactly the way she liked it. "So what's new with you?"

"Well." Elizabeth bit into another cookie. Damn these things were moreish. "The big news is I got a new job."

"Get out." Chris gaped at her. "So soon."

"I start Monday." Elizabeth told her the story.

Chris was thrilled for her. She said all the right things to reassure Elizabeth. This was what their friendship was about.

"And how are things with Sam?" Chris sipped her coffee. "Is he still rocking your world?"

Elizabeth's face heated and she rolled her eyes. "I never said he rocked my world."

"Yeah, but we can all see that he does." Chris chuckled. "Things still good with you guys?"

"Great. Perfect." And she didn't sound nearly as convincing as she was going for, because up came one of Chris's eyebrows. "What's going on?"

She battled to put it into words because it was more a feeling than something she could enunciate. "That thing you said to me about swapping one dominant male for another—"

"I was wrong about that," Chris said. "Sam is nothing like your dad and he makes you happy. He tries to put your needs first."

"I know that." Elizabeth didn't know how not to sound like a brat. "And he really does try."

"But?"

"You know, with my dad, I get pushed into the background because he has to be the center of attention. He has to have everything. Jane is the same." A characteristic people like Leonard also shared. "And I put up with them, and people like them, because I know how."

"And?" Chris crunched a cookie, her gaze intent on Elizabeth.

Buying time, Elizabeth sipped her coffee. "My mom once said something to me that's stuck with me. She said that just because we can manage difficult people, it doesn't mean we have to."

"But Sam isn't difficult," Chris said. "I think he may be feeling the L word."

"He does." Elizabeth got a smug glow as she said that. "He told me he did."

Chris whooped. "Way to go, Sam." Then she stared at Elizabeth. "So why aren't you farting sunshine and roses?"

"Do you think part of why I'm with Sam is because all I know is difficult?" She couldn't maintain the eye contact with Chris, and she fiddled with her mug. "Sam isn't difficult, but the situation is. With my dad and Jane, I take second place because of who they are. With Sam I take second place because of what he is, his career and his lifestyle."

"That's a tough one." Chris blew out a breath. "And I'm not really sure I have an answer for you."

"Me neither." Elizabeth felt a dull weight settle in the center of her chest. "I love Sam, I really do, but I'm not sure I can be second best for the rest of my life. And I really don't like how needy and whiny this is making me."

CHAPTER
THIRTY-FIVE

ELIZABETH TOOK the call from Chris at six a.m. This couldn't be good news. "Chris."

"Elizabeth." The seriousness of Chris's tone would have gotten her attention if the earliness of the call hadn't. "Sweetie, I've got some bad news."

Words that got anyone's heart going. "What? Did Sam get hurt? Dad?"

"Lizzie, it's Jane," Chris said. "The news came over the police dispatch about ten minutes ago. I made sure first before I called."

The blood drained south and every sound grew more acute. "What happened?"

"There was a car accident on the four seventeen. Five teen girls involved. They've taken them to Ottawa Hospital."

The world tilted around her, and she couldn't make her stupid brain work. "Are you sure it's Jane? Where was she going? What?"

"Elizabeth." Chris's voice was calm and clear. "I checked, and it's Jane. Your dad is being notified now, and I've sent Maddy to get you."

Some part of her knew she should do something, but she

couldn't think what. "Is she okay? Jane. She's okay though, right."

"Sweetie," Chris said, and Elizabeth really didn't like that tone. "It's not good. You need to get dressed, and Maddy will take you to the hospital."

She stood. "I'll get dressed."

"That's right," Chris said. "Maddy won't be long."

Elizabeth stumbled into some clothes, vaguely making sure they looked reasonable. She dragged her hair into a ponytail and brushed her teeth.

The doorbell rang as she was pulling her shoes on.

Maddy stood there, her face stricken. She wrapped her arms around Elizabeth. "Let's get you to the hospital."

"Sure." Elizabeth looked around not sure what to take. Suddenly her brain refused to cooperate.

Maddy brushed past her and picked up her phone, her purse and her house keys. "Come on. Your dad will need you."

"Right." Elizabeth scoffed. Chris said they were informing her dad, and he hadn't called her. Not one missed call from him. "Then you don't know my dad."

On the drive to the hospital, she tried to get her head together.

Maddy dropped her off at triage and went to park.

Walking through the automatic doors, the first face Elizabeth saw was Chris's. In her uniform Chris looked so official, and the reality of the situation body slammed Elizabeth.

She went straight to Chris. "Tell me."

Chris led her past reception and into the hospital. "From what we know so far, the girls were all packed up like they were on a road trip. The car was full of baggage, and they had their passports with them."

The trip she'd told Jane not to go on. She'd gone anyway. Wasn't that so fucking Jane, and suddenly she wanted to shake her sister. God, let that be a possibility.

Forcing the panic down, she concentrated on what Chris was telling her.

"According to witnesses and the trucker they hit, they changed lanes. He swerved but he couldn't avoid them. He hit them and spun them into oncoming traffic."

"Oh, God." Her legs refused to move.

Chris came back for her and put her arm around her. "The driver is the best off and is conscious. I have to go and talk to her. The three girls in the back took the worst of it."

Elizabeth didn't need Chris to tell her. "And Jane was in the back."

"Yes."

Chris caught the attention of a passing nurse. "Jane Rogers. Do you have an update on her condition?"

The nurse glanced at Elizabeth. "Family?"

"Sister."

Pointing down a short corridor, the nurse said, "Your father is waiting in there. He got here a couple of minutes go. The doctor will be out as soon as she can."

"Thanks." Chris fell into step with Elizabeth.

Elizabeth stopped her. "Let me talk to him alone. You go and do what you have to do."

"You sure?" Chris hugged her tight. "I'll be right back. You hang in there, Elizabeth. I've seen people walk away from much worse. She's young, and she's strong."

It was ridiculous how she could draw comfort from such trite words, but she did.

Dad sat in the waiting room, his gaze fixed on the silent television in the corner. The morning news was playing.

"Dad?"

He glanced at her and then went back to the television. "They called you."

"Yes." She sat on the chair to his left. "Have you heard anything?"

"Just that she was unconscious when they brought her in. Nonresponsive they say. They're working on her."

Hundreds of questions crowded her brain, but now wasn't the time. "I'll call Mom." She got her phone out.

Dad scowled at her. "Why?"

Elizabeth didn't even bother to answer but stood and walked to the far side of the waiting room. She left a message for her mother to call her urgently.

Then she called Sam. Voicemail. She couldn't remember what she said, but she didn't go into much detail. Just that Jane was in hospital and he should call her. Or something close to that.

"Any news?" Maddy walked into the waiting room.

Elizabeth shook her head. "We're waiting for the doctor."

"I'll get some coffee," she said. "Are you hungry?"

Elizabeth shook her head. "But Dad might be."

"I'll get something anyway." Maddy kissed her cheek and then hurried away.

Not able to sit still, Elizabeth paced the length of the waiting room. Surely someone knew something by now. She was on the verge of finding a person when a young doctor entered the waiting room and approached Dad. "Mr. Rogers?"

Dad stood and shoved his hands in his pockets. "Is she—"

"Jane suffered considerable injuries," the doctor said, her brown eyes full of empathy. "Mostly concentrated on the left side of her body. The side of impact."

"What injuries?" Elizabeth didn't recognize that voice as her own.

"She's broken her left tibia and fibula. Her leg bones," she said. "She also suffered broken ribs down that side of her body. Fortunately none of the ribs punctured her lungs, but her left lung did collapse from the impact."

Elizabeth dropped into a seat. How could anyone take this kind of damage?'

"We have the lung re-inflated, but for now we have her on a

respirator. There was also a minor brain hemorrhage, but we believe that has stopped."

Dad rocked from his toes to his heels. "Anything else?"

"Not now." The doctor shook her head. "But the next twenty-four hours are critical, and we'll be keeping a very close watch on her. Once she's stabilized, we'll move her to ICU, and you'll be able to see her."

After the doctor left, Dad went back to staring at the silent television. She knew he had to be feeling it, but outwardly nothing showed.

Imagine being her mother and living with his coldness for thirty years, living with a man who not only refused to acknowledge his own feelings, but dismissed everyone else's as well. Elizabeth couldn't do it.

God, she wished Sam was there.

Maddy reappeared with coffee and sandwiches.

"Thank you." Dad unwrapped a sandwich and bit into it. He ate it still watching his silent television. She told herself it was a coping mechanism, but it didn't piss her off any less.

He hadn't even called her to let her know about Jane. "Were you planning to call me and let me know about Jane?"

"You're here aren't you?" Dad scowled at her. "I didn't need to call you."

"Yes, but were you going to, if Chris hadn't?" It hadn't occurred to him that she might need a father, or that they could lean on each other.

The only surprise was that it still had the power to affect her. "Listen." She turned to Maddy. "This might take a while, so I don't expect you to wait."

"I'm not going anywhere." Maddy stirred sweetener into her coffee. She glanced at Dad. "And maybe you need someone. I'm sure Sam will be here when he can."

When he could. While her sister was fighting for her life, Sam was chasing a disc of vulcanized rubber around the ice, and all for the amusement of the masses.

None of it was fair.

"Sam?" Dad turned to her. "What has Sam got to do with it?"

"I called him and told him." Elizabeth stared at the sandwich Maddy had given her. She couldn't bring herself to even unwrap it.

Dad gaped at her. "Why would you call him?"

"He's her boyfriend." Maddy looked at Dad in shock. "Why wouldn't she call him?"

"Boyfriend." Dad snorted. "Sam doesn't have time for women and them needing stuff from him."

"Plenty of players are married," Maddy said.

Elizabeth touched her arm and shook her head. She appreciated Maddy's effort, but it would fall on fallow ground.

"Some are, yes." Dad puffed up, as always hating to be contradicted. "But they are jobbing players, not the Sams of this world."

"Gretzky was married." Maddy didn't give up easily.

Dad waved his hand and went back to his television. Then he turned again. "Sam is going through a critical point in his career. He doesn't need distractions. He needs to concentrate on his game."

"I think that's up to Sam to decide." Maddy crossed her arms. "And so far, it looks like Elizabeth has been a real asset to his career."

Dad scowled at her. "Who are you again?"

"I'm with Chris," Maddy said. "I'm her girlfriend."

"Right." Dad nodded. "But what you're not is family and I'd like you to leave. My daughter has been in a car accident, and I don't need to be arguing with you about what's best for Sam."

Maddy looked contrite. "I'm sorry. You're right. That was insensitive of me."

"Why don't you see if you can find Chris?" Elizabeth looked at Maddy. Her trigger to soothe troubled waters went core deep. She leaped into action before she could think about it.

"If you're sure that's best." Maddy glanced at Dad.

Elizabeth managed a smile. "This is nothing new."

"Okay." Maddy got to her feet and adjusted her miniskirt. "I'm sorry about Jane, Mr. Rogers. We're all hoping and praying she makes a full recovery.

Dad grunted and picked up the third coffee Maddy had brought.

Shortly after that, Mom rang back, and Elizabeth had to tell her as much as she knew. She left Mom planning to fly back immediately.

Time went by, and the news gave way to cartoons on the television.

Dad didn't seem to care but kept his gaze locked on the screen.

She wished she knew a way to make him speak to her.

Finally, after another two hours, a nurse came in. "You can see her now."

They followed the nurse into a small room with an observation window.

Jane lay in the bed, bristling with tubes. Her skin looked waxy and unreal. A respirator huffed and sighed as it breathed for her. Around the bed hung bottles and bags filled with fluids draining to and from Jane's body.

And Elizabeth nearly lost it.

Dad choked and had to draw in a steadying breath. Elizabeth took his hand in hers. He didn't clasp hers back, but he didn't break the contact either.

A monitor beeped the steady rhythm of Jane's heart.

"We have her heavily sedated," the nurse said, keeping her voice low. "We don't expect her to wake until tomorrow morning."

Dad cleared his throat. "But she'll be fine, won't she?"

"She's young and she's healthy." The Nurse gave him a sympathetic smile. "And those are the best things in her favor."

Jane's hand lay inert on the pale-yellow bedding.

Needing the connection, Elizabeth touched Jane's hand. "Hey, Janey. It's Elizabeth. Dad and I are here."

"She can't hear you," Dad said.

Elizabeth didn't care. "I've called Mom and she's on her way. But you need to get better, Jane. You need to fight and get better again."

Jane had been the sweetest baby and so much younger than Elizabeth. She had helped Mom feed and change her. The baby had fascinated her, and she had spent hours playing with her.

Each phase of Jane's growth and development had been more fascinating than the last. They'd all spoiled her because she had been cute and pretty and so delightful when she got her own way.

Until she'd hit her mid-teens, and then things had changed. Jane had grown demanding and hostile. As she grew older, her petulance when she didn't get her own way had bloomed into rage-filled rants.

If only she'd been firmer with Jane about this road trip. If only she'd made more of an effort to impress on Dad how worried she was about Jane's willfulness.

But no, she'd been obsessed with Sam and their burgeoning relationship. She'd taken all the energy she used to pour into her family and lavished it on her relationship with Sam.

It wasn't her fault Jane got hurt; she knew that. But since she'd been seeing Sam her life had undergone a rapid series of changes. Look at her job.

Those changes had consequences, and she hadn't been prepared for them. Things had moved so fast that she had been playing catchup the whole time.

She didn't know what a healthy relationship looked like. It made her second guess everything that happened with her and Sam. It made her unsure and insecure.

And her preoccupation had put distance between her and her family. She'd promised Mom she would watch out for Jane.

Well, she'd failed. Spectacularly.

———

Guy drove Sam to the hospital, breaking several traffic regulations along the way. Who knew Guy even had it in him?

The entire drive, Sam kept trying Lizzie's cell, but she must have turned it off because he kept getting voicemail.

He had been trying since he'd checked his messages after his matinee game against New York. Eventually in frustration, he'd tried Maddy and she'd broken the news to him.

Guy drew up outside the entrance. "Go."

Sam barely heard him, as he was already moving, ducking and weaving through people as he went.

Lizzie would be desperate, and her fucking father would be useless.

Dammit!

This was the downside to his job. Family events got missed, important occasions unmarked, and you were not always there when those you loved needed you most.

Chris had told him Jane was in ICU, and he stopped a nurse to ask.

She pointed him in the right diction. "Hey! Aren't you—"

"Yup." Sam leaped into the lift as the doors were closing.

The occupants stared at him. A few had no idea who he was, but to his left a couple had their gazes glued to him.

Any second now they would get up the courage to ask.

"Umm...excuse me?" It was the woman who found her voice first. "Are you Sam Stone?"

"Yes." He focused on the floor numbers above the lift door.

The man leaned forward. "Great game today."

"Thanks." He forced a smile. Fans didn't know what was going on in his life and sucking this shit up was part of the job. "The team played well."

"Yeah." The guy chuckled "But you got a hat trick."

He had. His fourth of the season, but he couldn't give a crap about that. He needed to get to Lizzie.

"Is everything all right?" The woman looked at him with concern.

"No." He didn't have it in him to invent a lie. "My girlfriend's sister has been hurt. I didn't know until the end of the game."

"Lizzie?" The woman's face dropped. "Oh, I'm so sorry. We'll be saying prayers for her, Sam. And for you."

This was the thing with the fans, sometimes they were so damned kind. "Thanks." Emotion choked his voice. "I'll let her know."

The lift door opened on his floor and Sam sprang for the gap.

He pushed through a set of double doors into ICU. The first thing he saw was Lizzie standing outside a room looking so fucking forlorn and brittle it broke his heart.

"Lizzie." He reached her in three strides and got his arms around her. He kissed her temple. "I'm so sorry, baby."

"Sam?" She stiffened, and then she relaxed and slid her arms around his waist. Her voice hitched. "S-Sam."

Sobs shook through her and Sam kept her as close to him as he could. He felt so helpless and useless. He could take on a two-eighty-pound enforcer and slam him into the boards, but he couldn't take any of the pain from this woman he loved.

All he could do was hold her. So, he did until the worst of the sobs stopped, and she grew calm. She peered up at him. "You came?"

"Of course, I came." He wiped her tears away with his thumbs. "Can you tell me what happened?"

She led him to a sterile, pitiless waiting room as she told him about Jane. It didn't sound good, but Sam kept that to himself.

Paul stood when he entered. "Sam." He frowned. "We didn't expect you."

"I came as soon as I could." He sat down next to Lizzie, wrapping his hand around hers. "How you holding up?"

Paul shrugged and looked down at his clasped hands. "It's not ever really something you expect to happen." He looked up.

It was hard to believe it sometimes, but in that moment, Sam could see how much Paul cared. "They say she's young and strong."

"That's good." Sam didn't know what else to say. He kissed Lizzie's hand. "Do you need anything?"

"No thanks." She shook her head. Then she took a deep breath. "Could I talk to you outside?"

"Sure." He kept hold of her hand as she led him out of ICU into the corridor beyond.

"Thanks for coming, Sam," she said in a stiff little voice that sounded nothing like his Lizzie.

"Now you sound like your dad."

"God forbid." She forced a strained laugh.

Sam's nape prickled like it did when he knew he was about to take a hit on the ice. "You holding up okay, Lizzie?"

"Yes. No." She gave a half sob, half laugh and looked up at the ceiling. "I can't do this, Sam."

"This?" He hated what his gut was screaming at him. "You mean Jane being hurt? I don't think anyone—"

"No, Sam." She lowered her eyes to him, and tears flowed down her face. "I mean us."

Even sensing where she was heading, it still hit him like a truck. "Is this because I couldn't get here sooner?"

He'd heard the other players talk in the locker room about when things got difficult with their families.

"No." She choked the word out. "It's not that, because that's a symptom of a bigger problem."

Oh, he got it all right. "The bigger problem being what I do for a living."

"Not just you." She dropped her gaze. "It's that and how it affects me. What it means for me. What it does to me."

He reached for her. This fucking hurt, and he couldn't let her do this to them. What they had was awesome. "Lizzie, baby, you're not thinking straight. Jane has been hurt and you're—"

"No, Sam." She fended off his hands. "I'm thinking straight

for the first time in weeks. I'm sure there are people who can do this, be with famous people, but I'm not one of them."

"But you have been doing it." He wanted to yell at her. He wanted to shake some sense into her. He wanted to hold her until she stopped talking shit. "We're good together, Lizzie. You're the best thing that ever happened to me."

She flinched. "But this is not the best thing that ever happened to me."

"Fuck!" That sucker punched him, and he had to take a deep breath to absorb the blow.

"Not because of you." She touched his arm. "Because of me. I'm not strong enough, Sam. I'm not big enough." When she dropped her hand, he wanted to howl. "My life is small, contained and I need it to stay that way, or everything goes out of control. I'm out of control now."

"Lizzie?"

"Please, Sam." She folded her arms and hunched her shoulders. "I can't do this. Let me go."

What choice did he have? Her sister was lying in ICU, and the woman he loved was begging him not to make it difficult for her.

The ICU doors swished shut behind her.

"Sam!" Guy ran down the corridor. He caught sight of Sam and stopped and paled. "No, don't tell me she's…"

Like a dead man walking, Sam approached Guy. "Jane isn't dead."

He picked up pace as he headed for the elevator.

"What is it?" Guy dropped into place beside him and grabbed his shoulder. "What happened?"

In a wooden voice he managed to respond. "I'm not good for Lizzie. My life is too big for her, and she doesn't like being out of control."

Guy's face fell. "Shit!"

Sam pressed the elevator call button. "Oh, I think this definitely qualifies as a fuck."

CHAPTER
THIRTY-SIX

THE NEXT FORTY-EIGHT hours were the longest of Elizabeth's life. She didn't allow herself to think about Sam and focused all her energy on Jane.

Jane had made it through the first night, which was encouraging. Somewhere in the middle of the next day, they lowered her sedation, and a few hours later, she woke for the first time.

After he'd seen her, Dad went to the canteen for something to eat, and Elizabeth stood on her own in the corridor outside the waiting room. She didn't know what to do with herself. Part of her was so relieved Jane would live, and another part was still cycling through all the things that could still go wrong.

The ICU doors opened, and Mom rushed through them. Face drawn and anxious, Mom went straight in to see Jane, leaving Elizabeth alone with Danica.

Danica had the same blue eyes as Sam, but the rest of Sam must have been inherited from his father. He'd been a pro athlete who hadn't quite made it to the pros. He now lived in the States with a new family. Sam had once tracked him down but hadn't made any effort to further the relationship from there.

"How is she?" Danica put her arms around Elizabeth. "We

came straight here, but we had to jump around from one flight to the other."

To her horror, Elizabeth's facade chose that moment to crumble and her voice trembled as she replied, "Jane is much better today. She has a long way to go, but she might be out of the woods."

"Lizzie." Danica pulled her into a hug. The only other person in the world who called her Lizzie, and Elizabeth broke.

As she sobbed into Danica's shoulder, Danica murmured soothing words and rubbed her back. "There now. It's going to be okay."

Only it wouldn't.

Elizabeth managed a smile for Danica and sat down in the waiting room to give Mom a chance to see Jane alone.

Jane might have residual damage from her accident.

And Sam was gone.

She hadn't heard a word from him since she'd broken things off. Not that she blamed him. He'd told her he loved her, and she'd told him goodbye.

When Mom came out of Jane's room, she looked pale and exhausted. She dropped into the chair beside Elizabeth. "God." Her voice shook and she buried her face in her hands. "We nearly lost her. Dear God, I can't..."

This time Mom collapsed, and Elizabeth held her. She cried a bit more with Mom until Dad entered the waiting room.

When he caught sight of Mom, he stopped. "So you came?"

"Of course I came, Paul." Mom sighed as if she couldn't be bothered to get into it. After thirty years, Elizabeth didn't blame her. "Our daughter got into a car accident and her life was in danger."

Dad grunted and found the remote for the television. A hockey game flickered on the screen.

"Oh!" Danica pointed. "It's Sam's team."

That went right though Elizabeth like a rusty razor blade, but she didn't have the right to pine over Sam now. Jane was lying in a hospital bed, still fighting for her recovery.

Mom took her hands. "How are you, darling?"

"I'm fine." Elizabeth dragged up some composure. The last thing Mom needed right now was to worry about her. "Of course, this thing with Jane...but I'm fine."

"Hmm." Mom glanced at Danica who glanced at the screen. Then Mom turned to Dad. "How did this happen, Paul?"

"What do you mean how did this happen?" Dad scowled at her. "Your daughter got into a car with a group of her friends to go on a trip I'd forbidden and got into an accident."

Mom sighed and turned back to her. "Did you know?"

"She wanted me to persuade Dad to let her go. I said no." Guilt took a vicious jab at her. "I should have known she wouldn't listen."

Dad grunted.

"Jane doesn't like being told no," Mom said. "And you're not her parent. I should have checked her behavior long ago, before the consequences got this serious." She rubbed a hand over her face. "God, I should never have left her when she was like this."

"Mom." Elizabeth took her mother's hands. "You needed to take the opportunity. None of us knew Jane would go this far."

"Didn't we?" Mom gave a hollow little laugh. "I think it was more a case of none of us wanted to believe she was this out of control."

"You shouldn't have left her," Dad said. "A girl needs her mother when she's at the phase Jane is. You left."

Danica gasped and stared at him. "She didn't leave Jane; she left you," she said. "And Jane has two parents."

Dad threw her a look of disgust and went back to the television.

"Anyway—" Danica crouched at Mom's feet. "I don't think you two taking the blame for Jane's actions is helping. Aren't we partially in this situation because Jane never takes responsibility for her own actions?"

Dad made a noise like a growl and stalked out of the waiting room muttering something.

"Let him go." Mom waved a hand in his direction. She turned back to Elizabeth. "How bad has he been?"

"He's been okay." She forced some light into her voice. "You know what he's like. He—"

"Elizabeth." Mom took her hands. "I know he's your father, but you don't need to make excuses for him. How has he really been?"

"The same." Her pretense crashed around her. "Horrible enough to me to make me want to leave in the first place, and then angry with me for not staying."

Mom stood and went to the window and stared out. "I've been doing a lot of thinking while we were away."

Danica took her place beside Elizabeth.

"I've taught you to be your father's whipping post." Mom hunched her shoulders.

Elizabeth hated her mother thinking that. "No, you haven't. You put up with him for years."

"Exactly."

"Besides, Mom, shouldn't we be concentrating on Jane right now?" Elizabeth didn't like Mom taking the blame for any of it.

"I should have left years ago," Mom said. "I should have left when he first started treating me like I didn't matter. But I thought I could change him. I thought I was doing the right thing, making the marriage work and all that."

"Weren't you?"

"No." Mom turned to face her. "The truth is that I was too frightened to get out. I didn't want to be a single mother with two children to raise, and I didn't trust Paul not to cut me off without a cent."

Elizabeth didn't want to have that conversation. Her mother's honesty had consequences she wasn't ready to face. "It doesn't matter."

"Yes, it does." Mom dropped into place on the other side of

her. "When things like this happen, it's a reminder that life is short. If we don't say these things when we should, the moment passes, and they never get said." She cupped Elizabeth's cheek. "I'm sorry, Elizabeth. I'm sorry for showing you how to try to please someone who can't be pleased, and I'm sorry for not standing up for you when I saw him doing the same things to you as he did to me."

"Why are you telling me this?" Elizabeth didn't want to cry, didn't want to be any bother. Inside her, a little girl whispered not to make more trouble for mommy and not to make mommy sadder than she already was.

"Because you need to know before you make a very big mistake." Danica took her hands. "I spoke to Sam."

"Oh." Then she realized the full impact of what Danica had said. "Oh."

"He's hurting, Lizzie, and he doesn't understand why you left him."

The idea of Sam hurting carved a piece out of her already raw insides. "I didn't want to hurt him."

"But I do understand what's going on," Mom said. "I think you're scared, darling. You don't know what a good relationship looks like and you're scared Sam will become your father."

Danica gave a wry laugh. "But Sam is nothing like Paul, Lizzie. Sam is kind and warm and he loves you. He believes in you and wants the best for you."

"I don't think I can be a hockey girlfriend." Her voice came out small and desperate, because a huge part of her still wanted to be that.

Danica shrugged. "I certainly didn't want to be a hockey mother. You know how hard I made it for Sam to play. But I try to live with the parts I don't like and enjoy the perks it offers."

"With hockey I'll always be second, just like with Dad."

"No." Mom hugged her. "I'm not saying it will be easy, but you'll always be first with Sam, and he won't play hockey forever."

Elizabeth's head felt crammed with all she had to think about. "Can't we concentrate on Jane?"

"I am concentrating on Jane." Mom patted her hand. "But I think all of us, you included, need to give Elizabeth some attention."

———

Sam felt like crap. He ached, and he was in pain, and none of it was from the game he'd played.

In fact, he'd played a great game and gotten one goal and two assists. Those had gone a long way to seeing the Titans into the playoffs.

Around him, his teammates cheered and broke out the drinks. After all it had taken for the team to get there, he should have been celebrating with them.

Dawson sat on the bench beside him. "This is not a happy face."

"I'm happy." Sam shrugged. "I'm cheering on the inside."

"Uh-huh." Dawson passed him a bottle of Molson. "We're letting this into the locker room but just for tonight. You had one helluva game."

"Thanks." Sam stripped off his shin pads, wincing at the stink of hockey gear. "You didn't suck yourself."

"Yeah." Dawson sniffed. "But I'm hot shit. Ask anyone."

Sam snorted and sipped the Molson. God, he felt like a huge part of him was missing ever since Lizzie had kicked his ass to the curb.

"I broke up with Kathy," Dawson said.

That was news, and Sam stared at him. "Yeah? What brought that on?"

"You." Dawson grabbed another beer from the cooler. "Watching your face the last few days, since Elizabeth…"

"Dumped me." Nope it didn't hurt any less. "So, what? You thought misery would like some company?"

"Nah." Dawson leaned his elbows on his knees.

Celebrations cranked up a notch as someone sprayed champagne over everyone.

"The way it hit you when Elizabeth left," Dawson said. "I don't feel like that, and I never did. It made me realize I want that kind of connection."

That made Sam want to laugh. "That's not really working for me right now."

"Yeah." Dawson shrugged. "But you're not going to let her go, right?"

"Well, no." Sam had been hanging back because of Jane. Elizabeth had more than enough to deal with. Jane was already out of ICU, and they were talking of sending her home to recuperate. "I haven't worked out my play yet."

"That's what I figured." Dawson stretched his legs out. "Because, you know, it's not like we'd ever want to make this choice, but if it came to hockey or an Elizabeth in your life…"

Sam totally agreed. "There really isn't a choice."

CHAPTER
THIRTY-SEVEN

ELIZABETH'S new word was getting a lot of practice as she carried on a text conversation with Jane. *No,* she typed, *I don't think you living with me is a good idea.*

After ten days, Jane had left hospital. It had taken her twenty-four hours of living with Mom to launch her attack. Mom had decided to learn from her mistakes and was taking a harder line with Jane. Even Dad had stood firm with her spending her convalescence with Mom.

Immediately, Jane went on the attack. *You're so selfish. You have all that space to yourself.*

Nope, it washed right off her. She didn't even bother with a justification that she had her condo because she paid for her condo. Jane was only interested in her capitulation. *Still, no.*

Jane went for the jugular. *I nearly died, Beth.*

I was there. Elizabeth really had to get going. It was opening night for *South Pacific* and her first challenge since she'd taken the job at Mountain Vista. *I'm so happy you're recovering, and I love you, but you're not coming to live with me.* She put her phone away.

"Elizabeth." Leonard had reached the point in opening night when a stiff whisky was needed. He appeared backstage and threw himself into a chair. "It's impossible." His top lip quivered. "I cannot do this."

Elizabeth handed him her hip flask because it was that or smack some sense into him. "Of course you can."

Leonard whimpered and took a sip. "We shall open to an empty house." He covered his eyes with his hand. "I shall be ruined. My reputation will never survive."

Elizabeth peeped through the curtains. Even she was surprised by the size of the audience. "Actually, Leonard, I think we have a full house."

"A full house?" He perked up, and then slumped again. "Jerry will forget his lines. Not once has he remembered them all."

"Jerry will be fine." Elizabeth responded by rote. Leonard went through galloping self-doubt every opening night. Keeping him distracted was almost working in distracting her from the persistent ache in her chest.

God, she missed Sam. She wanted to be able to text him about Leonard and have him make her laugh. Everything seemed dull and colorless since she'd broken up with Sam.

This was what she'd said she wanted, her ordinary life back. Funny, but she didn't remember it as being quite so gray.

"Elizabeth!" Leonard sat up. "Have we checked the props?"

"We've checked the props." For the fourth time, but it beat dwelling on Sam.

"But—"

"The props are fine, Leonard." She handed him the hip flask.

A stir from the audience side of the curtain grabbed Leonard's attention, and he sprang to his feet. He peered through the curtain. "Elizabeth!" Turning to her, he gave her a huge smile. "Darling, girl. You have made me the happiest of men." With a chuckle, he rubbed his hands together. "It would not surprise me if the local media followed them."

Not really understanding, Elizabeth peeked through the curtains.

Sam!

She stared, sure he would disappear again. But it was him. Sam was making his way down the central aisle in the theatre, and he had Guy and Dawson with him.

Tears blurred her vision and she swiped them away. Despite everything, Sam had still come, and he'd brought the others with him.

Elizabeth dashed her tears away.

Marc Gracie followed the three hockey players. The four weren't making much progress, as they kept getting stopped by fans.

She couldn't take her eyes off Sam. He looked tired and was sporting a slight bruise along his jaw. They'd come straight from a playoff game, which the team had won, and thereby won the first series.

Okay, so she hadn't managed to stop herself from following Sam's games. Who was she kidding? She had stayed glued to the television for every single one.

"Elizabeth," Leonard said. "Could you please pay attention to your director?"

"Leonard." She really didn't want to, but she dragged herself away and faced Leonard. "I understand that you're nervous but getting fussy with me is not your stress relief."

"You must speak with Myrtle." Leonard looked ready to burst into tears. "She is refusing to wear her Spanx."

Elizabeth went off to deal with Myrtle, but her head was full of Sam. He had come.

She didn't know what that meant, but he was there in the same building with her, and she wanted to rush to the front of house and…

What?

Breathe the same air as him. Touch him.

Except she'd given up the right to do any of that, and she hadn't spoken to Sam since that day in the hospital. She wished she knew what his being there meant.

She had lain awake nights knowing that Sam wouldn't be alone for long. Women would line up to be with him.

She was being stupid. He was probably there because Danica had asked him to be. Except he'd never done that before they'd gotten together.

Her head spinning, she knocked on the women's dressing room door, and popped her head around the corner. "Myrtle, we've had the Spanx discussion, and without them, the costume doesn't fit." She snagged the grass skirt behind the door. "And the grass skirt is still a hard no."

There was that word again. It got easier each time she used it.

The show took longer than ever, or so it seemed to her. She wanted to get to the end and maybe find out why Sam was there. Maybe even talk to him.

She sat backstage, one part of her running the show and another trying to stop herself from being so delighted Sam was there.

It was getting harder and harder to remember that she'd broken up with him, and it really shouldn't matter to her what he did.

Her reasons for the breakup seemed so flimsy and ridiculous that she couldn't even really understand why she'd done it.

But she'd had good reasons, valid reasons, and they had made so much sense to her.

Hadn't they?

"Elizabeth." Leonard glared at her. "The curtain?"

She cued the curtain for the end of the show and stood at an angle backstage where she could see Sam.

Guy whistled loudly as the actors bowed.

Dawson was clapping enthusiastically and doing a good show of looking like he was having the time of his life. He leaned over and whispered something to Sam, which made Sam laugh.

Sam had the best laugh. It came from his belly and crinkled up his face. She missed his laugh.

She missed everything.

But she'd blown it. She knew Sam well enough to know he wouldn't set himself up for another round of rejection. He had his fair share of pride, and she'd trampled all over it.

The applause died, and the cast flooded off the stage, laughing and chattering, high on the adrenalin rush of their performance.

The audience filed out of the theatre, swallowing Sam up with them.

Trying to block out the pain, Elizabeth threw herself into the post-performance cleanup. There was plenty to do, and she got to it.

Leonard had left for the front of the theatre already.

She put the props away and made sure everything onstage was fine for the crew to strike the set.

In the dressing rooms, the cast was still chattering away. She would make sure they were all out before she left.

"Elizabeth?" Dawson stood behind her with his hands in his back pockets.

His handsome face made her think of Sam again, but she managed a smile. "Craig." She took the hand he held out and kissed his cheek. "Thank you so much for coming."

"Are you kidding me?" Dawson spread a hand on his broad chest. "I love the theatre."

Elizabeth snorted, and Craig's face broke into a smile. "Okay, Sam asked me to come with him."

She couldn't stop her smile from sliding off her face. "That was nice of him. It was nice of you too."

"Lizzie." Dawson touched her shoulder. Then he surprised the hell out of her by pulling her into a hug. Broken heart aside, a Craig Dawson hug was a shot straight to the ovaries. Taller than Sam, and as solid, he wrapped her in muscle and clean smelling man. "My boy looks about as crappy as you do."

"He does?" As much as she didn't want Sam to be hurting,

she kind of did as well. Because if he was hurting, it meant he hadn't forgotten her.

Dawson chuckled and pulled back enough to see her face. "You probably don't know this, but I broke up with Kathy."

"Oh, I'm sorry." It seemed the right thing to say.

Dawson shook his head. "Don't be. What Kathy and I had wasn't the real thing. Not like you and Sam have."

"Had." A small sob got away from her. "We don't have it anymore."

"Of course you do." Craig gave her a small shake. "Men like Sam, Guy, and I don't have to look far to find a woman happy to share our lives."

Elizabeth had no idea how that was supposed to be helping. "Okay."

"But what we very rarely find is someone like you. You think you can't be with Sam because you have a normal life, and that's what you want, but that's exactly the reason you should be with him." Craig bent his knees and met her gaze. "You keep him grounded. You provide the real in a world that can get so fucking crazy it can eat you alive. You see him, Lizzie. You don't see Sam Stone, forward for the Titans. You see Sam when he's having a shitty day. When he's having a great day. When he's getting through one day and into another."

"I'm scared," she whispered, "that I'll disappear."

"That's not possible." Craig gave her another hug. "You are Sam's true north, and he knows that. Let the rest of the world see what they want. You and Sam know the truth, and that's all that matters."

————

When Elizabeth left Mountain Vista, the parking lot was nearly empty. Only night shift's cars were in the staff lot; all the visitors had gone. Until she saw the empty parking lot, she hadn't realized that some part of her had harbored hope that Sam might wait for her. Chill spring wind chased an empty chip packet across bare asphalt. And now she was seeing metaphors in litter, and that really had to stop.

Shivering against the wind, she hurried to her car and climbed in. The chip packet took off on a gust and crumpled against the chain-link fence.

A text chimed on her phone, and hope flared, only to dim again. It was Mom telling her she was going for a drink with Danica and congratulating her on the performance.

Mom should be taking herself out for a drink with her bestie. She had looked good tonight, dressed in a new red sweater and trendy jeans. She had spent years with a man who didn't make her happy because she was too scared of being without him. As uncomfortable as her marriage had been, it had been familiar.

Elizabeth turned on the ignition and got the heat going.

Predictably, Dad had not come to the show. Or he might have, and she hadn't noticed. Dad had treated her like an extension of Mom, and as such, only worthy of his notice when it pertained to him. They had been the minions to his Felonious Gru.

Well, Sam had come to the performance, and the minions had gotten their own movie.

She sent her mother a text before she lost courage.

The phone rang. "Darling." Mom sounded breathless. Chattering voices and glasses clinking underscored her voice. "We got your text."

Then Danica's unmistakable whisper. "Ask her."

"I am about to ask her." Mom sounded impatient.

"Do it now."

"I'm doing it."

"Do it."

"Darling," Mom said into the phone, "why do you want to know where Sam is?"

Oh, these two. And she would be laughing right now but her

stomach was a ball of nerves. "He and I have some talking to do."

"Tell her he misses her," Danica said.

Her Mom huffed. "I'm fairly sure she can hear you."

"Does he?" Elizabeth grasped at the drifting straw. "Does he really miss me?"

"Every minute of every day." Danica came on the line. "And he's spending the night at my house. And we'll be home much, much later. And the key is in its usual spot."

Laughing, Elizabeth hung up. Her courage faltered with the loss of connection. Then she took a deep breath. After thirty years, her mother was out there being the self she wanted to be.

It took twenty minutes to get to Danica's house and another fifteen of quaking in the car before she climbed out and approached the house.

The walkway was swept, and light shone from inside. She hesitated about knocking, and then went with what Sam would do. Full steam ahead and damn the torpedoes.

She got the spare key out and took another frigid five minutes hesitating to put it in the lock. It was crazy. She could go away and come back in the morning when she knew what to say. She was a planner, not an impulse person anyway.

The door opened, and Sam stood there. "Lizzie, I swear to God, both of us are going to freeze our balls off before you put that key in the lock."

Hair damp from a shower, Sam had changed into track pants and a long-sleeve T-shirt. He looked breathtaking and real and every thought she had slid away. "Er...hi."

"Hi?" He raised an eyebrow. "That's all you've got for me?"

"Umm...I was working on the rest." Her tongue felt huge and ungainly.

Growling, he gripped her arms and pulled her into the house. "Get in here."

She stood in the front hall, frozen and uncertain.

"Shoes." Sam pointed. "Or my mom will have your ass."

Danica would too, so Elizabeth bent and removed her shoes. Then hung her coat.

"Come on." Sam led her into the kitchen and leaned his lean hips against the counter.

Elizabeth had nothing. She stood there studying her white ankle socks against the dark wood floor.

"Want some help?" Sam raised an eyebrow.

She breathed a sigh of relief. "Please."

"You came by to thank me for coming to your show and bringing Dawson and Trapper. Also that Gracie prick."

"Yes." She stopped before she nodded a crick in her neck. "It was very nice of you, and we raised so much more money because of it."

"You're welcome." He folded his arms across his broad, sculpted chest. "Is that all?"

"No."

He studied her, looking nervous and unsure of himself. "I can't help with this part, Lizzie."

"Okay." She squared her shoulders. This was Sam. She'd known him since they could both toddle. She'd called him names, hit him with a hockey stick, and even sugared his bed. Then she'd fallen in love with him and he with her. She'd left him. This was her play. "I also came to say I'm sorry."

He watched her. Some of the tension eased out of him.

"I should never have said what I said at the hospital, but at the time it all felt like too much."

"I get that, Lizzie." His tone gentled. "But this is me, and this is my life."

"I know that, and I also know that I am strong enough to be in that with you. I can be your safe place if you'll let me." She raised her chin and took the leap. "I love you, Sam. I miss you like hell. Nothing is the same without you. My days are flat and dull without you in them. And it's not that I can't survive you, Sam, because if you turn me down, the sun will come up tomorrow and the earth will keep turning, but I don't want to be without you. I choose you, and that means everything about you." She took a deep breath for the biggie. "And I want you back. I love you, and I want you to love me back."

Sam watched her. The silence in the kitchen shrieked. Finally he sighed. "You know, Lizzie, if we're going to make this work, you're going to have to let me be better at something. At least some of the time."

She didn't know what else he was babbling about but the making things work thing she heard loud and clear. She crossed half the distance between them and stopped. "What are you talking about?"

"That was an awesome fucking speech, Lizzie." He grinned at her, his beautiful generous heart in his eyes. "That was so much better than what I had planned." He closed the distance between them and stopped when their toes touched. "I was coming to see you in the morning. I had this speech planned about teammates and working together. You know, making the play together."

"How very romantic." She couldn't resist a second longer and slipped her arms about his waist. Pressing her face into his neck she drew the scent of Sam deep into her bones. "I missed you so much."

"I'm not much of a romantic, Lizzie, and I'm pretty sure I'm crap boyfriend material. I forget important dates, and on the off chance I remember, I'll probably be playing that day anyway." He rested his cheek against her hair. "But I'm your crappy boyfriend, Lizzie."

She laughed against the warm skin of his neck. "I think you should stop talking and take me to bed."

"In my mother's house." He sounded shocked.

Elizabeth wriggled far enough back to see his face. "Sam Stone, I know for a fact this is not the first time you've had a girl in your room."

"I knew it." He frowned down at her. "I knew you were spying on me."

"Oh, please." She rolled her eyes. "I have much better things to do."

Sam's face softened and he kissed her. "I don't."

Yeah, he had her there. "Me neither."

There are currently two books in the Ottawa Titans series. Don't miss #2, Hooking, as team captain, Craig Dawson's love life heads for the penalty box.

———

———

Buy your next read directly from me at my Shopify store
Sarah Hegger Books

For first dibs on news, deals, and giveaways, and so much
more, join the @Home Collective

Or if Facebook is more your thing, join the Sarah Hegger
Collective

Anything and everything you need to know on my website
http://sarahhegger.com

ABOUT THE AUTHOR

Born British and raised in South Africa, Sarah Hegger suffers from an incurable case of wanderlust. Her match? A hot Canadian engineer, whose marriage proposal she accepted six short weeks after they first met. Together they've made homes in seven different cities across three different continents (and back again once or twice). If only it made her multilingual, but the best she can manage is idiosyncratic English, fluent Afrikaans, conversant Russian, pigeon Portuguese, even worse Zulu and enough French to get herself into trouble.

Mimicking her globe trotting adventures, Sarah's career path began as a gainfully employed actress, drifted into public relations, settled a moment in advertising, and eventually took root in the fertile soil of her first love, writing. She also moonlights as a wife and mother. She currently lives in Ottawa, Canada, filling her empty nest with fur babies. Part footloose buccaneer, part quixotic observer of life, Sarah's restless heart is most content when reading or writing books.

f

PRAISE FOR SARAH HEGGER

Drove All Night
"The classic romance plot is elevated to a modern-day,
wholly accessible real-life fairy tale with an excellent mix of
romantic elements and spicy sensuality."
Booklife Prize, Critic's Report

Positively Pippa
"This is the type of romance that makes readers fall in love not
just with characters, but with authors as well."
Kirkus Review (Starred Review)

"What begins as a simple second-chance romance quickly
transforms into a beautiful, frank examination of love, family
dynamics, and following one's dreams. Hegger's unflinching,
candid portrayal of interpersonal and generational
communication elevates the story to the sublime. Shunning
clichés and contrived circumstances, she uses realistic, relatable
situations to create a world that readers will want to visit time
and again."
Publisher's Weekly, Starred Review

Hegger's utterly delightful first Ghost Falls contemporary is what other romance novels want to grow up to be." –
Publisher's Weekly, Best Books of 2017

"The very talented Hegger kicks off an enjoyable new series set in the small Utah town of Ghost Falls. This charming and fun-filled book has everything from passion and humor to betrayal and revenge." –
Jill M Smith, RT Books Reviews 2017 – Contemporary Love and Laughter Nominee

Becoming Bella
"Hegger excels at depicting familial relationships and friendships of all kinds, including purely platonic friendships between women and men. Tears, laughter, and a dollop of suspense make a memorable story that readers will want to revisit time and again."
Publisher's Weekly, Starred Review

"...you have a terrific new romance that Hegger fans are going to love. Don't miss out!"
Jill M. Smith – RT Book Reviews

Blatantly Blythe
"Ms. Hegger has delivered another captivating read for this series in this book that was packed with emotion..." Bec, Bookmagic Review, Harlequin Junkie, HJ Recommends.

Nobody's Fool
"Hegger offers a breath of fresh air in the romance genre." – Terri Dukes, RT Book Reviews

Nobody's Princess
"Hegger continues to live up to her rapidly growing reputation

for breathing fresh air into the romance genre." – Terri Dukes, RT Book Reviews

"I have read the entire Willow Park Series. I have loved each of the books … Nobody's Princess is my favorite of all time." Harlequin Junkie, Top Pick

ALSO BY SARAH HEGGER

Urban Fantasy

The Cré-Witch Chronicles

Prequel: Cast In Stone

Vol l: Born In Water

Vol ll: Purged In Fire

Vol III: Raised In Air

Vol IV: Cradled In Earth

Vol V: Joined In Spirit

Forged In Fate a novella exclusive to Sarah Hegger Books

Sports Romance

Ottawa Titans Series

Roughing

Hooking

Contemporary Romance

Passing Through Series

Drove All Night

Ticket To Ride

Walk On By

Running On Empty

Ghost Falls Series

Positively Pippa

Becoming Bella

Blatantly Blythe

Loving Laura

Hunter Brothers Series
Nobody's Angel
Nobody's Fool
Nobody's Princess

Medieval Romance
Written under **Sarah Edwards**
Sir Arthur's Legacy Series
Sweet Bea
My Lady Faye
Conquering William
Defying Roger
Henry's Honor

Love & War Series
The Marriage Parley
The Betrothal Melee

Western Historical Romance
Written under **Sarah Edwards**
The Soiled Dove Series
Sugar Ellie

Standalone
The Bride Gift
Bad Wolfe On The Rise
Wild Honey